**Praise for #1 *New York Times*
bestselling author Linda Lael Miller**

"Miller's masterful ability to create living, breathing
characters never flags....Miller's romance
won't disappoint."
—*Publishers Weekly* on *McKettrick's Pride*

"Miller is the queen when it comes to creating
sympathetic, endearing and lifelike characters.
She paints each scene so perfectly readers hover
on the edge of delicious voyeurism."
—*RT Book Reviews* on *McKettricks of Texas: Garrett*

"Linda Lael Miller creates vibrant characters and
stories I defy you to forget."
—#1 *New York Times* bestselling author
Debbie Macomber

**Praise for *New York Times* bestselling author
Cathy McDavid**

"McDavid's characters are wonderful, and her story
really showcases the hardships and love it takes to
blend families."
—*RT Book Reviews* on *Cowboy for Keeps*

"McDavid's story strikes at the heart with its sensitive
storyline and nearly perfect character interpretations."
—*RT Book Reviews* on *Waiting for Baby*

LINDA LAEL MILLER

The daughter of a town marshal, Linda Lael Miller is a *New York Times* bestselling author of more than one hundred historical and contemporary novels. Linda's books have hit #1 on the *New York Times* bestseller list six times. Raised in Northport, Washington, she now lives in Spokane, Washington. Visit www.LindaLaelMiller.com

CATHY McDAVID

Cathy makes her home in Scottsdale, Arizona, near the breath-taking McDowell Mountains, where hawks fly overhead, javelina traipse across her front yard and mountain lions occasionally come calling. She embraced the country life at an early age, acquiring her first horse in eighth grade. Dozens of horses followed through the years, along with mules, an obscenely fat donkey, chickens, ducks, goats and a potbellied pig who had her own swimming pool. Nowadays, two spoiled dogs and two spoiled-er cats round out the McDavid pets. Cathy loves contemporary and historical ranch stories and often incorporates her own experiences into her books.

#1 *New York Times* **Bestselling Author**

LINDA LAEL
MILLER

Wild About Harry

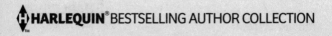

HHARLEQUIN® BESTSELLING AUTHOR COLLECTION

Recycling programs
for this product may
not exist in your area.

ISBN-13: 978-0-373-18081-3

WILD ABOUT HARRY
Copyright © 2014 by Harlequin Books S.A.

The publisher acknowledges the copyright
holders of the individual works as follows:

WILD ABOUT HARRY
Copyright © 1991 by Linda Lael Miller

WAITING FOR BABY
Copyright © 2009 by Cathy McDavid

Printed in U.S.A.

CONTENTS

Dear Reader,

I hope you'll enjoy this blast from the past, the story of Amy Ryan, a young widow with two children, and Harry Griffith, dashing Australian businessman and Amy's late husband's best friend.

It's been a while since the tragedy, but Amy still isn't really living. She loves her kids, but behind that brave and beautiful face of hers, she's just surviving. Marking time.

Then one fateful night, Amy wakes up from a sound sleep to find her husband's ghost standing at the foot of the bed. Is he even real? Amy doesn't know. But the message he brings is all too clear: she's got to move on, let go of past sorrows and open her closed-for-business heart to love, with all its risks.

He even has just the right man in mind—Harry Griffith.

The very next day, Amy gets a call from Harry, as the matchmaker ghost predicted, and the whirlwind begins.

I hope you'll come along for the ride.

With love,

Linda Lael Miller

WILD ABOUT HARRY

#1 New York Times Bestselling Author

Linda Lael Miller

For Jim Lang,
who married the girl with snowflakes in her hair,
thereby proving what a smart guy he really is.

Chapter 1

Amy Ryan was safe in her bed, drifting in that place where slumber and wakefulness mesh into a tranquil twilight, when she distinctly felt someone grasp her big toe and wriggle it.

"Amy."

She groaned and pulled the covers up over her head. Two full years had passed since her handsome, healthy young husband, Tyler, had died on the operating table during a routine appendectomy. She *couldn't* be hearing his voice now.

"No," she murmured. "I refuse to have this dream again. I'm waking up right now!"

Amy's toe moved again, without orders from her brain. She swallowed, and her heart rate accelerated. Quickly, expecting to find eight-year-old Ashley's cat,

Rumpel, at the foot of the bed playing games, she reached out and snapped on the bedside lamp.

A scream rushed into her throat, coming from deep inside her, but she swallowed it. Even though Tyler was standing there, just on the other side of her blanket chest, Amy felt no fear.

She could never be afraid of Ty. No, what scared her was the explicit possibility that she was losing her mind at thirty-two years of age.

"This can't be happening," she whispered hoarsely, raising both hands to her face. From between her fingers, she could still see Tyler grinning that endearing grin of his. "I've been through counseling," she protested. "I've had grief therapy!"

Tyler chuckled and sat down on the end of the bed.

Amy actually felt the mattress move, so lifelike was this delusion.

"I'm quite real," Tyler said, having apparently read her mind. "At least, *real* is the closest concept you could be expected to understand."

"Oh, God," Amy muttered, reaching blindly for the telephone.

Tyler's grin widened. "This is a really lousy joke," he said, "but I can't resist. Who ya gonna call?"

Amy swallowed and hung up the receiver with an awkward motion of her hand. What *could* she say? Could she dial 911 and report that a ghost was haunting her bedroom?

If she did, the next stop would be the mental ward at the nearest hospital.

Amy ran her tongue over dry lips, closed her eyes tightly, then opened them again, wide.

Tyler was still sitting there, his arms folded, charming smile in place. He had brown curly hair and mischievous brown eyes, and Amy had been in love with him since her freshman year at the University of Washington. She had borne him two children, eight-year-old Ashley and six-year-old Oliver, and the loss of her young husband had been the most devastating experience of Amy's life.

"What's happening to me?" Amy rasped, shoving a hand through her sleep-rumpled, shoulder-length brown hair.

Tyler scratched the back of his neck. He was wearing slacks and a blue cashmere cardigan over a tailored white shirt. "I look pretty solid, don't I?" He sounded proud, the way he used to when he'd won a particularly difficult case in court or beaten a colleague at racquet ball. "And let me tell you, being able to grab hold of your toe like that was no small feat, no pun intended."

Amy tossed back the covers, scrambled into the adjoining bathroom and frantically splashed cold water on her face. "It must have been the spicy cheese on the nachos," she told herself aloud, talking fast.

When she straightened and looked in the mirror, though, she saw Tyler's reflection. He was leaning against the doorjamb, his arms folded.

"Pull yourself together, Amy," he said good-naturedly. "It's taken me eighteen months to learn to do this, and I'm not real good at sustaining the energy yet. I could fade out at any time, and I have something important to say."

Amy turned and leaned back against the counter, her hands gripping the marble edge. She sank her teeth into her lower lip and wondered what Debbie would make of this when she told her about it. *If* she told her.

Your subconscious mind is trying to tell you something, her friend would say. Debbie was a counselor in a women's clinic, and she was working on her doctorate in psychology. *It's time to let go of Tyler and get on with your life.*

"Wh-what did you want to-to say?" Amy stammered. She was a little calmer now and figured this figment of her imagination might give her an important update on what was going on inside her head. There was absolutely no doubt, as far as she was concerned, that some of her gears were gummed up.

Tyler's gentle gaze swept her tousled hair, yellow cotton nightshirt and shapely legs with sad fondness.

"An old friend of mine is going to call you sometime in the next couple of days," he said after a long moment. "His name is Harry Griffith, and he runs a multinational investment company out of Australia. They're opening an office in Seattle, so Harry will be living here in the Puget Sound area part of the year. He'll get in touch to offer his condolences about me and pay off on a deal we made the last time we were together. You should get a pretty big check."

Amy certainly hadn't expected anything so specific. "Harry?" she squeaked. She vaguely remembered Tyler talking about him.

Tyler nodded. "We met when we were kids. We were both part of the exchange student program—he lived here for six months, and then I went down there and stayed with Harry and his mom for the same amount of time."

A lump had risen in Amy's throat, and she swallowed it. Yes, Harry Griffith. Tyler's mother, Louise, had spoken of him several times. "This is crazy," she said. "*I'm* crazy."

Her husband—or this mental *image* of her husband—smiled. "No, babe. You're a little frazzled, but you're quite sane."

"Oh, yeah?" Amy thrust herself away from the bathroom counter and passed Tyler in the doorway to stand next to the bed. "If I'm not one can short of a six-pack, how come I'm seeing somebody who's been dead for two years?"

Tyler winced. "Don't use that word," he said. "People don't really die, they just change."

Amy was feeling strangely calm and detached now, as though she were standing outside of herself. "I'll never eat nachos again," she said firmly.

Ty's gentle brown eyes twinkled with amusement. When he spoke, however, his expression was more serious. "You're doing very well, all things considered. You've taken good care of the kids and built a career for yourself, unconventional though it is. But there's one area where you're really blowing it, Spud."

Amy's eyes brimmed with tears. During the terrible days and even worse nights following Tyler's unexpected death, she'd yearned for just such an experience as this. She'd longed to see the man she'd loved so totally, to hear his voice. She'd even wanted to be called "Spud" again, although she'd hated the nickname while Tyler was alive.

She sniffled but said nothing, waiting for Tyler to go on.

He did. "There are women who can be totally fulfilled without a man in their lives. You aren't one of those women, Amy. You're not happy."

Amy shook her head, marveling. "Boy, when my subconscious mind comes up with a message, it's a doozy."

Tyler shrugged. "What can I say?" he asked reasonably. "Harry's the man for you."

"*You* were the man for me," Amy argued, and this time a tear escaped and slipped down her cheek.

He started toward her, as though he would take her into his arms, then, regretfully, he stopped. "That was then, Spud," he said, his voice gruff with emotion. "Harry's *now*. In fact, you're scheduled to remarry and have two more kids—a boy and a girl."

Amy's feeling of detachment was beginning to fade; she was trembling. This was all so crazy. "And this Harry guy is my one and only?" she asked with quiet derision. She was hurt because Tyler had started to touch her and then pulled back.

"Actually, there are several different men you could

have fulfilled your destiny with. That architect you met three months ago, when you were putting together the deal for those condos on Lake Washington, for instance. Alex Singleton—the guy who replaced me in the firm—for another." He paused and shoved splayed fingers through his hair. "You're not cooperating, Spud."

"Well, excuse me!" Amy cried in a whispered yell, not wanting the children to wake and see her in the middle of a hallucination. "I *loved* you, Ty. You were everything to me. I'm not ready to care for anybody else!"

"Yes, you are," Tyler disagreed sadly. Quietly. "Get on with it, Amy. You're holding up the show."

She closed her eyes for a moment, willing Tyler to disappear. When Amy looked again and found him gone, however, she felt all hollow and broken inside.

"Tyler?"

No answer.

Amy went slowly back to bed, switched out the light and lay down. "You're losing it, Ryan," she muttered to herself.

She tried to sleep, but images of Tyler kept invading her mind.

Amy recalled the first time they'd met, in the cafeteria at the University of Washington, when she'd been a lowly freshman and Tyler had been in his third year of law school. He'd smiled as he'd taken the chair across the table from Amy's, and she'd been so thoroughly, instantly besotted that she'd nearly fallen right into her lime Jell-O.

After that day, Amy and Tyler had been together every spare moment. Ty had taken her home to Mercer Island to meet his parents at Thanksgiving, and at Christmas he'd given her a three-carat diamond.

Amy had liked Tyler's parents immediately; they were so warm and friendly, and their gracious, expensive home practically vibrated with love and laughter. The contrast between the Ryans' family life and Amy's was total: Amy's father, one of the most famous heart surgeons in the country, was a distant, distracted sort of man, totally absorbed in his work. Although Amy knew her dad loved her, in his own workaholic way, he'd never been able to show it.

The free-flowing affection among the Ryans had quickly become vital to Amy, and she was still very close to them, even though Tyler had been gone for two years.

Alone in the bed where she and Tyler had once loved and slept and sometimes argued, Amy wept. "This isn't fair," she told the dark universe around her.

With the morning, however, came a sense of buoyant optimism. It seemed only natural to Amy that she'd had a vivid dream about Tyler; he was the father of her children and she'd loved him with her whole heart.

She was sticking frozen waffles in the toaster when Oliver and Ashley raced into the kitchen. During the school year she had trouble motivating them in the mornings, but now that summer had come, they were up and ready for day camp almost as soon as the morning paper hit the doorstep.

"Hey, Mom," Oliver said. He wore a baseball cap low on his forehead and he was wearing shorts and a T-shirt with his favorite cartoon character on the front. "Kid power!" he whooped, thrusting a plastic sword into the air.

Ashley rolled her beautiful Tyler-brown eyes. "What a dope," she said. She was eight and had a lofty view of the world.

"Be careful, Oliver," Amy fretted good-naturedly. "You'll put out someone's eye with that thing." She put the waffles on plates and set them down on the table, then went to the refrigerator for the orange juice. "Look, you two, I might be home late tonight. If I can't get away, Aunt Charlotte will pick you up at camp."

Charlotte was Ty's sister and one of Amy's closest friends.

Ashley was watching Amy pensively as she poured herself a cup of coffee and joined the kids at the table.

"Were you talking to yourself last night, Mom?" the child asked in her usual straightforward way.

Amy was glad she was sitting down because her knees suddenly felt shaky. "I was probably just dreaming," she said, but the memory of Tyler standing there in their bedroom was suddenly vivid in her mind. He'd seemed so solid and so *real*.

Ashley's forehead crumpled in a frown, but she didn't pursue the subject any further.

Fortunately.

After Amy had rinsed the breakfast dishes, put them into the dishwasher and driven the kids to the park, where camp was held, she found herself watching for Tyler—waiting for him to come back.

When she'd showered and put on her best suit, a sleek creation of pale blue linen, along with a blouse, she sat on the edge of her bed and stared at the telephone for what must have been a full five minutes. Then she dialed her best friend's number.

"Debbie?"

"Hi, Amy," Debbie answered, sounding a little rushed. "If this is about lunch, I'm open. Twelve o'clock at Ivar's?"

Amy bit her lower lip for a moment. "I can't, not today...I have appointments all morning. Deb—"

Debbie's voice was instantly tranquil, all sense and sound of hurry gone. "Hey, you sound kind of funny. Is something wrong?"

"It might be," Amy confessed.

"Go on."

"I dreamed about Tyler last night, and it was ultra-real, Debbie. I wasn't lying in bed with my eyes closed—I was standing up, walking around—we had an in-depth conversation!"

Debbie's voice was calm, but then, she was a professional in the mental health field. It would take more than Amy's imaginary encounter with her dead husband to shock this woman. "Okay. What about?"

Amy was feeling sillier by the moment. "It's so dumb."

"Right. So tell me anyway."

"He said I was going to meet—this friend of his—Harry somebody. Who names people Harry in this day and age? I'm supposed to fall in love with this guy, marry him and have two kids."

"Before nightfall?" Debbie retorted, without missing a beat.

"Practically. Ty implied that I've been holding up some celestial plan by keeping to myself so much!"

Debbie sighed. "This is one that could be worked out in a fifteen-minute segment of any self-help show, Ryan. You're a healthy young woman, and you haven't been with a man since Ty, and you're lonely, physically and emotionally. If you want to talk this out with somebody, I could give you a name—"

Amy was already shaking her head. "No," she interrupted, "that's all right. I feel foolish enough discussing this with my dearest friend. I don't think I'm up to stretching out on a couch and telling all to some strange doctor."

"Still—"

"I'll be all right, Deb," Amy broke in again, this time a little impatiently. She didn't know what she'd wanted her friend to say when she told her about Tyler's "visit," but she felt let down. She hung up quickly and then dashed off to her first meeting of the day.

Amy often marveled that she'd made such a success of her business, especially since she'd dropped out of school when Tyler passed the bar exam and devoted herself entirely to being a wife and mother. She'd been totally happy doing those things and hadn't even blushed to admit to having no desire to work outside the home.

After Tyler's death, however, the pain and rage had made her so restless that staying home was impossible. She'd alternated between fits of sobbing and periods of wooden silence, and after a few weeks she'd gone numb inside.

One night, very late, she'd seen a good-looking, fast-talking man on television, swearing by all that was holy that she, too, could build a career in real estate trading and make a fortune.

Amy had enough money to last a lifetime, between Tyler's life insurance and savings and her maternal grandmother's trust fund, but the idea of a challenge, of building something, appealed to her. In fact, on some level it resurrected her. Here was something to *do,* something to keep her from smothering Ashley and Oliver with motherly affection.

She'd downloaded the program and signed up for a seminar, as well.

Amy absorbed all the sessions in the program. The voice was pleasant and the topic complicated enough that she had to concentrate, which meant she had brief respites from thinking about Tyler. Under any other circumstances, Amy would not have had the brass to actually do the things suggested by the program and seminar, but all her normal inhibitions had been frozen inside her, like small animals trapped in a sudden Ice Age.

She'd started buying and selling and wheeling and dealing, and she'd been successful at it.

Still, she thought miserably as she drove toward her meeting, Tyler had been right, she wasn't happy. Now that the numbness had worn off, all those old needs and hurts were back in full force and being a real estate magnate wasn't fulfilling them.

Harry Griffith smiled grimly to himself as he took off his headphones and handed them to his copilot, Mark Ellis. "Here you are, mate," he said. "Bring her in for me, will you?"

Mark nodded as he eagerly took over the controls, and Harry left the cockpit and proceeded into the main section of the private jet. Often it was filled with business people and assorted hangers-on, but that day Harry and Mark were cutting through the sky alone.

He went on to the sumptuous bedroom, unknotting his silk tie with one hand as he closed the door with the other. He'd had a meeting in San Francisco, but now he could change into more casual clothes.

With a sigh Harry pulled open a few drawers and took out a lightweight cable-knit sweater and jeans, still thinking of his friend. He hadn't been present for Ty's services two years before. He'd been in the outback, at one of the mines, and by the time he'd returned to Sydney and learned about Tyler's death, it was three weeks after the fact.

He'd sent flowers to Tyler's parents, who'd been like a second mother and father to him ever since his first visit to the States, and to the pretty widow. Harry had never seen Amy Ryan or her children, except on the front of the Christmas cards he always received from them, and he hadn't known what to say to her.

It had been a damn shame, a man like Tyler dying in his prime like that, and Harry could find no words of comfort inside himself.

Now, however, he had business with Tyler's lovely lady, and he would have to open this last door that protected his own grief and endure whatever emotions might be set free in the process.

Harry tossed aside his tie and began unfastening his cuff links. Maybe he'd even go and stand by Tyler's grave for a while, tell his friend he was a cheeky lot for bailing out so early in the game that way.

He pulled the sweater on over his head, replaced his slacks with jeans, then stood staring at himself in the mirror. Like the bed, chairs and bureau, it was bolted down.

Where Tyler had been handsome in an altar-boy sort of way, Harry was classically so, with dark hair, indigo-blue eyes and an elegant manner. He regarded his exceptional looks as tools, and he'd used them without compunction, every day of his life, to get what he wanted.

Or most of what he wanted, that is. He'd never had a real family of his own, the way Tyler had. God knew, Madeline hadn't even tried to disguise herself as a wife, and she'd sent the child she'd borne her first husband to boarding school in Switzerland. Madeline hadn't wanted to trouble herself with a twelve-year-old daughter, and Eireen's letters and phone calls had been ignored more than answered.

Harry felt sick, remembering. He'd tried to establish a bond with the child on her rare holidays in Australia, but while Madeline hadn't wanted to be bothered with the little girl, she hadn't relished the idea of sharing her, either.

Then, after another stilted Christmas, Madeline had decided she needed a little time on the "the continent," and would therefore see Eireen as far as Zurich. Their plane had gone down midway between New Zealand and the Fiji Islands, and there had been no survivors.

Harry had not wept for his wife—the emotion he'd once mistaken for love had died long before she did—but he'd cried for that bewildered child who'd never been permitted to love or be loved.

Later, when Tyler had died, Harry had gotten drunk—something he had never done before or since—and stayed that way for three nightmarish days. It had been an injustice of cosmic proportions that a man like Tyler Ryan, who had had everything a man could dream of, should be sent spinning off the world that way, like a child from a carnival ride that turned too fast.

"Mr. Griffith?"

Mark's voice, coming over the intercom system, startled Harry. "Yes?" he snapped, pressing a button on the instrument affixed to the wall above his bed, a little testy at the prospect of landing in Seattle.

"We're starting our descent, sir. Would you like to come back and take the controls?"

"You can handle it," Harry answered, removing his finger from the button. He thought of Tyler's parents and the big house on Mercer Island where he'd spent some of the happiest times of his life. "You can handle it," he repeated gravely, even though Mark couldn't hear him now. "The question is, can I?"

Amy had had a busy day, but she'd managed to finish work on time to pick up Oliver and Ashley at day camp, and she was turning hot dogs on the grill in her stove when the telephone rang.

Oliver answered with his customary "Hey!" He listened to the caller with ever-widening eyes and then thrust the receiver in Amy's direction. "I think it's that guy from the movies!" he shouted.

Amy frowned, crossed the room and took the call. "Hello?"

"Mrs. Ryan?" The voice was low, melodic and distinctly Australian. "My name is Harry Griffith, and I was a friend of your husband's—"

The receiver slipped from Amy's hand and clattered against the wall. Harry Griffith? *Harry Griffith!* The man Tyler had mentioned in her dream the night before.

"Mom!" Ashley cried, alarmed. She'd learned, at

entirely too young an age, that tragedy almost always took a person by surprise.

"It's okay, sweetheart," Amy said hastily, snatching up the telephone with one hand and pulling her daughter close with the other. "Hello? Mr. Griffith?"

"Are you all right?" he asked in that marvelous accent.

Amy leaned against the counter, not entirely trusting her knees to support her, and drew in a deep breath. "I'm fine," she lied.

"I don't suppose you remember me…"

Amy didn't remember Harry Griffith, except from old photographs and things Tyler had said, and she couldn't recall seeing him at the funeral. "You knew Tyler," she said, closing her eyes against a wave of dizziness.

"Yes," he answered. His voice was gentle and somehow encouraging, like a touch. "I'd like to take you out for dinner tomorrow night, if you'll permit."

If you'll permit. The guy talked like Cary Grant in one of those lovely old black-and-white movies on the Nostalgia Channel. "Ah—well—maybe you should just come here. Say seven o'clock?"

"Seven o'clock," he confirmed. There was brief pause, then, "Mrs. Ryan? I'm very sorry—about Tyler, I mean. He was one of the best friends I ever had."

Amy's eyes stung, and her throat felt thick. "Yes," she agreed. "I felt pretty much the same way about him. I-I'll see you at seven tomorrow night. Do you have the address?"

"Yes," he answered, and then the call was over.

It took Amy so long to hang up the receiver that Oliver finally pulled it from her hand and replaced it on the hook.

"Who was that?" Ashley asked. "Is something wrong with Grampa or Gramma?"

"No, sweetheart," Amy said gently, bending to kiss the top of Ashley's head, where her rich brown hair was parted. "It was only a friend of your daddy's. He's coming by for dinner tomorrow night."

"Okay," Ashley replied, going back to the table.

Amy took the hot dogs from the grill and served them, but she couldn't eat because her stomach was jumping back and forth between its normal place and her windpipe. She went outside and sat at the picnic table in her expensive suit, watching as the sprinkler turned rhythmically, making its *chicka-chicka* sound.

She tried to assemble all the facts in her mind, but they weren't going together very well.

Last night she'd dreamed—only *dreamed*—that Tyler had appeared in their bedroom. Amy could ascribe that to the spicy Mexican food she'd eaten for dinner the previous night, but what about the fact that he'd told her his friend Harry Griffith would call and ask to see her? Could it possibly be a wild coincidence and nothing more?

She pressed her fingers to her temples. The odds against such a thing had to be astronomical, but the only other explanation was that she was psychic or something. And Amy knew that wasn't true.

If she'd had any sort of powers, she would have foreseen Tyler's death. She would have *done* something about it, warned the doctors, anything.

Presently, Amy pulled herself together enough to go back inside the house. She ate one hot dog, for the sake of appearances, then went to her bathroom to shower and put on shorts and a tank top.

Oliver and Ashley were in the family room, arguing over which program to watch on TV, when Amy joined them. Unless the exchanges threatened to turn violent, she never interfered, believing that children needed to learn to work out their differences without a parent jumping in to referee.

The built-in mahogany shelves next to the fireplace were lined with photo albums, and Amy took one of the early volumes down and carried it to the couch.

There she kicked off her shoes and sat cross-legged on the cushion, opening the album slowly, trying to prepare herself for the inevitable jolt of seeing Tyler smiling back at her from some snapshot.

After flipping the pages for a while, acclimating herself for the millionth time to a world that no longer contained Tyler Ryan, she began to look closely at the pictures.

Chapter 2

The next day, on the terrace of a busy waterfront restaurant, Amy tossed a piece of sourdough bread to one of the foraging sea gulls and sighed. "For all I know," she confided to her best friend, "Harry Griffith is an ax murderer. And I've invited him to dinner."

Debbie's eyes sparkled with amusement. "How bad can he be?" she asked reasonably. "Tyler liked him a lot, didn't he? And your husband had pretty good judgment when it came to human nature."

Amy nodded, pushing away what remained of her spinach and almond salad. "Yes," she admitted grudgingly.

A waitress came and refilled their glasses of iced tea, and Debbie added half a packet of sweetener to hers, stirring vigorously. "So what's really bugging you? That you saw Tyler in a dream and he said a guy named Harry Griffith would come into your life, and now that's about to come true?"

"Wouldn't that bother you?" Amy countered, exasperated. "Don't look now, Deb, but things like this don't happen every day!"

Debbie turned thoughtful. "The subconscious mind is a fantastic thing," she mused. "'We don't even begin to comprehend what it can do."

Amy took a sip of her tea. "You think I *projected* Tyler from some shadowy part of my brain, don't you?"

"Yes," Debbie answered matter-of-factly.

"Okay, fine. I can accept that theory. But how do you account for the fact that Tyler mentioned Harry Griffith, specifically and by name? How could that have come from my subconscious mind, when I never actually knew the man?"

Debbie shrugged. "There were pictures in the albums, and I'm sure Tyler probably talked about him often. I suppose his parents must have talked about the guy sometimes, too. We pick up subliminal information from the people around us all the time."

Her friend's theory made sense, but Amy was still unconvinced. If she'd only conjured an image of Tyler for her own purposes, she would have had him hold her, kiss her, tell her the answers to cosmic mysteries. She would never have spent those few precious moments together talking about some stranger from Australia.

Amy shook her head and said nothing.

Debbie reached out to take her hand. "Listen, Amy, what you need is a vacation. You're under a lot of stress and you haven't resolved your conflicts over Tyler's death. Park the kids with Tyler's parents and go somewhere where the sun's shining. Sunbathe, spend money with reckless abandon, *live* a little."

Amy recalled briefly that she'd always wanted to visit Australia, then pushed the thought from her mind. A trip like that wouldn't be much fun all by herself. "I have work to do," she hedged.

"Right," Debbie answered. "You really need the money, don't you? Tyler had a whopping insurance policy, and then there was the trust fund from your grandmother. Add to that the pile you've made on your own with this real estate thing—"

"All right," Amy interrupted. "You're right. I'm lucky, I have plenty of money. But work fills more than just financial needs, you know."

Debbie's look was wryly indulgent, and she didn't speak at all. She just tapped the be-ringed fingers of her right hand against the upper part of her left arm, waiting for Amy to dig herself in deeper.

"Listen," Amy whispered hoarsely, not wanting diners at the neighboring tables to overhear, "I know what you're really saying, okay? I'm young. I'm healthy. I should be...*having sex* with some guy. Well, in case you haven't noticed, the smart money is on celibacy these days!"

"I'm not telling you to go out and seduce the first

man you meet, Amy," Debbie said frankly, making no apparent effort to moderate her tone. "What I'm really saying is that you need to stop mourning Tyler and *get on with your life*."

Amy snatched up her check, reached for her purse and pushed back her chair. "Thanks," she snapped, hot color pooling in her cheeks. "You've been a real help!"

"Amy..."

"I have a meeting," Amy broke in. And then she walked away from the table without even looking back.

Debbie caught up to her at the cash register. "My brother has a condo at Lake Tahoe," she persisted gently. "You could go there for a few days and just walk along the shore and look at the trees and stuff. You could visit the house they used in *Bonanza*."

Despite her nervous and irritable mood, Amy had to smile. "You make it sound like a pilgrimage," she replied, picking up her credit card receipt and placing it neatly in a pocket of her brown leather purse. "Shall I burn candles and say, 'Spirits of Hoss, Adam and Little Joe, show me the way'?"

Now it was Debbie who laughed. "Your original hypothesis was correct, Ryan. You are indeed crazy."

It was an uncommonly sunny day, even for late June, and the sidewalks were crowded with tourists. Amy spoke softly, "I'm sorry, Deb. I was really a witch in there."

Debbie grinned. "True, but being a friend means knowing somebody's faults and liking them anyway.

And to show you I do have some confidence in your reasoning processes, expect my cousin Max over tonight." She paused to think a moment, then her pretty face was bright with inspiration. "Max will wear coveralls and pretend to be fixing the dishwasher or something. That way, there'll be a man in the house, in case this Griffith guy really is an ax murderer, but Mr. Australia will never guess you were nervous about having him over."

Amy wasn't crazy about the idea, but she had neither the time nor the energy to try to talk Debbie out of it. She had an important meeting scheduled and, after that, some shopping to do at the Pike Place Market.

"I'll call you tomorrow," Amy promised, as the two women went in their separate directions.

Because she didn't know whether to go with elegant or simple and typically American, Amy settled on a combination of the two and bought fresh salmon steaks to be seasoned, wrapped in foil and cooked on the backyard barbecue. She made a potato salad as well, and set out chocolate éclairs from an upscale bakery for dessert.

She was setting the picnic table with good silver when a jolting sensation in the pit of her stomach alerted her to the fact that she wasn't alone.

Amy looked up, expecting to see Debbie's cousin Max or perhaps even Tyler. Instead, she found herself tumbling end over end into the bluest pair of eyes she'd ever seen.

"Hello," the visitor said.

Oliver, who had apparently escorted their guest from the front door, was clearly excited. "He sounds just like Hugh Jackman when he talks, doesn't he, Mom?" he crowed.

The dark-haired man was incredibly handsome—Amy recalled seeing his picture once or twice—and he smiled down at Oliver with quiet warmth. "We're mates, me and Hugh," he said in a very thick and rhythmic down-under accent.

"Wow!" Oliver shouted.

The visitor chuckled and ruffled the boy's hair. Then he noticed Ashley, who was standing shyly nearby, holding her beloved cat and looking up at the company with wide eyes.

"My name is Ashley Ryan," she said solemnly. "And this is my cat, Rumpel. That's short for Rumpelteazer."

Amy was about to intercede—after all, this man hadn't even had a chance to introduce himself yet—but before she could, he reached out and patted Rumpel's soft, striped head.

"Ah," he said wisely. "This must be a Jellicle cat, then."

Ashley's answering smile was sudden and so bright as to be blinding. She'd named Rumpel for one of the characters in the musical *Cats:* Tyler had taken her to see the show at Seattle's Paramount Theater several months before his death. Ever since, the play had served as a sort of connection between Ashley and the father she had loved so much.

"Harry Griffith," the man said, solemnly offering his hand to Ashley in greeting. He even bowed, ever so slightly, and his mouth quirked at one corner as he gave Amy a quick, conspiratorial glance. "I'm very glad to meet you, Ashley Ryan."

Amy felt herself spinning inwardly, off balance, like a washing machine with all the laundry wadded up on one side of the tub. She reached out, resting one hand against the edge of the picnic table.

Harry's indigo eyes came back to her face, and she thought she saw tender amusement in their depths. He wore his expensive clothes with an air only a rich and accomplished man could have managed, and Amy concluded that he was used to getting reactions from the woman he encountered.

It annoyed her, and her voice was a little brisk when she said, "Hello, Mr. Griffith."

His elegant mouth curved slightly, and the ink-blue eyes danced. "I'm very glad to make your acquaintance, Mrs. Ryan. But since Tyler was one of my best friends, I'd be more comfortable having you call me Harry."

"Harry." The name came out of Amy's mouth sounding like primitive woman's first attempt at speech. "My name is Amy."

"I know," Harry answered, and, oddly, his voice affected Amy like a double dose of hot-buttered rum, finding its way into her veins and coursing through her system. Leaving her dizzy.

"S-sit down," Amy said, gesturing toward the picnic table.

"I'd like that," Harry replied. "But first I'd better tell you that there's a man in coveralls out front, ringing your doorbell."

Debbie's cousin Max, no doubt. Although she knew intuitively that she wouldn't need protection from a make-believe dishwasher repairman, Amy was relieved to have something to do besides standing there feeling as if she were about to topple over the edge of a precipice.

"Please," Amy said. "Make yourself at home. I'll be right back." As she hurried into the house, she couldn't help remembering what Tyler had said, that she was meant to marry Harry Griffith and have two children by him. She was glad no one else could possibly know about the quicksilver, heated fantasies *that* idea had produced.

Sure enough, she found Debbie's cousin peering through the glass in the front door.

She opened it. "Max? Listen, you really don't need—"

"Can't be too careful," the balding middle-aged man said, easing past Amy with his toolbox in hand. Then, in a much louder voice, he added, "Just show me to your dishwasher, and I'll make short order of that leak."

"You do understand that the dishwasher isn't broken?" Amy inquired in a whisper as she led the way to the kitchen.

He replied with a wink, set his toolbox in the center of the table, took out a screwdriver and went right to work.

Amy drew three or four deep breaths and let them out slowly before pushing open the screen door and facing Harry Griffith again.

He had already won over both the kids; Ashley was beaming with delight as he pushed her higher and higher in the tire swing Tyler had hung from a branch of the big maple tree a few years before. Oliver was waiting his turn with uncharacteristic patience.

Amy had a catch in her throat as she watched the three of them together. Until that moment, she'd managed to kid herself that she could be both mother and father to her children, but they were blossoming under Harry's attention like flowers long-starved for water and sunlight.

She watched them for a few bittersweet moments, then went to the grill to check the salmon. The sound of her children's laughter lifted her heart and, at the same time, filled her eyes with tears.

Amy was drying her cheek with the back of one hand when both Oliver and Ashley raced past, arguing in high-pitched voices.

"I'll do it!" Oliver cried.

"No, *I* want to!" Ashley replied.

Rumpel wisely took refuge under the rhododendron beside the patio.

"What...?" Amy turned to see Harry Griffith standing directly behind her.

He shrugged and grinned in a way that tugged at her heart. "I didn't mean to cause a disruption," he said. "I guess I should have gone back to the car for the cake myself, instead of sending the kids for it."

Amy sniffled. "Did you know Tyler very well?" she asked.

Harry was standing so close that she could smell his aftershave and the fabric softener in his sweater, and together, those two innocent scents caused a virtual riot in her senses. "We spent the better part of a year together," he answered. "And we kept in touch, as much as possible, after high school and college." He paused, taking an apparent interest in the fragrant white lilacs clambering over the white wooden arbor a few yards away. "I probably knew Ty better than most people—" Harry's gaze returned to her, and her heart welcomed it "—and not as well as you did."

Smoothly, one hand in the pocket of his tailored gray slacks, Harry reached out and, with the pad of his thumb, wiped a stray tear from just beneath Amy's jawline. Before she could think of anything to say, the kids returned, each carrying one end of a white bakery box.

Harry thanked them both in turn, making it sound as though they'd smuggled an important new vaccine across enemy lines.

"I guess we'd better eat," Amy said brightly. "It's getting late."

Oliver and Ashley squeezed in on either side of Harry, leaving Amy alone on the opposite bench of the picnic table. She felt unaccountably jealous of their attention, suddenly wanting it all for herself.

"Mom says you and Dad were buddies," Oliver announced, once the salmon and potato salad and steamed asparagus had been dealt with. He was looking expectantly at their guest.

Harry put his hand on Oliver's wiry little shoulder. "The very best of buddies," he confirmed. "Tyler was one of the finest men I've ever known."

Oliver's freckled face fairly glowed with pride and pleasure, but in the next instant he looked solemn again. "Sometimes," he confessed, with a slight trace of the lisp Amy had thought he'd mastered, "I can't remember him too well. I was only four when he…when he died."

"Maybe I can help you recall," Harry said gently, taking a wallet from the hip pocket of his slacks and carefully removing an old, often-handled snapshot. "This was taken over at Lake Chelan, right here in Washington State."

Ashley and Oliver nearly bumped heads in their eagerness to look at the picture of two handsome young men grinning as they held up a pair of giant rainbow trout for the camera.

"Your dad and I were seventeen then." Harry frowned thoughtfully. "We were out in the rowboat that day, as I recall. Your aunt Charlotte was annoyed with us and she swam ashore, taking the oars with her. It was humiliating, actually. An old lady in a paddleboat had to come out and tow us back to the dock."

Amy chuckled, feeling a sweet warmth flood her spirit as she remembered Ty telling that same story.

After they'd had some of Harry's cake—they completely scorned the éclairs—Amy sent both her protesting children into the house to get ready for bed. She and Harry remained outside at the picnic table, even after the sun went down and the mosquitoes came and the breeze turned chilly.

"I'm sorry I didn't make it to Ty's funeral," he said, after one long and oddly comfortable silence. "I was in the outback, and didn't find out until some three weeks after he'd passed on."

"I wouldn't have known whether you were there or not. I was in pretty much of a muddle." Amy's voice went a little hoarse as the emotional backwash of that awful day flooded over her.

Harry ran his fingers through his hair, the first sign of agitation Amy had seen him reveal. "*I* knew the difference," he said. "I needed to say goodbye to Tyler. Matter of fact, I needed to bellow at him that he had a hell of a nerve going and dying that way when he was barely thirty-five."

"I was angry with him, too," Amy said softly. "One day he was fine, the next he was in the hospital. The doctor said it would be a routine operation, nothing to worry about, and when I saw Ty before surgery, he was making jokes about keeping his appendix in a jar." She paused, and a smile faltered on her mouth, then fell away. She went on to describe what happened next, even though she was sure Harry already knew the tragic details, because for some reason she needed to say it all.

"Tyler had some kind of reaction to the anesthetic and went into cardiac arrest. The surgical team tried everything to save him, of course, but they couldn't get his heart beating again. He was just…gone."

Harry closed warm, strong fingers around Amy's hand. "I'm sorry," he said.

One of the patio doors slid open, and Amy looked up, expecting to see Ashley or Oliver standing there, making a case for staying up another hour. Instead, she was jolted to find cousin Max, complete with coveralls and toolbox.

Amy was horrified that she'd left the man kneeling on the kitchen floor throughout the evening, half his body swallowed up by an appliance that didn't even need repairing. "Oh, Max…I'm sorry, I—"

Max waggled a sturdy finger at her. "Everything's fine now, Mrs. Ryan." He looked at Harry and wriggled his eyebrows, clearly stating, without another word, that he had sized up the dinner guest and decided he was harmless.

In Amy's opinion, Max couldn't have been more wrong. Harry Griffith was capable of making her feel things, remember things, want things. And that made him damn dangerous.

"Mr. Griffith was just leaving," she said suddenly. "Maybe you could walk him to his car."

Harry tossed her a curious smile, gave his head one almost imperceptible shake and stood. "I've some business to settle with you," he said to Amy, "but I guess it will keep until morning."

Amy closed her eyes for a moment, shaken again. She knew what that business was without asking, because Tyler had told her. This was all getting too spooky.

Harry was already standing, so Amy stood, too.

"It's been a delightful evening," he said. "Thank you for everything."

His words echoed in Amy's mind as he walked away to join Max. *It's been a delightful evening.* She wasn't used to Harry's elegant, formal way of speaking: Tyler would have swatted her lightly on the bottom and said, *Great potato salad, babe. How about rubbing my back?*

"You're making me sound like a redneck," a familiar voice observed, and Amy whirled to see Tyler sitting in the tire swing, grinning at her in the light of the rising moon.

She raised one hand, as if to summon Harry or Max back, so that someone else could confirm the vision, then let it fall back to her side. "It's true," she said, stepping closer to the swing and keeping her voice down, so the kids wouldn't think she was talking to herself again. "Don't deny it, Ty. You enjoyed playing king of the castle. In fact, sometimes you did everything but swing from vines and yodel while beating on your chest with both fists."

Tyler, or his reflection, raised one eyebrow. "Okay,

so I was a little macho sometimes. But I loved you, Spud. I was a good provider and a faithful husband."

Instinct, not just wishful thinking, told Amy that Ty's claim was true. He'd been the ideal life partner, except that he'd thrown the game before they'd even reached halftime.

"Go ahead, gloat," Amy said, folding her arms. "You told me Harry Griffith would turn up, and he did. And he said something about discussing business with me tomorrow, so you're batting a thousand."

Tyler grinned again, looking cocky. "You thought you were dreaming, didn't you?"

"Actually, no," Amy said. "It's more likely that you're some sort of projection of my subconscious mind."

"Oh, yeah?" Tyler made the swing spin a couple of times, the way he'd done on so many other summer nights, before he'd single-handedly brought the world to an end by dying. Somewhere in that library of albums inside the house, Amy had a picture of him holding an infant Ashley on his lap while they both turned in a laughing blur. "How could your subconscious mind have known Harry was about to show up?"

Amy shrugged. "There are a lot of things going on in this world that we don't fully understand."

"You can say that again," Tyler said, a little smugly.

He still couldn't resist an opportunity to be one up on the opposition in any argument, Amy reflected, with affection and acceptance. It was the lawyer in him. "Debbie's theory is that you represent some unspoken wish for love and romance."

Tyler laughed. "Unspoken, hell. I'm telling you straight out, Spud. You're not going to find a better guy than Harry, so you'd better grab him while you've got the chance."

Only then did Amy realize she hadn't felt an urge to fling herself at Tyler, the way she had before. The revelation made her feel sad. "Doesn't it make you even slightly jealous to think of me married to someone else?"

Amy regretted the words the instant she'd spoken them, because a bereft expression shadowed Tyler's handsome features for several moments.

"Yes," he admitted gruffly, "but this is about letting go and moving on. Think of me as a ghost, or a figment of your imagination, whatever works for you. As long as you get the message and stop marking time, it doesn't matter."

"*Are* you a ghost?"

Tyler sighed. "Yes and no."

"Spoken like a true lawyer."

He reached out one hand for her, as he would have done before, but once again he pulled back. He didn't smile at Amy's comment, either. "I'm not a specter, forced to wander the earth and rattle chains like in the stories they used to tell at summer camp," he told her. "But I'm not an image being beamed out of your deeper mind, either. I'm just as real as you are."

Amy swallowed hard. "I don't understand!" she wailed in a low voice, frustrated.

"You're not supposed to," Tyler assured her gently. "There's no need for you to understand."

Amy stepped closer, needing to touch Tyler, but between one instant and the next he was gone. No fade-out, no flash, nothing. He was there and then he wasn't.

"Tyler?" Amy whispered brokenly.

"Mom?" Ashley's voice made Amy start, and she turned to see her daughter standing only a few feet behind her, wearing cotton pajamas and carrying her favorite doll. "Did Mr. Harry go home?"

Apparently Ashley hadn't heard her mother talking to thin air, and Amy was relieved. She reached out to stop the tire swing, which was still swaying back and forth in the night air.

"Yes, sweetheart," she said. "He's really a nice man, isn't he?"

Ashley nodded gravely. "I like to listen to him talk. I wish *he* was still here, so he could tell us a kangaroo story."

"Maybe he doesn't know any," she suggested, distracted. If Tyler had known what she was thinking earlier, had he also discerned that his widow felt a powerful attraction to one of his best friends?

"Sure, he does," Ashley said confidently as they stepped into the kitchen together. Amy closed and locked the sliding door. "Did you know they have yellow signs in Australia, with the silhouette of a kangaroo on them—like the Deer Crossing signs here?"

Amy turned off the outside lights and checked to make sure all the leftovers had been put away. The dishwasher showed no signs of Max's exploratory surgery. "No, sweetheart," she said, standing at the sink now and staring out the window at the tire swing. It was barely visible in the deepening darkness. "I didn't know that. I guess it makes sense, though. Off to bed now."

"What about the story?"

Amy felt tears sting her eyes as she stared out at the place where Tyler had been. That was what her life was these days, it seemed, just a place where Tyler had been.

Harry sat on the stone bench beside Tyler's fancy marble headstone, his chin propped in one palm. "Damn it, man," he complained, "you didn't tell me she was beautiful. You didn't say anything about the warm way she laughs, or those golden highlights in her hair." He sighed heavily. "All right," he conceded. "I guess you did say she was a natural wonder, but I thought you were just talking. Even the Christmas cards didn't prepare me…"

He stood, tired of sitting, and paced back and forth at the foot of Tyler's grave. It didn't bother him, being in a cemetery at night. He wasn't superstitious and, besides, he'd been needing this confrontation with Tyler for a good long time.

"You might have stuck around a few more years, you know!" he muttered, shoving one hand through his usually perfect hair. "There you were with that sweet wife, those splendid children, a great career. And what did you do? In the name of God, Tyler, why didn't you *fight?*"

The only answer, of course, was a warm night wind and the constant chirping of crickets.

Harry stopped his pacing and stood with one foot braced against the edge of the bench, staring down at the headstone with eyes that burned a little. "All right, mate," he said softly, hoarsely. "I know you probably had your reasons for not holding on longer—and that's not to say I won't be wanting an accounting when I catch up with you. In the meantime, what's really got under my skin is, well, it's Amy and those terrific kids."

He tilted his head back and looked up at the moon for a long time, then gave a ragged sigh. "We were always honest with each other, you and I. Nothing held back. When I laid eyes on that woman, Ty, it was as though somebody wrenched the ground out from beneath my feet."

While the damning words echoed around him, Harry struggled to face the incomprehensible reality. He hadn't been with Amy Ryan for five minutes before he'd started imagining what it would be like to share his life with her.

He hadn't thought of taking Amy to bed, though God knew that would be the keenest of pleasures. No, he'd pictured her nursing a baby…his baby. He'd seen her running along the white sand on the beach near his house in northern Queensland, with Ashley and Oliver scampering behind, and he'd seen her sitting beside him in the cockpit of his jet.

This was serious.

He touched his friend's headstone as he passed, and started toward the well-lighted parking lot. "If you know what's good for you, Harry," he muttered to himself, "you'll give the lady her money and then stay out of her way."

Harry got behind the wheel of his rented vehicle and started the engine. Nothing must be allowed to happen between him and Amy Ryan, and the reason was simple. To touch her would be to betray a man who would have trusted Harry with his very life.

Chapter 3

Amy didn't sleep well that night. She was filled with contradictory feelings; new ones and old ones, affectionate and angry ones. She was furious with Tyler for ever dying in the first place, and with Harry Griffith for thawing out her frozen emotions. She was also experiencing a warmth and a sense of pleasant vulnerability she'd never expected to know again.

After Oliver and Ashley had gone to camp, Amy didn't put on a power suit and go out to network with half a dozen potential clients as she normally would have done. Instead, she wore jeans and a pastel blue sun top and pulled her heavy shoulder-length hair back into a ponytail. She was in the spacious room that had once been Tyler's study, balancing her checking account and listening with half an ear to a TV talk show, when the telephone rang.

Amy pushed the speaker button. "Hello?"

Harry's smooth, cultured voice filled the room. "Hello, Amy. It's Harry Griffith."

"I know," Amy answered automatically, before she'd had a chance to think about the implications of those two simple words. She laid down her pen and turned away from her banking, feeling vaguely embarrassed. She wanted to say something witty, but of course nothing came to mind; in an hour or a day or a week, when it was too late, some smidgen of clever repartee would come to mind in a flash.

"I enjoyed last night's visit with you and the children," he went on, and Amy leaned back in her chair, just letting that wonderful voice roll over her, like warm ocean water. "Thank you for inviting me, Amy."

Amy closed her eyes, then quickly opened them again. She needed to be on her guard with this man, lest she say or do something really foolish. "Uh...yes... well, you're very welcome, of course." *That was really brilliant, Ryan,* she added to herself.

"I'd like to return the favor, if I might. I've made an appointment to look at a rather unique house over on Vashon Island tomorrow, and I could really use some company—besides the real estate agent, I mean. Would you and Ashley and Oliver care to go out and offer your opinion of the place?"

Amy's heart warmed as she thought how her son and daughter would enjoy such an outing, especially when it meant close contact with Harry. She wasn't exactly averse to the idea herself, though she couldn't quite admit that, even in the privacy of her own soul.

"It would give you and me a chance to discuss that business you mentioned last night." That was the best attempt at setting up a barrier Amy could manage.

Harry sighed. "Yes, there is that. Shall I pick the three of you up tomorrow, then? Around nine?"

A sweet shiver skittered down Amy's spine. "Yes," she heard herself say. But the moment Harry rang off, she wanted to call him back and say she'd changed her mind, she couldn't possibly spend a day on Vashon. She would tell him she had to clean the garage or prune the lilac bushes or something.

Only she had no idea where to reach the charming Mr. Griffith. He hadn't left a number or mentioned the name of a hotel.

Feeling restless, Amy pushed the speaker button on the telephone and thrust herself out of her chair. So much for balancing her checking account; thanks to Harry's call, she wouldn't have been able to subtract two from seven.

Amy paced in front of the natural rock fireplace, wondering where all this unwanted energy had come from. For two years, she'd been concentrating on basic emotional survival. Now, all of the sudden she felt as though she could replaster every wall in that big colonial house without even working up a sweat.

She dialed Debbie's private number at the counseling center.

"I'm going crazy," she blurted out the moment her friend answered.

Debbie laughed. "Amy, I presume? What's happened now? Have you been visited by the ghost of Christmas Weird?"

Amy gave a sigh. "This is serious, Debbie. Harry Griffith just called and invited me to go to Vashon Island with him tomorrow, and I accepted!"

"That *is* terrible," Debbie teased. "Think of it. After only *two years* of mourning, you're actually coming back to life. Quick, head for the nearest closet and hide out until the urge passes!"

Rolling her eyes and twisting the telephone cord around her index finger, Amy replied, "Will you stop with the irony, please? Something very strange is going on here."

Debbie's voice became firm, reasonable. She had become the counselor. "I know a crazy person when I see one, Amy, and believe me, you're completely sane."

"I saw Tyler again last night," Amy insisted. "He was sitting in the backyard swing."

"Your deeper mind is trying to tell you something, Ryan. Pay attention."

"You've been a tremendous help," Amy said with dry annoyance.

Debbie sighed philosophically. "There go my fond hopes of writing a bestselling book, becoming the next self-help guru and appearing on TV."

"Debbie."

"Just relax, Amy. That's all you have to do. Stop analyzing everything and just take things one day at a time."

Amy let out a long breath, knowing her friend was right. Which didn't mean for one moment that she'd be able to *apply* the information. "By the way, thanks for sending your cousin Max over last night. My virtue is safe."

Debbie chuckled. "Too safe, methinks. Talk to you later."

Amy said goodbye and hung up. She went into the kitchen and turned on the dishwasher. Almost immediately, water began to seep out from under the door.

"Great," she muttered.

As the rest of the day passed, Amy discovered that her normal tactics for distracting herself weren't working any better than the dishwasher. She had absolutely no desire to contact prospective clients, make followup calls or update her files.

At two o'clock, a serviceman came to repair the damage Max had unwittingly done to the dishwasher. Amy watched TV, having no idea who the characters were or what in the world they were talking about. She was relieved when it was finally time to pick the kids up at day camp.

The announcement that Harry had invited the three of them to spend the next day on the island brought whoops of delight from Oliver and a sweet smile from Ashley.

After those reactions, Amy could not have disappointed her children for anything.

That night in bed, she tossed and turned, half hoping Tyler would appear again so she could give him a piece of her mind. Of course, she reasoned, he probably *was* a piece of her mind.

When the first finger of light reached over the mountains visible from Amy's window, Oliver materialized at the foot of her bed. He scrambled onto the mattress and gave a few exuberant leaps.

"Get up, Mom! You've only got four hours to get beautiful before Harry comes to pick us up!"

Amy pulled the covers over her head and groaned. "Oliver, children have been disowned for lesser offenses."

Oliver bounded to the head of the bed and bounced on his knees, simultaneously dragging the blankets back from Amy's face. "This is your big chance, Mom," he argued. "Don't blow it!"

Shoving one hand through her rumpled hair, Amy let out a long sigh. "Trust me, Oliver—while I may appear hopeless to you, I have not quite reached the point of desperation."

The words were no sooner out of her mouth when Tyler's accusation echoed in her mind. *You're not happy.*

The assertion would have been much easier to deal with if it hadn't been fundamentally true. Amy loved her children, and she found her work at least tolerable. She had good health, a nice home and plenty of money.

Those things should have been enough, to her way of thinking, but they weren't. Amy wanted something more.

By the time nine o'clock rolled around, Amy had put on jeans and a navy sweater. She wore light makeup and a narrow white scarf to hold her hair back from her face.

"Am I presentable?" she whispered to Oliver with a twinkle in her eyes, when the doorbell sounded.

Oliver had already rushed to answer the door, but Ashley examined her mother with a pensive frown and then nodded solemnly. "I suppose you'll do," she said.

When Amy saw Harry standing there on the porch, looking rakishly handsome even in jeans and a white cable-knit sweater, her heart raced the way it did when she was trying to get in step with a revolving door.

His too-blue eyes swept lightly over Amy, but with respect rather than condescension. "G'day," he said.

The children's laughter seemed to startle Harry, though he looked suavely good-natured, as usual.

"You sounded like Hugh Jackman again," Amy explained with an amused smile. She was grateful to the children for lightening up the situation; if it had been left to her, she probably wouldn't have been able to manage a word. "Come in."

Harry smiled at the kids and rumpled Oliver's hair. Then, as if he hadn't already charmed the eight-year-old right out of her sneakers, he bowed and kissed Ashley's hand. The effect was oddly continental, despite the child's diminutive size.

Minutes later, after making sure that Oliver and Ashley's seat belts were properly fastened, Harry joined Amy in the front seat.

"You're quite competent at driving on the right-hand side of the road," she remarked, strictly to make conversation, when Harry had backed the van out onto the quiet residential street. An instant later, Amy's cheeks were flooded with color.

Harry's grin could only be described as sweetly wicked. "I've spent considerable time in the States," he responded after a time.

Amy ran the tip of her tongue over dry lips. With Tyler, there had always been so much to talk about, the words had just tumbled from her mouth, but now she felt as though the fate of the Western hemisphere hung on every phrase she uttered.

Lamely, she turned to look out the window, all the while riffling through the files in her mind for something witty and sophisticated to say.

"Mom isn't used to dating," Oliver put in from the back, his tones eager and earnest. "You'll have to be patient with her."

Harry chuckled at Amy's groan of mortification, then sent a seismic shock through her system by innocently touching her knee.

"It's all *right,*" he assured her in his quiet, elegant, hot-buttered-rum voice. "Why are you so nervous?"

Why, indeed, Amy wondered. Maybe it was because she was really beginning to believe that a ghost had set her up for a blind date!

"Oliver was right on," she said after a few moments of struggling to get her inner balance. "I'm not used to—socializing."

Harry grinned, skillfully shifting the van into a higher gear and keeping to the right of the yellow line on the highway. "Dating," he corrected.

Amy's color flared again, and that only amused him more.

"No wonder Ty was so crazy about you," he observed, keeping his indigo gaze on the traffic.

Foolishly pleased by the compliment, if mystified, Amy did her best to relax.

The lull obviously worried the children; this time it was Ashley who leaned forward to put in her two cents' worth.

"Once Mom went out with this dude who sold real estate," the little girl said sagely. "Rumpel bit his ankle, and the guy threatened to sue."

Amy shook her head and closed her eyes, beyond embarrassment. Then she risked a sidelong glance at Harry. "Rumpel has always been an excellent judge of character," she admitted.

Harry laughed. "All the same, I'll watch my manners when the cat's about."

The thought of Harry Griffith *not* watching his manners made a delicious little thrill tumble through Amy.

Presently they arrived in west Seattle, and Harry took the exit leading to the ferry terminal. He paid the toll and drove onto the enormous white boat with all the savoir faire of a native.

Ashley and Oliver were bouncing in their seats, but Amy made them stay in the van until the boat had been loaded. Their eagerness carried a sweet sting; riding on ferry boats had been something they did with Tyler. He'd taken them from stem to stern and, on one occasion, even into the wheelhouse to meet the captain.

The four of them climbed the metal stairway to the upper deck, Oliver and Harry in the lead, and then walked through the seating area and outside. The wind was crisp and salty and lightly tinged with motor oil.

While Oliver and Ashley ran wildly along the deck, exulting in the sheer freedom of that, Amy leaned against the railing as the heavy boat labored away from shore.

She was only too conscious of Harry standing at her side, mere inches away. He was at once sturdy as a wall and warm as a fire on a wintry afternoon, and Amy was sure she would have sensed his presence even in a pitch-black cellar.

"Have you seen pictures of this place we're going to look at?" she asked, and she sounded squeaky in her effort to keep things light.

Harry shook his head. "No, but the agent described it to me. Sounds like a terrific place."

Amy swallowed. So far, so good. "You'll be renting it, I suppose?"

"Buying," Harry responded. "My company is opening offices in Seattle. I'll be here about six months of the year."

Amy had a peculiar, spiraling sensation in the pit of her stomach. "Oh." She was saved from having to make more of that urbane utterance when Ashley and Oliver returned to collect Harry. They each took a hand, and in moments he was being led away toward the bow.

Wishing she'd had a chance to warn her son and daughter not to promote her like some revolutionary new product about to hit the supermarket shelves, Amy watched the trio stroll away in silence.

When Harry returned from inside, he brought coffee in plastic cups. The kids had a cinnamon roll but, instead of eating it, they were feeding bits and pieces to the gulls.

"They're very beautiful children," he said. The sadness in his tone resonated inside Amy like a musical chord.

"Do you have any kids?" she asked.

Harry sighed and stared at the receding shoreline and city. "I had a stepdaughter once. She died with her mother in a plane crash."

Amy winced inwardly. Losing her husband had been torment enough. To lose Tyler *and* one or both of her children would have been unbearable. "I'm so sorry," she said.

Harry's smile was dazzling, like sunlight mixing with sparkling water early on a summer morning. "It's been a long time ago now, love. Don't let it trouble you."

"Have you any other family?" Amy wasn't to be so easily turned aside.

"My mother," Harry answered with a grin. "She's a Hun, but I love her."

Amy laughed.

"What about your mother?" Harry asked. "Is she beautiful, like you and Ashley?"

Once again, he'd used an invisible emotional cord to trip her. She tightened her grip on the railing and felt her smile float away on the tide. "She died when I was four. I don't remember her."

It seemed perfectly natural for Harry to put his arm around her shoulders. Amy felt comforted by the gesture. "You've had a great deal of loss in your life," he said gently. "What about your father? Do you have one of those?"

Amy nodded, squaring her shoulders and working up a smile. "He's a doctor, always busy. I don't see him much."

"Do I detect a note of loneliness?" Harry asked, letting his arm fall back to his side again. He seemed to know intuitively when to touch and when not to, when to talk and when to keep silent.

A denial rushed into Amy's throat. Lonely? She had her beautiful children, her friends, her job. "Of course I'm not—"

"Lonely," Harry finished for her, arching one eyebrow.

Amy sighed. "Okay," she confessed, "so sometimes I feel a little isolated. Doesn't everybody have moments like that?"

The wind lifted a tendril of Harry's perfect hair. "Some people have *decades* like that," he replied, leaning against the railing now, bracing himself easily with both forearms. "Even lifetimes, poor souls."

A brief boldness possessed Amy. "What about you?" she asked. But an instant later she wished she could call the question back because it made her look like such a naive fool. Of course a rich, handsome, sophisticated man like Harry Griffith would never be subject to such a forlorn emotion as loneliness.

"There were days—nights, more particularly—when I honestly thought I'd die of it," he confessed, looking Amy directly in the eye.

She didn't think Harry was lying, and yet she couldn't imagine him in such a state. He was obviously a jet-setter, and women were probably willing to wrestle in the mud for the chance to be with him.

He smiled. "I can see by your expression that you're skeptical, Mrs. Ryan," he teased.

Harry Griffith was as suave and handsome as Cary Grant had been in his youth, and Amy could well imagine him as an elegant jewel thief. "Well, it's just—"

He cupped her chin lightly in his hand and stroked her lips with the pad of his thumb, making them want to be kissed. "Being surrounded by people doesn't make a person immune to emotional pain, Amy."

She could feel herself being pulled toward him by some unseen inner force. Harry's mouth was descending toward hers, at just the right angle for the kiss she suddenly craved, but Oliver prevented full contact.

"Mom?" he shouted, tugging at her sleeve. "Hey, Mom? When we get to the island, is it okay if I go swimming?"

Amy pulled back from Harry. Her frustration knew no bounds, and yet she spoke to her son in reasonable tones. "Puget Sound is too cold for swimming, Oliver," she said. "You know that."

Harry reached out to rumple the boy's hair affectionately, an understanding grin curving his lips, and Amy liked the Australian all the more for being so perceptive.

Soon they reached the island, driving ashore in Harry's van. He brought a small notebook from the catch-all space between the front seats and consulted some hastily scrawled directions with a thoughtful frown. After that, he seemed to know exactly what he was doing.

Within fifteen minutes, they pulled up beside the kind of place northwest artists loved to sketch. It was a lighthouse, built of white stone, with a long house stretching out in one direction, its many windows sparkling in the sunshine. On the other side was a fenced courtyard, complete with rose bushes, stone benches and a marble fountain.

Amy drew in her breath. "Harry, it's wonderful," she said.

A perfect gentleman, Harry had come around to her side of the van. Perhaps it was an accident, and perhaps it wasn't, that her midsection slid the length of his when he lifted her down. "Then I'll have no choice but to sign the papers," he said, his mouth very close to hers again.

Oliver and Ashley were sizing up the lighthouse, heads tilted back, eyes wide.

"I'll bet you can see all the way to China from up there!" Oliver crowed.

Ashley gave him a little shove. "Don't be a dummy. You'll only be able to see Seattle."

An expensive white car came up the cobbled driveway and stopped behind Harry's van. A tall, artfully made-up woman with champagne-blond hair got out. She was wearing a trim suit in the palest pink, with a classic white blouse, and Amy suddenly felt downright provincial in her jeans and sweater.

"Mr. Griffith?" the woman asked, smiling and extending her hand. As she drew closer, Amy let out her breath. The real estate agent was strikingly attractive, but she was also old enough to be Harry's mother. "I'm Eva Caldwell," she added. Her bright eyes swept over Amy and the children. "And this must be your family."

Harry only grinned, but Amy was discomfited by the suggestion. No matter what her subconscious mind had to say through very convincing images of her late husband, Harry Griffith was not the sort of man to want a ready-made family. He was the type that married a beautiful heiress and honeymooned on a private yacht somewhere among the Greek Islands.

"We're just his friends," Ashley piped up.

"Very good friends," Harry confirmed, giving Ashley's shoulder a little squeeze.

Mrs. Caldwell jingled a set of keys, her smile at once warm and professional, and started toward the double mahogany doors leading into the addition. "The lighthouse, of course, was the original structure. The other rooms were built around the turn of the century..."

The inside of the place was as intriguing as the outside. On the lower level was a living room with beamed ceilings. It stretched the width of the house, and the wall of windows gave a startling view of the water. The floors were pegged wood, and there was a massive fireplace at one end, with brass andirons on the hearth and built-in bookshelves on both sides.

On the far side of the room was an arched doorway leading to a hallway. There were four bedrooms beyond that, the master suite with a natural rock fireplace of its own, and up a short flight of stairs was a large loft, offering the same view of Puget Sound as the living room.

There was a door leading from the loft into the lighthouse itself. The kids rushed up the spiral staircase ahead of Mrs. Caldwell and Harry and Amy, in their excitement to see China or, failing that, Seattle.

"A place like this ought to come with a ghost, by all rights," Harry remarked.

If he'd tossed Amy a leaky plastic bag filled with ice, Harry couldn't have startled her more. She stopped on the stairs and stared at him, feeling the color drain from her face, wondering if he somehow knew she was seeing things and wanted to make fun of her.

"Amy?" He stopped, letting Mrs. Caldwell go on ahead. She was still talking, unaware that her prospect was lagging behind. "What's the matter?"

The calm reason of his tone and manner made Amy feel silly. Of *course* he didn't have an inkling that she'd seen Tyler, and as brief as their acquaintance had been, she knew Harry was above needling another person in such a callous way.

"Nothing's the matter," she answered finally. Her smile felt wobbly on her lips.

Harry frowned, but then he reached out to her, as naturally as if they'd always been together. Just as naturally Amy took his hand and they climbed the rest of the way together.

In the top of the old but well-maintained tower was a surprisingly modern electric light.

"The lighthouse is still used when the weather gets particularly nasty," Mrs. Caldwell explained.

"I can see Seattle!" Oliver whooped from the other side of the little causeway that surrounded the massive, many-faceted lamp.

"He's apparently given up on China," Harry whispered with a slight smile and a lift of one eyebrow.

Amy felt just the way she once had as a kid at summer camp, when she'd fallen off a horse and knocked the wind out of her lungs. Remarkable that just a hint of a smile could have such an effect.

"Spend as much time looking as you'd like," Mrs. Caldwell said, holding out a single key to Harry. She gave him brief directions to her office, which was near the ferry terminal, and asked him to stop by before he left.

When Ashley and Oliver raced back downstairs to check out the yard, Harry and Amy remained where they were.

Amy read the sober expression in Harry's eyes as consternation. He frowned again, as though she'd said something he was forced to disagree with, and then pulled her close and kissed her.

The gentle, skilled prodding of his tongue made her open to him, and she gave an involuntary moan, surrendering even before the skirmish had begun.

Harry held her hips in his hands, pressing her lightly against him. He nibbled at her lower lip and tasted the corners of her mouth, and still the gentle conquering went on.

Finally, though, Harry thrust himself back from her. He was breathing hard as though he'd just barely managed to escape a powerful undercurrent.

"I'm sorry," he said, and although Amy knew he had to be talking to her, it was almost as though he were addressing someone else.

An apology was probably the last thing Amy had wanted to hear. She was still responding, body and spirit, to the kiss, still reeling from the way she'd wanted him. She cleared her throat delicately and led the way downstairs without a word, using the time with her back to Harry to regain her composure.

"What do you think of the place?" he asked sometime later, when the four of them had built a driftwood fire on the beach and brought a cooler and a picnic basket from the van.

"It's wonderful," Amy answered, feeling her cheeks go warm as an echo of Harry's thorough kiss tingled on her mouth.

Harry surveyed the beautiful lighthouse pensively as he roasted a marshmallow over the fire. "It's big," he countered.

Ashley and Oliver were running wildly up and down the beach, their cheeks bright with color, their laughter ringing in the salty air. Amy couldn't remember the last time she'd seen them enjoy an outing so much.

She put a marshmallow on another stick and watched it turn crisp and bubbly over the flames. "I imagine you can see the ferry lights from the living room at night," she said a little dreamily.

Harry ate the sticky marshmallow he'd just roasted, and Amy imagined that his lips would taste of it if he kissed her again. For a long moment she honestly thought he was about to, but then he started gathering the debris from their picnic on the beach.

Amy helped, and by the time they reached the real estate office, Ashley and Oliver were already asleep in the back of the van and a light rain was falling.

Waiting in the van, watching the windshield wip-
ers whip back and forth over the glass, Amy felt sad,
as though she were leaving the one place where she
really belonged.

Chapter 4

Harry Griffith was not a fanciful man. He dealt in stark realities and played for very high stakes, and he hadn't done an impetuous thing since he was seven years old.

For all of that, he signed the papers to buy the lighthouse when he'd only meant to drop off the keys. He couldn't stop imagining Amy in the massive living room, reflected firelight glittering in her golden brown hair. Or in his bed, her trim yet lush body all soft and warm and welcoming.

If that wasn't enough to haunt a man for days, the mingled sounds of the children's laughter and the tide whispering against the shore were still echoing in his mind.

"I'm sure you'll be very happy on the island," Mrs. Caldwell said.

"I'm sure I will," Harry agreed, but he wasn't thinking about the view or the clams and oysters he could gather. He was obsessed with Amy Ryan, had been practically from the moment he'd met her.

Mrs. Caldwell smiled. "Do let me know if there's anything else I can do," she said. She and Harry shook hands, and then he turned and sprinted out into the rain to rejoin Amy and the children in the van.

Amy looked every bit as nervous and unsettled as he felt.

"I bought the house," he announced, the moment he'd closed the door and put the key into the ignition. Again Harry had taken himself by surprise; he'd definitely decided, only moments before, that he wouldn't mention the purchase to Amy until they knew each other better.

She seemed a bit bewildered, but there might have been just a glimmer of pleasure in those wonderful hazel eyes, too. Harry, who was usually such a good judge of people, couldn't be certain.

"You won't find a more charming place anywhere in the country," she said after a few moments of silence.

Harry glanced back over one shoulder at the sleeping children. "Do you think they'll wake up for dinner? We could stop somewhere on the other side..."

Amy shook her head. "Thank you for offering," she said softly, "but I think it would be best if I took them straight home. They've had a pretty full day as it is, and any more excitement would probably put them on overload."

Harry felt another new emotion: chagrin. Maybe he'd offended Amy by kissing her earlier that day in the lighthouse, made her wonder what kind of friend he could have been to Tyler. God help him, Harry had known better than to do what he did, but he hadn't been able to stop himself.

His vocal cords seemed to be on automatic pilot, yet another unfamiliar experience. All his adult life, except for those few whiskey-sodden days after he'd learned of Tyler's death, Harry had been in complete control of all his faculties. Now, suddenly, nothing seemed to follow its usual order.

"Tomorrow night, then?" he asked, before he could measure the words in his mind.

She smiled at him with a certain sweet weariness that made him want to give her comfort and pleasure. "Oliver and Ashley will be spending the day with Tyler's folks," she said, and he wondered if she expected him to withdraw the invitation because of that.

"But you won't be?"

Amy shrugged one strong but delicate shoulder. "I'd be welcome if I wanted to go. But I think both the kids and Mom and Dad Ryan need time to interact without me hovering around somewhere."

Harry rode the crest of foolhardy bravado that seemed to be carrying him along. "Fine. Then you'll be free to have dinner with me."

He sensed that she was carrying on some inner struggle, he was aware of it all the while he paid the toll and drove onto the Seattle-bound ferry, and the fear that she would refuse was as keenly painful as a nerve exposed to cold air.

"I'd like that," she finally said, her voice soft and cautious.

With some effort, Harry held back a shout of gleeful triumph—the sensation was rather like scoring the winning goal in a soccer match—and managed what he hoped was an easy, man-of-the-world smile.

"So would I," he agreed. "So would I."

Charlotte Ryan's voice echoed off the walls of Amy's closet as she plundered the contents for something suitable for that night's heavy date. Small, with sleek dark hair and inquisitive brown eyes, Charlotte was one of Amy's closest friends. Tyler had always referred to her as "my favorite sister," subsequently making light of the fact that she was his *only* sister.

She came out carrying a sophisticated silver-lamé sheath with a gracefully draped neckline.

"This is perfect," Charlotte announced. "Which isn't to say you couldn't give a lot of that stuff in there to the Salvation Army and start fresh with a whole new wardrobe."

The glittery dress was expensive, and one of the few garments in Amy's closet that wasn't a holdover from the fairy-tale time before Tyler's death. She'd bought it a few months ago for a banquet honoring her father and hadn't worn it since.

"Maybe it's too fancy," Amy fretted. "For all I know, we're going to a waterfront stand for fish and chips."

"With Harry Griffith?" Charlotte countered, laying the dress carefully on the bed. "Not on your life, Amy. The man is class personified. Mark my words, he'll be wearing a tux and holding flowers when he rings the doorbell."

Amy's heart rate quickened at the romantic thought, and she was instantly ashamed of the reaction. Tyler would be so hurt if he knew the depths of the attraction she was feeling for Harry Griffith.

Immediately her mind presented a counterpoint to its own suggestion, reminding her that it had been Tyler who'd told her she was supposed to marry Harry, even bear his children.

It was all too confusing.

Charlotte was waving one hand back and forth in front of Amy's face. "Yo, sister dear," she teased. "Are you in there?"

Amy busied herself finding panty hose in her bureau drawer. "How long is it supposed to take to get over...well, to get over becoming a widow?"

Her sister-in-law was silent for a long moment. Then she laid a gentle hand on Amy's shoulder. "I don't think there are any written rules about that. But I do know Ty wouldn't want you to spend the rest of your life grieving for him, Amy."

Tears burned in Amy's eyes and thickened in her throat. "I loved him so much."

Charlotte came around to face Amy and give her a quick hug. "I know," she said. "But, Amy, he's gone, and you're still young..."

"It's Ty's fault that I'm so hesitant to get into another relationship, you know," Amy sniffled. "Marriage to him was so wonderful, nothing else could possibly be expected to equal it."

Charlotte's eyes widened, and she chuckled. "That's the damnedest reason for staying single I've ever heard! You're scared of finding another husband because you were *too happy* the first time?"

"I know it sounds crazy," Amy insisted, pushing her bureau drawer shut with a thump, "but Tyler Ryan would be a very hard act to follow."

"Don't expect me to argue," Charlotte said, her eyes moist with emotion. "I loved my brother a lot. He was an original. But you can't just hide out in your career for the next forty years, waiting to join him in the great beyond. You've got to get out there and *live*."

"Who says?" Amy asked, but she knew Charlotte was right. Life was a precious gift; to waste it was the unpardonable sin.

Charlotte gave Amy a little shove toward the bathroom. "Get in there and take a long, luxurious bubble bath. I'll drop the kids off at Mom and Dad's."

Amy sniffled one last time. "Thanks," she said hoarsely, giving her sister-in-law another hug.

Taking Charlotte's advice to heart, Amy filled the

tub in her private bathroom, adding generous amounts of the expensive bubble bath her father had given her for Christmas the year before. She pinned up her thick hair and hung her long white terry-cloth robe on the hook on the inside of the door.

Amy stripped and sank gratefully into the warm, soapy water.

"Charlotte's right," Tyler announced suddenly, so startling Amy that she barely kept herself from screaming. "Harry is a classy guy."

Tyler, dressed in a vaguely familiar blue-and-white sweater, stood with one foot resting on the toilet seat, elbow propped on his knee, chin resting in his palm.

"You might have knocked or something!" Amy hissed, when she was finally able to speak.

"Knocked?" Ty looked downright offended. "We were married once, in case you've forgotten."

Amy sighed. "Of course I haven't forgotten. And what do you mean, we *were* married?"

Tyler shrugged and pretended a sober interest in the composition of the shower curtain. "You know. I'm here, you're there. And you've got a lot of time left on your hitch, Spud, so you'd better get your act together."

She started to rise out of the water, felt self-conscious, and decided to keep herself cloaked in the piles of iridescent bubbles. Then she narrowed her eyes. "Are you saying that you plan to go on to wherever you're going without me?" she demanded.

"The bargain was 'till death do us part,' darlin'. And don't look now, but death done parted us."

Amy felt a wrenching sensation deep within her, a tearing away that seemed decidedly permanent. "You've met someone!"

Tyler grinned. "It doesn't work that way on this side, Spud. And even if there were some kind of celestial dating service, I have too much work to do to take time out for a relationship."

He looked so real, as if she could reach out and touch him and he'd feel solid under her hand. She made no effort to do that, however, because the memory of the way he'd pulled back from her the other time was still fresh in her mind.

Amy leaned back against the blue plastic bathtub pillow and closed her eyes. "I'm hallucinating," she said. "When I open my eyes, you will be gone."

But when she looked again, Tyler was still standing there. "Are you through?" he asked a little impatiently. "I told you before, Amy...my energy is limited and I don't have time to play 'is he or isn't he?'"

Amy's mouth dropped open, and she closed it again.

"Harry's taking you to the Stardust Ballroom," Tyler went on. "He's very attracted to you, but he's also having some conflicts. It bothers him that you were my wife."

Amy waited, in shock.

"You've got to reassure Harry somehow, before he comes up with some excuse to go back to Australia and stay there. I'm counting on you, Amy."

There was an urgency in Tyler's tone that troubled Amy, but she had her hands full just trying to cope with *seeing* him. She blinked, that was all, just blinked, and when she looked again her husband's ghost was gone.

Relaxing in the bathtub was out of the question, of course. In fact, Amy wasn't sure she shouldn't call 911 and have herself trundled off to the pot-holder-weaving department of the nearest hospital.

She jumped up, grabbed her robe and wrapped it around herself without taking the time to dry off. The thing to do was call Harry and beg off from their dinner date. She could claim illness, since there seemed to be every possibility she was losing her mind!

The trouble was, Amy still didn't have Harry's number, nor did she know where he was staying.

But the Ryans might. Surely Harry had contacted Tyler's parents, since he'd lived in their home as an exchange student for six months, back in high school...

Amy was about to dive for the telephone when her eyes fell on the spray of white lilacs lying on her pillow. Their lovely scent seemed to fill the room.

The blossoms were Tyler's special signature. In the old days, before the great and all-encompassing grief that had practically swallowed Amy's very soul, he'd often cut a bouquet in the backyard and presented them to her in just this way.

Her eyes stung. "Oh, Tyler," she whispered.

Since she knew she'd obsess if she stayed home, Amy went ahead with the preparations for her dinner date. She applied makeup, put on the shimmery dress and did her hair up in a loose bun at the back of her

head. A few tendrils of sun-streaked blond hair were
left to dangle against her cheeks and neck.

She was in the den, pacing, when the doorbell rang.

Opening the door, Amy found Harry waiting on the
step. He was wearing a tux, just as Charlotte had predicted, and he looked like an advertisement for some
exclusive European wristwatch. In one hand he carried
a delicate bouquet of exotic pink-and-white blossoms.

His blue eyes darkened slightly as he looked at
Amy, then he smiled and held out the flowers, along
with a long white envelope.

"You must surely be the most beautiful woman in
the whole of the Western hemisphere," he said, his
voice a low, rumbling caress that struck sparks in some
very tender parts of Amy's anatomy.

"Come in," Amy said, sounding a lot more composed than she felt, stepping back to admit him. She
admired the velvety pastel lilies for a moment, then
turned the envelope over, as if its back might reveal
its contents.

"Your dividend on Tyler's investment in the opal
mines," Harry explained, his voice a bit gruff. He
cleared his throat, but it didn't seem to help much.
"Obviously I forgot to give it to you yesterday."

Amy hesitated.

"Open it," Harry prompted, closing the door.

She tore off the end of the envelope and slipped
the check out. As financially secure as Amy was, the
amount still came as a pleasant shock. It was enough
to buy a decent house outright.

"Tyler must have made a very large investment," she mused.

"Actually, he put up the accumulated birthday money from his grandmother," Harry explained.

Amy went into the den and put the check between the pages of her personal journal. Harry stood with his back to her, in front of the stone fireplace, looking at the row of pictures on the mantel.

When he turned to face Amy, the thought flew into her mind that she could probably achieve some distance between them by telling Harry she'd seen Tyler on three different occasions. Odd that she was more frightened of this living, breathing man than of a dead one.

"Shall we?" he said, offering his arm.

Amy couldn't bring herself to mention her hallucinations. "Just let me put these lilies in water," she said hastily, turning to hurry into the kitchen for a shallow bowl.

Floating in that fiery crystal, the flowers were so beautiful that they made Amy's throat swell.

There was a white limousine, complete with driver, waiting at the curb. Harry helped Amy into the backseat, which was upholstered in suede of a smoky blue, and climbed in beside her.

"I forgot to thank you for the dividend check," Amy said, feeling awkward and shy again. She couldn't help remembering the kiss she and Harry had shared the day before; just the thought of it made her go all warm and achy inside.

Harry gave an elegant shrug. "It's rightfully yours," he said. Then he reached out and lightly entwined his finger in one of the wisps of hair bobbing against Amy's cheek. "Such a bewitching creature," he added, as if musing to himself rather than speaking to her. "If a being as lovely and magical as you can exist, then surely there must be unicorns somewhere in this world as well."

Amy felt dizzy. "That's some line," she said, after a few moments of being totally inarticulate.

He smiled. "Oh, it's not a line," he assured her suavely. "I meant every word."

Amy believed him, although she knew she should have had her head examined for it. Next, he'd be telling her that no other woman had ever understood him the way she did, and asking her to come to his hotel room to view his etchings.

She ran the tip of her tongue over her lips. The gesture was quick, over in a second, but Harry followed it with his eyes, and it seemed that time stopped for a little while. That she and Harry were alone in the universe.

For all of the thrumming attraction she'd felt ever since she'd met this man, their second kiss startled her completely.

Harry tasted her lips expertly, as though they were flavored with the finest wine, sending little shocks reverberating throughout her system. He might have been kissing her much more intimately, given the responses the contact wrought in her, and when his hand cupped her breast, she gave a whispered moan and tilted her head back.

He sampled her neck, the tender hollows beneath her ear, the pulse point at the base of her throat.

Harry apparently remembered the driver, even if Amy, to her vast chagrin, did not. He drew back from her, smiled in a way that made her heart and throat collide at breakneck speed, and caressed her cheek with the side of his thumb.

He didn't have to say he wanted to make love to Amy; his eyes told her clearly enough.

Minutes later, when the limousine was purring at a downtown curb, the driver came back to open the door. Amy was grateful for the cool breeze that met her as she stepped out onto the sidewalk.

She was also enormously relieved, because the restaurant was not the Stardust Ballroom, as Tyler had predicted. That made things a little less spooky.

The place was shadowy and elegant, with candles flickering in the centers of the tables, and the atmosphere was intimate. Amy hoped the dimness would hide her bright eyes and glowing cheeks—it wouldn't do for Harry to guess how thoroughly he'd aroused her.

Amy had seafood salad and Harry had a steak, and they both drank a dry, velvety wine. When the meal was over, they danced.

For all that there were other couples around, the experience was another alarmingly intimate one for Amy. The way Harry held her close was in no way inappropriate, but the scent and substance of him excited her in a way nothing in her life had prepared her for. Her breasts and thighs were cushioned against the granite lines of his frame, and Amy's body was responding as though she were naked beneath him, in a private place.

He had guessed what was happening, evidently, for a half smile curved his lips. He gave no quarter.

His lips moved, warm, against her temple. "There's no going back now, love," he warned in a ragged whisper. "It's going to happen—tonight, tomorrow, next week."

Amy knew Harry was right, but as much as she wanted him, the idea of such total surrender terrified her.

He traced her mouth with the tip of one index finger. "So beautiful," he said.

"C-could we sit down, please?"

Harry led her back to their table and seated her with as much grace as if she'd been a princess.

She couldn't meet his eyes, and her cheeks felt as hot as the tip of the candle's flame. After all, she'd practically come apart in the man's arms, and all because of the way he'd been holding her.

Harry reached out to curve his finger under her chin. "We have time, Amy," he reminded her.

Amy was relieved when he didn't ask her to dance again, though. She wasn't sure how much intimate contact she could take without making an absolute fool of herself.

They had Irish coffee and then left the restaurant.

"I think I have a headache coming on," Amy lied, once they were settled in the limousine again. Inside, she was still quivering from the tempestuous desire he'd awakened in her.

Harry grinned. "We can't just go off and leave the driver, now can we?" he teased.

Amy glanced nervously toward the front. There was no sign of the chauffeur. "Maybe I could just take a cab…"

But Harry shook his head before she'd even finished the suggestion. "When I take a lady out," he said in his rich accent, "I always take her home again. Come here, Amy."

She was overwhelmingly conscious of Harry's aftershave, the softness of the suede seats, the gentle command in his dark blue eyes. She tried to think of Tyler and, to her utter frustration, found that she couldn't remember what he'd looked like. Although she would have testified in a court of law that she hadn't moved, Amy suddenly found herself in Harry's arms again.

He kissed her, that was all, and yet Amy felt herself melting like warm wax. For the first time ever, she actually wanted a man other than Tyler, and her emotions were as tangled as a string of garage-sale Christmas tree lights.

The tinted windows of the limousine provided a high degree of privacy; the fact that the driver could return at any moment lent the situation a sense of breathless urgency.

She heard the electric locks on the limousine's doors click into place, and that made her eyes go wide.

He did nothing more than kiss and hold her, and yet Amy felt like some succulent dessert. Everything seemed to be happening in slow motion, and Amy was helpless to stop the tide of fate. She was abashed to realize that, if Harry suggested heading straight for his hotel room, she would have agreed.

Suddenly, though, the locks clicked again, and Harry was sitting a respectable distance from her, looking as unruffled as if he'd just stepped from his barber's chair.

Amy, on the contrary, was in a state of blissful shock.

The driver got back into the car, and Amy heard Harry give him a familiar address—her own. The only emotion that exceeded her relief was her disappointment.

On the porch, Harry bent forward to kiss her lightly on the tip of her nose. "You were too delectable to resist," he told her. "I'll try to mind my manners a little better next time."

Amy's senses were still rioting, and she rocked slightly on her heels, so that Harry clasped her elbows to steady her. "You could come in and have coffee," she said, and then she bit her lip. She'd had virtually no experience at being a vamp, since she'd never been with another man besides Tyler.

His smile was sexy enough to be lethal, though there was an element of sadness in it, too. "If I came in tonight, Amy," he said, "I'm afraid I would want much more than coffee. And neither of us is ready."

With that, Harry kissed her on the forehead—it was a purely innocuous contact that left Amy feeling hollow—and walked away.

She had the presence of mind to turn the lock and put the chain on the door after he was gone, but just barely. She gave a little hiccuping sob when Rumpel appeared and wrapped her sleek, silky body around her ankles.

"Reowww," she said companionably.

In need of comfort, Amy scooped the small animal into her arms and hurried up the stairs.

All the while she was taking off her dress and washing her face and putting on cotton pajamas, Amy cried. She had turned some kind of emotional corner, and she knew there would be no going back.

Tyler's mother awakened her with a phone call at ten-thirty the next morning.

"Hello, Amy," Louise Ryan said warmly. "I'm calling to ask a very big favor."

Amy was only half-awake, and rummy from a night of alternate crying and soul-searching. "A favor?"

"John and I are leaving for Kansas, the first of next week…his side of the family is having a big reunion. We hadn't planned on going, but at the last minute we decided to live a little. And, well, we'd like to take Oliver and Ashley along on the trip, if you don't mind."

The breathless hope in her mother-in-law's voice brought a tender smile to Amy's mouth.

"Of course they can go, Louise," she said, marveling even as the words left her mouth.

The next few minutes were taken up with the making of plans; John and Louise planned to drive back to the midwest in their motor home, and they wanted to pick the kids up early Monday morning.

"Oliver tells me you've been seeing Harry Griffith," Louise said, when everything had been decided.

Just remembering last night's interlude in the limousine made color flow into Amy's cheeks, but she managed to make her voice sound normal. "I'm not *seeing* him, actually," she hedged. *You are, though,* challenged a voice in her mind. *And admit it, you'd like to do a lot more than that.*

"Harry is a wonderful young man," Louise said brightly.

"Yes," Amy agreed, keeping her tone strictly noncommittal. Despite the fact that she'd behaved like a teenager in the backseat of a Chevy the night before, she had a lot of reservations where Harry Griffith was concerned.

Amy swallowed, winding her finger in the telephone cord. She should tell Louise she'd been seeing Tyler, she knew that, but the risk was just too great. She depended on John and Louise Ryan—for all practical intents and purposes, they were the only family she had—and she didn't want them to think she was having a nervous breakdown or something.

"We'll bring the children home later this morning," Louise went on, apparently failing to notice the long lull on Amy's end of the conversation. "And thank you, dear, for letting us take them on the trip with us."

Amy said something ordinary, something she couldn't remember later, added a warm farewell and hung up. After she'd brushed her teeth and washed her face and generally made herself presentable, she went downstairs in shorts and a T-shirt to let Rumpel out.

She was having a much-needed cup of coffee when the doorbell rang, and when she reached the entryway, she found Harry standing on the step. He was wearing jeans and a Henley, and yet he managed to look as elegantly rakish as an old-time riverboat gambler.

"G'day," he said, leaning one shoulder against the doorjamb. "Is that offer of coffee still open?"

Amy hadn't prepared herself, mentally or otherwise, for an encounter with Harry, and she was caught off guard. She blushed, nodded, and stepped back.

"You know," Harry said with a grin, "it's perfectly charming, the way you do that."

"Do what?" Amy challenged. For some reason she couldn't have put a name to, she needed to contradict him.

"Color up like a naked virgin when the bathhouse wall has just collapsed," he answered. "Are the children about?"

Amy led the way into the kitchen. "No," she answered, grateful that her response only called for simple words. "They're with the Ryans, making plans for a trip."

Harry turned her when she reached for the cupboard where the mugs were stored, and she was trapped between his hard torso and the counter. He traced her mouth with the tip of one index finger. "Excellent," he said. "That leaves you with no rational excuse for refusing to fly to Australia with me tomorrow."

Chapter 5

Amy had every rational reason to refuse Harry's invitation to visit Australia with him. She *must* have rational reasons, she thought. It was just that she couldn't summon up a single one on such short notice.

Harry smiled his slow, knee-melting smile, only too aware, evidently, of her dilemma, then arched one eyebrow as if prompting her to produce a suitable answer.

"I don't have a visa for Australia," she finally said, flustered.

Harry outlined the edge of her jaw with a fingertip, sending fire racing through her system. "No worries, love," he said, his voice husky and low. "I can take care of that with a single telephone call."

Amy was trapped and she liked it, and the fact incensed her. "I can't just go flying off to another hemisphere with a man I hardly know!" she pointed out irritably.

He was so close, so solid, so warm. So male. "Ah," he said wisely, "but you *want* to know me quite well, don't you, Amy?"

Coming from any other man, the question would have sounded insufferably arrogant. From Harry, it was the unvarnished, pitiless truth.

"Yes," she confessed weakly, before she could stop herself.

Harry touched his lips to hers, with the lightest brushing motion, and a fiery shiver exploded in the core of her being, flinging rays of sweet heat into all her extremities. In fact, it was a wonder to Amy that her hair didn't crackle.

"Yes," he agreed with a sigh.

They just stood there like that, for an eternity, it seemed to Amy, and then he kissed her forehead.

"I think I'd better go now," he said reluctantly. He laid a finger to her nose. "Pack for a warm climate, love, and bring something for a glamorous occasion."

Amy didn't ask how he'd know when to pick her up. There was something mystical about the whole thing, something preordained. When it was time to leave, Harry would simply be there.

After he was gone, Amy went out into the backyard and stood by the tire swing.

"Tyler!" she demanded in an anxious, self-conscious whisper. "Where are you? I need to talk to you right now!"

There was no answer but for a breeze that ruffled the bushes burgeoning with white lilacs and carried their scent to Amy like a gift.

"This is important!" she pressed, feeling desperate. She knew what was going to happen if she went to Australia with Harry Griffith, and she was terrified. After all, she'd never been intimate with another man, before Tyler or after, and she felt as shy as a virgin.

"What's that, dear?" inquired a pleasant female voice.

Amy looked up to see Mrs. Ingallstadt, her neighbor, peering at her over the fence. The older woman was wearing a gardening hat and wielding clipping shears.

"I was just—" Amy paused to clear her throat and to work up a smile. "I was just thinking out loud, Mrs. Ingallstadt. How are you?"

"Well, my arthritis is going to be the death of me one of these days, and my gall bladder is acting up again, but otherwise I'm pretty chipper. Tell me, dear, how are you?"

Well, Amy thought, *I'm seeing things and I think I'm actually going to get on an airplane and fly away to another continent with a virtual stranger. Other than that, Mrs. Ingallstadt, I'm just fine.*

"I've been keeping busy." Recalling Mrs. Ingallstadt's fondness for white lilacs, and how Tyler had occasionally charmed the old woman with a bouquet, Amy walked over to one lacy bush and broke off several blossom-laden boughs. Without saying any more, she handed the flowers over the fence to her friend and neighbor.

Mrs. Ingallstadt beamed with pleasure, and Amy realized, with some chagrin, that she'd hardly exchanged a word with the woman in six full months. After Tyler's death, Mrs. Ingallstadt had been wonderful to Amy, and to Ashley and Oliver as well. She'd made meals, baby-sat and listened patiently when Amy was overwhelmed with grief. That first dreadful Christmas, when it seemed there would never again be reason to celebrate, the thoughtful neighbor had come into Amy's kitchen, pushed up her sleeves and proceeded to bake sugar cookies with the children.

"I'll just take these right inside and put them in water," Mrs Ingallstadt said happily. "I don't know why I haven't planted a few lilac bushes of my own. My husband was allergic to them, you know, but Walter's been dead these twenty years and I don't reckon anything could make him sneeze now."

Amy's grin was probably a little on the grim side. *Don't count on it,* she thought.

Later that day, when she'd vacuumed the upstairs hallway and gone through her closet four times, all the while insisting to herself that she *would not* do anything so impetuous as fly to Australia with Harry Griffith, Amy got her suitcases from the guest-room closet and laid them on her bed. Open.

Even then, she told herself she only meant to pack things for Ashley and Oliver to take to Kansas.

Still, when Louise brought the kids home from

Mercer Island in her shiny silver Mercedes, Amy had filled the luggage with her own best summer clothes.

She and Louise did the kids' things together. Louise Ryan was an attractive woman, tanned and obviously prosperous, and she was intelligent.

"How was your evening with Harry Griffith?" she asked, snapping the catches on Ashley's suitcase into place.

Color surged into Amy's face, and she didn't quite manage to meet her mother-in-law's gaze. She couldn't help wondering what Louise would think if she knew her son's widow was about to do something completely reckless and wanton.

"I like him," Amy finally replied. She was sure a greater understatement had never been uttered.

Louise smiled, her Tyler-brown eyes laughing. Her hair was a rich auburn color, frosted with silvery gray, and she claimed she was covered in freckles from head to foot. "A woman doesn't simply 'like' a man like our Harry," she said confidently, her gaze steady as she regarded Amy. "She either finds him totally intolerable or can't keep her hands off him."

Guess which category I fall into, Amy thought ruefully, her face going warm again. "I guess Tyler liked him a lot," she hedged, picking up Ashley's suitcase and lugging it to the doorway. Its weight didn't justify the effort, however, and she had a feeling Louise knew that.

"Tyler thought the world of Harry Griffith. So do the rest of us."

As understanding and progressive a woman as Louise was, Amy still couldn't make herself confide that she was wildly attracted to Harry. The thought reverberated inside her mind, however, like the silent toll of some mystic bell. "He's a nice man," was all she said.

After Ashley and Oliver had left the house with their grandmother, bag and baggage, Amy felt as insubstantial as an echo, bouncing aimlessly between one empty room and another. Finally, she went to the phone and dialed Debbie's home number, knowing she'd get an answering machine because her friend would be at the clinic.

"Hi," Amy said with a stilted effort at normalcy, "this is Amy. I just wanted to let you know that, well, I've completely lost my mind. Harry Griffith invited me to fly to Australia in his private jet, and God help me I'm going to do it." Color flooded her cheeks, even though she was talking to a whirring mechanism and not another human being. "Actually, *do it* isn't precisely the phrasing I was looking for, although I'm a grown woman and responsible person and if I want to do—anything—oh, never mind!" Amy forcibly stopped herself from rambling, drew a deep breath and let it out again. "I'm going to Australia, but I don't want you to worry about me because I know what I'm doing."

She hung up before adding, "I think."

Harry arrived an hour later, looking like a *GQ* model in his elegantly cut navy-blue suit. When he saw her luggage sitting in the entryway, he arched

one dark eyebrow and favored her with one of his
nuclear grins.

"Let's go, love," he said, reaching down to take the
handle of one suitcase in each hand. Rumpel purred
and curled around Harry's left ankle. "You have, I
presume, made arrangements for the cat?"

"Mrs. Ingallstadt will look after Rumpel," Amy
said, and even as she spoke she could hardly believe
she was really doing this crazy, impulsive thing. She
had always been the practical type, the one who balanced her checking account to the penny and color-
coded her sock drawer.

Harry's blue gaze drifted over her simple cotton
print dress with unsettling leisure. "Mmm. Well, then,
we're off."

They drove to the airport in Harry's rented van, and
Amy gnawed at her lower lip through practically the
whole trip. Once in a while, she even reached for the
door handle in an impotent stab at making a run for it.

Harry seemed amused.

"I suppose you're used to women who do this sort
of thing all the time," Amy said in stiff and testy tones,
clutching at her anger as though it were a lifeline.

He chuckled. "What sort of thing is that, my
lovely?" he teased, pulling the van to a stop next to a
sleek jet that stood gleaming on the tarmac beside a
private hangar.

"This is not at all like me," Amy insisted, when
Harry came around to her side to help her down.

He made an answering sound, a low rumble in his

throat, and then brushed her lips ever so lightly with his own. "Which is one of the many things that makes you so blasted appealing," he agreed with a philosophical sigh. For the first time, Amy realized that Harry didn't want this attraction between them any more than she did.

The idea was oddly painful, all things considered.

The pilot had already arrived and was in the process of a preflight check when Harry gave Amy a tour of the aircraft. There was a galley, glittering and efficient, and all the leather-upholstered seats were cushy and wide, built to swivel on their shiny steel bases. There was a bar, which didn't interest Amy—just the thought of combining liquor with altitude made her queasy.

"There are water closets back there," Harry said, gesturing toward a wide hallway at the rear of the cabin. "Take your choice."

For Amy, in those moments, curiosity was a refuge, a place she could scurry into and hide out from her fear of the inevitable. She ventured into the hallway and peered through two separate doorways.

Even though Amy's father was a heart surgeon, and she'd never known poverty in her life, those glitzy bathrooms came as a surprise to her, with their glass and marble.

Harry went past her with the suitcases, disappearing into yet another room. The master suite, no doubt.

The magnetism was powerful, and resisting it took a formidable effort, but Amy managed to grope her way back to the main cabin. She was standing behind one of the elegant seats, her fingers digging deep into the sumptuous upholstery, when Harry returned.

She smiled shakily. "You certainly have nice bathrooms," she said. The instant the words had left her mouth she longed to call them back, they sounded so silly.

Harry chuckled. "Yes," he agreed. His indigo eyes moved over her in a way that was, incomprehensibly, both arrogant and reverent.

Amy felt as though he'd deftly peeled her clothes away, and it seemed to her that the very air was pulsating with some elemental, unseen force—a power that emanated from Harry himself.

The intercom saved her from having to speak, which was fortunate because a troupe of heated fantasies had invaded her mind, crowding out all rational thought.

"The preflight check has been completed, sir," announced the pilot's voice, "and we have clearance for takeoff."

Harry walked over to the bar and pushed a button on a high-tech unit behind it, and his soul-searing gaze never left Amy once. "Fine," he said in a voice that was somewhat hoarse. "Thank you."

He crossed the cabin then and, smiling slightly, pressed Amy into a seat. The act of crouching beside her and fastening her seat belt was entirely innocent, and yet it left Amy feeling as though they'd engaged in half an hour of intense foreplay.

Harry took the seat nearest hers and fastened himself in. It was plain enough to Amy that he hadn't missed the significance of her bright eyes and flushed face.

Soon the plane was speeding down the runway. Harry held Amy's hand until they were aloft.

"There now," he said, unsnapping his seat belt and rising as casually as he might from an easy chair in his living room. "We're on our way. Would you like something to drink?"

Yes, Amy thought. *A double shot of the strongest whiskey you have.* "A diet cola would be nice," she said aloud.

Harry made no comment on her choice; he simply went about taking a can of soda from the refrigerator beneath the bar.

Amy unfastened her seat belt and thrust herself shakily to her feet. There was no going back now.

She crossed to the teakwood bar, which was bolted securely to the floor, and leaned against it, trying to look as though she did this sort of thing all the time.

"You must practically live in this plane, it's outfitted so well," she commented.

Harry was still behind the bar, and he handed Amy her cola. Then he grinned his endearing, soul-wrenching grin and said with a shrug, "I'm rich."

A nervous giggle escaped Amy, and she just barely kept herself from slapping one hand over her mouth. She'd never been more sober in her life, and yet she felt as though she were roaring drunk.

"Relax, Amy," Harry said, leaning forward slightly, bracing himself against the bar with wide-spread hands. "I'm not planning to heave you over one shoulder, haul you off to my bed and ravish you. When we make love—and we will, God help us—it will be because the desire is mutual."

Although Amy was relieved by this declaration, she was also damnably disappointed. And she certainly would have been better off without the caveman images Harry had just planted in her mind.

"Did you do that on purpose?" she demanded, only realizing she'd spoken the thought aloud when Harry laughed and answered her.

"Do what, love?" he countered, rounding the bar and laying his hands on either side of her narrow waist.

Amy swallowed hard. She was a modern woman, liberated and successful in her own right, but she couldn't help imagining what it would be like to be hoisted over Harry's shoulder like the willing captive of some sexy pirate. "Oh, God," she groaned.

Harry bent his head and tasted her mouth as though it were some rare and priceless delicacy, to be enjoyed at leisure.

Amy's heart began to pound and her breathing was audible.

Harry's lips strayed to her throat, the tender hollow beneath her ear. He took the glass from her hand and set it on the bar.

Amy's traitorous body was already preparing itself to receive him, already pleading for a fulfillment that had been denied it for over two years. "Oh, God," she said again, when Harry's hands cupped her breasts. His thumbs made her nipples go taut against the soft cotton of her sundress.

"Maybe," he speculated huskily, from the tingling space between Amy's shoulder and the base of her neck, "we'd better do something about this."

"D-do something about what?" Amy's voice trembled, like her body. The rumblings of an impending spiritual and emotional quake were making cracks in the wall she'd built around her innermost self, while, on the surface of her skin, a million tiny nerves quivered.

Harry touched the tip of his tongue to the corner of her mouth, and Amy had a melting sensation. In another minute, she'd be all over his shoes, like warm wax.

"About this attraction between us," he finally replied. Between light, teasing kisses, he added, "Amy, we're not going to have a moment's peace until we've made love."

The last of Amy's defenses crumbled then; she knew Harry was right. "Yes," was all she could manage to say, she was so overcome, so confused, so in need.

He lifted her easily, gently, into his arms and started toward the hallway and the one room Amy hadn't dared to explore earlier.

"Will the pilot know?" she asked warily.

Harry kissed the top of her head and chuckled. "No, love. Not unless you turn on the intercom."

The master bedroom was surprisingly spacious, even considering the luxurious proportions of that airplane. The floor was carpeted, the lighting dim, the air subtly tinged with Harry's very distinctive scent.

He set Amy on her feet at the foot of the bed and pushed a tendril of hair back from her cheek with a gentle forefinger.

"You're sure?" he asked.

She nodded, unable to speak, though every word in every dictionary in the world seemed to be waiting at the back of her mind, wanting to be part of some enormous declaration she couldn't begin to make.

He unzipped her sundress and eased the fabric down over her shoulders. When the dress was gone, Harry caught one finger under her bra strap and brought that down, too. She sucked in her breath and tilted her head back in surrender when he bent to sample her nipple as he'd tasted her lips earlier.

Tears trickled over Amy's temples and into her hair, not because she was ashamed or unhappy, but because it felt so wondrously good to give herself in this age-old way.

Presently, Harry bared her other breast and gave it proper and thorough attention, having tossed her bra aside. She was wearing only her satiny panties when he laid her on the bed.

The velvet softness of hundreds of rose petals cushioned her fevered flesh, and their lush scent perfumed the room. Amy was transfixed as she watched Harry strip away his clothes.

His body was lean and magnificent as he stretched out beside her. Taking a handful of the scattered pink, yellow and white petals, he sprinkled them over her and then bent to kiss the places where they landed. As he did this, he took her panties down over her hips and thighs, and they were lost in the blanket of blossoms.

Harry covered Amy with petals, and with the touch of each one to her quivering skin, she wanted him more.

"Harry, please," she finally rasped in desperation.

He raised her knees and knelt between them. He burrowed and nuzzled his way through the blossoms that sheltered her most vulnerable place, then scored her boldly with his tongue.

Amy gave a primitive groan of welcoming surrender and arched her back. Harry held her taut bottom in his hands and drank from her greedily.

Delirious with a terrifying, sweeping pleasure, Amy tossed her head from side to side. One forearm rested across her mouth, muffling the soft cries of wonderment and glory that she couldn't hold back.

And still Harry consumed her.

Finally, with a shout of joyous desolation, Amy reached her climax.

Even as he lowered her back to the flower-strewn mattress, Harry kissed the insides of Amy's thighs and the smooth moistness of her belly. She was beyond speech, beyond thought; all she could do was lie there in Harry's arms, her head resting on his strong chest. As pieces of her soul gradually wandered back from the far reaches of the universe, where her shattering release had flung them, Harry lightly caressed her shoulder blades, the small of her back, her bottom, her thighs.

Presently, he laid her on her back and settled his powerful frame between her legs. It seemed to Amy that every muscle in her body had melted—she could not possibly respond to this final stage of Harry's lovemaking—but she longed to be joined with him. The desire was far more complex than mere physical need.

He paused at her entrance and looked deeply into her eyes, silently asking her permission.

Amy nodded, tilted her head back, and closed her eyes.

Harry moved into her in a powerful stroke that awakened all her satisfied senses to an even keener need than before.

Amy's eyes flew open again, in startled surprise, and her fingers rushed to Harry's hard, sun-browned shoulders.

"Do you want me to stop?" he asked quietly, his manhood buried deep within her.

"No," Amy whispered in a frantic rush, shaking her head.

He withdrew slowly, until their joining was almost broken, and Amy felt genuine despair. But then Harry took her forcefully and she was completely, joyously lost.

As her body convulsed beneath his in the final moments of Harry's conquest, her cries echoed off the back of his throat.

Moments after she'd settled back to the mattress, completely exhausted, Harry wedged his hands under her hips to press her closer still. With a low groan, he faced his own moment of utter surrender.

At least half an hour must have passed before either of them had the breath to speak.

"Rose petals, huh?" Amy said, staring up at the ceiling. "You were pretty sure of yourself, weren't you?"

Harry was propped up beside her on one elbow. With the fingers of his other hand, he caressed a responsive nipple. "I was pretty sure of *you*," he countered.

Amy was holding a lot of things at bay in those moments. Like reality, for instance. "The flowers were a poetic touch," she said. "I guess you probably do that every time you bring a woman here."

He was silent for a long interval, during which he continued to tease her nipples, each in turn, with skillful fingers. "I've brought women to this bed before, of course," he said finally, unapologetically. "But those rose petals were for you and you alone, Amy."

What a line, observed the left side of Amy's brain. *If this is a dream, don't let me wake up,* countered the whimsical right side.

As if to prove his assertion, Harry gathered a hand-

ful of the bruised, fragrant petals and began to rub
them lightly against Amy's breasts and belly.

She moaned helplessly as he lowered his mouth to
her nipple, once again to drink from her.

They landed in San Francisco some two hours later
and although Amy's knees were still wobbly from
Harry's lovemaking, she'd managed to grab a shower
in one of the fancy airplane bathrooms and put on
evening clothes.

She wore a snowy-soft white jacket, with tiny iridescent beads stitched to it to lend a subtle sparkle, a
delicate camisole top, and black silk slacks.

As she and Harry descended the roll-away stairs to
the tarmac, a pearl-gray limousine whisked to a stop
beside the plane.

"Wow," Amy said. "You really know how to impress a girl."

Harry's grin was downright wicked. "You did seem
pretty impressed," he agreed, and Amy knew he was
referring to her unbridled responses to his lovemaking.

She felt a little anticipatory thrill, because she knew
she would return to Harry's bed that night.

They dined in a restaurant atop one of San Francisco's finest hotels, and since the requisite fog had
somehow failed to roll in, the view of the harbor and
the Golden Gate Bridge was unobstructed.

Amy had seafood of some kind—she would never
remember exactly what—and she indulged in one
glass of white wine. The sweet, pulsing daze she'd

been wandering in turned to a feeling of giddy adventurousness.

She wanted to neck in the rear of the limousine while they were driving back to the airport, but she was too shy to make the first move, and all Harry did was hold her hand and look at her as though she were a poem he wanted to memorize. Or a puzzle he couldn't solve.

They had barely returned to the jet when two men in suits appeared. Harry obviously knew them, but they produced Customs badges anyway, and Amy showed them her passport. She was heart-stoppingly certain they were going to say she couldn't leave the country.

"Have a good flight," one of them said to Amy with a smile, while the other shook hands with Harry.

When the Customs agents were gone, Harry went to the cockpit to confer with the pilot. Amy strapped herself in and waited.

After a few minutes, Harry's voice came over the intercom. "Sit tight, love," he said. "The flight check has been completed and we're about to take off."

They'd been airborne almost half an hour when Harry finally returned to the main cabin. With a chuckle he unfastened Amy's seat belt and pried her fingers loose from the arm rests.

"You're as beautiful as a moonflower," he said, holding her close and burrowing into the soft skin of her neck. "And despite the shower and that perfume you're wearing, I can still catch the scent of the rose petals."

He left her, just briefly, to dim the cabin lights and turn on soft music. Then Harry drew Amy into his arms and they danced, and for Amy that was almost as keenly erotic as lying naked in a bed of flower petals.

Emotionally, Amy was drowning. She thought of Tyler, in a desperate attempt to anchor herself to the only world she really knew, but suddenly he was only a sweet, fading memory.

The music went on and on, and Harry and Amy danced tirelessly. Then he took her hand and led her back to his bed.

Where before their lovemaking had had a fevered urgency, now it was leisurely and deliberate. Harry brought Amy to one release after another before he permitted her the final conquering she literally begged for, and the first light of dawn was sparkling on the blue waters of the sea when he finally allowed her to sleep.

The thump and lurch of landing brought her bolt upright in bed, her eyes wide. Harry was fully dressed, wearing charcoal slacks and a lightweight white sweater, his sleek, raven-black hair glistening in the morning light.

"Where are we?" Amy asked, pulling the sheets up under her chin even though she knew it was too late to hide herself from Harry.

"Honolulu," he answered, grinning at her rumpled hair and dazed expression. "We'll only be here long enough to refuel, do some maintenance and change pilots, so take your time getting dressed."

Blushing to recall how she'd behaved with this man, how she'd let him shape and maneuver her into every possible position for taking, Amy tried to get out of bed without letting go of the sheet. She wanted the blue terry cloth robe draped over a nearby chair, but Harry got to it before she did and held it out of reach.

"On second thought," he said, his dark blue eyes full of mischief and passion, "don't bother to get dressed at all."

Chapter 6

Amy settled into the airplane's big marble bathtub with a contented sigh. The intercom crackled out the announcement that the flight had been cleared for takeoff, and she gripped the sides of the tub as the craft hurtled down the runway and then catapulted into the air.

Some of Amy's bubbly bathwater slopped over onto the floor.

"They should have put a seatbelt in this thing," she muttered.

Harry's laughter came over the intercom, along with a few chuckles from the pilot.

"Push the white button on the panel, love," Harry told her. "*After* you get out of the tub."

Red in the face, Amy snatched up a towel and

scrambled out. She could hardly get to the intercom panel fast enough.

Once Amy was dried off and dressed, her hair toweled and then combed into a casual style, she made the bed. The crushed rose petals had mysteriously disappeared, but their luscious scent lingered.

Amy ventured out into the main cabin. She sat contentedly at one of the windows for a long time, looking down on the clouds—giant cotton balls stretched thin—as well as the sea, just enjoying the view.

She was surprised when Harry showed up, carrying a tray. He'd brought her a gigantic fruit salad, a croissant and a little pot of special Hawaiian coffee.

Amy gratefully accepted the food, but her tone of voice was testy. "Do the rest of the intercoms on this plane have minds of their own, or just the one in that particular bathroom?"

Harry grinned and sat down in another seat, facing her. He was wearing jeans and a light yellow sports shirt, but he still looked elegant enough to play for high stakes in Monaco. "No worries, love. That's the only one with temperament."

Amy popped a juicy piece of fresh pineapple into her mouth and looked out at the sea.

"What are you thinking?" Harry asked softly at great length.

She sighed, gazing at him with bewildered eyes. "I guess I'm waiting for the guilt to strike."

He took a strawberry from her bowl and touched it lightly to her lips. Amy opened her mouth to receive the tidbit and felt a sweet tension begin to curl up tight within her.

"Why would you feel guilty?" he asked quietly.

Amy was practically breathless. She was going to have to talk to Debbie when she got back to Seattle, find out why a simple thing like having a man put a strawberry to her lips felt so much like a sweet seduction.

"Because of Tyler," she said lamely. "Oh, I know we haven't done anything wrong." She wanted to tell Harry about her strange encounters with Ty, but she was afraid of the impression that would make.

Harry raised both eyebrows. "Well, then?"

"It's just that, well, I'd never been with anyone else—until you."

Resting his elbows on the arms of his chair, Harry made a finger steeple beneath his chin. He sat quietly, ready to listen, and if Amy hadn't already been crazy about him, that gesture would have done it.

"Instead of guilt," Amy stumbled on awkwardly, "I feel a sense of adventure and newness and excitement. Like, maybe I'm something more than a mother and an erstwhile wife."

Harry's dark brows knitted together in a momentary frown. "Maybe?"

Amy bit into a grape, chewing thoughtfully and then swallowing. "Tyler was a great guy," she finally said with a shaky sigh. "And God knows, I loved him. But I don't think it ever occurred to either of us that

I should have an identity apart from being a wife and mother."

"Mmm," Harry said.

Amy laughed. "If you ever get tired of being a venture capitalist, or whatever you are, you could be a shrink. You listen very well."

He took another strawberry between his fingers and traced the outline of her mouth with the morsel until her lips parted. Just when Amy thought surely he was going to take her to his bed, he asked, "How would you like to try your hand at flying the plane?"

Although her first instinct was to draw back and shake her head no, Amy made herself nod.

Moments later, she was in the cockpit, in the copilot's seat, wearing earphones and staring at the instrument panel in utter ignorance. The pilot had gone to the rear of the aircraft, and Harry was occupying his chair.

Over the next hour he taught Amy the function of most of the instruments and showed her how to gain and lose altitude. For a while, she was actually flying the aircraft herself, and the knowledge filled her with a kind of pride she'd never felt before.

Finally, however, Amy excused herself and left the copilot's seat to the man who had come on board in Honolulu. She found a book in Harry's room and settled into one of the comfortable seats in the main cabin to read.

Lunchtime came, and Harry clattered around in the galley, opening and shutting doors. A bell chimed, and he carried a tray forward to the pilot, then brought Amy a compact meal of Spanish rice and vegetables, along with a plate for himself.

They ate in comfortable silence, not needing to talk, and then Harry went back to the cockpit. Amy tidied up the galley, thinking that was the least she could do, since Harry had done the cooking, then returned to her book.

She was so absorbed in the story, a fast-paced spy thriller, that when Harry appeared, she was startled.

He took the book from her hands and set it aside, then unsnapped her seat belt. Again, Amy was electrified by a perfectly ordinary thing.

She knew what Harry wanted, and she wanted it, too, but the vamp in her made her offer a token resistance.

"What if I don't go to bed with you?" she whispered. Even though the blood was thundering in her ears, Amy hadn't forgotten the incident with the bathroom intercom, and she wasn't taking any chances on having the pilot overhear such an intimate conversation.

Harry ran his hands lightly over her thighs, easing her legs apart at the same time. "Then I'll have you right here," he said, his voice low, like thunder rumbling in a summer sky. After that, he kissed her, subjecting her to a preliminary conquering with his tongue. Then he bared her breasts.

"I'll go," Amy moaned, as he nibbled at her. "I'll go!"

Harry chuckled and lifted her legs, so that her knees rested over the arms of the seat. Then he opened the snap on her jeans.

"Harry," she pleaded.

He bent to nip at the crux of her womanhood and, despite the sturdy denim covering her, Amy felt the contact to the core of her being. She closed her eyes, loving the feeling of his hands cupping her breasts, and let her hips rise and fall as he bid them.

After tormenting her for at least fifteen minutes, he took her legs from the arms of the chair and relieved her of her jeans and panties, then put her back into position again. The first foray of his tongue tore a raw cry from her throat, but Harry granted no quarter. He slipped his hands under her bottom and then feasted in earnest.

When the first wave of satisfaction struck, Amy was grateful, because the sensations Harry was treating her to were so intense they were almost frightening. But that crest was followed by a second, higher one, and then a third.

As Amy shuddered with the volcanic force of her pleasure, she clasped Harry's shoulders in both hands. Her vision blurred and she cried out at the top of her lungs, but there was no helping that. She was totally out of control.

Her heart had almost settled back into its normal rate when he gathered her up and carried her to his bed.

The taking of Amy Ryan had only begun.

* * *

They landed in Fiji, then briefly, hours later, in Auckland, New Zealand, then in Sydney, where more Customs men came on board and inspected Amy's passport. Finally, they headed north again.

When Amy finally stepped off the plane, into a lush tropical climate, she was amazed to see colorful parrots flying free, as robins did at home in Seattle. The sea was as blue as India ink, lapping at sugar-white beaches, and a spectacular stone house loomed in the distance, as imposing as a castle.

"Where are we?" Amy asked, still in a fog from all the sweet, busy hours spent in Harry's bed.

He laughed and kissed her softly on the mouth. "Paradise," he answered. "The island is named Eden, and not without reason."

A Jeep was waiting at the edge of the private airstrip, and Harry flung the suitcases into the back with a practiced motion, then helped Amy onto the seat. The pilot was evidently staying behind to perform maintenance on the plane.

There was a working fountain in front of the house, and two Australian sheepdogs came bouncing across the yard, barking gleefully, to greet their master.

Harry took a moment to acknowledge the animals, then lifted Amy down from the Jeep.

"You'll be needing a bath and something to eat," he said, his accent sounding more pronounced than before. "Then you'll want to catch up on all that sleep I've deprived you of since we left Seattle."

An amiable housekeeper opened one of the stately double doors, and Amy stepped inside. She didn't notice much about Harry's house that first day, because she was too tired and distracted, and she was grateful when he led her upstairs to an airy suite filled with the distant sound of the tide.

He undressed her, like a child, and they showered together. Even as Harry tenderly soaped and rinsed her exhausted body, Amy could barely keep her eyes open.

At last, he wrapped her in a soft, giant towel and took her to bed. After pulling a T-shirt over her head, he tucked her under the covers and bent to kiss her forehead.

"Sleep well, love," he said.

Dimly, Amy was aware of Harry moving around the room, getting dressed again, and she wanted him beside her even though she hadn't the strength for even one more session of lovemaking.

"Harry," she whimpered, patting the mattress fitfully with one hand.

He chuckled. "No, love, not today. You're too tired."

Amy fought to open her eyes, marshalled all her strength to ask, "What about you? Aren't… you tired?"

Harry bent and planted a smacking kiss on her forehead. "On the contrary, my sweet little Yankee, I feel like I could take on the world with one hand lashed behind my back."

"Don't…go."

"Sleep," he ordered with mock sternness. Then he was gone and Amy slept.

The room was bright with sunshine when she awakened, alone in the big bed and fully rested. Her suitcase was nowhere in sight, but when Amy opened the top drawer of a beautiful antique bureau, she found some of her clothes neatly stacked inside.

Quickly she dressed. Beyond the glass doors leading onto the terrace, parrots made their raucous cawing sound and the tide recited its ancient, rhythmic poetry. After brushing her teeth, grooming her hair and applying lip gloss, Amy ventured out of the bedroom.

She was ravenously hungry and nervous because there was no sign of Harry in any of the enormous, rustic rooms that lay between his room and the kitchen.

The familiar housekeeper was there, stirring batter in a crockery bowl, and she greeted Amy with a gapped smile.

"There you are, then," the woman chirped gleefully. "If I hadn't seen you arriving with me own eyes just yesterday, I would have sworn you were nothing but a story our Harry had made up."

Amy was embarrassed, but she made an effort to be cordial. "My name is Amy Ryan," she said.

"Elsa O'Donnell," said the housekeeper, with a nod and a twinkly smile. "You'd be Master Tyler's widow, then. Oh my, but we was fond of that boy."

The reminder of her husband unsettled Amy a little. As much as she'd loved Tyler, she'd never responded to him in quite the way she did with Harry. She just nodded.

"Sit down," Elsa commanded good-naturedly, setting the mixing bowl aside. "I'll see about getting you some tea."

Amy glanced at the clock and saw that it was two-fifteen. She'd not only slept away the night, but a good part of the day as well.

By tea, Elsa meant a scone with jam and fresh cream, a plate of fruit, four delicate sandwiches and a pot of rich orange pekoe.

Amy consumed the repast as politely as she could, considering that she was famished, then asked shyly, "Is Harry around?"

"He's down at the beach, I imagine," answered Elsa, methodically putting away the ingredients of afternoon tea. "Headed straight for it after getting you settled yesterday, and was off to the water again this morning, right after breakfast."

Amy rinsed her cup and plate and silverware at the sink, then set them on the drain board. "If I walk down there, will I find him?"

"It's a big island," Elsa replied. "But I think you'll run across him. Just mind you don't go through the cane fields—there's snakes there."

Amy shuddered, but even the thought of snakes didn't dampen her excitement at being in a new place and, yes, the prospect of seeing Harry again had its attractions, too.

The sheepdogs joined her on the lawn, romping along beside her, and they were the ones who led her to Harry. He was in water up to his hips, examining the hull of a sleek sailboat, and his grin was as dazzling as the tropical sun.

"So then, Sleeping Beauty has awakened," he teased, making his way toward her. He wasn't wearing a shirt, just cutoffs dark and sodden and clingy with seawater. "Welcome to the land of Oz."

Amy, wearing shorts and a T-shirt herself, kicked off her sandals so she could feel the fine, pristine sand between her toes.

Harry met her on the beach, and his kiss, quick and innocent as it was, sent her senses tumbling in all directions, just as always. He curled two fingers under her chin and grinned again.

"If you're all rested up, love, I'd like to volunteer to wear you out again."

Amy laughed and twisted away from him, running toward the sparkling turquoise water. The dogs bounded after her, barking with delight at the game.

She and Harry splashed each other in the lapping tide, and Amy felt as though all the grief had been erased from her past, leaving only the joy.

"Who else lives on this island?" she asked later, when the two of them were sitting on the beach, their feet buried in the sand.

Harry brushed a tendril of hair back from her forehead. "Just Elsa and her husband, Shelt. He's the gardener."

Amy lay back with a sigh, looking up at an impossibly blue sky. Exotic flowers bloomed at the edges of the cove, orange ones, pink, violet and white. Birds that would only be seen in pet stores and zoos at home chattered in the trees, crazy splotches of living color.

"This really is a garden of Eden," she said, recalling what Harry had said when they'd first arrived on the island. "I wish we could stay here forever."

Harry stretched out beside her and gave her a brief but tantalizing kiss. "There's no reason why we can't. Live here with me, Amy. We'll start the world all over again."

Amy blinked, and her throat tightened with emotion. "I can't do that," she said. "I have two children, remember? They need to go to school and spend time with their friends and with Tyler's family."

Harry shrugged. "We'd live in the States half the year anyway, love. We could hire a nanny to look after Oliver and Ashley here on the island, and the Ryans would be welcome to visit at any time. They know that." He paused, gazing pensively out to sea. "There are worse things than growing up in paradise, you know."

Deep down, Amy knew Oliver and Ashley would be happy here. They adored Harry, just as she did, and his island would seem like heaven on earth to them. When he got bored with domestic life, however, and wanted to return to the jet set, they'd be shattered.

Losing Tyler had been enough trauma. Playing Swiss Family Robinson for a few months or years, then being abandoned again, would crush Oliver and Ashley, maybe destroy their ability to trust.

"I want a ride in the sailboat," Amy announced, as much to change the subject as anything.

"Tomorrow," Harry promised. He seemed troubled, distracted.

That night, it rained as it can only rain in the tropics. The droplets were warm as bathwater, and Amy stood on the terrace outside Harry's room, her face turned upward and her arms outspread to welcome the deluge.

"You're daft," Harry accused, but he laughed and kissed Amy and soon he was drenched, just as she was.

When he finally hauled her inside the house and began toweling her dry, she saw that the bed was literally mounded with orchidlike blossoms. Some were pink, some white, but all were beautiful.

A sweet ache constricted Amy's throat, and she stood still while Harry peeled away her sodden clothes, then his own. Finally, he laid her on the bed of flowers and made slow, gentle love to her.

In the morning it was as though the rain had never fallen, so fiercely did the sun shine on the sea and the dazzling sand. Amy awakened slowly, cushioned in crushed petals, but this time when she reached out, Harry was beside her.

"When are we going home?" she asked, dreading the answer. If it hadn't been for Oliver and Ashley, she would gladly have agreed to live on the island for the rest of her life.

Harry rolled onto his side and kissed her breast. "Never," he replied throatily. "Consider yourself kidnapped, a one-woman harem."

"Just promise never to give me back," she whispered, "no matter how high the ransom gets."

Moments later, ransom was the farthest thing from Amy's mind. She was into unconditional surrender.

After a leisurely shower together, and an equally unhurried breakfast in the kitchen, Harry and Amy took the picnic basket Elsa had packed and set out for the nearby cove where the sailboat was moored.

"Take your clothes off," Harry ordered, when they reached the shore.

"Already?" Amy countered, eyeing him skeptically.

He laughed. "Yes. If you don't want to get them wet when you wade out to the boat." With that, Harry removed his cutoffs and T-shirt, rolled the garments up and secured them under the handles of the wicker picnic basket. Balancing that on top of his head, he stepped into the water, magnificently naked.

Amy was considerably more self-conscious about stripping, even though she knew they were completely alone on that magical beach. Nonetheless, she followed Harry's lead, took off everything and marched into the water.

After tossing the basket onto the deck, Harry vaulted over the side and reached down to help Amy in after him. The weathered old boards were smooth and warm from the sun.

Amy could have languished there for a while, but

Harry gave her a playful swat on the bottom and said, "What's this? A mutiny before we even weigh anchor?"

Hastily, Amy rose and put her clothes back on, except for her shoes.

After a few minutes of busy preparation, they set sail.

"Where are we going?" Amy inquired, shading her eyes with one hand.

"That island over there," Harry answered, pointing.

Amy felt like an intrepid explorer. All her life she'd taken the safe and practical route, whenever a choice was offered. Now here she was in a foreign country, with a man she'd known only briefly, about to set sail in tropical seas.

So what if their destination was clearly in sight?

The water between Eden Island and its neighbor was so clear that Amy could see the reefs beneath the surface and the colorful fish that swam through intricate passages. When she saw a shark glide by, she drew back from the side of the boat, her mind filled with movie images.

Harry, who was working with the sails, smiled at her reaction. "What did you see, love? A great white?"

Amy felt the blood drain from her cheeks. "Do you mean to tell me that *Jaws* might be swimming around down there, at this very moment?"

Harry laughed. "A famous shark like that? Not likely, rose petal. He's living in the South of France and wearing sunglasses so his fans won't recognize him."

"Very funny," Amy replied grudgingly, peeking over the side of the boat again. The spectacle going on down there was just too good to miss.

When they reached the other island—if it had a name of its own, Harry didn't mention it—Amy was possessed by a remarkably pleasant feeling that she and Harry were completely alone on the planet.

The only sign that anyone else had ever visited the island before was a tree house wedged between two massive palms. Small boards had been nailed to the trunk of one of the trees to form a crude ladder, and the structure's thick roof appeared to have been woven from long, supple leaves.

"Yours?" Amy inquired.

Harry looked away. "I built it for my stepdaughter, Eireen. Unfortunately, Madeline—my wife—never gave the poor little thing a chance to be a child."

Amy touched his arm lightly, then pushed up non-existent sleeves—she was wearing a T-shirt—and started up the ladder.

"Best let me go first, love," Harry remarked presently, when she'd climbed about five rungs. "Could be snakes up there."

Amy was back on the ground with the speed and dispatch of a cartoon character. "Snakes?" she croaked.

Harry took a manly stance for effect, then began to climb deftly toward the tree house, the picnic basket in one hand. There was a rustling sound, followed by a fallout of leaves and dirt, then Harry peered down at her from a crudely shaped, glassless window.

"All clear, rose petal," he called.

Amy ran her tongue over her dry lips and then stepped onto the first rung, gripping another with both hands.

Although there were no snakes in the tree house, it was clear enough that other things had been nesting in there. For all of that, it was a lot of fun, yet another thing Amy had never done before.

"Come here," Harry said, and Amy went straight into his arms. It did not even occur to her to resist.

His kiss was one of thorough mastery; the slow dance of their tongues soon became a duel of passion. Amy felt as though a sudden fever had set in, and by the time Harry had removed her T-shirt, then her bra, then the rest of her clothes, she was weak with the need to surrender.

He enjoyed her, like some juicy tropical fruit, for a long, torturously sweet interval, wringing response after response from her. When he finally made her his own, she came apart in his arms as uninhibited as a jungle tigress with her mate.

After her senses were restored, Amy found herself lying on the floor of the tree house, where Harry had spread a soft blanket taken from the picnic basket. While Harry caressed her—he was lying quietly beside her, still recovering from his own invasion of heaven—Amy felt strong enough to permit herself memories of lovemaking with Tyler.

Her late husband had been a tender, considerate lover always, and Amy had learned a woman's secrets in his arms. She had to admit, though, that there had never been the sense of wild abandon she felt with Harry. It was a different sort of passion, more mature and more intense.

And far more dangerous.

He slid down to kiss the flat of her stomach. "Stay with me, Amy," he said hoarsely. "Please."

Harry had never said "I love you," nor had he asked her to be his wife. Amy was pretty sure he was marriage-shy after his first experience, and a sophisticated man of the world like him would *expect* an uncomplicated relationship with no strings attached.

"I can't," she said, as a soft tropical rain began to patter on the roof of dried leaves. She'd loved being married; Tyler had shown her just how marvelous a physical and spiritual partnership could be. For the first time since his death, Amy felt ready to make a real and lasting commitment to someone new.

They ate their picnic lunch naked, cozy inside the dank and dusty tree house, talking quietly, but the day had lost some of its magic.

When the rain let up, late that afternoon, they returned to the boat and sailed back to Harry's island.

Harry made a fire on the living-room hearth, because the rain had returned and there was a slight chill in the air.

That night, for the first time since their adventure had begun, Harry and Amy didn't make love.

They spent the next two days walking the beaches, soaking up the medicinal Queensland sun, playing backgammon on the terrace. Lying next to each other at night, they were unable to resist the magnetism, and while their lovemaking was as ferociously satisfying as ever, there was a distance about it. A certain reserve.

Amy's heart was heavy when they left the island on the morning of the third day; she thought she knew now how Eve must have felt when she and Adam had been driven from the Garden.

Harry kept himself busy in the cockpit of the jet, while Amy wandered aimlessly around the cabin, wishing the dream never had to end.

They landed in Sydney a few hours later, and Harry returned from the controls.

"You'll need an evening gown if you brought one," he said, as though speaking to a casual acquaintance instead of a woman he'd made love to in beds of flowers and in a tree house.

They rode downtown in yet another limousine, over the famous bridge, and their hotel suite boasted a view of the Opera House and the harbor.

Still, the mood was subdued, and Amy couldn't help thinking that, glamorous surroundings or none, Cinderella time was over. The glass slipper wasn't going to fit.

Chapter 7

Harry Griffith was a man who planned his life years in advance. He knew details about his future other people wouldn't even begin to consider until they'd passed the age of sixty.

One thing he had definitely *not* planned on, however, was falling in love.

He turned from the window overlooking Sydney Harbor when he sensed Amy's presence, and the sight of her standing there in her light blue, sleek-fitting dress practically stopped his heart. Still, cool reserve was Harry's strong point; he'd relied on the trait for so long that it was second nature to him now.

Amy's eyes were bright with a peculiar mixture of defiance and hope, and Harry made up his mind in that moment that he would sacrifice anything to have her for his own. His pride, his fortune—anything.

He took her to see *Madame Butterfly* at the Opera House, and then the two of them had dinner in an out-of-the-way restaurant Harry had always favored.

"What did you think of the opera?" Harry finally asked. The question came out smoothly, as the things he said nearly always did, but behind the facade his emotions were churning in secret.

Amy took a sip of her wine before answering. "I've seen it before, of course," she replied, looking uncomfortable. "I always cry and I always get angry because Pinkerton shows so little regard for Butterfly's feelings. He goes into the marriage planning to dump her later, for a 'real wife.'"

Harry felt a rhythmic, thumping headache begin behind his right temple. Only when it was too late, when they'd already taken their seats in the Opera House, had he realized that *Madame Butterfly* was probably a poor choice because it dealt with the subject of male treachery.

"All men aren't like Pinkerton, of course," he said quietly.

Amy didn't look convinced. "When a man travels a lot," she said distractedly, "there are temptations. I have a friend who used to be married to an airline pilot, and he had a playmate in every city between here and Buffalo, New York."

Harry arched an eyebrow. "Busy man," he allowed. "Amy, what is it? What's really troubling you?"

He saw the battle going on behind her beautiful hazel eyes and wondered whether he was winning or losing.

"I think I'm in love with you," she said, as though confessing that she'd contracted some embarrassing disease.

Staid, sedate Harry Griffith. It was all he could do not to leap onto his chair and shout the news to everyone in the restaurant. "That's a problem?" he asked.

"Yes!" she whispered furiously. "You're a rich man! You have your own jet and a private island!"

"I'll try to reform," Harry promised.

Amy's cheeks glowed pink, and her wondrous eyes were now glistening with tears. "I can't share you with all the other women you probably know. I won't!"

"You don't have to," he said reasonably.

She stared at him for a moment. "What?"

"Amy, you're not the only one who's fallen in love here."

She dropped her fork. "You're saying that you— that I—that we—"

"I love you, Amy. I thought you understood that when I kept asking you to stay with me—I believe I said something poetic about our starting a new world together."

She picked up her fork again and waved it like a baton. Her mouth moved, as though she would deliver a lecture, but no sound came out.

"I'm asking you to marry me," Harry said, figuring he'd better grab the opportunity to speak while her tongue was still tangled. "I'll sell the island and we'll spend all our time in the States. I'll wear baseball caps, drink beer and call you 'babe,' if that's what you want. And even though it goes without saying, I'm going to say it anyway—I'll never be unfaithful to you."

A tear scurried down Amy's cheek. "You'll get tired of us, Ashley and Oliver and me."

"No way," Harry answered, his voice sounding hoarse. "Amy, men *are* capable of making solid commitments. You know that. Tyler did."

She obviously had no argument. Tyler had made her happy, and Harry blessed his late friend for that, silently promising Ty, as well as himself, that he would never bring Amy anything but joy.

"I wouldn't want you to sell the island," Amy said after a long time. "If you did, we'd never be able to make love in the tree house again."

"Are you saying yes?" Harry inquired, leaning forward slightly in his chair.

"Yes," she replied, and then there were more tears. Happy ones, silvery in the candlelight.

Once again, Harry kept himself from shouting for joy, but just barely. He paid the check and, after the waiter had pulled back Amy's chair, helped her into her wrap. When they reached the waiting limousine, he opened the door for her and gave the driver very rational directions.

It was only when they reached the privacy of their hotel suite that he put his hands on either side of Amy's slender waist, hoisted her over one shoulder and carried her to bed for a proper celebration.

In the morning Amy and Harry went shopping. She bought a toy koala bear for Ashley and an outback hat for Oliver, and Harry bought an engagement ring.

He put it on her finger that afternoon, on board the jet, with Australia falling away behind them. Amy was pretty certain she could have flown home without an airplane, she was so happy.

Twenty-six hours later, they touched down in Seattle. Harry drove her home in his van.

"You're going to need some time to recuperate," he said, when they were standing in her kitchen. "I have some business to take care of in New York, but I'll call you when I get back."

Jealousy flared in Amy's heart, but she was too tired from all that traveling and lovemaking to nurture the flame. If she was going to love Harry, then she had to trust him as well.

"I love you," she said.

He kissed her, weakening her knees and causing her heart to catch. "And I love you," he replied, his voice a low rumble.

The first thing Amy did was call the number in Kansas that Louise had given her. She talked to both Oliver and Ashley, who were having a grand time at the reunion, but said nothing about her own trip or the wedding awaiting her in the future. Those were subjects she wanted to bring up in person.

"We'll be home next Tuesday, according to Grampa," Ashley said. "I'm bringing you something really neat."

Amy smiled, picturing an ashtray in the shape of Kansas or maybe a plate bearing a painting of the state bird. "I'll be looking forward to that," she said.

After saying goodbye, Amy immediately dialed her friend Debbie. She would listen to her voicemail messages later.

"What do you *mean,* you went to Australia with Harry Griffith?" Debbie demanded, the moment the receptionist at the clinic put Amy through to her office.

Amy smiled, perched on the edge of her desk and wrapped the phone cord idly around one finger. "He asked me to marry him," she said. "And I said yes."

Debbie gave a delighted cry, then apparently had second thoughts. "Wait a minute. You don't know him all that well."

"I know him as well as I need to," Amy replied quietly. "And what happened to all those lectures you were handing out before I left? I think the general theme was, 'Amy, you've got to put your past behind you and get on with your life.'"

Debbie sighed. "It sounded good in theory. Do you love this guy?"

"With all my heart."

"I'm coming right over. We'll go out for pizza and talk this through—"

"I'm not going anywhere," Amy sighed. "Not tonight. I just traveled from one hemisphere to another and I'm exhausted. I'm planning to have some soup, take a bath and crawl into bed."

"All right, we'll talk tomorrow, then," Debbie said breathlessly. "You're not going to live in Australia, are you?"

"Only part of the year," Amy answered, half yawning the words. "Goodbye, Debbie."

Before her friend could protest, Amy hung up.

She could barely see to heat soup, but she knew she needed nourishment, so she made herself a bowl of chicken and stars. After eating about half of the impromptu meal, Amy stumbled upstairs, had the bath she'd promised herself, put on a cotton nightshirt and fell into bed.

"It's about time you got home," commented a disapproving male voice.

Amy's eyes flew open, and she sat bolt upright in bed, reaching feverishly for the lamp switch. The subsequent burst of lights showed Tyler standing at the foot of the bed, one foot balanced on the antique blanket chest.

The fact that this had happened before did nothing to ease the shock. In fact, by that time Amy had half convinced herself that she'd never seen Tyler's ghost at all.

"What are you doing here?" she managed, staring at him, blinking hard and then staring again.

Tyler shoved one hand through his curly brown hair

and sighed. "I used to live here, remember? I used to live, period."

Amy tossed back the covers, meaning to scramble over to Tyler and see if she could pass her hand through him, like a projection from her father-in-law's old eight-millimeter movie camera.

But Ty stepped back, and the expression on his face, though a benevolent one, was unmistakably a warning. "Don't try to touch me, Amy," he said. "It dissipates my energy."

Kneeling in the middle of the bed that had once been theirs, Amy covered her face with both hands. "This is insane. *I'm* insane!"

"I told you before," Tyler sighed, "you're perfectly all right. Where have you been for the past week?"

Amy lowered her hands. "You don't know? That's weird. I thought you knew all, saw all."

"I'm confined to a certain area," Tyler explained somewhat impatiently. "And my time is running out. Where were you, Amy? And where are the kids?"

"Ashley and Oliver are in Kansas, with your parents," she answered, worried. "And I was in Australia, with Harry Griffith. What do you mean, your time is running out?"

Tyler turned away for a moment.

"Ty?"

He held up one hand. "It's okay, Amy. I knew you and Harry were going to hit it off—it was meant to be—but it's still a little hard to let go."

Amy's throat tightened, and her eyes filled with

tears. "You're telling me. Losing you was the worst thing that ever happened to me, Ty. If I could have held on to you even a moment longer, I would have."

When he turned to face her again, his eyes were suspiciously bright. He started to say something, then stopped himself.

Amy drew a deep breath and held it for a moment, struggling to regain her composure. She adored Harry, and she knew marrying him was the right thing to do, but Tyler had been her first love, the father of her children, and saying goodbye to him would not be easy.

"Will I see you again—someday?" she asked, clasping her hands together in her lap.

"Our paths may cross at some point," he answered gruffly. "Whether or not we'll recognize each other is another question. Be happy, Spud."

He started to fade.

"Tyler!" Amy cried. "Don't go!"

Between one instant and the next, however, Tyler disappeared completely.

Amy switched out the lamp and cried herself to sleep, and when Harry called the next morning, her throat was scratchy and she felt as though she hadn't slept in a week. He told her he'd be back the following day, and that he loved her, but that was all Amy could remember of the conversation.

"I saw Tyler again last night," she told Debbie, when the two of them met for pizza and salad at a restaurant near the clinic.

Debbie took the announcement in stride, just as she had before. "Part of the grieving process, I'm sure."

"He was really there!" Amy insisted.

"I believe that you believe that," Debbie replied. "Tyler came to say goodbye, didn't he?"

Amy couldn't deny that. She knew her grudging nod only confirmed her friend's theory that Tyler was some kind of subconscious manifestation.

"Do you still love him?" Debbie uttered the question subtly, spearing a cherry tomato from her salad bowl while she spoke.

"Tyler?" Amy searched her heart, and found a deep, sweet sadness there. "Not in the same way as before," she confessed, her voice barely audible.

"Separation complete," Debbie said.

"You think I'm crazy."

"I think you're a perfectly normal woman who loved her first husband to distraction. But you're young and you're healthy and now you care for somebody else."

Amy dried her eyes with a wadded napkin and sniffled. "Last night, you weren't quite so blithe about it."

"I was having a personal conflict," Debbie said matter-of-factly, every inch the professional. "You're my best friend, and I don't exactly relish the idea of seeing you move to Australia."

"I told you, it will only be for half the year."

"I'm not used to having to wait six months for a lunch date, Amy," Debbie pointed out. "This is going to create a serious gap in my social life. How do you think the kids will react to the news? And Tyler's parents?"

Amy sighed. "Ashley and Oliver adore Harry," she said. "The Ryans like him, too, of course, but I'm not sure how they're going to feel about being separated from their grandchildren for such long periods."

"They could visit," Debbie said practically.

"So could you," Amy pointed out.

Debbie beamed. "You're right. Will you introduce me to Hugh Jackman?"

"Why not?" Amy teased with a shrug. "I'll probably know everybody in Australia on a first-name basis."

Later, Amy stopped by the supermarket to buy milk, fresh vegetables, cat food and a magazine. When she arrived home, Mrs. Ingallstadt was there, feeding Rumpel.

"My goodness, you scared me!" the old woman said, laying one plump hand to her heart.

Amy smiled. "I'm sorry. I should have called, but I was so tired when I got home yesterday."

"That's all right, dear," Mrs. Ingallstadt said kindly. "You've got a very good cat here, though it seems to me the poor creature is a little on the jumpy side."

Amy had been taking groceries from the canvas shopping bag she always brought to the store with her, but she stopped. Something in Mrs. Ingallstadt's tone had put all her senses on the alert. "Jumpy?"

"Cats are generally unflappable, you know," the neighbor explained. "But every time I came over, she flung herself into my arms and meowed like there was no tomorrow. I could hardly get her to settle down to eat."

If the cat had seen Tyler, that would prove he was real and not a delusion. Wouldn't it?

"Maybe she saw a ghost," Amy said with a nervous giggle.

Mrs. Ingallstadt didn't smile. "I used to see my Walter sometimes—after he was gone, I mean."

Amy no longer made any pretense of being interested in the groceries. "Really? What was he doing?"

The old lady chuckled fondly. "Cleaning out the birdbath in the backyard," she said. "I saw him on and off for about three years, I guess. Then, once I knew I could make my way alone, he stopped paying me visits."

Pulling back a chair, Amy sank into it. "Do you think you really saw Walter, or was it just your imagination?"

"Oh, I think I really saw him," Mrs. Ingallstadt said confidently. "I may be old, but I know when I'm daydreaming. Walter was as real as you are."

Amy wanted to laugh and cry, both at once. Her emotions were so tangled she couldn't begin to sort them out. "Why do you think he came back?" she ventured after a few moments.

Mrs. Ingallstadt smiled. "He was looking after me the only way he could," she said. "Walter always promised he'd stand by me, no matter what." She approached and laid a hand on Amy's shoulder. "Are you all right, dear? You look a little peaky."

Amy couldn't tell her neighbor and friend about seeing Tyler, not then at least. But she was overjoyed to know she wasn't the only one who'd had such an experience.

That night she made herself a salad, ate and went to bed early.

In the middle of the morning, Harry arrived, carrying an enormous bag full of rose petals. He poured the cloud of white softness onto the living-room floor, laid Amy on top of them and made slow, exacting love to her.

While she was caught up in the last, fevered stages of response, he gently squeezed her bottom and spoke to her in low, soothing words.

She was drenched with perspiration when she finally lay still, caressing Harry's strong shoulders while he strained upon her and finally spilled his passion.

"I have a bed, you know," she said much later, when he was lying with his head on her breast. She entangled her finger in an ebony curl as she spoke.

He raised up far enough to look her in the eye. "Tyler's bed," he pointed out.

"Ty would approve of our getting married," Amy said. She was certain of that, since Tyler had told her so himself.

"I know," Harry agreed, caressing her intimately. "But a man's bed is sacred."

Amy gasped as his finger slid inside her. His thumb, meanwhile, was making slow revolutions of its own.

She used the last of her strength to rebel, to bait him. "You mean, if you—died—I couldn't bring my third husband to the tree house?"

Harry bent to nibble at a breast that was still wet from previous forays of his tongue. "Not a chance. I'd haunt you."

Amy's last coherent thought was *It wouldn't be the first time that had happened.*

Hours later, when she and Harry were eating home-made spaghetti in Amy's kitchen, she said boldly, "I want you to stay here tonight."

The swift flatness of Harry's answer surprised her. "No."

"We could sleep in the guest room," Amy said reasonably. She'd been alone for two years, and now that she had someone to share her life again, she didn't want to sleep solo.

Harry shook his head. "Tyler's house," he said.

Amy was frightened, although she couldn't have explained the sensation. "That didn't stop you from making love to me in the middle of the living room," she pointed out in what she hoped was an even voice.

"I was desperate," Harry replied. "We'd been apart."

"I don't believe this!"

"Believe it. I love you, Amy, and I'm convinced Tyler would be happy about our being together. But he was one of my best friends and making love to his widow, under *his* roof, is not my idea of a fitting memorial."

Now Amy understood why she was scared. Harry was going to think of Tyler every time they were intimate, and maybe it would get so it didn't matter where they were at the time.

"Suppose I told you I'd seen Tyler," she burst out, without thinking. "Suppose I said he'd *told* me you and I were going to be married and have two children!"

Harry pushed away his plate. "Then I'd say you weren't through grieving and the last thing you were ready for was a new relationship."

The room seemed to sway around Amy; she gripped the table's edge to steady herself.

"What's going on here?" she demanded. "Are you getting cold feet?"

"If anybody's entitled to ask what's going on, love, I am!" Harry roared, throwing down his napkin and shooting to his feet. "Are you over Tyler or not?"

Amy was stunned. Although she'd seen anger snapping in Harry's blue eyes, she'd never heard him yell before. She'd never even *imagined* him yelling. "Yes, I'm over him," she said in a small, stricken voice.

"But you've seen him?"

Amy wanted to say no, but she couldn't lie. Not to Harry. So she didn't say anything at all.

Harry bent and kissed her angrily on the mouth. Amy didn't know if he was mad at her or himself.

She followed him to the front door and stood on the step, watching him storm down the walk.

"I love you, Harry," she called after him.

"I love you!" he shouted back.

That weekend, he and Amy went to Vashon Island together, to get the lighthouse ready for occupancy. They washed windows and walls and bathtubs all day Saturday, and made love in front of the fireplace most of the night. On Sunday they chose furniture from the showroom of an exclusive Seattle department store.

Sunday evening, Amy broiled steaks for dinner, and they ate at the picnic table in her backyard.

She wanted to ask Harry to stay, but she didn't because she knew he'd say no. He'd been his old self at the lighthouse, but once they were back in Seattle, he acted as though Tyler were looking over his shoulder.

They indulged in a passionate kiss, there in the backyard, and Harry helped Amy carry the debris from their meal into the house. He rinsed their plates and utensils, and she loaded the dishwasher.

When that was done, Harry said good-night, promised to call the next day and left.

Amy was brewing a cup of decaf when Tyler put in another one of his appearances.

This time he was sitting at the kitchen table, his chin propped in one hand.

Amy set the coffee aside so she wouldn't spill it. "I'm not supposed to be here, actually."

"Then why—?"

"You're pregnant," he said, looking and sounding as pleased as if he'd accomplished the deed himself. "I just thought you might like to know that."

Instinctively, Amy put both hands to her flat stomach. "I can't be pregnant," she said. "I took precautions."

"Precautions don't mean diddly where The Plan is concerned," Tyler replied blithely. "It's a girl. Dark hair, blue eyes. She'd going to run Harry's company someday."

Amy felt dizzy. She'd barely come to terms with her feelings for Harry as it was.

"Tyler, I'm imagining you. You're not here and I'm not seeing you!"

"I hope not," observed a third voice.

Amy whirled to find Harry standing in the kitchen doorway. The expression in his eyes was bleak, resigned, and Amy knew he couldn't see Tyler.

"Do something!" Amy ordered Tyler frantically. "Show yourself, make a sound, tip over the table—something!"

"It's no use, Spud," Tyler said with a philosophical sigh. "Nobody can see or hear me but you. And the cat, of course. To show myself to Harry would take so much energy that I'd probably short out or something."

Amy turned to Harry. "He's really here," she cried. "Harry, I swear I'm not having delusions—Tyler is *right here!*"

Harry looked sad. "It's obvious that you're not ready for a new marriage, Amy." He collected his sweater, which he'd left draped over the back of a chair. "I'll call you sometime."

"Harry!"

"Now I know why they told me not to come back," Tyler muttered.

"Oh, shut up!" Amy yelled. She'd finally found happiness, and it was walking out the door.

Harry paused on the front step. "Do you want me to call your doctor or something?" he asked.

Amy bit her lower lip, held back all the fevered denials and angry defenses that rushed into her throat. It was too late now, Harry had heard her talking to someone he couldn't see or hear, and he thought she was in the midst of some emotional crisis.

"I'll be fine," she managed to say.

Harry got into his van, closed the door and drove away.

The next day Ashley and Oliver returned from their trip, bearing gifts from every tacky souvenir shop between Seattle and Topeka, or so it seemed. Amy was delighted to see them; they were, at the moment, her only viable reasons for not going crazy.

"That's a pretty ring," Oliver told her that night, when he'd had his bath and his story, and she was tucking him into bed.

Amy looked at the diamond engagement ring she would have to return and sighed. "It is pretty, isn't it?" she said sadly. "I only borrowed it, though."

"I missed you a whole bunch, Mom," Oliver confided. "A couple of times I even thought I might cry."

He whispered the final word, lest it fall on enemy ears. Ashley's, for instance.

Amy kissed her son on the forehead. "I missed you a whole bunch, too, and I *did* cry," she said.

"I know," Oliver replied. "Your eyes are all red and swelly, like they used to be after Dad died."

"I've got some problems," she told the child honestly, "but I'll work them out, so I don't want you to worry, all right?"

"All right," Oliver agreed, closing his eyes and settling into his pillow with a sigh. "'Night, Mom."

Amy went on to Ashley's room. Her daughter was sitting up in bed, busy writing in her diary.

"I guess that trip to Kansas must have been pretty exciting," Amy said gently, standing near Ashley's ruffly, stuffed-animal-mounded bed.

"It was," Ashley beamed, "but I'm glad I'm home. What did you do while we were gone, Mom?"

Amy kissed the little girl's warm cheek. "That's a long story, baby," she answered gently. "But someday I'll tell you all about it."

She switched out Ashley's light and left the room, and in the hallway Amy touched her stomach again, wondering.

If she was about to present Ashley and Oliver with a little sister, as Tyler claimed, she'd be doing that explaining sooner rather than later.

Chapter 8

Amy waited a full week for Harry to reach out and touch someone—namely, her. When he didn't, she tracked him down by calling the Ryans and asking for his office address and telephone number.

After summoning Mrs. Ingallstadt to look after the kids, Amy jumped into her car and set out for downtown Seattle.

Harry's investment firm was housed in one of the swanky, renovated buildings overlooking Elliott Bay. Clutching her courage as tightly as she clutched the handle of her purse, Amy took an elevator to the nineteenth floor.

A pretty receptionist greeted her from behind a tastefully designed desk when she entered the suite, and Amy felt another sting of envy. She was also more than a little nettled by the fact that she'd been going to marry the man and yet had had to call her former in-laws to find out where his office was located.

"I'd like to see Mr. Griffith, please."

The receptionist smiled. "I'll see if he's available. Your name?"

Amy swallowed, feeling at once foolish and belligerent. "Amy Ryan."

An exchange over the intercom followed, though Amy could only hear the receptionist's side.

"Go right in," the girl said, gesturing toward a heavy pair of mahogany doors.

Amy's bravado flagged a little, but she lifted her chin and squared her shoulders and walked boldly into Harry's inner office, closing the door behind her.

Harry sat behind an imposing library table desk, an antique from the looks of it, and he was as handsome as ever. His ebony hair gleamed in the subdued light coming in through elegantly shuttered windows, and he had taken off his coat to reveal a tailored white shirt and a gray silk vest.

"Amy," he said. He hesitated before standing, just long enough to rouse Amy's ire.

Eyes flashing, she stormed over to one of the sumptuous leather chairs facing his desk and sat down, practically flinging her purse to the floor.

"I haven't had a decent night's sleep in a whole week!" she announced.

One corner of Harry's mouth tilted slightly upward, but he didn't exactly smile. Which was a damn good thing, Amy figured, because she was in no mood to be patronized.

"Nor have I," he replied in a husky voice. Sinking back to his chair, he made a steeple with his index fingers and propped them under his chin.

Amy's pride was in tatters, but her temper sustained her. "If you want your ring back," she challenged, "that's just tough. I'm keeping it!"

Harry sighed. "It wouldn't fit me, anyway," he retorted quietly.

Amy rushed on, just as though he hadn't spoken. "And the reason I'm not giving it back is because I still love you," she blurted out, "and I think what we have together is too special to throw away!"

He rose from the chair again to stand at one of the windows, his back to Amy. "To have you for my own and then lose you," he said, "would be a thousand times worse than never having you at all."

She felt the wrench of his words to the very core of her soul, and before she realized what she was doing, she went to him and laid her cheek against his back.

"Harry, what if we visited my friend Debbie—she's a psychologist, and she could reassure you that I'm not crazy—"

He turned and took her shoulders gently in his hands. "I never said you were crazy, love. I said you needed some time to work things through. Having me around would only complicate the process."

Amy couldn't resist; she laid her hands against his smooth-shaven cheeks. "Okay, we don't have to get married next week or next month. But I want you in my life, Harry."

Harry sighed, pulled Amy close and propped his chin on the top of her head. She was practically drunk on the strength and substance and fragrance of him.

"You didn't say you needed me," he pointed out, after an interval of sweet, poignant silence.

Amy laughed, even though there were tears in her eyes. "It's not fashionable for a woman to say she needs a man. I could end up with people picketing in front of my house."

Harry kissed her forehead. "Well, I don't give a damn about fashion or any of that other rot," he said. "I'm perfectly willing to admit it, Amy—I need you, even if it's only to be my friend."

She drew back in his arms, feeling as if he'd given her a kidney punch. "Your—friend?"

He cupped her chin in his hand. "Yes, Amy, your friend. Things got too hot, too fast between us. I should have known better."

Amy swallowed, feeling wretched. She wanted Harry's friendship, of course, but she also desired him as a lover. The idea of never making love in a tree house again, or on a bed of rose petals, was a desolate one. "What do you mean, you should have known better?"

Harry smoothed her hair back from her cheek, and his smile was infinitely sad. "You're still grieving for Tyler, and I guess I am, too. It's impossible to tell whether what we feel for each other is real."

"Harry—"

He traced the outline of her mouth with one index finger. "Shh. We'll be mates, you and I. No need to complicate that with sex and marriage and all that."

Amy's cheeks were warm with color. "Were you trifling with me before?" she demanded.

He chuckled. "*Trifling?* You've been reading too many Victorian novels, Amy." He paused, seeing her ire, and cleared his throat. "It's because I love you," he concluded solemnly, "that I refuse to take further advantage of your emotional state."

She stepped back, because being so close to Harry made her ache in ways that would not be relieved in the foreseeable future. "I guess that's better than nothing," she concluded, speaking more to herself than to Harry. She turned and moved toward the door, as if in a daze.

Amy wondered how she was supposed to feel now. Happy? Sad?

She hadn't lost Harry exactly, but she hadn't really won him back, either. They were going to be *friends*.

Instead of going straight home, Amy drove across the Mercer Island bridge and made her way to her in-laws' gracious Tudor-style house. Louise met her at the door with a joyful hug.

"I'm relieved to see you're still speaking to me!" The older woman laughed. "After I let Ashley and Oliver buy you that awful Kansas ashtray, I thought your affection might cool a little."

They were in Louise's living room, about to have tea in delicate china cups that had belonged to Tyler's great-grandmother, before the older woman's expression turned serious.

"That's a very nice suntan you have," Louise said. "You didn't get that in Seattle."

Amy cleared her throat and looked away for a moment. Tyler was gone and she was an adult, free to do as she chose, but Amy still felt as though she were confessing to adultery. "While you and John and the kids were in Kansas," she finally said, "I went to Australia. With Harry Griffith."

Louise's smile was thoughtful, speculative, but not condemning. "I see."

Suddenly, without warning, Amy began to cry. She snuffled, and when Louise presented her with a box of tissue, blew her nose industriously.

"I take it you're in love with our Harry," Louise said with no little satisfaction. "Well, I think that's wonderful!"

Amy plucked a fresh batch of tissues from the box and blotted her mascara-stained cheeks. "You do?"

"Of course I do," Louise replied, reaching out to pat her daughter-in-law's hand. "You've been alone too long. All the better that it's Harry you've taken up with—for all practical intents and purposes, you'll still be our daughter-in-law."

"He wants to be my friend," Amy informed her gloomily. "He thinks I'm not ready for a new relationship."

"What gave him that idea?" Louise inquired in a calm tone, pouring more tea for herself and Amy.

Amy fidgeted in her chair. "It's—well—I just don't know how to tell you this!"

"How about just opening your mouth and spitting it right out?" Louise prompted matter-of-factly. She'd always been a proponent of the direct approach.

"I've seen Tyler—since he died, I mean. Several times."

To her credit, Louise didn't scream and run. She just drew her beautifully shaped eyebrows together for a moment in an elegant frown, then replied, "Oh, dear. I don't think that's very usual."

Amy shook her head miserably. "No, it isn't. But my neighbor used to see her late husband cleaning the birdbath, and Debbie says I'm not dealing with a ghost at all, but some projection from my deeper mind."

"Hmm," said Louise.

"Anyway," Amy went on, "Harry happened to walk in on one of my conversations with Tyler and now he thinks I haven't adjusted. For a whole week I didn't see Harry, and he didn't call. Now he wants to be—" she began to cry again "—*buddies*."

"I think things will work out, dear. You and Harry just need a little time, that's all."

"You don't think I'm weird for seeing Tyler?"

Louise smiled sadly and shook her head. "There were times when I thought I caught a glimpse of him myself, just out of the corner of my eye. When you love someone, they leave a lasting imprint on your world."

Amy wanted to tell Louise there might be a baby, a dark-haired, blue-eyed girl who would one day run Harry's empire, but she figured she'd done enough soul baring for one day. Besides, if Tyler was really a figment of her imagination, then the baby was nothing more than wishful thinking.

"You've been a big help," Amy said, gathering up what seemed like a square acre of crumpled tissue and carrying it to the wastebasket.

"Why don't you bring the kids over for dinner tonight?" Louise said eagerly. "I'll be all alone if you don't come."

Assuming her father-in-law was out of town playing golf or overseeing some investment property he and Louise owned in the eastern part of the state, Amy didn't question Louise's statement. "Sure," she said. "Why not?"

"See you at seven," Louise replied, "and dress pretty."

When Amy returned to Mercer Island that evening, wearing her green silk skirt with a lightweight white jacket, she was surprised to find Harry's van parked in the Ryans' driveway.

"Harry's here!" Oliver crowed, bounding out of the car a second after Amy had brought it to a stop.

Ashley was more circumspect, but Amy could see that her daughter was just as pleased.

As for Amy, well, her mother-in-law's final words were echoing in her ears. *Dress pretty.*

"I should have known you were up to something," Amy accused pleasantly, when Louise answered the door. "Did you call him up the minute I agreed to come to dinner?"

After hugging their grandmother, Oliver and Ashley rushed inside in search of Harry.

"As a matter of fact, yes," Louise answered.

When Harry stepped into the entryway, wearing gray slacks and a blue summer sweater, Amy could have sworn the earth backtracked on its axis for a few degrees before plunging forward again.

"Hello, Amy."

She resisted an urge to smooth her hair and her jacket. "Hello," she replied.

"I'll just leave the two of you to chat while I go and put the chicken on the grill," Louise announced busily. A moment later she was gone.

Amy just stood there, as embarrassed as if she'd crashed a private party. Ashley and Oliver appeared behind Harry, anxious for his attention.

Harry held his hands out to his sides, and Ashley and Oliver each took one, on cue. "We're going for a walk down by the water. Want to go along?"

Since her emotions were as raw as an exposed nerve, Amy opted out. "I'll stay here and help Louise with the chicken," she said.

Harry's ink-blue eyes swept over her once, in a way that used to precede a session of lovemaking. "You're not exactly dressed for barbecuing, but I guess that's your choice."

Having made this cryptic pronouncement, Harry turned and walked back through the big house, taking Amy's children with him.

Amy took an alternate route to the big deck overlooking the water and found Louise there, busily brushing her special sauce onto the chicken pieces she'd already arranged on the grill.

The elder Mrs. Ryan looked at her daughter-in-law quizzically. "Didn't you want to join Harry and the children on their walk?"

"I think Ashley and Oliver need to have him to themselves for a little while," Amy answered.

Louise smiled, watching with a wistful expression in her eyes as the three figures moved down the verdant hillside behind the house. "Tyler was a good father," she said. "It's not surprising that his children miss the presence of a man."

"They have their grandfathers and their uncles," Amy pointed out.

"That's not quite the same," Louise said, meeting Amy's eyes, "and we both know it. Children need a man who not only loves them, but loves their mother as well. And Harry loves you passionately."

Amy went to the deck railing, helpless to turn away, and stood watching, listening to her children's laughter on the evening breeze. Watching Harry and shamelessly wanting him.

"Harry's not sure what he feels," Amy mused. "He told me that himself. He thinks we need time."

"Harry may very well not be sure what he feels," Louise replied without hesitation, "but he's wildly in love with you. He might as well have the fact tattooed on his forehead."

Amy smiled at that image, though she felt more like crying. It seemed to her, in her present fragile mood, that love should be simpler than it was. With Tyler, romance had been as natural as breathing, and their relationship had progressed without a hitch.

Finally remembering her original plan to help with the chicken, Amy turned and started toward the grill.

"Stay back," Louise warned, brandishing her barbecue fork. "You're not dressed for this."

The sun was starting to dip behind the horizon when Harry, Ashley and Oliver climbed the wooden stairs behind the house to join the small party on the deck. Amy's heart started thumping painfully the minute Harry was within a dozen feet of her, and she wondered how on earth she was ever going to stand just being his friend.

Ashley and Oliver chattered nonstop, all through dinner, and Amy was relieved because that saved her from having to make conversation. The moment the meal was over, however, Louise enlisted the kids to help clear away the dishes, leaving Amy and Harry alone at the redwood picnic table Ty and his father had built one long-ago summer.

"I'm sorry," Amy said. She gazed at the city lights and their aura of stars because she still wasn't bold enough to look straight at Harry. "Louise seems to be throwing us together."

Their knees touched under the table, and Harry drew back as if he'd been burned. "She's a matchmaker at heart."

Amy swallowed. She'd made love with this man in a tree house, for heaven's sake, not to mention the bedroom of a fancy jet and on her own living-room floor. For all of that, she felt nervous with him, vulnerable and shy.

"Thank you for paying so much attention to the kids," she choked out. "They miss having a man around."

"It isn't an act of charity, Amy," Harry said quietly. She sensed that he was about to take her hand, but when she looked, he withdrew. "I love kids. I've always wanted a whole houseful of my own."

Amy considered telling him she might be pregnant, but decided against it. Her crazy confessions had gotten her into enough trouble. Besides, as much as she loved Harry, as much as she yearned to share her life with him, she didn't want him to marry her as a point of honor. When Harry became her husband, it had to be by his own choice, not by coercion.

"Let's go in," he said, when the silence grew long and awkward. "It's getting chilly."

"I noticed," Amy replied ruefully, but she wasn't talking about the weather.

* * *

For the next month Amy saw Harry only when she went to dinner at her in-laws' house, or when he could be sure Ashley and Oliver would be around to act as chaperons.

Right after Labor Day, school started, and Amy told herself it was time to start concentrating on her real estate deals again. Instead of putting on a power suit and going out to meet with a potential client, however, she jumped into the car and headed for the nearest drugstore the minute the school bus turned the corner.

In the end, though, Amy didn't have the nerve to go into that familiar neighborhood establishment and buy what she needed. She drove on until she found another one, where the proprietors were strangers.

Even then, Amy wore sunglasses and a big hat while making her purchase.

At home again, she tore open the box and rushed into the downstairs bathroom to perform the pregnancy test.

The process took twenty minutes, and the results were positive.

Amy sat on the edge of the bathtub, unable to decide whether she should mourn or celebrate. Her relationship with Harry was clearly over, except for his playing doting uncle to the kids, and nobody knew better than Amy did how hard it was to raise a child alone.

On the other hand, she had wanted another baby for a long time. In fact, she and Tyler had planned to have at least two more little ones—until fate intervened.

Amy needed desperately to talk to someone. After throwing away the paraphernalia from her test and washing her hands, she wandered out into the living room.

"Tyler?"

Nothing.

Struck by another impulse, Amy brushed her hair, applied fresh lip gloss and snatched up her purse and keys. Within minutes she was on the road again.

When she reached the cemetery where Tyler had been buried, she parked the car and sat behind the wheel for a while, struggling to contain her emotions.

Finally she walked up the hill to Tyler's grave. His grandparents and another Ryan son who'd died in childhood shared the well-maintained plot.

After looking around carefully and seeing nobody but a gardener off in the distance, Amy touched Tyler's marble headstone lovingly, then sat down on a nearby bench.

Five minutes passed, then ten, then fifteen. Amy wiped away a tear with the back of one hand.

"Oh, Ty, what am I going to do? You were right about the baby—I'm pregnant, and Harry's going to know the child is his. He'll insist on doing the honorable thing, and we'll have one of those terrible, grudging marriages—"

A breeze, warm because it was still early in September, ruffled the leaves of the trees and wafted through Amy's hair.

"Tyler, you started all this," Amy went on. "You've got to help me. You've got to tell me what to do."

There was no answer, and yet Amy thought she could sense Tyler's presence. Maybe it was only a silly fancy.

"I'm open to suggestions!" Amy said, spreading her hands wide in a gesture of acceptance.

An older couple stopped to look at her, probably wondering if they should scream for help, then hurried on, hand in hand.

"You're no help at all!" Amy whispered, bending a little closer to the headstone so her voice wouldn't carry. But it did help to sit there, talking to Tyler. Only when she was driving away did Amy realize that she'd said a goodbye of her own, final and complete.

She just wished there were a way to convince Harry that she'd turned the corner, that she was ready to love him with her whole heart. As for her body, well, that was *more* than ready to love Harry.

"Harry's living at the lighthouse now," Tyler's sister, Charlotte, announced that night, when she came to have supper with Amy and the kids.

Amy thought of the child growing within her and ached to share the news, but, much as she dreaded telling Harry, she knew he had to be the first to know.

"Oh?" Amy tried to sound unconcerned as she assembled a salad. "Is he dating anybody?"

Charlotte shook her head. "You're not fooling me with the casual act, Amy. You can hardly keep your hands off the man. What's going on between you two, anyway?"

"I wish I knew," Amy sighed. "He thinks I'm not over Tyler." She gazed out the kitchen window at the lilacs, withered now with the coming of fall, and felt sad because Ty had loved them so much.

Charlotte shrugged. "It's Friday," she said. "Why don't you go out to the lighthouse and talk things over with Harry? I'll stay here and look after the kids."

"I couldn't—"

"Why not?"

"It would be too forward."

Charlotte rolled her eyes. "Amy, you're not in junior high school. And you love this guy, don't you?"

Amy nodded. "I always thought it could only happen once."

"Well, don't blow it," Charlotte hissed happily. "Go! Get out of here!"

"What if he's with someone else?" Amy whispered. "I'd die."

"He won't be," Charlotte replied in a confident tone of voice, "but if you insist on being civilized, call first."

"No," Amy said resolutely. But when Charlotte and the kids were eating, she found she couldn't choke down a bite of the special eggplant dish she'd made.

Finally she went into the den and closed the door.

She didn't have to call information, or Louise, for Harry's new number. It was branded on her mind in steaming digits.

He answered on the third ring, with a gravelly and somewhat impatient "Hello?"

Amy wondered despairingly if she'd pulled him away from a glass of wine, a crackling fire and a willing woman. "Hello," she finally managed to say.

"Amy?" Her name echoed with alarm. "Are you all right? Has something happened to one of the kids?"

She cleared her throat. "No," she said as quickly as possible. "I mean, yes, I'm all right, and no, nothing has happened to Ashley or Oliver. I just...wanted to talk with you."

He was silent, waiting for her to go on, but she couldn't tell whether it was a receptive silence or an impatient, angry one.

"Do you think I could come out there? There's a ferry in half an hour, and I can catch it if I hurry."

It was agony, waiting for his answer. "All right," he finally said, and again, his tone betrayed none of his emotions.

Amy dropped her toothbrush into her purse, grabbed her coat and gave Charlotte the okay sign from the dining-room doorway.

After saying good-bye to Ashley and Oliver, carefully avoiding any explanation of her destination the whole while, Amy rushed out to her car.

She made the ferry with only seconds to spare.

Finding the lighthouse, once she reached the island, was easy. The structure's giant electric lamp was shining in the darkness, guiding her.

When she pulled up in front of Harry's spectacular

house, he came out to meet her, his blue eyes searching her face worriedly in the glow from above. He took her arm and shuffled her inside and across a glistening hardwood floor to the fireplace.

"What's this about?" Harry asked. "Are you all right?"

Amy could no longer carry the burden alone, and besides, her secret was going to be obvious enough in the months to come. She needed to tell Debbie and Louise and Charlotte, in order to enlist their support, and she couldn't do that until Harry knew.

"I'm going to have a baby," she said bluntly.

Harry's mouth dropped open. "I thought...?"

"That I was protected? So did I. But sometimes babies just decide they're going to be born, no matter what."

His hands closed on her shoulders, firmly but with a gentleness that touched her heart. He pressed her into the big leather chair they'd picked out together, that happy day before things had fallen apart.

"I'm not sick, Harry," Amy pointed out practically. "Just pregnant."

"When?" He croaked the word, paused to clear his throat, and started again. "When will the little nipper be joining us?"

"In the spring," Amy answered, wishing there truly could be an *us*.

Harry was completely beside himself. He paced and ran one hand through his usually impeccable hair, and

Amy would have laughed if the situation hadn't had such a serious side.

She knew she was about to get everything she wanted, for all the wrong reasons. And those reasons might well poison her relationship with this man forever. He'd soon view her the same way he'd seen Madeline—as a manipulator and a schemer.

"We'll have to be married right away," he said.

"No," Amy replied. "We can't get married."

Harry was quietly outraged. "Then what the hell are we going to do? You're not going to bring *my* child into this world with no claim to his rightful name! And don't suggest living together, because that wouldn't be good for Ashley and Oliver."

"I wasn't going to suggest living together," Amy said. "I think we should just go on as we have been." *Even though it's torture,* she thought, *that's better than it would be to look into your eyes and see contempt, or boredom, or God help us both, hatred.*

He took her hand, pulled her easily to her feet. "I think I know how to convince you," he said. And then he slanted his mouth over hers for a commanding kiss, and Amy thought she'd faint with excitement and relief.

Chapter 9

The fact that he knew better didn't keep Harry from making love to Amy. Nor did the realization that she was carrying his child; *that* only made her more attractive.

No, Harry could no more have turned away from her than a starving man could resist hot cornbread dripping with butter.

They didn't even get as far as the bed, but instead sank to the Persian rug on the hearth. Their clothes melted away and their tongues mated and then, suddenly, their bodies were engaged in the ancient struggle, twisting and writhing and colliding with sweet, fevered violence.

Arched beneath him, Amy threw her head back and gave a long, guttural cry. Tendrils of her hair clung to the moisture on her forehead and cheeks, and her eyes stared sightlessly past him, past the ceiling and the night sky.

Harry's own climax was fast approaching when he saw surprise in her features, felt her sated body come alive once more under his hips, heard her murmur with joyous desperation, "Oh, God, Harry, it's going to happen—again!"

Harry drove deep inside her, and she came apart in his arms, chattering senselessly, enfolding him in her strong, slender legs. A sound that was half sob and half shout of triumph tore itself from Harry's throat, and he stiffened upon Amy, surrendering what she demanded of him.

For several long moments, his body spasmed violently in response to her gentle conquering. Then he collapsed beside her on the rug in front of his fireplace.

"We'll be married as soon as we can get the license," he said a long time later, when he had regained enough strength to speak.

She shook her head, which had been resting placidly on his shoulder until that moment.

"No, Harry, we won't. I don't want it to be like this."

Harry swallowed a growl of frustration; this was no time to be macho. He was proud of the fact that he spoke so calmly. "Tell me what you want, Amy, and I'll give it to you."

She raised herself on one elbow, and the firelight

bathed her satiny, naked flesh, making Harry want her all over again. "I want you to want me, for *me*. Not because I'm carrying your baby, not because you feel obliged to look after your good friend's widow, but because you're absolutely wild about me."

He raised her fingers to his lips and kissed the knuckles lightly, one by one. "I thought I just proved that."

"You just proved that you wanted *a woman,* Harry. I refuse to buy the delusion that someone else couldn't have satisfied you just as completely."

Harry sighed. God, but women were a frustrating lot, always attacking a man's pure logic with their reasonable implausibilities. The bloke who figured out what in the hell they really wanted would make millions.

"I love you," he said. "You know that."

She laid her head on his chest again and started making circular motions on his belly with one hand. If she kept that up, he'd be out of his mind in about five seconds. "I know we have good chemistry," she argued sweetly. "I also know that you were perfectly willing to end everything between us until you found out about the baby."

With another sigh, Harry shoved splayed fingers through his hair. "All right, rose petal, jump to whatever conclusions that might look comfortable. But add this to the list of things you know—I have rights where this child is concerned and I *will not* sacrifice them."

He felt her shiver in his arms, but when she executed her special vengeance, her hand was damnably strong and steady.

"Oh, God," he rasped, closing his eyes.

Amy was kissing her way down over his chest, his rib cage, his midriff. "Even prayer won't help you now, Harry Griffith." She purred the words, but not as a kitten would. Oh, no. This was a lioness.

Harry gave a strangled gasp of pleasure when she claimed him.

The next morning, Amy awakened in Harry's bed. She'd spent the night in heaven, but now, as she sat there alone, she returned to earth with a painful thump. Nothing had really been resolved, nothing had changed.

She sat bolt upright and looked wildly around for her clothes.

With perfect timing, Harry entered the room, carrying a tray with a coffee cup, a covered plate and a newspaper on it.

"Where are my things?" Amy demanded, embarrassed to remember how she'd behaved the night before. Merciful heavens, this man could turn her into a harlot with a touch or a single kiss.

He grinned, setting the tray across her lap. "What clothes?" he asked innocently.

"The ones I was wearing last night, when I arrived," Amy answered tightly. She wanted to spurn the food he'd brought, but she'd had a world-class workout and she was hungry. She lifted the lid from the covered plate and nibbled at a piece of fresh pineapple.

"Oh," Harry replied, in a tone of great revelation, standing back from the side of the bed, "you're speaking of the garments you tore off, in your eagerness to surrender yourself to me in front of the fireplace last night." He paused, rubbing his chin. "I'm afraid I burned them."

Amy's fork clattered to the tray. *"You burned them?"*

Harry nodded. "Essentially, rose petal, you're a prisoner of love. Unless you want to make the trip back to Seattle in the altogether, of course."

She narrowed her eyes. "You're making this up!"

"See for yourself," Harry said, gesturing toward the door leading to the living room. "Of course, I feel honor bound to tell you that you'll be taking a big chance, just walking past me. There's something about impending fatherhood that makes me—well—eager."

Color flooded Amy's face, but it was a blush of chagrin and not anger. She'd just realized that she didn't mind the prospect of being Harry's toy for a while, and that insight embarrassed her greatly.

"What are the conditions for my release?" she asked after sitting there for a long time, staring at Harry like a fool.

He raised an index finger. "Oh, there is only one. You'll have to become my wife."

Amy closed her eyes, took a deep breath and let

it out again. With that she was calm. She wouldn't scream and yell.

She opened her eyes and her mouth at the same time, and when she did she found that Harry was gone.

Furiously Amy stuffed down the rest of her breakfast. Then, wrapping herself in the bedspread, she got up and started going through Harry's bureau drawers.

She put on a pair of his briefs in place of underpants, but he didn't have anything that could be adapted to serve as a bra. After adding tailored wool slacks, a cinched belt, a striped, button-down shirt, socks and a pair of loafers that flippity-flopped when she walked, Amy stormed defiantly into the living room.

"I'm leaving," she said.

A corner of Harry's mouth quivered, but he didn't laugh. He didn't even smile. He closed the book he'd been reading and rose from his chair. "How? I've hidden your car, not to mention your purse, and if you try to walk to the ferry terminal in my clothes, the police will probably pick you up and haul you off to some shelter."

Amy stomped one foot. "Harry, this isn't funny."

His blue eyes swept over her. "That's your opinion, rose petal. I think it's hilarious." Another sweep of his eyes left her feeling weak. "Come here," he said.

Although reason and pride dictated that she must stand her ground, instinct prevailed. Amy stepped out of the loafers and walked slowly across the room to Harry.

Methodically, he untucked the shirt she'd borrowed, then unfastened the belt buckle. The slacks fell straight to the floor, and Harry chuckled when he saw the briefs beneath.

Reaching smoothly, boldly inside the flap, he cupped her femininity in his hand, making a circular motion with his palm.

"Harry," she whimpered, helpless to twist away from him because he'd already made her need what he was doing to her.

"Open the shirt, Amy," he said. "I want to see your breasts."

She obeyed him, moving slowly and deliberately, like some creature under a spell. All the defiance she could come up with was "You can't make love to me in the living room in broad daylight, Harry."

"Watch me," he replied. Then, still caressing her, he plunged one finger deep inside her and, at the same moment, bent to take one of her nipples greedily into his mouth.

He brought her to the very edge of release, made her coast back to earth just short of satisfaction, then carried her high again.

Finally, sitting in his leather wingback chair, he positioned Amy on his lap, facing him, her knees draped over the arms. She was transfixed when he took her, letting out a long, low, primitive cry of pure animal pleasure.

His hands gripping the quivering flesh of her hips, Harry rocked Amy back and forth until she was literally out of her mind with passion. He sucked her breasts, first one and then the other, while she shivered again and again and again.

Finally Harry climaxed, too, and she was allowed to sag forward against him, her forehead propped on his shoulder.

"You didn't really burn my clothes," she managed, after some time.

"Oh, yes I did," he replied. "Marry me."

Amy trembled, still filled with him, her legs still balanced over the arms of the chair. "No."

He took her to the master bath, bathed her languid body thoroughly in the big marble tub, then, in his room, placed her atop a bureau and had her again.

If Amy had told Harry she didn't want to make love, he would have respected her wishes and left her alone. The trouble was, he was very good at arousing her, and by the time he'd gone through all the steps, she was more than ready to cooperate.

Her responses this time were just as wild, just as violent, as before. Harry had opened some well of need inside her, some region of surrender that had never been reached before.

"Marry me," he said intractably, kissing her shoulder blades, when she finally stopped howling in raucous appeasement.

"Absolutely not," Amy gasped with the last of her defiance.

Harry began to massage her bottom with both hands, although he did not withdraw from her depths because he had somehow stopped himself on the brink of satisfaction and he was still hard inside her.

Slowly, rhythmically, he began to move—in, out, in, out.

Amy groaned and clutched the edges of the bureau. "Oh, no," she whimpered, feeling the treacherous pressure begin to build inside her. "Oh, Harry, don't make me—"

He did make her, though.

More than once.

"Harry," she said, much later, huddled in his bed again, with the covers pulled to her chin, "I have children. I must get back to them."

"Louise and Charlotte are looking after the nippers," Harry replied. Fresh from the shower, he was wearing a dark blue terry robe with a hood, and his dark hair, only partially dry, was combed.

"What did you tell Louise?" Amy wanted to know.

"That I've made you my love slave and she shouldn't look for you to return to the city anytime soon," Harry replied, turning to stand in front of the dresser mirror.

"You didn't!" Amy cried in mortified disbelief, her cheeks hot with humiliation.

"Sure I did," Harry answered. "But don't look for the sheriff to come and save you, rose petal. Louise thought being a plaything might do you some good."

Amy snatched up a pillow and flung it at him, missing by a wide margin. "She did not. Louise is a very modern woman. She would never approve of this!"

Harry picked up the pillow and hurled it back with deadly accuracy. "She also comes from a generation where women married the men who made them pregnant. She thinks I should keep you here until I've made you see reason."

Amy swallowed, no longer sure what to believe. It was no small irritation to her pride that she secretly loved this game Harry was playing with her, and even though she was exhausted, she could hardly wait to see where he would make love to her next.

"You're a bastard, Harry Griffith," she sulked.

"And you're a hot little number who needs to be taken on a regular basis."

Again, it was the truth in Harry's statement that made Amy so angry.

"I hate you!" she yelled.

"Mmm-hmm," he answered distractedly. "It's going to be a man-sized job keeping you properly pleasured. Of course, I'm—" he paused, cleared his throat "—up to the task."

Amy screamed in frustration. "Damn you, Harry, get me some clothes and take me home, right now!"

He wrapped her in a heavy bathrobe of navy velvet and led her out to the living room, where he settled her in a chair by the hearth, then built up the fire. He brought her food, fruit and bread, and a snifter of brandy, and for a while she thought Harry was beginning to see reason.

Instead, he was resting up for another round.

Once she'd eaten, he took her back to bed and made love to her again.

"Will you marry me?" Harry inquired implacably, when she was dangling from the edge of ecstatic madness.

"Yes!" Amy cried. "Oh, Harry—oh, God—*yes!*"

Her reward left her drenched with perspiration and weak from her own straining efforts.

Harry finished what he'd begun, and after a long time, he got up and found oil to rub into every inch of her skin. Finally, then, he allowed her to sleep.

The next day a judge arrived with a special license, and Louise, John and Charlotte appeared with the children. Louise had brought along a flowered sundress for Amy to wear, along with casual clothes, nightgowns and underwear for later.

"You're sure you're okay with this?" Amy asked her children, when the three of them were alone in one of Harry's guest rooms. She hadn't told them, of course, how Harry had burned her clothes and made love to her repeatedly. "You really want a stepfather?"

"We really want *Harry,*" Ashley clarified.

"We're going to live in Australia, on an island!" Oliver crowed, hardly able to contain his enthusiasm at this good fortune. "Wow!"

Amy was looking forward to becoming Harry's wife, but she was also reluctant. She couldn't get past the idea that none of this would be happening if she hadn't told Harry she was expecting his baby.

The wedding was to be held in Harry's living room, that evening, by the light of a hundred candles. All the rest of Tyler's family came over for the occasion, and since Amy's father couldn't take enough time off from being a world-renowned surgeon to make the trip, John Ryan gave away the bride.

Oliver was to be the best man, Ashley the maid of honor.

Amy went to the master bedroom to be alone and gather her thoughts before the ceremony, and what she found there practically stopped her heart in midbeat.

In the middle of the bed, fragrant and lacy and totally impossible, lay an armload of white lilacs.

Mentally Amy searched the lighthouse grounds, and she found no lilacs. They couldn't have come from the mainland, either, because there had been a hard freeze the last week in August and all the flowers were gone.

Slowly, her eyes filling with happy tears, Amy approached the bed and lifted one of the lovely fronds into her hands. She was drawing in its unforgettable scent when she heard the door open.

Harry was standing there.

"Did you have these shipped in from somewhere?" she asked, knowing the answer before he spoke. Harry had sent for caviar and champagne, but his contribution to the ceremony was a massive bouquet of pink roses, already in full bloom. Amy knew their petals would become her marriage bed and, for all the time

she'd spent exploding in Harry's arms, she was ready
to give herself again.

"No," Harry answered, coming to her side and taking up one of the boughs with a frown. "I thought
these were gone for the year."

Someday, Amy thought, she would tell him that
white lilacs had been special to her and Tyler. Someday, she would say that Tyler had found a way to offer
his blessing on their marriage, but now wasn't the time
for explanations and Amy knew it.

She made a wreath of the lush lilacs for her hair,
and when it came time for the ceremony, she drew a
deep breath, said a prayer and went out to be married.
Somehow, she would find a way to make Harry love
her, truly love her, for real.

In the meantime, she would take whatever happiness she could find, wherever she found it.

The Ryans took Ashley and Oliver back to Seattle
after the wedding, and Harry drove Amy to the jet.
When the plane was high in the air, bound for some
mysterious honeymoon destination, he left the pilot to
handle the controls and joined Amy in the main cabin.

"You are beautiful, Mrs. Griffith," he said in a
hoarse voice, taking off his suit jacket and draping it
casually over the back of one of the seats. As he loos-
ened his tie, he went on. "If you would be so good as to
go into our bedroom and take off your clothes, please."

Amy could hear her own heartbeat, thundering
as loudly as the jet's engines. "You're incredible,"
she said.

He smiled easily. "Thank you," he said, with a slight bow of his head.

Amy went to the master suite as she'd been bidden. The bed was mounded with pink rose petals, just as she'd expected, and there was a bottle of sparkling cider on the nightstand, cooling in a silver bucket.

"I thought champagne might be bad for the baby," Harry said from the doorway.

Amy was touched, but she wished she could matter to Harry as much as this child she was carrying. "Where are we going?"

Harry closed the door and kicked off his shoes. "I'm taking you to the morning star and back again," he said.

She couldn't believe it, not after the marathon they'd already put in. "I meant, for our honeymoon," she retorted dryly.

"Wait and see," he answered.

Soon rose petals were drifting down off the edges of the bed like pink rain, and Amy had made more than one trip to the morning star before the plane touched down.

She looked out and saw an isolated airstrip, a lot of desert and cactus and a proud hacienda of white stucco.

"Mexico?" she asked, kneeling on the bed and peering through the porthole.

"Yes," Harry answered, pulling her back down beside him.

Later, they went into the house, which was clean,

well furnished and vacant. The pilot refueled the jet, went through a flight check and took off again.

"Is this your place?" Amy inquired, amazed. There was a pool out back, filled with inviting crystal-clear water, and the main bedroom had air-conditioning, a terrace and its own hot tub.

Harry smiled. "Belongs to a friend," he answered, setting their suitcases down at the foot of the massive bed. "Not a bad place to be a prisoner of love, is it?"

Amy blushed furiously at the reminder. "I gave in to your demands," she pointed out. "By all rights, I should no longer be classified as a captive."

"You may get a reprieve someday," Harry responded easily. "Time off for good behavior and all that. Louise is going to interview governesses for the kids so we can leave for the island soon."

Amy sat down on the bed. "You certainly are anxious to get back to Australia," she said, worried.

Harry stood near enough to touch the tip of her nose with an index finger. "Never fear, rose petal," he began. "I'm not planning to dump you and the nippers there and then go off and chase women. I want my baby to have the best possible start in life, and a calm, peaceful environment for its mother seems like a good beginning."

No protests came to mind. The kids, who would have been her best excuse for staying in Seattle, were eager to visit the island. Harry had promised them each a pony, and Tyler's folks were already making plans to visit.

The honeymoon lasted a week, though afterward those delicious days and nights ran together in Amy's mind, indiscernible from each other. She and Harry swam and made love, talked and made love, ate and made love, played tennis and made love.

Then they went back to Seattle, where Amy put her house on the market, said good-bye to her friends and family, packed summer things for herself and the children, put Rumpel into Mrs. Ingallstadt's loving care, and did her best to absorb the fact that her life had changed forever.

It wouldn't have been accurate to say she was unhappy—she was married to a man she loved desperately and was expecting his child—but there was an undercurrent of suspense. Harry was doing what he saw as his duty, and it didn't matter that he did such a damn good job at pretending to like it.

Amy's happiness was underlaid with a sense of urgency, of barely controlled anxiety.

The children thrived on the long, often-interrupted journey from Seattle to Australia. Both of them took their turns at the plane's controls, and when they stopped in Hawaii for a day, they explored their surroundings with energetic delight. The same thing happened in Fiji and Auckland, New Zealand and finally Sydney.

Once again, there was no problem with Customs. Ashley and Oliver were permitted into the country on the strength of Amy's passport and, she suspected, because Harry Griffith was their stepfather.

Returning to Harry's private isle, which Oliver promptly renamed Treasure Island, was like having the gates of Eden swing open again. It was a second chance.

The governess Louise had selected, a pretty brown-haired girl who had been doing graduate work at the University of Washington, was waiting when they arrived, as were Elsa and Shelt O'Donnell. Evidently, Amy thought testily, the nanny had taken a direct flight.

Although Amy's pregnancy was in its early stages, it had already begun to take its toll. She was exhausted from the trip to Australia, even though Harry had taken every opportunity to let her rest.

She hadn't been able to sleep on the plane, though she'd tried. Instead, she'd mindlessly read one book after another, and five seconds after she'd closed the last cover, she'd forgotten what the story was about. When she wasn't reading, she was in one of the swanky bathrooms, being violently sick.

Amy concluded that she just wasn't cut out to be a jet-setter.

When they finally reached their destination, she slept for two days straight, waking up only to eat and bathe and go to the bathroom, and although he was in bed beside her at regular intervals, Harry didn't once make love to her. She supposed the inevitable withdrawal had already begun, and for the first time in her life she was irrationally jealous of another woman.

Mary Anne, the governess, to be precise.

"You're just saying Louise hired her," Amy said pouting one night, when she and Harry were sitting on the terrace outside their room. The children were asleep and the sky was scattered with gaudy stars that were bigger and brighter than they had any business being. "You probably handpicked Mary Anne yourself, because of her great body."

Harry bent over her chair, gripping the arms, his nose less than an inch from Amy's. "You're very fortunate that you're pregnant, rose petal," he said. "If you weren't, I'd turn you over my knee, bare your backside and paddle you soundly for saying that."

Amy stuck out her lip. "You wouldn't dare. Modern American men don't do such things."

"Maybe they don't," Harry replied softly, "but I'm not an American and I'm not especially modern, either. It would behoove you to remember that."

A tear slipped down Amy's cheek. "She's so pretty."

With a warm chuckle, Harry gathered Amy up, sat down in the chair she'd occupied before, and cradled her on his lap. "If I didn't know better, Amy-girl," he said soothingly, holding her close, "I'd think Tyler did you wrong. What on earth gives you the idea that I'm constantly on the prowl for other women?"

"You wouldn't really spank a grown woman," Amy said, ignoring his question. But she laid her head against his shoulder, feeling fat and frumpy and very worried.

"Don't test the theory," Harry warned. "Australian men are still a generation or two behind the times, love. I would never get myself into a drunken rage and beat you or anything like that, but a few smart swats on the bottom never hurt."

"That depends on whose bottom it is," Amy reasoned. She had an unsettling feeling that Harry was totally serious.

Harry laughed and kissed her soundly on the forehead. "I will never, ever, be unfaithful," he promised in a sincere tone of voice a few moments later. "So stop worrying."

"What about when I'm fat and cranky and I'm retaining water?"

"You're cranky now, love, and no doubt you're retaining water, too." He opened her robe, baring one of her breasts to the attentions of an idle index finger. "And all I can think about is taking you to my bed and having you, thoroughly and well."

A delicious shudder ran through Amy, and when Harry bent to take her nipple between his lips and tease it mercilessly, she gasped.

Both her breasts were wet, their peaks hard and tingling, when Harry carried his bride inside and arranged her gently on his bed.

He laid aside her robe, like the wrapping on a gift, and never took his eyes from her as he stripped away his clothes.

He made her body tell all its secrets over the course of that magical night, and he had Amy so thoroughly and so well that, a couple of times, she thought she glimpsed the far side of forever.

Chapter 10

The following week Harry left the island on business for the first time. Late that afternoon a tropical rainstorm blew in, hammering at the roof and tapping at the panes and making Ashley and Oliver rush, giggling with nervous excitement, from one window to another.

"Do you think it's a hurricane?" Amy asked Mary Anne, who was reading a book next to the fireplace. Amy had already come to terms with the fact that her children's teacher was a good person, not likely to engage in frolics with the master of the house, and the two women were becoming friends.

Mary Anne smiled. "Just a regular spring storm," she said.

It still seemed weird to Amy that mid-October

could qualify as spring, but in Australia it did. "It doesn't appear to be bothering the kids."

Mary Anne closed her book, the pleasant expression lingering on her pretty face. "Kids are born adventurers," she agreed. "Is there anything I could get you, Mrs. Griffith? Some tea, maybe, or a glass of lemonade?"

Amy shook her head, feeling guilty for all the uncharitable thoughts she'd once harbored for this bright, intelligent young woman. "Thanks, no. I'm all right."

But she wasn't, and Mary Anne seemed to know that as well as Amy did. Amy was imagining Harry in cosmopolitan Sydney, dressed in one of his tuxedos, surrounded by sexy blondes, brunettes and redheads at some swanky party.

The next day, however, the storm blew out and Harry blew in. He brought fancy saddles for the kids, whose promised ponies had been waiting in the stable on their arrival, and for Amy there was a sketch pad and the biggest selection of colored chalk she'd ever seen.

She began to sketch the fabulous birds roosting in the trees just outside her walls. Startled at her own ability, Amy progressed to drawing images of Shelt and Elsa and Harry and the kids. When Ashley and Oliver were busy studying and Harry was either away or working, Amy's new interest in art positively consumed her.

Harry brought oil paints and canvases when he returned, and so many art books that Shelt had to make two trips to the landing strip to pick them all up.

In November, Amy and Harry went to Sydney on their own to take in a concert, have elegant dinners in gracious restaurants and do some preliminary shopping for the holidays. Amy visited her doctor, who pronounced her in good health, and she and Harry made love all of one afternoon and half the night.

When they returned to the island, Amy felt restored and renewed.

In early December they flew back to Sydney, this time taking Mary Anne and the kids with them. Although it was the height of summer, it was also Christmastime, and the clean, beautiful city was decorated for the holidays.

Harry and Amy took the kids and their governess to see *The Nutcracker* at one of the city's better theaters, then everyone shopped. Mary Anne sent presents to her family via airmail, and when they returned home, there were boxes galore awaiting them at the mainland post office.

They decorated a towering artificial tree, even though the sun was dazzlingly bright on the water. It seemed to Amy that there were presents hidden everywhere, and Ashley and Oliver were having the time of their lives.

Amy couldn't quite trust Harry's commitment— every time he left the island, she was on pins and needles until he returned. She had progressed by that point to making her own exquisite gift wrap, though, complete with hand-painted angels and other heralds of Christmas, and she did her level best to keep busy.

"Happy, love?" Harry asked, late Christmas Eve, when they'd filled the kids' stockings and played Santa.

Her emotions were complex and very confusing, and she supposed a lot of them could be ascribed to her pregnancy. For all of that, Amy was insecure as she had never been insecure before. Despite her art and her beautiful children and the much-wanted baby tucked away between her heart and her soul, Amy felt cut off from Harry. It seemed to her that the only time they were really close was when they were in the throes of lovemaking, unable to speak coherent words, flinging themselves at each other as if in battle.

Not being able to put her condition into words, Amy started to cry instead.

Harry put an arm around her and drew her close beside him in bed, one hand resting in a proprietary way on her rounded stomach. "There now, love," he said, his lips moving against her temple. "Your hormones are in a bit of a muddle, but it'll all come right in the end. You'll see."

Tell me you love me, Amy thought. "That's easy for you to say, Harry," she said aloud. "You're not pregnant."

"Darn good thing, too," he confirmed good-naturedly, "or we'd get nothing done for fending off photographers from all the tacky tabloids."

Amy laughed in spite of herself. "If I were you, I'd hate me," she said.

Harry rolled over to look deeply into her troubled eyes before he kissed her. "Hate you?" he countered hoarsely, after he'd left Amy dizzy from the intimacy of their contact. "Never."

Normally he would have made love to Amy then. Instead, he just cuddled her close, sighed contentedly and went to sleep.

The next day was a noisy riot of rumpled gift paper, food, presents and laughter.

On New Year's, Elsa and Mary Anne took the Christmas tree down and put it away, and Amy got out her oils and canvas and started to paint.

Harry took Amy to Sydney for another doctor's appointment at the end of the month and again in February.

The first week in March, just as winter was getting off to a fine Australian start, Amy went into labor.

This time she didn't go to the doctor, he came to her on board Harry's jet, bringing a nurse and an anesthesiologist with him.

Sara Tyler Griffith was born in her parents' bedroom, with a tropical storm threatening to make the seas run over onto the land. She was a lovely child, with the blue eyes all babies have, and a rich shock of dark, dark hair. Just as Ty had predicted.

Harry held his daughter, his beautiful eyes glistening with wondrous tears, while the doctor and nurse saw to Amy's care.

Amy looked at her husband and this innocent, trusting child, and couldn't help being happy, at least for the moment. She had practically everything she'd ever wanted, and so what if there were slight imperfections in the fabric of her life? So what if Harry didn't truly love her and she still wondered what he did when he was away from home? Nobody had everything.

A day later, when her milk came in, Amy nursed Sara, stroking her tiny, doll-like head, and told her, "You'll be more your daddy's girl than mine, I think, but I guess I can live with that." She smiled. "Just between you and me, Sara Griffith, you'll be running the family business someday. I have that on good authority."

There was a timid knock at the door, and Ashley and Oliver trailed in, drawn to their sister and at the same time wondering how her presence would affect their places in the scheme of things.

"I'm going to need lots and lots of help from the two of you," Amy told her older children solemnly. "Raising a baby is a very hard job, even if it is fun most of the time, and I'm counting on you."

"What about Harry? Is he going to help?" Ashley asked reasonably.

The words stung. Harry adored the baby, although he seemed to hold just as high an affection for Ashley and Oliver, but he'd already started drawing away from Amy. He slept in one of the guest rooms, and when he paid a visit, it was always to see his daughter, not his wife. Soon he was traveling as much as ever, and when Sara was two and a half months old, Amy's unhappiness rose to tremendous proportions.

It was time, she decided when Harry called from Brisbane to say he'd be staying over a few days longer on business, for a confrontation.

Boldly Amy called the mainland and ordered a helicopter, since Harry had taken the jet. She kissed Ashley and Oliver goodbye and, carrying Sara while Shelt hauled the heavy diaper bag, she boarded the whirlybird and was soon on her way.

The pilot obligingly landed the copter on the roof of Harry's hotel, and not one but two bellhops were waiting to carry baggage.

"I'd like you to deliver our things to Room 373," Amy said to one of the young men, feeling more and more nervous as the elevator swept from the roof to the third floor. What was she doing?

If she caught Harry with another woman, she was going to be devastated. And if she didn't, he would be furious with her for not trusting him.

She bit her lower lip, holding Sara a little too tightly, when one of the bellhops knocked at the door of Harry's suite.

There was no answer, so the gentleman opened the door himself, using a special key, and escorted Amy inside.

Harry's clothes were hanging in the closet, but only Harry's clothes, and the dresser drawers contained his things alone. The scent of his cologne lingered in the air, but there was no tinge of perfume.

By that time Amy was beginning to feel really foolish. "I need to join one of those self-help groups for clingy women," she muttered to herself after the bellhops had taken their tips and left. She wanted to flee, to pretend she'd never done this stupid, suspicious, sneaky thing, but Sara was hungry and Amy herself was tired to the core of her spirit.

She lay down on the bed to nurse Sara, and she was lying there, half-asleep herself, when the door opened and Harry came in. Amy felt a pang when she saw the realization that she didn't trust him register in his wonderful indigo eyes.

"Well, Amy," he said, extending his arms from his sides in a gesture of furious resignation, "have you looked under the bed and checked the medicine cabinet for lipstick?"

Tears welled in her eyes. "I'm sorry," she said.

Harry bent to kiss his sleeping daughter's downy head, then took the infant and laid her gently in her portable crib. He had no kiss for Amy, however, only quiet, well-controlled outrage.

"What a pity you didn't come here because you wanted to be with me," he said bitterly. "Damn! I suppose you'll be hiring a private investigator next and having me followed!"

Amy sat up, trying to close her blouse, but Harry held her hands away, kneeling astraddle of her hips on the bed. He stared at her breasts for a long time, then, with a helpless groan, fell to her.

Because he hadn't touched her in so long, Amy was

instantly on fire. And the anger pulsing in the room only made the interval more exciting.

Harry enjoyed one nipple, then the other, until he had Amy tossing helplessly on the bed. Then, with no more foreplay than that, he lifted Amy's cotton skirt and took her in one powerful stroke.

Amy gripped the underside of the headboard in both hands and held on, her back arched so high that only her head, shoulders, and heels were touching the bed. Her release began as Harry delved into her, and she went wild when he grasped her hips and bid her take him deeper and deeper.

Finally, with a burst of rasped swearwords and an involuntary buckling of his body, Harry reached his climax.

Amy had been as thoroughly satisfied as he had, if not more so, and that was what made her next words so hard to say. "I'm leaving, Harry. I'm going back to the States."

Her husband was quiet for so long that Amy feared he hadn't heard her. On another level, she *hoped* he hadn't, so that she could back down, pretend she'd never voiced the decision.

Then, still inside her, he raised himself on his palms and glowered as he searched her eyes. *"What?"*

She tried to squirm out from under him, but he'd pinned her, and there was no going anywhere until he set her free.

"You were right before," she said with breathless misery. "We're not ready for marriage, either of us.

You're angry and frustrated all the time, and I'm turning into a shrew. So I want to go home."

He searched her eyes with angry blue ones for a long, long moment. "You'll damn well leave Sara here if you do."

Amy shook her head. "I'll never walk away from my baby, Harry," she vowed.

Harry flung himself onto his back and glared up at the ceiling, his breathing ragged, his scowl black as clouds before a tropical storm. "Damn it all, woman, you would drive a saint to drink!"

"You're going to let us go?"

He turned to meet her eyes. "Not in a million years, love," he said, his voice totally void of all traces of affection, "but I will take you back to the lighthouse. Maybe a miracle will happen and you'll be the woman I married again."

His words hurt Amy almost as much as finding him in the middle of a romantic tryst would have. She turned onto her side and cried silently, her heart breaking as she listened to the roar of the shower, the familiar, once comforting sounds of a man dressing, the crisp closing of the door.

Sara, blissfully unaware that her parents were at war, slept undisturbed in her little bed.

Within the week, the family was back in the States and, a few days after their return, they were settled in the lighthouse. Ashley and Oliver were immediately enrolled in elementary school, and Mary Anne went back to her studies at the university. Harry spent all day, every day, in the city, throwing himself into his work, and sent a steady stream of aspiring housekeepers for Amy to interview.

She finally selected an English grandmother type, Mrs. Hobbs, because the woman reminded her of Mrs. Ingallstadt. If nothing else, it was a relief not to have to review résumés and ask questions anymore.

"Main problem with you, mistress," Mrs. Hobbs announced one afternoon, when Amy was curled up in Harry's big leather chair, Sara nearly asleep at her breast, "is that you're tired. Begging your pardon, ma'am, but you've got dark circles under your eyes and every time I look at you, I want to cry because you seem so sad."

Amy gently lowered her daughter, put her bra in place and closed her blouse.

"I have everything," she confided forlornly. "It's shameful for me to feel so discontented."

"Maybe you should see your doctor," the gray-haired woman ventured kindly. "There are them as gets gloomy because there's chemicals off balance in their brain."

Smiling at the housekeeper's phrasing, Amy carried Sara to her crib and looked out the bedroom window at the choppy gray waters of Puget Sound. "I'm pretty sure my brain's all right," she said. *It's my heart that might not hold up.*

Mrs. Hobbs was puttering with the bedspread, even though it was mid-afternoon and the master suite was always the first room to be cleaned, after the kitchen. "Mr. Griffith be home tonight?" she asked casually.

Amy stiffened. How astute this Englishwoman was. She'd only been in the house a few days and already she knew there was trouble. "No," she said, hugging herself because she felt a chill. "Mr. Griffith won't be home. He has a late meeting tonight and conferences all day tomorrow."

The weekend ahead looked desolate from Amy's viewpoint: Ashley and Oliver would spend it with the Ryans on the mainland, and Harry, of course, would be working.

The housekeeper picked up the pink-and-gray plaid woolen afghan at the foot of the bed and refolded it, even though it had been perfectly arranged in the first place.

"Forgive me, ma'am," she said, lowering her eyes when Amy looked at her directly, "but it wouldn't hurt if you was to doll yourself up a little and spend some time in the city, with your husband."

Amy looked down at her baggy gray sweat suit, and a grin tugged at the corners of her mouth, even though she wanted very much to cry. "Are you insinuating that I'm not on the cutting edge of fashion, Mrs. Hobbs?"

The woman's already ruddy face was flushed with conviction. "Yes, ma'am."

The idea of going to Seattle, of perhaps finding some common ground with Harry, some way to reach him, was appealing. But Amy couldn't forget the last time she'd paid him an unscheduled visit, back in Brisbane. He'd been furious at her for mistrusting him.

"I have a small baby," Amy reminded Mrs. Hobbs and herself.

"She's big enough to be left for a day or so, ma'am. It's not like I haven't looked after a nipper or two in my time, you know. You'd just have to leave some milk."

Amy sighed. She could speak honestly to Mrs. Hobbs, and that was a great relief, because Amy had felt alone for a long time. "My husband wouldn't appreciate a visit from me," she admitted sadly, at the same time yearning to shop and see a play and eat in an elegant restaurant, all without having to nurse her baby or change a diaper. "He'd think I was checking up on him."

"That's easy to remedy," Mrs. Hobbs said briskly, fussing with the pillow shams. "You just play hard to get, Mrs. Griffith. You check into another hotel—not his—and then you call and leave a message, saying you're in town. After that, you go out and buy yourself some fine new clothes, and if it's a while before you return Mr. Griffith's messages when he calls, so much the better."

The plan appealed to Amy, whose unhappiness was rapidly escalating into sheer panic. Her marriage was turning out exactly as she had feared it would. If the relationship was to have any chance at all, she would have to stop mooning around and *do something*.

"You're right," she said excitedly. Then, impulsively, she gripped the housekeeper's sturdy shoulders and kissed her soundly on the cheek. "God bless you, Mrs. Hobbs, you're right!"

Amy packed hurriedly and made sure there was an ample supply of milk for Sara, who was already living mostly on baby food, anyway. When it was time for Ashley and Oliver to cross to West Seattle to meet their grandparents at the terminal, Amy kissed her infant daughter goodbye, rallied all her willpower, and got onto the ferry with them.

It wasn't easy; she and Sara had never been separated before, and the pull of maternal instinct was very strong indeed. In fact, a couple of times Amy thought she might not be able to keep herself from diving overboard and swimming back.

On the other hand, she wanted to reach out to Harry, to try to make things right between them again. She closed her eyes against a sudden swell of tears, remembering how he'd said he hoped a miracle would happen and she would turn back into the woman he'd married.

Am I so different? she wondered miserably, watching through blurred eyes as Oliver and Ashley ran happily up and down the deck on the other side of the window.

She looked down at herself.

Amy was only about five pounds heavier than she'd been before her pregnancy, but she *had* been neglecting her exercise program. She hadn't had a good haircut in weeks, and she often went for days without wearing makeup.

She felt a stirring of hope, because clothes and exercise and makeup and haircuts were all things within the realm of her control. Amy had read enough pop psychology to know she could change nothing about Harry, much less his feelings toward her, but she couldn't help hoping that he might be willing to meet her halfway.

After the boat docked and the Ryans had collected Ashley and Oliver, Amy drove downtown. Since Harry was staying in a suite at the Hilton, she took a room in the Sheraton.

She called his office and left a message with the puzzled receptionist, who had offered to put her through to Harry immediately. "Just tell him I called," Amy said brightly, and then she hung up.

The phone was ringing fifteen minutes later when she was leaving the room, but Amy didn't stop to answer it. She knew Mrs. Hobbs wasn't calling about Sara because she'd just talked to the woman, and that left Harry.

Let him wonder, Amy thought, closing the door on the insistent jangling.

She walked to the nearby Westlake Center, an urban answer to the shopping mall, boasting several levels of good stores, and bought bath salts and special soaps and lotions. After that, Amy entered an upscale lingerie boutique and purchased a sexy floral nightgown and some silky lingerie.

Down the street from the mall, at Nordstrom, her

favorite department store, Amy selected a black crepe
sheath and a glittery jacket to match.

When Amy returned to her room to drop off her
packages and hang up the dress and jacket, the message light on her phone was blinking. She dialed the
registration desk and was told that Mr. Griffith had
called twice, once from his office, once from his hotel.
He'd left both numbers, as if Amy wouldn't know
them.

"Thank you," Amy said with a smile. Then she took
the elevator down to the lobby, had her hair cut and
styled in the swanky hotel salon and charged the whole
obscene price to Harry's American Express card.

On her return, Amy found two message envelopes
just inside the door. Both were from Harry.

Feeling better all the time, and blessing Mrs. Hobbs
for a genius, Amy yawned, set the messages aside and
rustled through the bags for her soap and bath salts.
She indulged in a long, luxurious soak in the tub, ignoring the telephone when it rang. She and Mrs. Hobbs
had worked out a system earlier; if the housekeeper
needed to reach Amy for any reason, she would ring
twice, hang up and ring twice again.

Amy must have fallen asleep for a little while, because the bathwater got cold. She was just reaching
out to turn the spigot marked Hot when she heard the
outer door open.

"Thanks, mate," she heard Harry say.

"Thank *you,* sir," a bellhop replied, obviously re-
ceiving a big tip for letting Harry into the room.

"I think I'll complain to the management," Harry announced, stepping into the bathroom just as Amy was rising, towel wrapped, from the tub. "I could have been anybody, but all I had to do was tell them I was your husband."

Amy smiled, though she felt almost as nervous as she had the first time she'd met Harry Griffith. "I told the concierge to keep an eye out for you," she admitted. Then she made a shooing gesture with one hand. "Get out of here, please. I want to dress."

"It's not like I've never seen you naked," Harry reasoned, frowning. He was leaning back against the sink counter, his arms folded, his dark brows drawn together. "What are you trying to do, Amy?"

She put a hand to his arm and eased him through the doorway. "I'm planning to have a luxurious dinner and see a play. Tomorrow I plan to shop."

Amy closed the door and locked it.

"You're doing all this alone?" Harry called from beyond the barrier.

"Yes," Amy answered, smiling at her reflection in the mirror. She liked her sleek new haircut; it made her look both sexy and mischievous. She waited a few beats before adding, "Unless, of course, you'd like to accompany me. I wouldn't want you to think I was crowding you, or checking up on you, or anything like that."

"Amy, this is silly. Open the door!"

Amy reached for a makeup sponge and a new bottle of foundation and leaned toward the mirror. "I'm busy," she chimed. "Maybe you could come back later."

"Damn it, I'll break this thing down if you don't let me in."

"You wouldn't do that," Amy reasoned, blending her foundation skillfully with the sponge. "Trashing a hotel room would definitely be unHarrylike. Besides, the management would be furious."

She heard him sag against the door, probably in exasperation, and her heart took wings. Maybe he didn't love her in the classical sense, maybe his attachment to her was largely sexual, but there was no denying that Harry cared.

When she turned the knob, he practically fell into the bathroom. Staring at her in angry bewilderment, he said, "I don't like being kept from my own wife."

"Tough," Amy replied, bending close to the mirror to begin applying her eye shadow. "I'm through walking on eggshells, Harry. I'm going to live my life, with or without your approval."

He filled the doorway, glowering, a human storm cloud. "What about Sara? Where does she fit into your plans, Mrs. Griffith? And where is she, by the way?"

"Sara is with Mrs. Hobbs. She's going to be one of those modern babies who goes everywhere with her mommy. I'll buy a carrier of some sort."

"Right. And when she gets hungry, you can just whip out a breast in the middle of a board meeting!" Obviously Harry was losing his perspective as well as his temper. He shoved a hand through his hair, making it unperfect. "Damn it, Amy, you can forget the whole crazy idea! You're not dragging my daughter through the corporate world like a rag doll!"

Amy finished shadowing her right eye and started on her left. "Actually I was thinking in terms of attending art school. I've got real talent, you know, and in this day and age, a woman needs to know how to support herself."

Harry, the cool, the calm, the collected man of the twenty-first century, looked as if he were going to pop an artery. His voice, when he spoke, was low and lethal. "Even if you didn't have me to look after you, Amy, you would never need a job. Between what Tyler left you and the proceeds from selling the house—"

"There are other reasons to work besides money," Amy said, reaching for a green kohl pencil and starting to line her eyes. "Like knowing you mean something, knowing you're strong and you're interesting and you're worth something all on your own. The subject isn't open to debate, Harry—I'm going to art school, whether you like it or not."

Out of the corner of her eye, Amy could see that her husband's jaw was clamped down tight, as though he'd just bitten through a piece of steel. "Fine," he said. And when the door of the hotel room slammed, Amy wondered if her wonderful plan had backfired.

Chapter 11

Harry paused in the doorway of his office, his hand still on the light switch, thinking he'd finally lost his mind, once and for all.

He blinked, looked again and, sure as hell, Tyler was there, sitting in Harry's leather chair, feet propped on the tidy surface of his antique desk.

"You're really seeing me," his friend assured him with a sigh. Ty's hands were cupped at the back of his head, and he looked pretty relaxed for someone who'd been dead in the neighborhood of three years.

Harry rubbed his eyes with one hand. It was the problems with Amy that had pushed him over the brink, he was certain of that. "This is ridiculous," he said.

Tyler sighed again and hoisted his feet down from

Harry's desk. He was wearing clothes Harry vaguely remembered: jeans and a University of Washington sweatshirt. "Look, old buddy, I don't have all night here, so listen up. I had to get special permission from the head office to make this appearance, and this is positively the last time they'll let me come back. You're blowing it, man."

Harry went to his private bar and poured himself a brandy. A good, stiff drink might jump-start his brain circuits and blast him back to reality.

When he turned around, however, Tyler was as substantially *there* as ever. He was leaning against the edge of the desk now, his arms folded, his eyes full of pitying fury.

"Do you realize what you have?" the apparition demanded. "Amy is wonderful and sweet and bright, and damn it, she loves you! There must be a million guys out there—" Tyler gestured toward the bank of windows behind the desk "—just wishing to God they could meet somebody like her! She adores you, you lucky bastard!"

Harry shoved one hand through his hair, thinking what a remarkable mechanism the human mind is. He would have sworn his dead friend was really standing there, every bit as real as Amy or the janitor downstairs dust mopping the lobby, or the doorman out on the street.

"Wrong," he said forcefully. "Amy's planning to leave me and become some kind of barefoot Bohemian, painting pictures and carrying my daughter around on her back like a papoose."

Tyler laughed, and the effect was remarkably authentic. It gave Harry a pang, remembering the old days, when he and Ty had thought the whole world was funny. "Oh, the art school thing," Tyler said. "As you Aussies say, 'No worries, mate.'"

The game was becoming alarmingly easy to play, and Harry put his brandy aside, unfinished. "You mean, she's going to change her mind about art school?"

"Hell, no," Tyler answered with a cocky grin. "You really started something when you gave her those art supplies—even Amy didn't know she had a talent for painting. In three years she'll be having her own shows in some of the best galleries in the country."

Harry sagged into a chair. Damn, but this was elaborate. He hadn't known he was harboring so many possibilities in his subconscious mind. "And that's supposed to keep me from worrying?" he muttered. He'd already had a sample of the new Amy, the woman who was bent on living her life to the fullest, with or without him, and he wasn't sure he liked her. One thing he had to admit, though, she was exciting.

"Relax," Tyler said. He crossed the room to touch one of the crystal liquor decanters on Harry's bar. Harry figured a genie would probably come out of the thing, thus laying to rest all doubt that Harry had lost his sanity. "Amy's becoming the person she's supposed to be, and you'll be a world-class fool if you try to stand in her way."

"How," Harry began raggedly, closing his eyes, "am I supposed to live without her? Tell me that."

"You won't have to live without Amy if you'll just quit trying to drive her away," Tyler replied without missing a beat.

Harry's eyes flew open. "I haven't been trying to drive her away!" he hollered.

Tyler grinned indulgently. "Sure you have, Harry. You're afraid to let go of your emotions and really care about Amy and the kids because of what happened before, in your first marriage."

A sense of bleakness swept over Harry, practically crushing him. He'd had such high hopes back then, for himself and Madeline and little Eireen, before he'd learned just how cruelly unpredictable life can be.

"I see you're not trying to deny that," Tyler observed, pacing back and forth a few feet in front of Harry, his hands clasped behind his back. Except for the clothes, this was probably the way his friend had looked in the courtroom, authoritative and confident.

But not dead, of course.

"You're not here."

"Amy kept saying that, too. Did you like the white lilacs I sent for the wedding?"

Harry's mouth dropped open, but he didn't speak because he couldn't.

"Look," Tyler said, beginning to summarize, "I don't really give a damn whether you believe I'm here or not, because what you think about me doesn't matter. But you and Amy have to make it work—there's a lot riding on it."

For the first time since his friend's death, Harry thought he might actually break down and weep. He loved Amy, thoroughly, totally, as he'd never loved another human being, but Tyler had been right earlier. He was terrified of letting his guard down completely where Amy was concerned, because losing her would kill him.

"You'll find her in front of the Fifth Avenue Theater," Tyler said. He was standing at the windows now, looking through the shutter slats at the city lights. "She's carrying an extra ticket in her purse and hoping against hope that you'll have the good sense to show up. Don't drop the ball, Harry. Don't lose her."

"Next," Harry sighed, "you're going to offer to show me how the world would be if I'd never been born, right?"

Tyler chuckled. "Sorry, that's a Christmas bit. Good-bye, Harry, and good luck."

Before Harry's very eyes, Tyler vanished. He was there, then he wasn't. It was weird.

Harry got his coat and wandered out of the office, through the swanky reception area and over to the elevators. He rubbed his chin as he waited, then looked at his watch.

It was seven-ten, and curtain time at the theater was usually eight o'clock. His hotel was connected with the theater by a walkway—

She *had* said she was going to the theater.

That was how he knew, Harry was sure of it. He'd only imagined Tyler because he was so stressed out, so lonesome for his wife. It was a spiritual longing, as well as a physical one, intense enough to explain his hallucinations.

He went back to the Hilton, glanced at the telephone—the message light wasn't blinking—and then took a hot shower. He shaved and put on fresh clothes, and when he passed through the underground shopping center and climbed the stairs to the Fifth Avenue Theater, Amy was standing there on the sidewalk.

She was so beautiful, in her clingy black dress, sexy jacket and high heels, that Harry was momentarily immobilized by the sight of her. He just stood gaping at her, his hand gripping the stair railing.

Amy must have felt his gaze, because she turned and smiled, and Harry tightened his grasp on the railing, as much off balance as if he'd been punched in the stomach.

"Hello, Harry," she said gently.

"You really mean it, about this art school thing?"

Worry flickered in her hopeful eyes. "I really mean it," she confirmed softly.

He finally broke his inertia and joined her in the line of theatergoers waiting to be admitted.

"You look fantastic," he said, not quite meeting her eyes.

He could feel her smile, warm as sunlight. "Thanks, Harry. You look pretty good yourself."

He turned, unable to resist the pull anymore, and went tumbling, head over heels into her eyes.

She linked her arm with his. "I love you, Harry," she said.

Harry felt something steely and cold melt within him. "And I love you," he whispered raggedly.

They went into the theater with the crowd, and sat there in their seats, holding hands. Harry was never able to remember, without a reminder from Amy, what play they saw that night, because his mind was everywhere but on the stage.

After the final curtain, they had a late dinner at an expensive, low-key restaurant.

Harry felt as nervous as a kid on his first date.

He wondered what she would say if he told her she wasn't the only one who'd ever had a delusion, that he'd seen Tyler, too.

"I think I'm going round the bend," he finally confessed, because he wanted to be honest with Amy. Completely honest.

She arched one delicate brow and took a sip of her wine. "Oh? Why is that?"

"Because when I went back to the office after our conversation in your room, fully intending to lick my wounds and whimper a little, Tyler was there."

Amy set the wineglass down, very slowly. Her cheeks were pale, and although her throat worked visibly, no sound passed her lips.

"Not that I believe I saw a ghost or anything like that," Harry was quick to clarify.

Amy reached for her wineglass again, her hand shaking as she extended it. She closed her eyes and took three or four gulps before looking at Harry squarely again and agreeing, "Of course not."

Harry sighed. "The human mind is a fascinating thing," he ruminated, hedging.

"What did Tyler want?" Amy asked in a small voice.

"He delivered a lecture, essentially," Harry said, frowning, "and I must confess that he was pretty much on target. Obviously my subconscious mind had worked the whole thing out beforehand."

"Obviously," Amy said in a whisper. Her beautiful eyes were very wide, and Harry could see the pulse at the base of her throat.

It made him want to kiss her there, as well as a few other places.

"I've been a fool, Amy," he went on, after clearing his throat and shifting uncomfortably in his chair. "I thought I could keep myself from loving you, and thereby keep my heart from being broken to bits, but it didn't work. Practically every stroke of good fortune in my life can be traced back to you—not only did you give me yourself, but Ashley and Oliver and Sara, too. God in heaven, Amy, I love you more than I ever believed could be possible, and it hurts—and I'm scared."

Tears brimmed in her eyes, and she reached across the table to grip Harry's hand. "Me, too. Everything just sort of fell into place with Tyler—we met, we got married, we had kids. I was happy, and I think he was, as well. Then I met you and suddenly everything was complicated."

Harry lifted her hand to his lips and kissed the knuckles lightly. A bittersweet sense of homecoming filled him. It was not like returning after an hour's absence, or even a week's. No, it was as though an eternity had passed, during which he'd been deprived of this woman he needed more than air, more than light, more than water.

"Give me a second chance," he said. "I'm a chauvinist, but I can reform."

Amy laughed softly. "Don't reform too much. There are things I like about the caveman approach."

Harry raised his eyebrows. "Such as?"

"Such as being your love prisoner," Amy said, leaning closer and uttering the words in a breathless tone that made Harry's loins pulse and his heart start to hammer.

"Is it warm in here?" he inquired, tugging at his collar.

Amy's smile was slow and hot and saucy. He felt her toe make a slow foray up his pant leg. "Steaming," she answered.

Harry practically tore his wallet from his inside pocket, fished out a credit card, and threw it at the first waiter to pass by. They were out of the hotel and onto the bustling night streets within minutes.

"My place or yours?" Amy teased.

"Which is closer?"

"Mine."

"Yours it is."

They entered Amy's room a few minutes later, and she snatched up a shopping bag and immediately disappeared into the bathroom again.

Harry paced, listening as the water ran and the toilet flushed and various things clinked and rattled. Finally he paused outside the door. "Amy?"

"Be patient, Harry."

He tried, he honestly tried. He went to the telephone and ordered champagne, then called the hotel florist for a dozen of whatever flower they happened to have on hand.

Both the carnations and the champagne arrived before Amy came out of the bathroom, but the wait was worth it. She was wearing a gossamer floral nightgown, of the very thinnest silk, and it clung to her womanly curves in a way that made Harry's heart surge into his throat.

"My God," he rasped.

Amy walked past him, her hips swaying, her soft skin exuding the scent of lavender. The bellhop had opened the champagne before leaving the room, and Amy poured a glass for herself and one for Harry.

"Let's offer a toast," she said, holding out his glass.

He accepted it with a slightly unsteady hand.

"To us," she said. "To you and me and Ashley and Oliver and little Sara—and whoever else might happen to come along in the next couple of years."

Harry swallowed. "You mean, you're willing to

have another child? But you've been so tired, and there's art school—"

"Other women have done it. I'll manage, Harry, with a lot of help from you and Mrs. Hobbs."

Now it was Harry who had tears in his eyes. He set his champagne aside and laid his hands on Amy's waist, pulling her close to him. "God, Amy, how I love you," he breathed.

She put down her glass, slid her arms around his neck, and drove him crazy by wriggling against him.

"Prove it," she said.

"Oh, I will," he answered.

Harry was as good as his word. He buried his fingers in Amy's hair and gently but firmly pulled her head back for his kiss. When his mouth crushed hers and his tongue gained immediate entry, Amy nearly fainted. It had been so long.

She peeled off Harry's jacket while their tongues battled, then wrenched at his tie and ripped open his shirt, sending little buttons flying in every direction.

Amy didn't care about shirt buttons. She pushed the fabric savagely aside, sought a masculine nipple with her tongue and nibbled until Harry was moaning under his breath.

"This time," she said, "you're *my* prisoner. You have to do everything I tell you, and give me everything I want."

Harry moaned as she unfastened his belt buckle. "Amy—"

"I want to hear you crying out, for once," Amy said, kissing her way down his belly, baring his navel. "I want to hear you beg, the way I always do."

"Ooooh," he rasped, as she knelt and pushed down his slacks, her hands moving strong and light on his buttocks, molding and shaping him, pushing him into the pleasure she so willingly offered.

Amy enjoyed her husband, and the beautiful, angry, hungry sounds he was making, and she was greedy about it. His firm flanks began to flex under her palms and, with a gasp, he leaned forward to brace himself against the dresser.

Amy granted him no quarter.

"Amy…" he pleaded, a man in delirium. "Oh, God, Amy, I'm going to—"

She stopped, just long enough to finish the sentence for him, and then she was insatiable again.

Harry stiffened, with a low, primitive cry, and she made him experience every nuance, every degree of sensation, every shade of ecstasy. When she finally released him, it was clear that he could barely stand.

Their clothes were mysteriously gone. Amy didn't remember shedding her own garments or stripping away Harry's, but when they fell onto the big bed in the center of the room, they were both naked.

"I'll have to have vengeance for that," Harry said, after a long time, rolling onto his side to begin kissing Amy's stomach.

"For what?" Amy teased, but a little gasp of antic-

ipation betrayed her as Harry's mouth drew danger-
ously near the center of her femininity.

"For turning me inside out," Harry answered in a
rumbling voice, then took her boldly into his mouth.

She cried out, but it was only the beginning. Harry
teased her unmercifully, for what seemed like hours.

Amy was wild, untamed, primitive in her responses. She cried, she pleaded, she moaned and
groaned and cursed, and finally, in a long, shattering
spasm, she lost all control.

Although he had what he wanted, Harry was not a
benevolent captor.

He folded her close, and held her, and stroked her,
until she was ready again. When he entered her, it was
a sudden, fierce invasion, and her eyes rolled back in
her head.

"Look at me, Amy," he ordered.

She opened her eyes and stared up at her husband
dreamily.

"I want to see you responding to me," Harry said.
"I want to see you belonging to me..."

Amy dug her heels into the bed and rose and fell
under Harry with graceful desperation. She needed
him, wanted him, so much, that giving herself was
heaven. "Put a baby inside me, Harry," she choked
out. "Please—give me your baby."

At her words, he seemed to lose control. He groaned
and threw his head back, as fierce as a stallion having his mare. "I love you, Amy," he struggled to say.

She ran her hands up and down the straining muscles of his back, soothing, tormenting, urging him on. "I love you," she answered breathlessly, meeting him thrust for thrust, heartbeat for heartbeat, dream for dream.

Finally, in one blinding, spectacular collision, the joyous miracle happened and their two souls mated, just as their bodies did.

Later, much later, Amy lay with her head on Harry's shoulder, exhausted, nibbling at his heated skin.

"We never made love in the tree house again," she said, as he entwined one finger in a lock of her hair.

Harry drew in a deep breath, let it out slowly. "If ever I've heard a good reason for going back to Australia, that's it. We'll leave as soon as Oliver and Ashley are out of school."

Amy smiled in the cozy darkness and kissed Harry's shoulder. "And come back before classes start at my art school," she negotiated.

"Deal," he said, after a lengthy and very philosophical sigh.

Down on the sidewalk, beside the hotel, stood Tyler, unseen by the city dwellers hurrying past him, looking up at one certain window. He was about to return to a place where there was no darkness and no pain, but during those few precious moments, he was a living, breathing man again.

He could hear the noise of passing cars, a plane overhead, people chattering as they rushed along. He felt the solid cement of the sidewalk beneath his feet and smelled the peculiar mix of salt water, pine and exhaust fumes that was Seattle. He also felt no small measure of satisfaction because he knew Harry and Amy had a long, rich life ahead of them.

Tyler had accomplished his mission. Amy and Harry would live and love, laugh and cry. They would decorate Christmas trees together and balance checking accounts and shop for snow tires. They would fight sometimes, but they would have a glorious time making up.

It was all written in the book.

Tyler sighed and lifted one hand in farewell. "Goodbye," he whispered. And then he walked away, into the waiting light.

One year later...

The tree house was just as Amy remembered it, dusty and primitive and wonderful. Harry gave her a mischievous pinch on the bottom as she climbed the last rung and scrambled inside.

It had taken them a little longer than they'd expected to reach this very special, very private place— Amy had completed her classes at the art school, and she worked on her painting for several hours every day.

Sitting there, with her blue-jeaned legs drawn up, she made a mental note to draw a sketch of the tree house. She would frame the picture, and when she and

Harry and the kids were far away in the States, she could look at the drawing and remember.

"I think you're crazy, wanting to spend the night here," Harry remarked, dusting off his pants. "If the mosquitoes don't eat us alive, the rain will come through and give us our deaths."

Amy laughed. "Me, Jane," she said. "You, Tarzan. And don't you forget it, buster!"

Harry opened the canvas bag he'd brought along, taking out food, a blanket and a small sterno-powered stove. "Alas," he said, "all we need now is a monkey."

Amy's smile was broad; she could feel it stretching her face. She waited for Harry to look up and see her kneeling there, beaming, and laid her hands to her flat stomach. "We already have three monkeys," she answered. "I guess one more won't hurt."

Harry's befuddled expression made her shriek with laughter, scaring all the beautiful birds from their roosts in the tree.

When the beating of wings finally died down, he said, "You mean, you're—?"

"Again." Amy nodded. "I think it's a boy this time."

Harry swallowed visibly, scrambled over to her and covered both her hands with one of his own, as though by doing that he could somehow make contact with this new child. His indigo eyes glistened with tears of wonder.

Amy rose up on her haunches to kiss Harry's eyelids, first one and then the other. She tasted his tears.

"Do you know how much I love you, Harry

Griffith?" she asked, one hand on either side of his handsome face.

His voice was gruff. "How much?" he asked.

Her answer was a kiss, deep and fiery. "That much," she said, when it was over.

Harry broke away to spread the blanket on the floor of the tree house. His motions were graceful and quick, and when he reached for Amy, she came to him willingly, with laughter and love and the purest joy.

He kissed her, subjecting her to a tender invasion of his tongue, and then laid her on the blanket and began removing her clothes with deft, methodical hands.

"I can't wait, Amy," he said, tossing her jeans aside and bending her knees and pushing her legs wide of each other. "I've got to be inside you, part of you, now."

She opened his jeans, pushed them down, along with his briefs. "Come in, Mr. Griffith," she whispered.

In the depths of the night, the rain came.

Harry lay awake on the floor of the tree house, listening, holding a sleeping Amy close by his side. He supposed he should wake her and insist that they go back to the shelter and safety of their house on the other island, but he didn't have the heart to awaken his wife. She was tired and she'd given him everything and she looked like an angel, lying there.

Idly, he caressed her. Soon, her beautiful body would ripen, her breasts would grow heavy with milk to nourish his child. He smiled, even though his vision was suspiciously blurred. He wondered if Amy would be as crabby this time around as she'd been while she was carrying Sara.

He decided he didn't care.

She moved against him, inadvertently setting him on fire again. Some men were put off by pregnancy, he knew, but knowing Amy was going to bear a child— his child—made him yearn for her in a way that went beyond the physical into a realm he didn't begin to understand.

"Harry?"

He kissed her temple. "Shhh, it's all right. Sleep."

She played with his nipples and the hair on his stomach. "Harry?" Her tone was serious.

"Mmm?"

"Are you happy about the new baby? Really happy?"

"Ecstatic," he answered.

"Oliver says if he doesn't get a brother pretty soon, he's joining the Foreign 'Region.'"

Harry laughed. Oliver was a miniature version of Ty, and Harry loved the boy as much as if he'd been his own, by blood. "Promises, promises," he said.

"You've been so good to them, Harry—Ashley and Oliver, I mean. Anyone would think they were as much yours as Sara is."

"They *are* as much mine. In a funny sort of way, I think Tyler gave them to me. He knew I could be trusted to love his children as deeply as he did."

She sniffled against his shoulder. "I really saw him," Amy said half to herself after a long moment had passed.

"So did I," admitted Harry, who had long since come to terms with the fact that Tyler had really been in his office that night, when Harry's and Amy's marriage had been in crisis.

"Do you think Ty's happy, wherever he is?"

Harry thought the question through, even though he'd done as much many, many times before.

"Yes, rose petal," he said sincerely. "He's happy."

Amy raised her head far enough to plant a row of tantalizing kisses along Harry's jawline. "I think I just felt a raindrop land on my backside," she said.

Harry chuckled and gave said backside an affectionate squeeze. "I love a sophisticated woman," he replied.

Amy nudged him with one elbow, pretending to be angry. "Oh, yeah?" she joked. "What's her name?"

* * * * *

Dear Reader,

I'm so excited about the rerelease of *Waiting for Baby*. This has always been one of my favorite stories. The hero, Jake Tucker, is something of a bad guy in book one of the series, *Cowboy Dad*. This is his chance for redemption, and he takes it. Writing a character who goes through such a big transformation was definitely a challenge. I'm glad to say Jake listened to me—he really was stubborn in that first book!

Lilly Russo is a delight. She's endured a tragic past and has this one chance at making her dreams come true. First, however, she must turn Jake from a lion into a lamb. If anyone can, it's Lilly. I also loved writing the large cast of secondary characters, many of whom are special needs. I tried to portray them honestly but also with compassion and humor. I thank my volunteer work with special-needs adults during college for help with that.

If you enjoy *Waiting for Baby*, then be sure to look for my next new release, *Most Eligible Sheriff*, coming in March of 2014. This is the final book in my Sweetheart, Nevada miniseries and wraps up the story of this small honeymoon town's recovery in the wake of a devastating forest fire.

Warmest wishes,

Cathy McDavid

PS I love hearing from readers. Visit my website, at www.cathymcdavid.com, to sign up for my newsletter or email me.

WAITING FOR BABY

New York Times Bestselling Author

Cathy McDavid

Chapter 1

Lilly Russo wasn't looking forward to meeting with the man who'd so unceremoniously dumped her a mere three weeks ago. She'd do it, however, and just about anything else for the clients of Horizon Adult Day Care Center. They were too deserving, too much in need, too dear to her to lose out on a golden opportunity because of her pride.

"Mr. Tucker will be with you in a few minutes."

"Thank you."

If his assistant knew that her boss and Lilly had recently engaged in a brief affair, she gave no indication.

"Would you care for coffee or water while you wait?"

"I'm fine, thank you."

Lilly attempted a smile and sat on the closest piece

of furniture, which happened to be an overstuffed couch, and instantly sank like a stone into its soft cushions. She should have chosen the chair by the window instead. Then she would've been able to stand gracefully when the assistant or, worse, Jake Tucker himself came to collect her for their appointment.

While she waited, she studied the comfortable and charmingly appointed lobby. The rustic, Western flavor of the mountain guest resort was as apparent here as everywhere else on the ranch. Green checked curtains framed large picture windows. Heavy pine furniture, much of it antique, sat on polished hardwood floors covered by colorful area rugs. Paintings depicting nature scenes and wild animals indigenous to Arizona's southern rim country hung on the walls.

Lilly had been acquainted with Jake Tucker—manager of Bear Creek Ranch and landlord of the mini mall where the day-care center was located—for almost two years. They'd first met here in his office, when she'd become the day care's new administrator and her predecessor had introduced her to Jake. Since then she'd visited the ranch only a few times. But at the Labor Day cookout nine weeks ago, Jake had suddenly taken notice of her and asked her on a date.

If Lilly knew then what she did now, she'd have saved herself a heap of heartache and refused his invitation.

The assistant appeared in Lilly's line of vision. "Mr. Tucker will see you now."

She pushed out of the couch, wobbling only once, much to her relief. If it hadn't been so important to make a businesslike impression on Jake, she'd have worn something other than a slim-fitting suit and high-heeled pumps. He wouldn't guess by looking at her how much his abrupt breakup had hurt. Not if *she* could help it.

"Follow me, please." Jake's assistant led Lilly behind the busy front desk to an open office door. She gestured for Lilly to enter before discreetly moving aside.

The moment of truth had arrived.

Mentally rehearsing her pitch, Lilly stepped into Jake's office. She came to a halt when the door closed behind her. Lilly's stomach, already queasy to begin with, knotted into a tight ball.

Jake sat behind a large, ornate desk reading a computer screen, his profile to her. He turned his head to look at her, and she was struck anew by his intelligent hazel eyes and strong, square jaw. Memories of cradling that face between her hands while they made love flooded her.

She promptly lost track of what she'd planned to say.

He stood and extended his hand across the desk. "Good morning, Lilly. How are you?"

His greeting jump-started her befuddled brain. "Hello, Jake."

She stepped forward and accepted his handshake. His grip was confident and controlled and reminiscent of when their relationship had been strictly professional. But she'd seen him in those rare moments when he lost control and gave himself over to passion. That was the Jake she found most attractive, the one she'd fallen for harder than she would've thought possible.

"Thanks for seeing me on such short notice." She cleared the nervous tickle from her throat and sat in one of the two visitors chairs facing his desk.

"I would've come to the center on my next trip to town," he said, resuming his seat.

"I felt our meeting should take place here, since what I want to discuss involves Bear Creek Ranch."

"Is that so?" he asked and leaned forward.

He wore his sandy brown hair a little longer than when she'd first met him. It complemented his customary wardrobe of Western shirts and dress jeans—and was surprisingly soft when sifted through inquisitive fingers.

"Yes." Lilly struggled to stay on track.

She couldn't afford to mess this up. The facility's clients and staff were depending on her to make their hopes and dreams a reality.

Besides, she and Jake weren't an item anymore, their personal relationship over. Hadn't he made that abundantly clear three weeks ago? He could get down on his knees and crawl across the floor and she wouldn't agree to see him again.

Lilly Russo didn't court misery. She'd already had enough in her life, thank you very much.

"As you know," she went on, finding her stride, "the center isn't just a babysitting service for emotionally and mentally challenged adults. One of our goals is to provide clients with recreational activities that enhance their life experience, either by intellectually stimulating them or teaching them skills they can use outside the center."

"You have a great program there."

"I'm glad you think so because we'd like your help with a project."

"What kind of help?"

Someone who didn't know Jake quite so well might have missed the subtle change in his expression from mild interest to wariness. Lilly suspected the wariness had more to do with his feelings toward her and their breakup than not wanting to help the center. She rallied against a quick, yet intense, flash of pain and continued with her pitch.

"The center's revenue comes from a variety of sources, including donations. Some of those donations are in the form of equipment or furniture or even small appliances rather than money. We've received an item that I initially thought was unusable. But after some consideration, I've changed my mind. Dave, our owner, and the staff, agree with me that if we can find a suitable place to board this…item, it might prove to be very valuable and enjoyable to our clients."

"Board?"

Trust Jake to pick up on the one key word in her long speech.

"Yes. A mule."

"Someone's given you a *mule?*"

"Tom and Ginger Malcovitch. You may know them."

"I do." Jake frowned.

Lilly knew why. Ginger's brother and Jake's ex-wife had recently announced their engagement. In fact, it was right after their announcement that Jake had asked Lilly out on their first date.

Unfortunately, she hadn't seen the connection. Not until the night he'd ended their relationship.

She pushed the unhappy memories to the back of her mind, determined not to let anything distract her. "The mule is old and very gentle, though slightly lame in one leg. But not so lame that he couldn't be led around a ring carrying one adult."

"Your clients?"

She nodded. "I'm sure you've heard of the positive effect animals can have on the mentally, emotionally and even physically challenged. They seem to have an ability to bond with these individuals in a way people can't."

"I saw something on TV once."

"Yes, well, the benefits animals have on the elderly and disabled is a documented fact." She wished he'd sounded more enthusiastic.

"And you think this mule will help your clients?"

"I'm convinced of it." She gathered her courage. "In addition to corralling the mule with the horses on the ranch, we'd need to use your riding equipment. In exchange, our clients who are able to will do some work for the ranch."

"What kind of work?"

"Mucking out stalls. Feeding. Cleaning and oiling saddles and bridles. Whatever simple tasks can be accomplished in a morning or an afternoon."

"How often would you come out?"

"Three times a week. More if I can recruit additional volunteers."

Horizon employed ten full-time caretakers, including two nurses and several student volunteers from the nearby college. Outings required one caretaker for every two clients and put a strain on the center's regular staff. She doubted Dave and his wife would agree to hire more employees.

Jake expelled a long breath and sat back in his chair.

Lilly sensed she was losing him and panicked. "I've spoken with our CPA. She tells me the cost of boarding the mule would be a tax deduction for the ranch."

"It's not just money."

"You've offered to help the center in the past."

"I was thinking more along the lines of repairs and maintenance. Not providing jobs for your clients."

"Work in exchange for boarding our mule isn't exactly a job."

"There's an issue of liability." Jake spoke slowly and appeared to choose his words carefully.

Lilly's defenses shot up. "Because they're disabled?"

"Because they'd be neither guests nor employees. I'm not sure they'd be covered by our insurance in the case of a mishap."

"Oh. Of course." Insurance wasn't an obstacle Lilly had considered, and she chided herself for her short-sightedness. "I understand. You have to do what's best for the ranch."

"I'll call our agent later today. Check with him on how the policy reads."

The wheels in Lilly's mind turned. "What if our insurance covered the clients while they were on the ranch?"

"Does it?"

"I'll find out. If not, maybe Dave could have a special rider added."

Jake drummed his fingers on the desktop. "Even if I end up agreeing to your proposition, I'll still need to take it to the family for their approval."

Here was an obstacle Lilly *had* considered. Jake managed Bear Creek Ranch but it was owned equally by eight members of the Tucker family, including him.

"I'd be happy to meet with them," she said, hope filling the void left by her earlier disappointment.

"Let's wait a bit. That may not be necessary."

She sat back in her chair, unaware that she'd inched forward.

"Your clients would also have to keep a reasonable distance from the guests. Please don't take this the wrong way, but they might make some people uncomfortable, and I have to put our guests' interests first."

Was Jake one of those "uncomfortable" people? Lilly compressed her lips and paused before replying. She encountered this discomfort on a regular basis. And not just at work.

It had started with her ex-husband, immediately following their son Evan's birth. She'd also seen it in the expressions of countless friends and relatives who had visited during the two months little Evan resided in the hospital's neonatal intensive care unit. Then later when they brought him home, still hooked to machines and monitors. The discomfort prevailed even at Evan's funeral seven months later.

Differences and abnormalities, Lilly had sadly learned, weren't always tolerated. All she could do was try to show people that special needs individuals were frequently affectionate and charming.

"That won't be a problem," she told Jake. "The people we choose to bring will be closely supervised at all times. At least one staff member for every two to three adults."

"That should be acceptable."

"Good." She made a mental note to contact the college regarding more student volunteers.

"I'll let you know what the family says." Jake rose.

Lilly did likewise. "Do you know when that might be?" She started to mention the Malcovitches impending house sale, then bit her tongue. Another reminder of Jake's ex-wife's engagement wouldn't advance her cause. "We need to find a place for the mule this week."

"Saturday's the earliest I can get everyone together. If you're stuck, you can board the mule here temporarily."

"Really?" She couldn't help smiling. His offer was both unexpected and generous. "Thank you, Jake."

He came around the desk toward her, a spark of interest lighting his eyes. "It was nice seeing you again, Lilly."

As they walked toward his office door, his fingers came to rest lightly on her elbow. The gesture was courteous. Not the least bit sexual. Yet, she was instantly struck with an image of that same hand roaming her body and bringing her intense pleasure.

Oh, no. She didn't need this now. Not when she'd finally resigned herself to their breakup.

"I'll call you in a day or two about our insurance policy." She casually sidestepped him, the movement dislodging his hand.

"Take care, Lilly."

Was that concern she heard in his voice? Did he regret the ruthless manner in which he'd informed her they were through? A more plausible explanation was that she'd only heard what she wanted to.

But then, there was that look on his face....

"You, too, Jake." She left his office before she could jump to a wrong conclusion, barely acknowledging the young woman seated at the workstation behind the front desk.

Lilly's thigh-hugging skirt hampered her hasty retreat across the lobby. She slowed before she tumbled down the porch steps. From now on, she vowed, whatever happened between her and Jake Tucker would be strictly business. Forget all those looks and touches and vocal inflections. She wasn't going to endanger a valuable program for the center. Nor was she risking her heart on the basis of a few misread signals.

Buttoning his flannel-lined denim jacket, Jake headed out the main lodge and along the uneven stone walkway leading to the parking lot. A gust of wind swept past him, sending a small pile of leaves and pine needles dancing across the hard-packed dirt.

He held the crown of his cowboy hat, dropped his chin and walked directly into the chilly breeze. Fall came quickly to this part of the state and stayed only briefly before winter descended. Within the last few weeks, the temperature had dropped twenty degrees. By next month, frost would cover the ground each morning. Soon after that, snow.

Bear Creek Ranch was always booked solid during the holiday season, which stretched from late October through the first week of January. Nestled in a valley at the base of the Mazatzal Mountains, it was surrounded by dense ponderosa pines and sprawling oak trees. Bear Creek, from which the ranch derived its name, ran crystal clear and icy cold three hundred and sixty-five days a year. Fishermen, both professional and amateur, flocked from all over the southwest to test their skill at landing record-breaking trout.

Jake had lived on the ranch his whole life—until two years ago when he'd walked in on his then-wife with another man. Given the choice, he'd have sought counseling and attempted to repair his and Ellen's deteriorating marriage, for the sake of their three daughters if nothing else. Ellen, on the other hand, had wanted out and promptly divorced him.

Because he wanted his daughters to grow up in the same home he had, enjoy the same country lifestyle, remain near the close-knit Tucker family, Jake had let Ellen keep their house on the ranch until their youngest child graduated from high school. He'd purchased a vacant lot a few miles up the road. There, he'd built a lovely—and terribly empty—house on a hill with a stunning view no one appreciated.

Never once did Jake dream Ellen would bring another man into *his* home to sleep in *his* bed, eat at *his* table, live with *his* daughters. The very idea of it made him sick. And angry. That anger had prompted him to invite Lilly on a date.

Seeing her for the first time since he'd botched their breakup, watching the brave front she put on, had reminded him of the genuine liking he'd had for her and still did. He'd been a jerk for treating her so poorly—but not, he reasoned, for letting her go.

As difficult as their breakup had been for both of them, it was for the best. Jake had jumped the gun with Lilly, something he'd realized when she'd begun to pressure him for more of a commitment. His daughters were having trouble coping with their mother's upcoming marriage and the prospect of a stepfather. A new woman in Jake's life would've added to those troubles, and his daughters came first with him. He'd chosen wisely, he felt, to call it quits with Lilly before too many people were hurt or, as in her case, hurt worse.

Climbing into his pickup truck, he took the main road through the ranch to the riding stables. He pulled up beside a split-wood fence his grandfather had built fifty years ago and parked.

"Howdy, Jake." Gary Forrester, the ranch's manager of guest amenities, came out from the barn to greet him. He carried a metal toolbox in one hand. In the other, he jangled a set of keys to one of the ATVs the hands regularly used to get around the property.

"Hey, Gary. You off somewhere?"

"The number-three pump went on the fritz this morning. I'm on my way up the hill to see if I can talk sweetly to it." The older man had a real knack with finicky pieces of machinery, coaxing them to work when they were beyond repair. Hired thirty-plus years ago by Jake's grandfather, he'd become a permanent fixture on the place.

"I won't keep you long, I promise." Jake ambled toward the holding corral where a dozen horses milled quietly in the warm noontime sun. The other dozen or so were out carrying guests on one of the many scenic trails winding through the nearby mountains.

"I can spare a minute." Gary set the keys and toolbox on the ATV's wide seat and joined Jake at the corral. "What's on your mind?"

"Any chance we have room for another animal?"

"Sure. You found one?"

"Not exactly." Jake rested his forearms on the piped railing. "This one would be a boarder."

"Hmm." Gary raised his weathered brows. "That's a new one. Didn't think we were in the boarding business."

"We're not. The Horizon Adult Day Care Center has come by a mule and is looking for a place to keep it." Jake didn't need to elaborate. Gary was familiar with the center. It was located in the same small shopping plaza as the antique store co-owned by his wife and Jake's aunt. "An old, lame mule, so I'm told."

Gary pushed his cowboy hat back and scratched the top of his head. "What in the tarnation are they doing with a mule?"

"The Malcovitches donated it." The reminder of Ellen's fiancé triggered another surge of anger in Jake. He quickly suppressed it.

"Why?"

He summarized Lilly's plan to use the mule as a teaching tool and positive influence on the center's clients. "I haven't decided anything yet. There are some insurance issues to resolve. And I wanted to bounce the idea off you, seeing as the work the clients do will fall under your domain."

"Are them people up to the task? Cleaning out pens doesn't take much know-how, but it's physically demanding, and they gotta be able to follow directions."

"Ms. Russo seems to think they are." Jake's voice involuntarily warmed when he spoke Lilly's name.

Did Gary notice? Jake wasn't sure how much the employees knew about his former relationship with Lilly or what conclusions they'd jumped to. Bear Creek Ranch was a small community, and as much as the family tried to minimize it, people gossiped.

"What about the guests?" Gary asked.

"Obviously, nothing the center does here can interfere in the slightest with the ranch's operation."

Gary nodded. The guests—their comfort and enjoyment—were his top priority. "We might want to put the mule in by himself for a while. Just to be on the safe side. Some horses take unkindly to long ears."

"I don't think he should be allowed on any trails,

either, until we determine just how lame he is. Make sure he's ridden only in the round pen for now."

"Sounds like you've already decided."

"No. But I will take Ms. Russo's proposal to the family."

Gary's eyes twinkled with amusement. "That ought to be interesting."

Jake didn't dispute his statement. The Tuckers were close but they didn't always agree on what was best for the ranch—and each other. Gary knew that better than anyone. Thirty years of working and living side by side with his employers had given him an inside track. Their relationship had recently become further entwined when Gary's daughter had married Jake's former brother-in-law.

"We're meeting on Saturday," Jake said. Pushing away from the railing, he turned toward his truck, mentally composing his argument to the family in favor of Lilly's plan. Tax deduction and goodwill aside, it was the right thing to do. The Tuckers had a longstanding history of giving back to the community.

"I'll have Little José ready one of the stalls," Gary said.

"No rush."

Jake's words were wasted on his manager. The stall would be fit for a Kentucky Derby winner by quitting time today.

"Not that my opinion counts, but I think helping the center is a good idea." Gary had fallen into step beside Jake. Midway between the ATV and Jake's truck, they paused to finish their conversation. "Ms.

Russo is a fine lady with a heart of gold. She works her tail off for them folks."

"Yes, she does."

Was that a subtle reprimand in Gary's tone or was guilt coloring Jake's perception? Probably a little of both.

"Lord knows some of them need a fighter on their side. It'll be my pleasure having her around."

Jake's, too. More than he would've guessed and for reasons in no way connected to the center, its clients or an old, lame mule about to find a new home on the ranch if he had any say in the matter.

He cautioned himself to tread carefully. The reasons he'd broken off with Lilly in the first place hadn't changed. If anything, they'd intensified. As his ex-wife's wedding approached, his daughters were becoming more sullen and starting to act out, especially his oldest, Briana. Asking them to accept yet another change, in this case Lilly, wasn't fair and would only make the situation worse.

Lilly had the right idea: keep things on a professional level, for everyone's sake.

But after seeing her today, Jake knew it wouldn't be easy.

Chapter 2

Lilly bent over the compact porcelain sink and turned the right faucet on full blast. Forming a cup with her hands, she splashed cold water on her face. A quick glance in the mirror confirmed that her efforts fell short of the desired effect. Her complexion remained as pale as when she'd woken up that morning.

With a flick of her wrist, she shut off the water, snatched a coarse paper towel from the dispenser and blotted her face dry. When she was done, she reached into her purse and removed a small bottle of antacid tablets, popping two in her mouth. She doubted they'd cure what ailed her.

Since last Thursday when she'd met with Jake, her stomach had been in a chronic state of queasiness. Despite her best efforts, her plan for the center still hadn't come together. And at the rate things were progressing, it might never.

Keeping her word to Jake, she'd contacted the Horizon day care's owners over the weekend, and Dave had assured her the insurance was adequate to cover clients and staff while they were visiting the ranch. Yesterday afternoon, the appropriate documentation was faxed to Jake's office. His assistant had verified its receipt but volunteered no additional information in response to Lilly's probing, other than to inform her that Jake would be in touch.

Lilly's anxiety had increased when the Malcovitches called a short while ago to tell her that if she didn't have the mule picked up by tomorrow, they were giving him to someone else. She immediately placed another phone call to Jake and received the same cryptic message from his assistant. Lilly's nerves couldn't take much more.

Popping a third antacid tablet, she returned the bottle to her purse and silently chided herself for letting Jake's failure to call back upset her to the point of making her ill. He'd said he'd be in touch and he would. Jake was nothing if not dependable. All she had to do was wait.

Giving her wispy bangs a quick finger-combing, she spun on her heels, opened the bathroom door and was immediately halted in midstep. Mrs. O'Conner was right outside and standing behind her wheelchair was Georgina, the center's head caregiver.

"Sorry." Georgina backed up Mrs. O'Connor's

wheelchair to let Lilly pass. "She says she has to go. Now." Georgina rolled her eyes.

Lilly understood. Mrs. O'Connor "had to go" five or six times a day, whether she truly needed to or not.

"How are you doing today, my dear?" Lilly stooped to Mrs. O'Connor's level and laid a hand on her frail arm. "You seem sad."

Mrs. O'Connor raised watery eyes to Lilly. "My cat's missing."

"Oh, I'm sorry to hear that."

"She's been gone three days now." Mrs. O'Connor sniffed sorrowfully. "Such a good kitty."

Lilly straightened but not before giving the older woman a reassuring squeeze. "I'm sure she'll return soon."

"I hope so."

According to Mrs. O'Connor's daughter, the cat had expired of old age more than a year earlier. There were days Mrs. O'Connor remembered and days she didn't. The Horizon staff had been asked by her daughter to play along whenever the cat was mentioned.

The O'Connors were typical of the center's clients. Caring for elderly and emotionally or physically challenged adults wasn't always easy. Families needed breaks to run errands, attend to personal business, go to dinner or one of a thousand other things most people took for granted. If family members worked outside the home, those breaks were even more important. The Horizon Adult Day Care Center helped by providing quality care in an attractive facility and at an affordable price.

After the death of her son, Evan, and the divorce that followed, Lilly had reevaluated her priorities and decided on a change in careers. The satisfaction she derived from earning a fat paycheck and driving a nice car waned in comparison to making a difference in people's lives. At first, she'd contemplated working with children but that would have been too difficult. When she heard about the administrative position at the Horizon Center, she knew she'd found what she was looking for. Accepting the position, she left her job at Mayo Clinic Arizona and moved from Phoenix to the considerably smaller town of Payson.

There'd been times during her thirty-two years when Lilly was happier, but never had she felt more valued or appreciated.

"Do you need any help?" she asked Georgina.

"I think we can manage." Maneuvering Mrs. O'Connor's wheelchair to clear the bathroom doorway, Georgina set about her task with the cheery smile that made her such an asset to the center.

"If my daughter phones about my cat, will you come get me?" Mrs. O'Connor called as the door was closed.

"Right away."

Lilly traveled the short hall that opened into the main recreational room. There was, as usual, a flurry of activity and a cacophony of noisy chatter. She was stopped frequently—by both clients and staff members—on the way to her office, located near the main entrance.

"Lilly, Mrs. Vega has taken the TV remote again and refuses to tell me where she's hidden it."

"Try looking in the microwave."

"M-M-Miss R-R-Rus-s-so. S-s-see wh-what I d-d-draw."

"Very nice, Samuel."

"The soda machine is out of Pepsi again."

"You know you're not supposed to drink caffeine, Mr. Lindenford. It makes you agitated."

And on it went.

Lilly's official title was administrator, which involved running the office, supervising the personnel, maintaining the financial records and overseeing customer relations. Some days, however, she felt more like a babysitter. Not that she minded.

Lilly no sooner reached the entrance to her office door and sighed with relief when she was stopped yet again.

"Is it true we're picking up the mule tomorrow?"

She spun around. "Jimmy Bob, where did you hear that?"

The young man hung his head in shame. "Georgina told me."

He was lying. They both knew it. Like many people with Down's syndrome, Jimmy Bob was a sweet, kind soul with boundless energy and a quick, hearty laugh. He was also a chronic eavesdropper, sneaking quietly up and listening to conversations that weren't any of his business. Because it was impossible for him to keep a secret, he always confessed what he'd heard, usually in the form of a lie so as not to implicate himself. Fortunately, he was also very likeable.

Lilly took pity on him. His woe-is-me expression never failed to win her over despite resolutions to the contrary.

"Sucker," she mumbled under her breath, then said out loud, "We *hope* to be able to pick up the mule tomorrow. We're not sure yet."

"When will we be sure?"

A glance at the phone on her desk and the glaring absence of a flashing red message light made her heart sink. Jake still hadn't called. Was he avoiding her? Had the family rejected her plan, and he was trying to think of an easy way to let her down?

"I don't know, Jimmy Bob. By the end of today, maybe, if all goes well."

His face broke into an enormous grin, his earlier shame evidently forgotten. "Can I ride him tomorrow? I'm a good rider. Ask my mom. She took me riding at the ranch. You know, the one with the big white barn." He started whistling an off-key rendition of the theme to *Bonanza*.

Bear Creek Ranch had a red barn. Jimmy Bob must be referring to Wintergreen Riding Stables, which were located about a mile outside town heading toward Phoenix.

"*If* we get the mule and *if* your mother agrees, you can ride him. But that won't be tomorrow, honey."

Jimmy Bob stopped whistling and his enormous smile collapsed.

"Maybe by Friday." She patted a cheek that bore

severe acne scars along with the slightest hint of facial hair. "I promise, when we finally take our first trip to see the mule, you'll go with us."

She meant what she'd said. If Jake agreed, they would need their more able-bodied clients to keep Horizon's end of the bargain. Jimmy Bob wasn't only enthusiastic, he was strong and fit and cooperative. Other clients, like Samuel, weren't capable of performing any chores but would be able to interact with the mule, possibly ride it while being led around a ring.

Jimmy Bob's smile showed signs of reemerging.

"Would you do me a favor?" Lilly asked.

He bobbed his head.

"Go to the supply closet and bring me a ream of paper, okay?"

He shot off to do her bidding. Lilly didn't really need a ream of paper. She had two stacked beside her printer from previous attempts to distract Jimmy Bob.

Sitting at her desk, she debated placing another call to Jake and was startled when the phone rang. It was answered by Gayle who was currently manning the welcome desk in the main room. The four to five caregivers always on duty took turns at the desk, rotating every hour or so. Ten seconds later when the caller wasn't put through to her, Lilly gave up hope that it was Jake.

She lifted a manila folder from a wire rack on the corner of her desk and withdrew the monthly bank statements. Normally, she could reconcile a bank statement in her sleep, but today the numbers refused to add up. Her chronic indigestion wasn't helping matters. How long until those damn antacids kicked in?

How long until Jake called?

Lilly jumped to her feet. It wasn't quite lunchtime, but she couldn't tolerate the waiting anymore. A break from the center might be the perfect remedy to settle her nerves. She stopped at the welcome desk to inform Gayle that she was leaving.

But Gayle forestalled her. "Any chance you can postpone lunch a few minutes?"

"Why?" Lilly inquired.

She inclined her head in the direction of the front door. Lilly turned to see Jake striding across the room straight toward her.

Jake sensed every pair of eyes on him but he didn't react.

Activity and chatter ceased by degrees until the hiss of a wheelchair-bound woman's portable oxygen tank was the only sound in the room. Three people abruptly leapt out of their seats to trail his every move, like predators stalking prey. He looked behind him and smiled. One of the trio, a young man, smiled back. The other two glared openly. Jake was an experienced businessman and accustomed to holding his own under pressure. But for some reason, his confidence wavered, and he didn't like it.

"Good morning, Lilly," he said when he reached her.

"Hi, Jake."

"Are you all right?"

"I'm fine."

She didn't appear fine. Fatigue shadowed her eyes and when she first caught sight of him, her cheeks had paled. Shock at seeing him? He supposed he should have called first. But the family trust attorney's office was only a few minutes away, and since a signature was required on the contract, Jake had decided to stop in and deliver it in person.

His self-appointed security detail crowded in around them. Jake shifted, resisting the urge to tug on his suddenly tight shirt collar. If Lilly noticed, she gave no indication.

"Is there somewhere we can talk?" Glancing around, he added, "Alone."

"Come with me." She motioned for him to follow. His security detail came, too. Once he and Lilly had crossed the threshold into her office, she informed the group to "Wait here" and shut the door on their unhappy faces. "Sorry," she told Jake. "New visitors always create a stir. They weren't intentionally ganging up on you."

"No problem." When she didn't stop scrutinizing him, he added, "Really."

"Don't be embarrassed. Special-needs individuals often make people feel ill at ease."

"I'm not ill at ease."

She didn't believe him. He could tell by her narrowed eyes.

Could it be true? Jake didn't consider himself a snob but the fact was, he'd had little interaction with "special-needs" people other than his grandfather. Jake had been away at college during most of Grandpa Walter's decline and, as a result, missed the worst of it.

"I'm—" he started to say ignorant then changed it to "—inexperienced."

"You're not alone." She didn't act offended at his remark. Quite the contrary. "Would you like a tour of the facility?" Pride rang in her voice. "You're our landlord, after all, and I don't think you've seen the place since I took over."

What she said was true. With the exception of his aunt's antique store located in the same plaza, Jake rarely dropped by his tenants' businesses. Not unless there was a problem, which wasn't the case here. And during the short time he and Lilly had dated he had always picked her up at her house rather than work. He'd told himself it was a matter of convenience for both of them, as most of their outings took place in town. Now he wondered if he hadn't been unconsciously keeping their relationship from progressing by avoiding her work and the ranch.

"Thanks, but I can't." He hated disappointing Lilly. She obviously loved the center and showing it off. "I'm meeting someone for lunch, and I only have a few minutes." As if a switch had been flicked, she sobered, and Jake didn't know why. Had he insulted her by declining her offer of a tour? He certainly hadn't meant to.

"Please, sit." Lilly gestured at the visitor's chair facing her desk.

"I'd rather stand if you don't mind. I've been sitting all morning and will be again all afternoon."

Her office had a glass window opening out to the

main room. He turned to face it, and a dozen heads swivelled to stare at him. The young man who'd smiled earlier waved exuberantly. Without thinking, Jake raised his hand in return.

"Did you get the insurance certificate we faxed over?" Lilly asked.

"Yes. It's exactly what we needed." He stepped away from the window and held out the envelope he'd been carrying. "Our attorney also suggested we draw up a contract."

"Does that mean…" She took the envelope and turned it over in her hands. "Has the family agreed?"

"For once, we were completely unanimous." Jake hadn't needed to twist one arm or press a single point. "I didn't tell you earlier because I couldn't meet with our attorney until this morning."

"Oh, wow." Lilly's face, always so expressive, lit up. "I can't believe it."

Her delight was contagious, and he chuckled. "There are one or two conditions you should know about."

"Oh?"

Jake sobered. He hadn't yet determined how he felt about the stipulations the attorney had insisted on putting in the contract. "As you can imagine, liability is our main concern. Our attorney suggested that someone in charge, specifically you or the owner, accompany the clients on their visits. At least for the first several months until we determine how well the program is going."

"I doubt Dave can go. He and his wife commute

regularly to Apache Junction where they just opened a second center."

"Then I guess it'll have to be you."

He could see the uncertainty in her eyes and wondered if she harbored the same doubts he did about the prospect of them constantly running into each other at the ranch.

"Okay." She nodded resignedly. "Whatever it takes."

"You sure?"

"Positive." She relaxed. "I'm not about to let a few scheduling conflicts get in the way of this program."

"I'm glad."

"Thank you, Jake." Setting the envelope on her desk, she took a step toward him, and hesitated. Then, evidently going with her first instincts, she closed the distance between them. "Thank you so much."

Before he could say anything, she linked her arms around his shoulders. He automatically returned the hug and was instantly lost when she laid her head in the crook of his neck. They had, after all, done this before. Often.

He might have gone on holding her, might have let himself enjoy the memories her nearness evoked, if not for a loud bang on the window. Lilly gasped and sprang back. Jake swung around to see what had caused the noise.

One—no, make that two dozen—of the center's clients and staff stood crowded outside the window, some with their noses or fingertips against the glass.

"Are we getting the mule?" The young man's muffled shout barely penetrated the insulated window.

Lilly nodded, fidgeting nervously. Her previously pale cheeks shone a vivid red.

Their audience cheered. Lilly motioned for them to go on about their business. Her order went unheeded. "Now," she mouthed, and still no one moved.

Jake couldn't help himself and laughed.

"This isn't funny," Lilly scolded and retreated behind her desk.

He could see her point, though for a moment or two, it had been nice holding her.

"What next?" she asked him and glowered at the window. Some of their audience had fortunately dispersed. The rest ignored her silent warning and remained glued to the spot.

"You and Dave review the contract. If it meets with your approval, sign it and send it to my office."

"What about the mule?"

"I'll arrange to have him picked up, unless you have access to a truck and horse trailer."

"We don't."

"Is tomorrow early enough? I remember you said you were in a hurry."

"Tomorrow's perfect. I'll let the Malcovitches know."

The reference to his ex-wife's fiancé's family didn't generate nearly the anger it usually did. If anything, Jake felt good. Damn good. His charitable deed accounted for some of his elevated mood. He suspected Lilly's hug was responsible for the rest.

"I have to leave. I'm late for my meeting."

"I'll walk you out." She came around from behind the shelter of her desk.

At the entrance to the center, he got another hug. This one, however, was from the young man who'd waved. Not Lilly.

Jake watched Lilly's long legs emerge from the open car door. Her delicate shoes were sexy as hell and completely inappropriate for traipsing around a stable. Her wool slacks weren't much better. At least she'd had the sense to wear a warm coat. She must have flown out the door and sped the entire drive from Payson, considering what good time she'd made.

"Is that him?" she asked. Breathless and eager, she tentatively approached the mule tied to the hitching post in front of the barn. Her long black hair, usually twisted in a braid or gathered in a ponytail, fell loose around her shoulders, framing her face and emphasizing her large brown eyes.

"It is." Jake couldn't look away. Only after he'd stared his fill did he invite her to come and stand by him. Together, they turned their attention to the ranch's newest boarder and the man standing beside him. "That's Doc Mosby. He's giving the mule a quick examination."

"He's not sick?"

"Just a precaution." Jake stooped to pick up an empty feed bucket and set it on one of the grain barrels. "Our attorney suggested the mule be vet-checked on arrival and regularly after that, since he's lame."

"Oh." Lilly observed the vet at work, her brow knitted with worry. "Did you receive the contract?"

"Our attorney's still reviewing the changes your boss made."

"Oh," she said regretfully. "I was hoping to get started by Friday."

"Even if the contract's not finalized, you can bring a small group on Friday morning to see the mule and tour the stables."

"Not to sound ungrateful because I truly appreciate this, but how big is *small?*"

"No more than six clients at a time."

"Another of your attorney's suggestions?"

"Don't be mad. It's his job to watch out for the family and the ranch."

"I'm not mad. If six is our limit, then that's what we'll bring."

The vet was bent over, one of the mule's hooves braced between his legs. Using a pick, he dug around inside the hoof. Jake and Gary had their own suspicions about what had caused the animal's lameness. It would be interesting to see if the vet also concluded it was a deformity.

"Doc Mosby was out here anyway to examine one of our pregnant mares," Jake explained to Lilly. "I'll just have him add the charge for Big Ben to his bill. Your clients can work it off, along with the other expenses."

"Big Ben?"

"That's the mule's name."

A smile touched the corners of Lilly's mouth. "It fits."

Jake agreed. The mule stood as tall as any of his horses and was considerably wider than most. "My guess is his mother was a draft horse."

"What kind?"

"A Belgian. They're similar to the Budweiser Clydesdales you see in the TV commercials, only sorrel."

"And sorrel is?"

"The color of his coat. A kind of red like Big Ben. Clydesdales are usually a darker shade of brown."

She sighed miserably and shook her head. "I think I might've gotten myself in over my head. Everything I know about horses and mules could fit into a thimble."

"You'll do fine." He smiled encouragingly. "And we have plenty of experienced ranch hands around to help."

"I hope it wasn't too much of an inconvenience to pick up Big Ben today," she said, changing the subject to a safer one.

"Not at all. I sent Little José."

"Make sure you add that expense to the others." She gave a small laugh. "At this rate, we'll be here every day for a year working off our bill."

Against his better judgment, Jake was liking their arrangement more and more. He seized the chance to study her while her attention was on Doc Mosby and the mule.

At the time of their breakup, Jake had been completely positive that continuing their relationship was a mistake. He liked Lilly and hadn't wanted to string her along when there was no hope whatsoever for a future together.

That hadn't been his initial feeling, though. In the beginning, their dating arrangement had been exactly the enjoyable distraction he'd needed to take his mind off his ex-wife's engagement and help him move on. But things had quickly become complicated, in large part because of his daughters, although they weren't the only obstacle.

Once he and Lilly became intimate, the complications increased. Not because there was anything wrong with the sex. Quite the opposite, in fact. But Lilly didn't give herself to just anyone. Sex came with a commitment from her *and* him.

Jake had held her in his arms after they made love that last time, stared into those gorgeous brown eyes that brimmed with hope and expectation and realized, with a sinking heart, that he couldn't offer her what she wanted, what she needed. Not anytime soon. To continue as they were would have been unfair to Lilly. So, instead of postponing the inevitable, he had broken up with her the following day, telling himself he'd done it for her sake.

But after their meeting in his office last week, it had occurred to him that his actions weren't entirely noble and were calculated to spare *him* grief, not her.

"Good boy." Doc Mosby dropped Big Ben's hoof and patted his round rump, then came over to chat with Jake and Lilly.

"Lilly, this is our vet, Dr. Greg Mosby," Jake said.

"Lilly Russo is the administrator of the adult day care center that owns the mule."

"Nice to meet you." Doc Mosby pulled a handkerchief from his back pocket and wiped his hands before shaking Lilly's.

"What do you think?" Jake asked.

"Well, I'd say he's in pretty good shape overall. A little fat—" Doc Mosby patted his protruding stomach "—but aren't we all? I suspect he's been standing in a pen too long. Exercise should shave off a few of those extra pounds."

"How lame is he?"

"Some. Corrective shoeing will help. He was born with a slight deformity to his right front hoof, and it's gotten worse with age. It causes his foot to turn in." Doc Mosby demonstrated with his hand.

"A birth defect?" Lilly's interest was visibly piqued, which, in turn, piqued Jake's.

Doc Mosby grinned. "I reckon you could call it that."

"If you want to return him to the Malcovitches—"

"No, no!" Lilly cut Jake short. "He's perfect for us. A mule with a birth defect helping people who are themselves physically challenged."

"Have your farrier insert a leather wedge between the shoe and the hoof," Doc Mosby explained. "It should straighten the hoof and reduce the pain."

"Can he be ridden before then?"

"I wouldn't recommend it."

Lilly's smile dimmed.

Jake touched her arm. "I'll call the farrier, have

him come out here Friday morning. That way, the people in your program can watch Big Ben being shoed firsthand."

She instantly brightened. "Oh, that would be wonderful!"

Clapping the vet on the shoulder, Jake gestured at Gary with his other hand. "You ready to look at that mare?"

"Sure."

Gary, who'd been standing nearby, took charge of the vet, leaving Jake alone with Lilly.

"Is it all right for me to pet Big Ben?" she asked.

"Would you like to walk him to his stall?"

"Yes!"

Jake went over and untied the mule's lead rope. Big Ben ambled obediently alongside Jake, his large feet clip-clopping in the dirt.

"Here."

She took the rope. Bunching it in her fingers, she gazed up at Jake. "What now?"

"You walk, he follows."

"Just like that?"

"With him. Not so with all horses or mules. But this guy's a teddy bear."

"I walk." She took a tentative step.

"That's it."

"He's not following."

"Keep going."

She did. The heels of her completely inappropriate shoes wobbled and dust coated her expensive slacks.

Big Ben finally extended one foot and lifted his huge head to snuffle her hair.

"Hey! That tickles." Lilly raised her hand, not to push the animal away but to stroke his nose.

Big Ben snorted and nuzzled her cheek, clearly enamored.

He wasn't the only one.

Jake found himself attracted to Lilly all over again.

He would have to watch himself closely in the coming weeks and months. Lilly deserved more than he could give her. She deserved a man ready, willing and able to commit.

Chapter 3

"Put your seat belt back on, Jimmy Bob."

"But we're here."

Lilly turned around and gave the young man a hard stare. She sat in the front passenger seat of the center's specially modified van. Beside her, driving the van, was Georgina. The student volunteer accompanying them sat in the rear.

"Not yet," Lilly told Jimmy Bob. "We just pulled in to the ranch entrance. The stable is another mile from here."

Jimmy Bob rarely rebelled but he did so today, his normally cherubic face set in stone, his arms folded. Lilly attributed his stubbornness to excitement. Since he'd learned yesterday morning that he'd be one of the six people accompanying Lilly on the center's first trip to see Big Ben, he'd been bouncing off the walls. His high-strung behavior earned him frequent reprimands from the staff members and his family. This morning, he'd reached emotional overload, becoming surly and rebellious. Not uncommon behavior for individuals with Down's syndrome.

Lilly couldn't allow Jimmy Bob to ignore the rules, today or any other day. Anyone riding in the van obeyed them or wasn't permitted to go on the next outing.

"Pull over," she said.

Georgina slowed and eased the vehicle safely to the side of the bumpy dirt road. She knew the drill, and once they were stopped, she put the van in Park and shut off the ignition.

"Damn it to hell, Jimmy Bob," the woman sitting beside him shrieked. "Put your freakin' seat belt on."

"Don't swear, Miranda," Lilly scolded.

"He's screwin' it up for everybody." Jimmy Bob's seatmate clutched the sides of her head in an exaggerated display of theatrics. A lock of wildly curly hair had come loose from her ponytail and stuck up like a rooster's comb.

"Jimmy Bob," Lilly implored in a tone that was midway between firm and coaxing.

"Can I ride the mule first?"

"We're not riding Big Ben today. The farrier has to put new shoes on him."

"When we do get to ride the mule, can I be first?"

"Oh, puleeze!" Miranda banged her head repeatedly against the padded rest behind her. "Quit being such a damn baby."

"Miranda. You're not helping." Lilly aimed a warning finger at her.

Miranda slapped a hand over her mouth to muffle her groan.

Lilly cautioned herself to remain calm. Though her patience was often tested by the people in her care, she hardly ever lost it. Had her son lived, she would've made a good mother.

Her throat closed abruptly and tears stung her eyes. Lilly didn't know why. It had taken a while, but in the two and a half years since Evan's death, she'd finally stopped crying at every reminder of him.

"What's wrong, Miss Russo?" Jimmy Bob didn't miss a thing.

"Nothing."

He grabbed his seat belt and buckled it. "I'm sorry. I didn't mean to make you mad at me."

"I'm not mad." She smiled at him, still fighting her unexpected weepiness. What had come over her today and why?

She wondered if seeing Jake so often lately and the memories stirred by those encounters had anything to do with her fragile mood. Lilly had come to care deeply for him during the six weeks they'd dated, which was why she'd pressured him for a greater commitment, ultimately triggering their breakup. And as much as she'd wished things could be different, she was afraid her feelings for him were as strong as ever.

Visiting the ranch two or three times a week wasn't

going to be easy and made her wish that her boss was around more to share the responsibility.

Georgina started the van and pulled back onto the road.

"It's about freakin' time," Miranda exclaimed, flinging her arms every which way.

Lilly didn't react to the outburst, which was done solely to attract attention. She spent the rest of the drive preoccupied with her own thoughts. Maybe Jake wouldn't be there. He'd informed her that his manager, Gary Forrester, would oversee their visits and the chores they performed.

She'd just about convinced herself that the likelihood of running into Jake was nil when the stables came into sight—and so did his familiar pickup truck.

Lilly's heart involuntarily raced. With anticipation, not dread.

Georgina parked next to Jake's truck. Jimmy Bob was first out the door. No surprise there. Lilly went around to the side of the van and, along with Georgina and the student volunteer, helped the remaining five clients out.

"Stay together."

She'd gone over the rules with each of them repeatedly. Nonetheless, she anticipated disobedience. Jimmy Bob didn't disappoint her.

"Look! There's the mule."

"Jimmy Bob, come back!

Big Ben was tied to the same hitching post as the previous day. Tail swishing, he stood calmly, demonstrating what Lilly hoped was a personality ideally suited to her clients. He didn't so much as blink when Jimmy Bob came charging at him.

"Hey! Don't ever run up to an animal like that. You'll get yourself kicked."

The reprimand came from a teenage, female version of Jake. His oldest daughter, Briana. Lilly recognized her from the Labor Day cookout at the ranch. The girl cut in front of Jimmy Bob before he reached the mule. The young man came to a grinding, almost comical, halt.

"Just because an animal looks calm," Briana scolded Jimmy Bob with an authority beyond her years, "doesn't mean he is. Be careful."

He gazed down at her, slack-jawed.

"Did you hear me?"

"You're pretty."

She shook her head and huffed in exasperation. "Come on," she said after a moment. "I'll introduce you to Big Ben."

Jimmy Bob followed like a devoted puppy.

Lilly considered intervening, then decided against it. Jake's daughter seemed capable of handling herself, and while Jimmy Bob might be stubborn sometimes, he was trustworthy and didn't have a mean bone in his body.

"Are you ready, Mr. Deitrich?" Lilly shoved the sliding van door closed after the elderly man had climbed out.

"Where are we?" He gazed around in obvious confusion.

"Bear Creek Ranch. Remember? We're here to visit our mule, Big Ben."

"There are no mules at Gold Canyon," he scoffed. "Everyone knows the old man won't have the sorry beasts. Claims they scare the cows."

"We're not at Gold Canyon Ranch." She grasped his arm securely and guided him toward the mule, where the rest of their group had gathered to gape in awe. At a respectable distance, thanks to Briana. "We're at Bear Creek Ranch."

Mr. Deitrich had Alzheimer's disease. It began when he was in his early sixties and, sadly, progressed rapidly. During his youth, he'd worked on a cattle ranch in Wyoming. His wife hoped the familiar setting of stables and horses would stimulate him mentally and possibly improve his condition.

Lilly didn't know if it would work, but was more than willing to try. As the only adult day care center of its kind in town and with a wide variety of client needs, Dave and the staff were open to any new ideas and approaches. It was one of the reasons Lilly had fought so hard for Big Ben.

"Does anyone know the difference between a horse, a donkey and a mule?" Briana stood with a hand on Big Ben's neck, conducting class. "No? Well, a mule has a donkey father and a horse mother."

"She's always liked being in the spotlight."

Lilly whirled around to find Jake standing behind her and sputtered a startled, "Hi."

"I hope you don't mind Briana helping. She's off school today for some reason."

"Not at all." Lilly tried to focus on the teenager and not her father, who, like Lilly, stood to the side.

Briana was so much like Jake, in looks and mannerisms and personality. She even pursed her lips in concentration the same way he did before answering the many questions her audience threw at her. Clearly she was knowledgeable about horses and happy to share that knowledge with others. Jake must have been very proud of his oldest. Lilly certainly would be if Briana were her daughter.

Suddenly a lump formed in the back of Lilly's throat and tears pricked her eyes. She blinked to counter the effect. What in the world was wrong with her today? Feeling vulnerable and not understanding why, Lilly hugged herself hard—only to let go with a small gasp that Jake fortunately didn't hear.

Her breasts hurt. A lot.

How strange was that? She'd noticed a tenderness this morning when she'd put on her bra but forgot about it in the next instant. Casting a sideways glance at Jake, she hugged herself again. Her breasts were definitely sore.

She must be having a raging case of PMS, she decided. That would explain her weepiness and the mild off-and-on stomach upset she'd been experiencing. Or maybe her birth control prescription needed adjusting. She hadn't responded well initially to the pill she was on and required several dosage modifications. What other explanation could there be?

Unless she was pregnant...

"Here comes the farrier," Jake said, nodding at an old pickup truck rumbling down the road.

Lilly composed herself and muttered, "Great." Swallowing did nothing to relieve the dryness in her mouth.

She couldn't be pregnant. It simply wasn't possible. She was on the pill *and* Jake had used condoms. Well, except for that one time when they'd gotten carried away in the hot tub at his house. But it shouldn't matter; the pill was nearly one-hundred-percent effective if taken every day, which she did without exception.

There had to be another explanation. Besides, she'd had her period a couple of weeks ago. Granted, it was a few days late and lighter than normal, but still a period. She'd even endured her usual cramping the day or two before.

"Who's ready for a tour of the stables?" Briana's question was met with great enthusiasm from everyone, especially Jimmy Bob, who was glued to her side. "Okay then, stay together. No wandering off. And no talking to the guests."

Lilly knew she should go with the group but her feet refused to obey her brain's command. When Jake tapped her on the shoulder, she practically jumped out of her skin.

"I'm going to talk to the farrier. Be back in a few minutes."

"Sure." She smiled weakly.

Watching Jake stride off, she decided that if she didn't feel better by tomorrow, she'd call her doctor and make an appointment. Another change in dosage, another switch to a different brand of pill and she'd be back to her old self.

She continued to delude herself for the rest of the morning and several days after that until it became impossible.

"How could this have happened?"

"The pill isn't infallible. And you only began taking it shortly before becoming intimate."

"He used a condom." *Most of the time.*

"They break. Leak. Come off."

"You've seen my records, you know my history. Before Evan, I had two stillbirths. One at five and a half months, the other at seven." Lilly's voice rose in pitch with each sentence she uttered.

Her doctor's voice, on the other hand, remained calm. "One thing you have to remember, Lilly, is this baby has a different father. The trisomy disorder that affected your previous children may have been a fluke combination of your DNA with your ex-husband's."

Lilly lifted her head, which had been propped in her hand, to meet Dr. Thea Paul's intense yet compassionate gaze. She liked the ob/gyn, who was a plain old small-town doctor and not a specialist in some obscure field of medicine Lilly didn't understand. She'd certainly had her fill of those back in Phoenix.

"I'm the carrier." She sniffed and wiped her damp cheeks. The emotions she'd been attempting to hold at bay overwhelmed her, and she blubbered, "That's what the other doctors told us."

Her fault the babies died. *Her* corrupt DNA.

It was why she'd vowed never to get pregnant again, why she was so diligent about birth control—at least, she'd *meant* to be diligent.

Dr. Paul got up from her chair, came around her desk and sat in the chair adjacent to Lilly's. She took Lilly's hand in hers. "Science and medicine aren't exact. I'm sure the other doctors explained your odds of having a healthy baby."

"Fifty-fifty. But that's not how it turned out." The chromosomal abnormality Lilly had passed on to her babies occurred only in males.

"Nature isn't exact, either," Dr. Paul said.

"I had my period." Lilly still resisted.

"Spotting, even heavy spotting, in the first trimester is common and can be confused with menstrual flow."

She wasn't reassured. Spotting and cramps had plagued her other three pregnancies. Accepting the tissue Dr. Paul offered, she blew her nose.

"This is all so…unexpected and…upsetting." She sobbed quietly. "God, you must think I'm a terrible person. All your other patients are probably thrilled to learn they're pregnant."

"Of course I don't think you're terrible," Dr. Paul said soothingly. "You've been through a lot and have every reason to worry about the health of your baby. There are several tests you can have that will determine—"

"No tests. They're too risky."

"Some are, that's true, but they can help you make an informed decision."

Lilly had heard of two patients at the hospital where she'd worked who'd miscarried after having amniocentesis. "There's only one decision to make. I'm having the baby."

Lilly's personal beliefs wouldn't allow her to terminate her pregnancy. It had been a contentious issue between her and Brad and a contributing factor to their divorce. When she became pregnant a second time, he'd insisted she undergo every available test.

She did as he'd asked. The results had revealed that the baby, also a boy, suffered from the same genetic disorder as his brother. After much pressure, Lilly succumbed to her husband's wishes and went so far as to schedule the termination but changed her mind at the last minute, to her husband's fury. For two long, agonizing months she carried the baby, knowing his chances of survival were slim to none but praying for a miracle.

The stillbirth broke her heart and nearly shattered her spirit.

With Evan, she'd stood her ground and refused all testing. What was the point when an abortion was out of the question? Fear and anxiety were her constant companion during that third pregnancy but so was hope for a girl and a different outcome. She wouldn't trade that feeling for the world, then *and* now.

"Your decision, of course." Dr. Paul squeezed Lilly's fingers. "And you can always change your mind later on."

"I won't."

Dr. Paul reached for Lilly's paperwork and made

some notations. "You feel strongly now, which is un-derstandable. That may change, however, when you talk to the baby's father."

Jake!

Lilly had been so busy the last few days denying the possibility of pregnancy, she hadn't considered what to tell him. Admitting her condition would be bad enough, especially when she'd assured him she'd been using birth control. Admitting the fact that their baby could be born deformed—if she even carried to term—was unimaginable. And grossly unfair to Jake. She knew firsthand the difficulties and potential agony facing them. He didn't. Worse, she was taking away his choice in the matter by choosing to have the baby regardless of his feelings.

"I can't tell him." She swallowed another sob. "Not yet."

"I'm your physician," Dr. Paul said. "It's not my place to advise you on personal matters. But as the father, he does have a right to know about the baby."

For one wild second, Lilly contemplated hiding her pregnancy from Jake. Then she remembered her agreement to accompany the center's clients on their visits to Bear Creek Ranch. He was no stranger to pregnant women and no dummy. He'd eventually fig-ure out her condition and realize he was the father.

"I need some time before I make any announce-ments." There was so much to consider. Her job. Her family. The expenses not covered by her health insur-ance. Astronomical medical bills had also contributed greatly to her marital problems with her ex-husband.

And then there was Jake.

Lilly started to rise. Her unsteady legs refused to support her, and she immediately dropped back into the chair.

"That's a good idea. And do think about the tests. I would be remiss in my duties if I didn't advise you to have them." Dr. Paul handed Lilly several sheets of paper. "Take these to the front desk. The nurse will call in your prescription for prenatal vitamins."

"Thank you." Lilly tried again to stand and managed it this time.

"Since you're a high-risk pregnancy, I'd like to see you every two weeks if your schedule allows it."

Lilly nodded and stumbled out of Dr. Paul's office. She paid her bill, scheduled her next appointment and gave the nurse the name and phone number of her pharmacy, all in a daze. The ground blurred on her walk across the parking lot to her car. She was barely aware of the return drive to the center and was surprised to find herself parked in her reserved space.

Sitting behind the steering wheel, she waited before leaving the car. Carefully, as if the slightest touch might harm the life growing inside her, she rested a hand on her abdomen.

Another baby. The last thing in the world she wanted, and, at the same time, the one thing she wanted with a longing that bordered on desperation.

A tiny seed of hope took root inside her. Was Dr. Paul right? Would this baby be born normal because the father was someone different? The tiny seed anchored itself more securely and began to blossom, filling Lilly with something she hadn't felt since her first pregnancy.

Joy.

A smile curved the corners of her mouth. The sigh escaping her lips was one of contentment, not despair. With a sense of elation, she opened the door and stepped out of the car.

She'd done no more than place one foot on the asphalt when the first cramp hit. The second was so severe, Lilly doubled over. Her breath came in spurts.

"Oh, God," she cried to herself. "Not again." Then, in a whisper, she pleaded, "Please don't take this baby from me, too."

Chapter 4

Jake looked up just as the beam from a pair of head-lights cut across his kitchen window. Ellen was dropping off the girls for their regular Wednesday-night dinner—late as usual. He didn't have to worry that she'd come inside. His ex-wife avoided him if at all possible these days, for which he was grateful.

He'd no sooner taken dinner from the oven than the girls tumbled through the back door. In the next instant, their lively antics filled the room, and Jake's loneliness vanished.

"Cheese pizza!" LeAnne shouted and ran immediately to the table, where Jake had set out paper plates and napkins.

"What? No hug?"

His youngest fled the chair she'd been ready to occupy and bounded into his arms. At seven, she was mostly arms and legs and long auburn hair that refused to stay out of her face. Briana and his middle daughter, Kayla, quickly followed suit.

Jake cherished his girls and had bent over backward to preserve his relationship with them during his divorce from their mother. At the time, it had rankled to give in to Ellen's outrageous demands, especially since she'd cheated on *him,* not the other way around. Now he was relieved that Ellen was unable to engage him in her petty power plays.

"Who else besides LeAnne is hungry?" Jake reluctantly released his children.

"Me." Kayla scrambled to beat her sisters to the table.

Jake cut the pizza into slices and served it. He wasn't much of a cook, usually taking his meals with either employees or guests in the spacious dining hall. After the divorce, he'd learned to prepare simple meals for himself and his daughters. Kayla and Briana were both picky eaters—Kayla hated vegetables and Briana didn't eat meat—which made the task a daunting one at times.

"How's school?" he asked once they were all seated.

His question earned him a round of frowns and one dismal head shake.

"You always ask the same thing," LeAnne objected.

"I'm interested." Jake washed his pizza down with a glass of fruit punch, something the younger girls loved and he tolerated.

"Mom's taking me into Payson tomorrow after school to get my learner's permit."

At Briana's announcement, Jake choked. He'd known this day was coming but it still took him by surprise. "Driving? You're only fifteen!"

"Fifteen and seven months. Which is when I can legally get my permit."

"Can I ride with Briana?" Kayla piped up.

"Absolutely not." Jake massaged a throbbing temple. When had his baby girl become old enough to drive? "Maybe I should go with you."

"It's all right. You don't have to."

Briana was being too blasé, a sure sign of something amiss. "I want to go," he said, applying pressure with the skill of an experienced parent. "It's a big day for you."

"What about work?" Panic widened her eyes.

Eyes, he suddenly noticed, made to look larger by mascara, their lids faintly tinted with blue shadow. He didn't recall giving Briana permission to wear makeup. Obviously, her mother hadn't seen the need to consult him on the matter.

"I'll leave early," he answered, searching for other unwanted signs of maturity, like piercings and tattoos and hickeys on her neck. Fortunately, there were none, or else she wouldn't be getting her learner's permit for another ten years.

"Really, Dad. It's okay."

He recognized that tone. Whenever he heard it, a sour taste filled the back of his mouth. "Travis is going," he said flatly. "Isn't he?"

All three girls stopped eating in midbite. Briana stared at her plate, guilt written all over her face.

Jake set his paper napkin on the table although he would've preferred to pound his fist against the unyielding surface. His ex-wife's fiancé was accompanying his daughter to get her learner's permit. The son of a bitch. Where did he get off? He wasn't Briana's father. He wasn't even her stepfather. Not yet.

"Please, Daddy." Briana's voice fell to a whisper. Translation: *Don't ruin this for me.*

"No. I'm sorry, honey." Jake could stomach a fair amount of insult but he drew the line at this.

"You promised I could get my permit as soon as I was old enough. And I've been studying for the test."

Though he recollected no such promise, he didn't dispute his daughter. Obtaining her learner's permit wasn't the issue. Rather, it was who went with her to the Department of Motor Vehicles. Or, more correctly, who *didn't* go with her.

"Fine, you can get it tomorrow."

"I can?"

"As long as Travis doesn't go with you. Your mother can take you. Alone," he stressed. "Or I will."

"Then you can take me." Briana's anxiety fled in an instant. She didn't care who went with her, only that she got to go.

"I'll call your mother and tell her."

Jake knew it wasn't fair of him to put Briana on the spot like this, yet he'd do it again in a heartbeat. Travis might be sleeping in Jake's bed but he sure as hell wasn't about to usurp Jake's place at his daughter's side during those all-important milestones.

"And I'd really prefer that only your mother or I give you driving lessons. Our insurance doesn't cover Travis."

"Yes, sir," Briana answered, cheerful once more. "I really didn't want him to go anyway."

In another moment, all three girls were eating and chatting as if no tense words had been spoken.

"What are you doing Friday after school?"

"I'm going to Mindy's for a sleepover," LeAnne said after a sip of fruit punch that left a pink mustache above her upper lip.

"I have an orthodontist appointment." Kayla peeled back her lips to show off her recently acquired braces.

Jake had foolishly hoped his daughters would be free and that he could squeeze in an extra visit this week. So much for spontaneity.

"What about you, Briana? We could have a driving lesson around the ranch. Early, before it gets dark."

"I...um..." She snapped her mouth shut, her indecision plain as day.

"Never mind," Jake grumbled. If she was going somewhere else with her mother and Travis, he didn't want to hear about it.

"She's giving riding instructions to those funny people with the mule," LeAnne piped up.

"Don't call them funny," Briana retorted hotly.

"Your sister's right, sweetie. That's not very nice."

LeAnne glanced around the table in a bid for support. "Well, they are."

Jake didn't know what baffled him more. Briana sacrificing her precious social time to work with Lilly's clients, or her quick and emotional defense of them.

"That's very good of you. I'm sure they appreciate it." Of his three daughters, his oldest was the only one to take a real interest in horses and the ranch.

"She spends practically every day there," LeAnne said with the conspiratorial demeanor of someone revealing a secret.

"Really?"

Jake hadn't been to the stables to check on Lilly's group in over a week. Not since last Tuesday when she'd acted so odd. He'd shown up, determined to be friendly and courteous, but drawing the line there. She'd appeared equally determined to avoid him and did everything from making flimsy excuses to turning on her heel and changing direction when she saw him coming. He eventually got the hint and made his own excuse to return to the office.

He hadn't spoken to her since, although he knew from Gary's reports that she'd accompanied her clients the required number of times as stipulated in their agreement.

What had brought about the sudden change in her? Had she sensed his lingering interest and decided to put a halt to it before things heated up again? If that was true, she had good reason to avoid him. He'd hurt her badly and too recently for her to have fully recovered.

Unless it was the other way around.

Could her abrupt retreat be because *she* had a renewed interest in *him* and didn't want to risk more heartache? While that scenario was somewhat tempting, he knew better than to consider it even for a moment.

"So I like giving riding instructions," Briana said, her tone defensive. "What's wrong with that?"

LeAnne shuddered. "They're strange."

"They have special needs." Jake stood and began clearing the table. He tapped Kayla on the shoulder and pointed to the refrigerator. She rushed over, opened the freezer compartment and gave a delighted squeal when she discovered the carton of ice cream he'd bought for dessert.

"I don't care," LeAnne continued with the typical unrestrained candor of a child. "They make me feel weird. Don't they make you feel weird?" She waited for Jake to answer.

He was torn between being honest and being diplomatic. Admittedly, there had been one or two moments at Horizon when he'd experienced some discomfort and one or two instances at the ranch last week when he'd had to force himself not to stare. It took an exceptional person to work with special-needs individuals, someone with an enormous capacity for caring.

Like Lilly.

"You feel a little weird at first," Briana said, showing a capacity to care as enormous as Lilly's. "But then you get over it and realize they're okay."

"She's right," Jake immediately agreed. "And what she's doing is very commendable." His gaze traveled from LeAnne to Kayla. "Don't either of you give her a hard time."

They nodded in synchronized solemnity.

"How 'bout you come with me on Friday?" Briana asked cheerfully. "You haven't been to the stables in a while."

"Sure." Jake smiled and dished out the ice cream. "I'd love to."

If he took Briana up on her offer, he'd get to spend extra time with her. Be a proud and doting father. Show his younger daughters that, like their sister, he accepted special-needs individuals. Also important, he'd see Lilly and reaffirm with her—and himself—that their relationship was strictly business.

His smile grew. Between going with Briana tomorrow to get her learner's permit and to the stables on Friday, the rest of the week was shaping up quite nicely.

"L-look at me, Miss R-Russo. I'm r-riding."

"You're doing great, Samuel."

Lilly waved at the beaming man who clung to the saddle horn for dear life. His undersized body rocked back and forth in rhythm to Big Ben's slow steps. They'd had quite a time getting Samuel to wear a helmet; he didn't like anything constricting on his head. He'd finally relented when someone else nearly got his turn on Big Ben.

Jimmy Bob led the mule and rider around a circular pen, his smile equalling Samuel's in size. There wasn't anything about the ranch Jimmy Bob didn't love. Even the dirtiest, most backbreaking chores were completed with enthusiasm.

"Keep up the good work," Lilly hollered to both men, pleased with Samuel's progress and his growing confidence.

So far, everything about the center's new program met or exceeded the staff's expectations. The clients were responding well to the mule and he to them. Corrective shoeing had helped with his limp, enough so Big Ben could be ridden for two hours at a stretch without tiring. Not that they worked him hard. Mostly he walked. Slowly. Twice, Jimmy Bob got the mule to trot a few paces and yee-hawed like a wild cowboy when he did. Big Ben responded with his usual calm.

It had required some trial and error, but they'd developed a successful routine, thanks in part to Jake's daughter, Briana, who'd generously spent several afternoons with them. She or one of the hands helped them groom and saddle Big Ben. Then each of the six clients was given a twenty-minute ride on the mule, always under the supervision of two people, one from the center and one from the ranch. Anyone not riding was assigned chores, also under the same supervision guidelines. When they were done, Big Ben was brushed down and returned to his stall, where he was duly rewarded with carrots and petting.

After a week and a half, the group from Horizon had figured out the chores, which mostly involved cleaning stalls and pens and raking the barn aisle. Lilly appreciated Jake's kindness. She didn't think they were anywhere close to earning back Big Ben's board or the wages he paid the ranch hands who helped them.

At the thought of Jake, she automatically glanced over her shoulder to search for any sign of his pickup truck. He hadn't dropped by to watch them since the Tuesday after her doctor's appointment, when she'd received the startling news that she was pregnant.

A baby. Lilly still couldn't believe it.

There'd been no more cramps since that last incident in her car, and she'd had no spotting like in her previous pregnancies, and every morning when she woke up free of pain, she thanked God with all her heart.

As the baby's father, he has a right to know.

Dr. Paul's words resounded in Lilly's head. Despite that, she'd decided to wait until her fourth month to tell Jake. What would be the point if she lost the baby in the early stages?

You're scared, she told herself.

Yes, she was—scared of telling Jake and, even more, of losing the child who'd already become so precious to her.

"Have you seen Briana?" Jimmy Bob asked when he and Samuel passed the railing where Lilly stood.

"I don't know if she's coming today."

"She said on Wednesday she'd be here after school."

"It's still early. Maybe she's not home yet."

Lilly had only the briefest glimpse of Jimmy Bob's crestfallen face before he and Samuel passed out of range. She worried a little about Jimmy Bob's adoration of Briana, concerned the teenager might unwittingly hurt the young man if he got carried away—as he often did. Jimmy Bob's affection knew no bounds. Lilly made a mental note to keep tabs on the budding friendship, prepared to step in if necessary.

Hearing the rumble of an approaching vehicle, she turned and suffered a moment's confusion at seeing Briana behind the wheel of Jake's truck. Hadn't he come with his daughter? And since when did she drive?

Then, when the truck pulled in to an empty spot, she saw Jake in the front passenger seat, motioning with his hands and giving Briana what appeared to be parking tips. After a moment, they emerged from the truck and headed toward the barn.

All at once, Jake looked Lilly's way.

Instantly, every nerve in her body went on high alert. Her eyes shot down to her waistline. Not that she was showing yet. At seven weeks, her clothes had barely started feeling tight. Still, she was glad her bulky coat completely concealed her upper half.

Loosening her fingers from their death grip on the pipe railing, she reminded herself to stay calm. No reason to assume Jake was here to see her, especially after her cool treatment of him the previous week.

She hadn't meant to be ill-mannered but having only learned about the baby so recently, she'd been in no frame of mind to deal with Jake and the ever-present attraction she felt when they were together.

Her hopes of escaping his attention—if that was indeed what she wanted—were dashed when he changed direction and walked straight toward her.

"They look like they're having fun." He nodded at Jimmy Bob and Samuel, who were making yet another round of the circular pen.

"They are. Very much."

He didn't wait for an invitation, simply stood beside her as if she'd been waiting for him all along. So close, his arm inadvertently brushed hers when he moved. The touch was no more than a whisper but enough to make Lilly keenly aware of his proximity.

Had she ever reacted like this with her ex-husband? Probably. At least in the beginning, when their relationship was new and thrilling. Sadly, they'd forgotten that initial magic in the wake of endless heartbreak and disappointment. Not to mention financial pressure. Had even one small thing gone differently, they might still be married.

But then Lilly wouldn't be pregnant now and hoping against all hope that a different gene combination would swing the odds for a healthy baby in her favor.

Then what? Either way, healthy baby or not, Jake would have a role in her life—a significant one.

"Can any of your clients drive?" Jake asked.

Lilly brushed a lock of wind-blown hair from her eyes, using that as an excuse to mentally regroup before answering. "Some of the older ones may have had a driver's license years ago but I doubt they're allowed on the road. If they were, they'd be capable of independent living and wouldn't need our services."

"I was talking about a tractor here, around the ranch."

"Hmm. I don't know."

"Does he drive?" Jake indicated to Jimmy Bob.

"He hasn't mentioned it, and trust me, Jimmy Bob would." Lilly's involvement in the lives of their clients was restricted to Horizon and what was in their files or told to her by them in the course of a normal work day.

They watched Briana show Samuel how to hold on to the reins properly and sit straight so his shoulders weren't hunched. Though standing and not riding, Jimmy Bob mimicked his friend.

"Do you think he'd like to learn?"

"I'm sure he would. The question is, would his parents consent?" She angled her head slightly to stare fully at Jake, something she'd been avoiding since he'd arrived. "What exactly are you getting at?"

He shifted and either consciously or unconsciously narrowed the space between them. Her awareness of him immediately intensified.

"We're short one hand this week. Little José went home to El Paso for his great-grandparents' fiftieth wedding anniversary. We need someone to drive the tractor and pull the flatbed trailer behind it."

"I…um…" Lilly wavered. Jimmy Bob's Down's syndrome wasn't as severe as most, but his capabilities were still limited.

"A tractor's much easier to operate than a car, and there's no traffic to contend with."

"Someone would have to teach him. Someone with a lot of patience."

"I had Briana in mind." He grinned. "She just got her learner's permit yesterday. I think she'd enjoy being the one giving instructions rather than taking them for a change."

"Is she competent enough? You said she just got her permit."

"That's true but she's been driving ATVs and the tractor around the ranch for years."

Lilly considered her concerns about Jimmy Bob's fondness for Briana. "A staff member would need to supervise them."

"Absolutely."

"And what about our agreement? Driving ranch equipment isn't in it. I'll have to check with our insurance agent about our coverage."

"I'll do the same. And amend our agreement if necessary."

"It's really up to Jimmy Bob's parents."

"Can you call them tomorrow? We're in a bit of a bind and could use his help. The Weather Channel's predicting rain, and we have to move the hay into the barn," Jake added by way of explanation.

"I guess I could."

Lilly was a little baffled by Jake's request. According to the terms of their agreement, the center's clients were obliged to perform whatever reasonable chores he or his manager asked of them. Filling in for an absent hand didn't strike her as particularly unusual. But she couldn't shake the notion that he had something else in mind.

"Seriously, do you really need Jimmy Bob? Don't you have plenty of ranch hands to drive the tractor?"

"Sure, but I thought he might enjoy it. And I want

to set a good example for LeAnne and Kayla. They're both a little…shy about special-needs individuals."

Lilly was touched. "That's very nice of you, Jake."

"If you're not too busy afterward," he said, his tone casual, "I have some ideas I'd like to run by you."

"About our agreement?"

"Yes. And a few other things, too."

"Okay." She remained dubious, not sure how she felt about being alone with Jake.

"We can use Gary's office."

"I need to—"

Her sentence was cut short by a stabbing pain in her lower abdomen.

No! Not here, not now. *Not again!*

A second pain followed the first one. She didn't need to see her face to know all color had drained from it. While not terrible, the cramps were unexpected and alarming and too much like the ones preceding her previous stillbirths. She fought the wave of mild dizziness overcoming her. Only her hand on the railing kept her from swaying. Tears filled her eyes, distorting her vision, and she uttered a small cry.

"Lilly, are you all right?" Jake's arm circled her waist.

"I, ah…" A third cramp robbed her of further speech. Vaguely she realized people were staring.

So, apparently, did Jake.

"Come on. Let's get you out of here."

Jake guided her toward the barn. Lilly didn't object. Without thinking, she leaned into him and rested her cheek on his jacket sleeve. Instantly, she relaxed.

A minute later—or was it several minutes?—a door appeared in front of her.

She glanced around, recognizing the room as an office. By the time he lowered her to a threadbare flowered couch, her pain had diminished, along with the dizziness.

Thankfully this episode, like the one in the parking lot the other day, hadn't lasted long or been too severe.

"You can stop fussing over me," she mumbled. "I'm fine."

"No, you're not." Stretching out her legs, Jake grabbed an old blanket, folded it into a square and positioned it under her raised feet. "You're pale, perspiring and shaking like a leaf."

"Am I?" Lilly touched her forehead and found it damp. "It's a little warm in here."

"Yeah, must be all of fifty-six degrees."

"Really, I'm okay." To prove it, she propped herself up on one elbow. "I had a charley horse in my leg, that's all."

He sat on the edge of one couch cushion and studied her intently. "Are you sure?"

She nodded, unable to verbalize another lie while he was staring at her with that concerned look in her eyes.

"Hey, boss. Is Ms. Russo all right?" Gary Forrester, Jake's manager, stuck his head in the door. "Want me to call 9-1-1?"

"No," Lilly insisted before Jake could answer.

"Give us a minute," Jake told Gary. "And pull my truck around if you don't mind."

"What for?" Lilly asked.

"In case I need to drive you to the emergency room."

"That won't be necessary." What she really wanted was to phone Dr. Paul and get her opinion before being rushed—again—to the emergency room, only to be sent home after several hours with instructions to rest and see her doctor the following day.

She refused, however, to call Dr. Paul in front of Jake.

"Just do it." He nodded at Gary who promptly left, closing the door behind him.

It suddenly occurred to Lilly how small the office was and how close she and Jake were on the couch. Not counting her impulsive hug at the center, they hadn't been this intimate since their dating days.

"I'd like to try sitting up," she said and struggled to get her balance. Jake helped by holding on to her elbow. His strong grasp felt familiar and reassuring. "Thank you," she said once both her feet were settled on the wood floor.

"Can you walk to the truck?"

"I'll be fine in the van."

"You're not going back to the center."

"Truly, I'm okay." She pushed off the couch. "See?"

She stood a total of two seconds before another cramp hit. She cried out, more in surprise than agony, just as Jake caught her and eased her onto the couch again.

"That's it. I'm taking you to the hospital now." He held her protectively, both arms around her.

"I want to call my doctor first."

"Your doctor? Damn it, Lilly, what's wrong?"

The combination of pain and fear and hormones and Jake was too much, and she started to cry. Before she knew it, the words spilled from her mouth. "I'm pregnant."

Jake stiffened, although he didn't withdraw.

Lilly wiped her eyes with the back of her hand. For better or worse, he knew about the baby. As the cramp waned and her breathing returned to normal, she waited for his reaction.

Chapter 5

"How far along are you?"

"About nine weeks."

Jake stared at the winding mountain road and tried to recall a time he and Lilly had failed to use protection. There'd been that one night in the hot tub at his place. He hadn't worried much because she'd sworn up and down the first time they made love that she was on the pill.

"Nine weeks," he repeated and calculated dates. Definitely the night in the hot tub.

Not two weeks later, he'd ended their relationship. Had she known then she was pregnant? Probably not. Something told him she was every bit as shaken by this turn of events as he was.

"When were you planning on telling me?"

He'd insisted on driving her home—would have driven her to Payson and the emergency room if her cramps hadn't subsided. A phone call to her doctor had eased their anxiety. Dr. Paul had prescribed complete bed rest for twenty-four hours and told her to go to the E.R. only if the camps continued or if Lilly began to spot. She further assured them by saying she'd call Lilly at home to check on her later that evening.

Lilly had initially refused Jake's offer of a ride home, citing the center's policy that two staff members had to accompany clients on field trips at all times. He countered by suggesting Briana go with Georgina in the van. Lilly finally relented, but only after additional persuasion by Jake and Georgina.

He and Lilly had spent the first half of the twenty-minute drive in complete silence. Jake had needed the quiet to recover from his initial shock. Even now he wasn't entirely ready to talk, but he knew they should.

"To be honest," Lilly said, her face toward the passenger window, "I was going to wait until I reached my fourth month, when I started showing. Around the middle of January."

"January!"

"The chance of a miscarriage lessens after the first trimester. If I…if anything happened—"

"You had no right to keep this from me." He hadn't meant to snap and instantly regretted his tone. "I'm sorry. I'm still trying to cope with…the news."

The baby. Why couldn't he say the words?

Because he'd just learned that he was going to be a father again.

"I don't blame you for being angry." She abandoned the passing scenery to look at him. "I didn't deceive you intentionally. I really was on the pill and I'm as shocked as you are."

"I'm not angry. Just upset. You should've told me from the start."

"I practically did. I've only known about it for the past two weeks."

"Come on. You said it yourself. If not for your cramps, we wouldn't be having this conversation until January."

She didn't disagree.

"Are you planning on keeping the baby?" he asked after a moment.

"Yes."

"I'll help." He wasn't sure what he could do; they had a lot of decisions to make. But he'd be there for Lilly and their child, before and after the birth. "If you need money—"

"At this point, money isn't the issue. It's whether or not I can carry to term." Her eyes suddenly misted with tears. "Or how long the baby will survive after the birth."

"Why wouldn't the baby survive?"

"The other three didn't."

Jake's hands froze on the wheel. He quickly corrected his steering when the passenger-side tires went off the road and onto gravel. "You've been pregnant before?"

She sniffed and dabbed at her eyes with the back of her hand. "The first two babies were stillborn, one at five and a half months and the other at seven. A blessing in disguise. At least that's what well-meaning people told me. My son, Evan, lived. His deformities weren't quite as severe as his siblings. But the machines could only do so much, and he didn't reach his first birthday."

"Good God, Lilly. I'm so sorry." She'd told him about her former marriage. Not a single mention, however, of stillbirths or a son. "Can I ask what was wrong with him?"

"All three of my children had a trisomy disorder. Most of their major organs didn't work right or, in some cases, were missing. Their limbs were also shrunken and their heads misshapen from tumors." Her voice became flat and robotic, as if she was trying to distance herself from what she was saying. "The cause was a chromosomal abnormality. Faulty DNA. Mine, to be specific. My chances of having a healthy baby are supposedly fifty-fifty. So far the odds haven't been in my favor."

"That must've been really hard on you." He winced at his lame and grossly inadequate response.

Lilly didn't seem to notice. Or maybe she'd already heard the same thing a thousand times before.

"I didn't plan to ever get pregnant again," she said sadly. "I went so far as to schedule the procedure to have my tubes tied, but chickened out at the last minute."

"Maybe this time you'll get lucky."

She turned back to the window. "It's easy for people who have healthy children to say that."

"You're right. I was thoughtless. The fact is, I can't begin to imagine what you've had to endure or how I'd act in your shoes."

She didn't respond, and they drove the remaining three miles to Lilly's house in silence. Jake wasn't finished talking but didn't pressure her to continue. He figured they both could use a break to regroup before the next round.

"I don't suppose you'd leave if I told you this isn't a good time," she said at the front door of her house.

"I would if you insisted—and if you promised to rest." Jake had walked her from his truck, observing her carefully for any sign of more cramps. There'd been none, but he was still cautious, not wanting another scare. "How are you feeling?"

"Better." She fished a ring of keys from her purse and unlocked the door.

"Has this happened before?" He accompanied her inside. "The cramps, I mean."

"Last week. And with my previous pregnancies." She choked on the word.

Jake went to her, put an arm around her shoulders and led her to the living room couch, where he arranged the pillows. "Lie down. I'll get you some water."

She nodded and did as he told her.

He knew his way around Lilly's kitchen, having visited her house during the time they'd dated. Drinking glasses were kept in the cupboard to the left of the sink. He removed two and filled them with ice and water. Once that was done, he paused. Five seconds stretched into thirty, then sixty.

There was no reason not to return to Lilly. Yet somehow he couldn't bring himself to leave the kitchen. Not until he'd sorted through some of what he was feeling.

She was having a baby. *His* baby. And from what she'd told him, one who might not be born normal—if at all. Jake had fathered three daughters, and while his ex-wife, Ellen, had fretted endlessly, he hadn't given potential complications of the pregnancies more than a moment's thought.

He remembered lying in bed one night just before Briana was born, his hand on Ellen's stomach. She'd asked him if he would still love their child even if he or she was born with something wrong. He'd answered yes, giving her the reassurance she needed, never really considering the reality of "something wrong." Those kinds of tragedies happened to other people, not him.

Now he'd have to consider it.

He'd also have to decide what to do if the baby *was* born normal.

Jake pushed away from the counter and took the glasses of water to the living room. Regardless of the baby's health, he and Lilly were in this together. Possibly for the rest of their lives.

He paused at the archway leading to the living room, brought to a halt by his sudden worry. His daughters were already having trouble coping with a stepfather. How would they feel about a new sibling? One who might be born with a chromosomal abnormality.

"I'd like to go with you to the doctor tomorrow."

Lilly braced a hand on the couch cushion and sat up straight. Surprise gave her voice an edge. "You don't have to do that. It's just a routine examination."

Jake handed her the glass of water before sitting down on the couch, which put them in close proximity. *Too* close.

"I want to. I'm the baby's father, and I have a responsibility to go with you."

"There really isn't much need at this stage." She took a sip of water and set the glass on the side table before her trembling fingers could give her away. Why hadn't she insisted he leave when they were standing outside her door?

"No need because you might lose the baby?" he asked, crossing his legs.

"Yes, that's part of it."

"Even more reason for me to be there."

She was no stranger to his stubbornness, having encountered it before. Those occasions, however, had involved the ranch or center's business, not her *personal* business.

"If your cramps return or the news isn't good," he said, "you don't want to be alone. You won't want to drive yourself home."

She reluctantly conceded that his argument had merit, and in all fairness, she couldn't refuse him. Like it or not, he had certain rights, along with duties and obligations. They'd have to decide on those, as well.

Pressing a palm to her cheek, she closed her eyes. It was too soon. Everything was happening too fast. She'd believed she'd have more time and more answers before informing Jake of her pregnancy. If only she could take back the last couple of hours...

"Are you okay?"

"Fine," she said and tried for a casual smile. "I just hate inconveniencing you."

"No problem. I can rearrange my schedule."

"Why not wait until later when I have an ultrasound?"

The instant she made the suggestion, she regretted it. Hadn't she told Dr. Paul no tests? Now she was committed. And worse, Jake would be in the exam room, viewing the monitor along with her. What if Dr. Paul found something irregular or of concern? Jake would ask questions, become involved, think he was entitled to participate in any and all decisions. Lilly wasn't sure she could handle bad news and his take-charge attitude.

God forbid he'd want her to terminate the pregnancy. He hadn't mentioned abortion so far, but maybe that was because he hadn't thought of it yet. Dr. Paul would likely bring up that option if the ultrasound indicated any...irregularities. Lilly's other doctors had.

So be it. Jake would have no more luck convincing her to end her pregnancy than her ex-husband had.

"I know about doctor visits and that they can be emotional," he said with a compassion she hadn't expected. "Remember, I have three daughters. I went with Ellen to the doctor's quite a few times."

Emotional didn't begin to describe Lilly's appointments. "Your ex-wife's pregnancies were all normal. Mine weren't."

"I'd like to talk with your doctor if I can."

She nearly fell off the couch. "About what?"

"Your genetic problems. The baby's health."

"Why?" Alarm stiffened her spine, and her face felt hot. "I'll tell you everything you need to know."

Wrong. She'd tell him only what she wanted him to hear and judging by the narrowing of his eyes, he'd guessed as much.

"What's really bothering you, Lilly? Surely your ex-husband went to the doctor with you."

Husband. Jake's question hit the nail square on the head. They weren't married. While he had rights when it came to the baby, he didn't where *she* was concerned, and she wasn't about to let him coerce her into doing something she didn't want to do, like Brad had.

"Everything's moving a little fast for me."

"For me, too."

"It's not the same." She shook her head. "For one thing, we aren't dating anymore."

"Lots of unattached couples have babies together and make it work."

"We aren't a typical couple experiencing a typical pregnancy."

"That's true," he said after a moment. "And you have every reason not to trust me. I handled our breakup badly. But I promise you I won't abandon you or this child. Regardless of…the circumstances."

Lilly huddled in the corner of the couch. Jake could be a steamroller when he made up his mind about something, and she wasn't about to let him into her life again, at least not anymore than necessary. He'd already walked out on her once when the situation between them was a whole lot less complicated. For all she knew, he might do it again, and she'd had her fill of men leaving her when the going got tough.

He reached for her hand. She hadn't realized how cold her fingers were until he wrapped them in his much warmer ones, and her instinct to pull away faded.

"What time is your appointment tomorrow?" He stroked the inside of her wrist with his thumb. It was something he'd done frequently when they were dating.

She remained mute, trying to resist the familiar sensations his touch evoked.

"Will you tell me if I promise to keep my mouth shut during the visit?"

"When have you ever done that?"

Though she'd been mostly serious, he laughed. "It won't be easy. But I'm a man of my word." He sobered, and his grip on her fingers tightened.

"True." She remembered the last promise he'd made to her. It was in this very room, on the night he broke up with her.

I won't make things any harder than they have to be by beating around the bush.

Jake had gotten right to the point, and she'd cried for three days afterward. If not for the unexpected gift of an old mule, she wouldn't have spoken to him for months. Neither would she be facing the dilemma of what to do about her appointment with Dr. Paul tomorrow.

"I'll stay in the waiting room during your exam," he said.

She frowned, not quite believing him. "I thought you wanted to talk to my doctor."

"I'm willing to hold off until you feel more comfortable about it." He resumed his mesmerizing stroking of her wrist.

Lilly supposed that if she stood her ground, she could put Jake off temporarily, though not indefinitely. Payson wasn't a large town, and there was only a handful of ob/gyns. He'd heard her mention Dr. Paul by name. Locating her office would be easy enough. It was even possible Ellen had gone to Dr. Paul, too. With his stubborn streak, she wouldn't put it past him to camp out in the parking lot until she arrived for an appointment and then follow her inside.

"Okay," she heard herself agreeing. "You can come, but only if you stay in the waiting room."

He smiled. "Deal."

No, Lilly thought. *Test.*

If he could contain his impulse to take charge and take over, if he stuck to the rules they both agreed to, then maybe they had a chance of being successful co-parents.

"What time is your appointment?" He took out his PDA.

"One-fifteen at the Payson Physicians Plaza. Suite two thousand and three."

"Would you like to stop for lunch on the way?"

"No, thanks." Between her morning sickness and nerves, she doubted she'd be able to eat.

"I'll pick you up at work."

"Fine," she said, biting her lower lip and hoping she didn't regret her decision.

"So, what did the doctor say?"

Jake leaned forward, his forearms balanced on the table. He'd spoken softly, Lilly presumed, so the few nearby diners and waitresses didn't hear him.

"Everything appears normal," she answered in an equally soft voice.

"What about the cramps and bleeding?"

"She says that's not uncommon in the first trimester. A woman's body goes through a lot of changes during pregnancy, and..." Lilly tried to recall exactly how Dr. Paul had put it. "Sometimes the changes cause side effects."

"But you're okay? And the baby's okay?"

"Yes." *For now.*

She twirled her glass of milk, noticing the faint trail of condensation it left on the scratched Formica. When he'd learned she'd skipped lunch, he'd insisted on taking her to the Hilltop Café—another of his tenants in the same small complex as Horizon and his aunt's antique shop—so she could have a quick bite before returning to work. Her first instinct had been to refuse, but then she thought better of it and ordered a small chef's salad to go with her milk. Skipping meals wasn't good for the baby or her own health and as often as not, eating settled her chronic nausea.

"Is that all she said?" Jake took a bite of the key lime pie he'd ordered with his iced tea.

"I'm supposed to take it easy for the next few weeks. Not lift heavy objects and rest as much as possible."

"Why don't I arrange for someone to clean your house? I can have one of the maids from the ranch come over."

"That's not necessary." The worry of being steamrolled returned, and Lilly's defenses shot up. "I can still lift a dust cloth and push a broom."

"Okay." The staccato pinging of fork tines on his now-empty plate left no doubt that Jake would be bringing up the subject again.

Trying to look at the situation from a different perspective, Lilly supposed his constant attempts to take charge could be construed as kindness. Maybe she was overreacting, looking for ulterior motives that weren't there. After all, Jake was a businessman, used to making decisions and delegating tasks. Sometimes he carried those same traits into other areas of his life.

"Call me if you need anything."

"I will." Lilly meant what she'd said.

If she truly needed help and couldn't get it elsewhere, she'd ask Jake. While she had friends in Payson, none of them possessed Jake's resources or had as much of a stake in her welfare. Her family was in Albuquerque. She'd left them and her closest friends and acquaintances when her ex-husband's employer transferred him to their Phoenix office seven years ago. After almost five years in Phoenix and two in Payson, she hadn't connected with anyone the way she had with Jake. She'd even contemplated a future with him.

Now, it seemed, she had one. Just not the one she'd envisioned.

"I really should get back to work." She wiped her hands on her napkin and set it aside. "Thanks for lunch."

"When's your next doctor's appointment?"

"Two weeks from today. Same time. You don't have to drive me," she added with what she hoped was firm insistence.

"I'd like to, if you don't mind."

He didn't say, "And I want to come into the exam room with you and meet your doctor," but she sensed it was on the tip of his tongue.

"All right," she said, deciding to pick her battles. Besides, having Jake along wasn't nearly the hardship she'd expected. He'd been considerate and sweet— when he wasn't trying to boss her around. Opening doors for her. Putting her at ease with small talk. Seeing to it that she ate.

"I want to be an involved father, Lilly. Before *and* after the baby is born."

"Will you still feel like that if this child has the same…birth defects as Evan?" She shuddered, remembering the horror and revulsion in her ex-husband's eyes. "Brad refused to hold Evan or even touch his tiny hand."

"I'm not like him," Jake said resolutely.

"Forgive me for not having complete faith in you. Until you've sat beside an isolette in a neonatal intensive care unit and watched your child struggle for every breath, praying he's going to survive his latest surgery and yet terrified about what kind of life he'll have if he does, you can't understand."

"No, you're right. The closest I've come to experiencing anything like that was when my sister died."

"Sorry." Lilly instantly regretted her hasty assumptions. "I'd forgotten about Hailey."

Jake's younger sister had lost her life in a riding accident several years earlier. She'd survived the fall long enough to make it to the hospital, lived long enough for her family to arrive at her bedside. Jake had told Lilly about his sister's tragic death the night they'd made love in the hot tub. The same night she'd gotten pregnant.

"She suffered such extensive brain damage that if she'd lived she wouldn't have been the same." His voice grew rough, and his gaze turned inward. "I hate to admit that after hearing the doctors' prognosis, I was almost relieved when she didn't make it. For her sake, not mine. Hailey would never have wanted to live out her life in a vegetative state, hooked up to machines and tubes that breathed and ate and went to the bathroom for her."

How well Lilly knew those machines and tubes.

Had she misjudged Jake? Been too hard on him? Was it possible that he, of all people, understood a little of what she'd been through and had a heart open enough to welcome a child like Evan?

When they were done eating, Jake paid the bill, and they left.

"You don't have to walk me to work," Lilly said outside the entrance.

He took her elbow and guided her down the walkway in front of the stores, their windows already decorated for the holidays. "It's a nice afternoon, and I can use the exercise after that pie."

Lilly smiled her first genuine smile all day. Whatever Jake did to stay fit worked like a charm. She'd seen every inch of him, skimming her fingers along the smooth ridges of his honed muscles, and knew him to be in great shape. He was one of those people who could eat ten pieces of pie every day and not gain an ounce.

"Remember, call if you need anything." They both hesitated outside the door to the center.

"Thanks. Again."

"Or if you just want to talk. You don't need a reason."

"Um, okay."

Lilly wasn't sure what to do next. Should she shake his hand? Hug him? Turn around and head to her office? He didn't leave, and the awkward minute lengthened into two.

"Daddy, Daddy!"

Jake's two youngest daughters came racing down the sidewalk, straight for him and Lilly.

"Hey, what are you doing here?" He opened his arms, and the girls flew into them.

"Mommy's dropping us off at Aunt Millie's store."

"Oh?" Jake glanced up the walkway.

So did Lilly. Her hand automatically went to her stomach, and she was infinitely glad not to be showing yet.

Jake's ex-wife exited a fire-engine red Mustang convertible and made her way toward them, heels clicking on the concrete.

"Jake. I didn't realize you'd be here." The smile she flashed Lilly was brief and disinterested. "Do you mind watching the girls for a few minutes? I was going to leave them with Millie while I did some shopping but I'm sure they'd rather stay with you."

"Not at all. I can take them home, too, if you want."

"That would be great."

"Where's Briana?"

"Some after-school function. I'll pick her up when I'm done." Ellen waved a hand before starting off. "See you later."

Lilly allowed herself to breathe again.

The girls hung on Jake's coat sleeves. "Can we go to the pet shop?" the youngest one asked. The store was a few doors down from Horizon.

"In a few minutes. Girls, do you remember Ms. Russo? You met her at the barbeque a while back." He indicated Lilly, and they nodded solemnly.

"Nice to see you again," Lilly said and winked. Jake was truly fortunate; his girls were charming.

"This is where Ms. Russo works." He pointed to the center's front door. "She's the administrator."

LeAnne examined the sign in the window, her brow furrowed in concentration, and tried to sound out the words. "The Hor-i-z-zon…"

"The Horizon Adult Day Care Center," Jake supplied.

LeAnne's eyes widened. "What's that?"

"Kind of like the summer program you and your sister go to. Only it's for grown-ups."

LeAnne and Kayla turned to each other, then burst into giggles. "Grown-ups don't need day care."

"Well, some do." Jake took the girls' hands. "Would you like to go inside and see for yourself?"

"Can we?" Kayla seemed wary but intrigued.

LeAnne, on the other hand, was reserved. "Is this where the funny people who come to the ranch are?"

"They're not funny, LeAnne."

"Yes, they are." She peered up at her father. "They make me feel weird."

Jake smiled apologetically. "Sorry…"

"Don't worry about it." Lilly wasn't offended by LeAnne's comment. Special-needs adults could be intimidating to young children.

"Mr. Tucker!" The door to the center flew open, and Jimmy Bob landed outside, a bundle of unconstrained excitement. "I saw you through the window. Why didn't you come inside?"

Lilly stepped sideways, having experienced the

force of Jimmy Bob's enthusiasm before. She needn't have bothered; she wasn't the young man's target. He rushed up to Jake and, although he was a good head shorter, enveloped him in a fierce bear hug.

"Thank you, thank you, Mr. Tucker, for Big Ben." Jimmy Bob buried his face in the front of Jake's jacket. "We love him so much."

"You're welcome." Jake awkwardly patted Jimmy Bob's back.

Lilly attempted to come to the rescue. "Jimmy Bob, you know you aren't supposed to be outside the center unless there's a staff member with you."

He stepped back from Jake, his jaw set in the determined line Lilly had come to recognize as meaning business. "*You're* a staff member."

He was, of course, right.

Georgina opened the door and sighed. "Jimmy Bob."

"I wanna stay." He hunched his shoulders.

"You can't, sweetie." Lilly took his arm. "Mr. Tucker and his daughters are leaving."

Jimmy Bob refused to budge. He'd spotted Kayla and LeAnne and stood rooted in place, grinning widely. "Hi! What's your names? Mine's Jimmy Bob. I come here almost every day."

The girls were rooted in place, too, but for different reasons, Lilly suspected. She recognized the trepidation in their small faces, LeAnne's especially. Jimmy Bob's effusiveness, though well-meaning, could be overwhelming.

"Daddy, I want to go." LeAnne yanked on her father's hand. "Now."

Kayla appeared a little less nervous than her sister but still uncertain.

"Girls," Jake reprimanded softly. "Don't be rude."

"It's all right. Let's go, Jimmy Bob." This time Lilly wasn't taking no for an answer.

"Is Briana your sister? She's my friend." Jimmy Bob ignored Lilly and leaned down to the girls' level. "Do you wanna be my friend, too?"

LeAnne cowered and backed away until she was half-hidden behind her father.

"Don't be afraid of me." Jimmy Bob's smile crumpled. "I won't hurt you." His disappointment was heart-wrenching.

"Come on, girls," Jake coaxed. "Be nice."

Lilly shook her head. "It's better if you don't force it."

"That's enough, big guy." Georgina took charge of the situation before it worsened and pulled on one of Jimmy Bob's arms. Lilly aided by pushing on the other and together they managed to get him inside.

"I am really sorry," Jake said, gesturing at his daughters. "They're not as comfortable around the center's clients as their sister is."

"It's okay. Really." Lilly stood in the doorway, glancing over her shoulder at Jimmy Bob and Georgina. "I'll see you later," she told him, suddenly anxious to get away. "Bye, girls." She let the door close.

She went directly to her office, her earlier optimism dwindling.

Jake and his oldest daughter, Briana, might very well be capable of welcoming a child like Evan but clearly the same couldn't be said of his other girls. Not that Lilly blamed them.

Sitting at her desk, she scolded herself for her short-sightedness. She'd been so caught up in herself and Jake, she'd failed to consider the rest of his family and their reactions to a possible special-needs baby. Until today.

Chapter 6

Jake's personal assistant, Alice, poked her head around the corner of his office door. "Your cousin Carolina is here. She wants to know if you have a few minutes for her."

"Sure. I'm expecting a call from Howard," he said, referring to the family trust attorney. "Go ahead and put him through when he phones."

Alice retreated and a moment later, Carolina breezed into the office.

"Hey." She sat in one of the visitor's chairs, reaching for a candy from the dish Jake kept on his desk. Tall, slim and with the trademark Tucker hazel eyes, she was the envy of her three sisters because of her ability to eat whatever she wanted and never have it show.

"What's going on?" Jake took a break from the maintenance reports he'd been reviewing and leaned back in his chair.

"I just came from the kitchen. Mom asked me to drop by."

"What's wrong?" Her mother, Jake's aunt, was also the ranch's wedding coordinator and worked closely with the kitchen staff.

"Nothing we weren't expecting. Eventually." Carolina shrugged. "Olivia's retiring."

"She's threatened that before."

"This time she's serious. Her husband gave his notice at the plant. Says they're boarding up the house and taking a three-month vacation to visit their kids in El Paso and Austin, even if he has to hog-tie her to the front seat of their motor home."

"I see."

Bear Creek Ranch's kitchen manager had been employed by the Tuckers since Jake was in the third grade. All during his teens, he'd rotated at different jobs, learning the family business from the ground up. Olivia had supervised him during his stint as a dishwasher and cook's helper. He might have been the owner's son, but she'd cut him no slack, instilling in him a work ethic he didn't appreciate until he was much older and had taken over the management of Bear Creek Ranch from his father.

"What are you going to do about it?" Carolina asked. "Olivia practically runs that dining hall single-handed."

"There's nothing I can do. She's been talking

about retiring for months." In hindsight, he should have started the recruitment process by now. Lilly's pregnancy had distracted him—from that and a lot of other things.

"You don't seem too broken up about this."

"I'll miss Olivia, of course. We all will. But I'm sure there's a qualified candidate out there."

"You'd better act fast. Olivia's husband's giving her until the end of January. That's just weeks away."

Carolina was the only person, besides his parents and Aunt Millie, who could order Jake around. If any of his employees or other family members so much as tried, they'd either be out of a job or put soundly in their place. Carolina was an exception because she'd filled the void left after his sister's death.

"I'll get Alice right on it." Jake didn't make a move to pick up the intercom.

Carolina studied him critically. "You care to tell me what's really bothering you? Or would you rather go on pretending that everything's fine?"

"Everything is fine."

"Please." His cousin sent him her I'm-not-buying-what-you're-selling look. "You've been out of sorts for two or three weeks now, and I'm starting to worry."

He thought for a moment and nodded. It was time he confided in someone about Lilly's pregnancy. Keeping everything inside was ruining his appetite, his sleep at night and his concentration. He didn't always appreciate Carolina's strong opinions, and they'd certainly had their share of disagreements, but she could also be a good listener, and he needed that right now.

"How much time do you have?"

"I'm going out, but not until later."

"A date?"

Carolina smiled coyly.

"Anyone I know?"

"Kevin Ward from the station."

Like most of the family, Carolina divided her days between the ranch and an outside job. She worked part-time as a roving reporter for Payson's second largest radio station, having landed the job seven months earlier when the station conducted a live broadcast from the ranch.

"Isn't he a little old for you?"

"He's forty-seven," she said with the air of someone who regularly dated men ten years her junior and twenty years her senior. "Why? What difference does it make?"

"None, as long as you're happy."

Jake had given up on his social-butterfly cousin years ago. In that regard, they were polar opposites. Carolina loved the single life, while he'd married young and begun having children almost immediately. Had Ellen not strayed, he'd probably still be married.

And Lilly wouldn't be pregnant now. At least not with his child.

A surge of excitement halted him in his tracks. He was going to be a father again. Jake had been so wrapped up in the complications of Lilly's pregnancy and their relationship—past and present—he'd forgotten about the thrill of impending fatherhood. In that instant, his perspective, along with his attitude, changed.

"You okay?" Carolina asked.

"Yeah. I just remembered something."

"Must've been important. You were seriously gone for a minute there."

He smiled. "It was important."

Carolina snatched another candy from the dish. "So, is it woman troubles that have you down?"

"What makes you say that?"

She laughed good-naturedly. "Let's face it, Jake, you're surrounded by them. Three daughters, an ex-wife, a mother, an aunt and four cousins," she ended, including herself and her three sisters. "I don't know how you and your dad stand it."

"We've developed a high tolerance," he answered jokingly.

"The only thing you don't have is a girlfriend— well, you did, but you blew it."

He didn't respond.

"Wait a minute." She put down the partially un-wrapped candy. "Did something happen that I don't know about?"

Jake inhaled deeply before speaking. "Lilly's pregnant."

"Wow!" Carolina's mouth hung open for a good five seconds. "You're not kidding."

"No, I'm not. She's about twelve weeks along. I've known for the last three."

"I guess that explains your recent mood."

"Sorry to be so irritable."

"Why haven't you said anything?" Carolina still looked shocked.

"Two reasons. Lilly isn't ready to make an announcement. So, no talking to anyone." He leveled a warning finger at her. "And I didn't want the girls to find out. Not until I was ready to tell them. They're already dealing with so much, what with the divorce and Ellen getting married next month." Briana had informed him recently in no uncertain terms that she refused to be her mother's maid of honor.

"Are you okay with being a dad again?"

"Sure."

"Is that hesitation I hear in your voice?"

Jake explained about Lilly's previous pregnancies, her son, Evan, and the end of her marriage.

"Wow!" Carolina repeated, then picked up the candy and popped it in her mouth. "The hell with my date tonight."

"Hey, don't cancel on my account."

"Trust me, this is more important." For several minutes, Jake answered her questions. When they were done, she asked, "Can I be honest without you getting offended?"

"When aren't you honest?"

"This is serious."

"All right." He sobered.

She paused, then proceeded cautiously. "Losing the baby would be hard. I'm not minimizing that, so please don't take this the wrong way."

"I'll try." He was starting to worry.

"But have you really considered the ramifications of having a severely handicapped child?"

"Well...I admit my knowledge is limited."

"It won't be easy."

"I was thinking about Grandpa Walter the other day and everything we had to go through with him. We managed, didn't we?"

"Oh, Jake. You can't compare taking care of him to taking care of a gravely ill child who depends on machines to survive. Lilly's husband couldn't deal with it, and they were in love."

"I have...feelings for her."

"You dated for six weeks. They were *married.*"

Jake remained silent. He hated it when his cousin found the holes in his arguments.

"The pressure is incredible," she went on. "You just told me her husband could hardly bring himself to hold his own child. Will you be different?"

"Yes!"

"What about your girls?"

He remembered that day at the center when Jimmy Bob had tried to make friends with Kayla and LeAnne and what a disaster that had been. Doubts crept in, and he pushed away from his desk. He'd have to work harder at convincing his youngest daughters that people with special needs were no different than everyone else.

"Sorry to upset you," Carolina said.

"It's okay. I need to face reality."

She shook her head. "Your parents will freak when you tell them."

Jake had been concentrating on his daughters and not his parents. He rubbed the back of his neck, the muscles there taut and aching.

"Is there anything I can do to help?"

"Thanks. I'll let you know if and when. Lilly and I need to make some decisions before I say anything."

"Not that I'm any kind of expert in these matters, but I don't think you should wait too long."

"I agree, but it's been hard pinning her down." He thought about their appointment at Dr. Paul's office last week, his second time accompanying Lilly. "She dodges every question I ask about the baby or our future together and insists on doing nothing until she's a lot farther along."

"I don't blame her," Carolina said. "From what you've told me, her pregnancy hasn't been easy so far. She must be afraid of losing the baby."

"And afraid I'll abandon her."

"You wouldn't do that!"

"I did once before."

"You broke up. That happens to couples. And you didn't know she was pregnant."

"She doesn't trust me to stick with her for the long haul. Especially if the baby's born with the same birth defects as the others."

"What about tests? Can't the doctors predict these things?"

"She mentioned having an ultrasound later on."

"Maybe you'll get some answers then."

"I hope so." Jake did want answers and prayed the news would be good.

"What about health insurance? Our group plan has restrictions."

"Good question." And another concern to add to Jake's growing list. He could wind up paying size-able out-of-pocket expenses, though it was a respon-sibility he was more than willing to assume. "Lilly probably has insurance, too, through the center. I'll have to figure out how to ask her without making her defensive."

Carolina's expression softened. "I'm sure every-thing will be fine. How can it not be with you as the dad?"

He smiled. "There are times I'm kind of excited about being a dad again."

"And who knows? You could have a son."

"Yeah." His smile widened.

He was about to suggest Carolina leave to get ready for her date when his intercom buzzed.

"That's Howard. I've been expecting his call." He picked up the receiver. "Yes, Alice."

"Lilly Russo just called. She said to tell you she's at the hospital emergency room and needs you to come right away."

Jake bolted out from behind his desk, grabbing his keys from the credenza on his way to the door.

"What's wrong?" Carolina chased after him.

"Alice will tell you."

He ran to the parking lot and climbed into the clos-est vehicle, which happened to be one of the old main-tenance trucks, and drove it straight through to Payson without stopping.

* * *

Lilly gave a start when the privacy curtain surrounding her hospital gurney was swept aside. Jake entered the small treatment area where she'd spent the last twenty-five minutes, supposedly resting but in reality going slowly crazy. She'd spent nearly as long in the waiting room out front and then again at the counter being admitted.

"You came," she blurted, fighting to contain her emotions.

"Are you okay?" He grabbed her hands, wrapping his strong fingers around them.

"Better." She laid her head back and closed her eyes. "The cramps have stopped, and the bleeding's a lot lighter."

"Bleeding? Has that happened before?"

"Yes, with all my previous pregnancies."

Hospital emergency rooms were scary and uncomfortable. The relief Lilly felt at seeing Jake was enormous. And disconcerting. He was competent and capable and exuded confidence. She supposed it was natural for her to rely on him and to call him first in this crisis. Most of his family and employees would do the same. But she didn't want to be like them, accepting his help and his presence in her life without question.

Not yet.

He bent to kiss the top of her head. Her eyes flew open and a sob escaped her lips. Embarrassed at her outburst, she turned her head.

"Shh." He pushed a lock of hair from her face. "Everything's going to be fine."

"I wish I knew that for sure."

Lilly had contacted the ranch looking for Jake in a moment of pure terror, when the cramps and bleeding were at their worst. Once the danger seemed to have passed, she began to regret her impulsiveness. Jake had a history of running scared when she made assumptions about their relationship and placed too many expectations on him.

She'd seriously contemplated retrieving her cell phone from her purse to call him back. She might have done it, too, if not for the strict instructions she'd been given to lie still and not strain herself. But now that Jake was here, comforting and reassuring her with warm, soft strokes of his fingertips, she was glad she'd phoned him in the first place, glad to have someone with her.

"What did Dr. Paul say?" He pulled a metal chair closer to the gurney and sat down. "Has she been in to see you?"

"Not yet. She's on her way. A lab technician came by a little while ago and drew blood." Her glance traveled to the bandage on the inside of her elbow, and she slipped her arm underneath the blanket. Why were emergency rooms always so damn cold?

"Hi, there."

The same friendly nurse who'd attended to Lilly earlier appeared from behind the curtain. She'd asked a hundred questions during the brief exam. Questions like, when did the cramps start? How severe were they? Do you feel dizzy or faint?

And the worst one of all, have you previously miscarried or lost a baby?

But the question the nurse asked now was even more disconcerting. "Are you ready to take a ride?"

"Where to?" Lilly attempted to sit up.

Jake restrained her by laying a hand on her arm.

"Down the hall a bit," the nurse said. "Your doctor just arrived, and she's ordered an ultrasound." The nurse dropped the clipboard she'd been carrying onto the gurney by Lilly's feet and raised the side rails. Straightening, she showered Jake with a thousand-watt smile. "Is this your husband?"

"Ah...no."

"I'm the baby's father," Jake said, standing.

"Then you'll want to come along." The nurse flipped a lever to release the brake.

Lilly fought an overpowering sense of disorientation and loss of control. Everything was moving so fast. Again. She didn't want any tests and had told Dr. Paul as much. Now, it seemed she was having one and Jake would be accompanying her. He might suggest terminating the pregnancy if the results indicated an abnormality, and she couldn't do that. Nor did she want to go through another pregnancy like her second, knowing all along her baby's chances of surviving were nil. Some might say that wasn't a very realistic attitude, but hope was the only thing that kept her going.

"Where's Dr. Paul? I need to talk to her first," Lilly

protested when the nurse positioned herself behind the gurney and began to push.

"She's signing the necessary paperwork and will be here in a minute."

Lilly remembered the last series of ultrasounds she'd undergone and the images that had appeared on the screen. She could still hear the "tap-tap" of the doctor's pencil as he pointed out the deformities to her and her ex-husband, Brad. Seeing similar images again today, learning the baby wasn't normal and might not survive, would devastate her.

No telling what it would do to Jake.

"Wait!"

"I know you're afraid. But I'm here with you." His voice, so close to her ear, was soothing, as if he could make everything okay just by saying so.

"What if the ultrasound shows…" She couldn't say the word.

"What if it doesn't?"

"I realize I'm being unreasonable but I don't want to…can't go through what I did before. I don't want to know that I'm carrying a damaged baby. I need to have hope."

"An ultrasound can give you that hope."

"It can also destroy it."

"Whatever it shows, we're in this together, Lilly."

Oddly enough, his reassurances worked, and she felt calmed.

He walked beside her down the hall. Lilly's ex-husband hadn't done that. Neither had he shielded her from the too-bright fluorescent lights, or touched her arm to let her know she wasn't alone in this ordeal. She'd needed Brad to be there. To share her misery and grief. To pray for a miracle. To lend his shoulder to cry on when the doctor delivered the dismal prognosis. Instead, he'd withdrawn and borne his suffering all by himself, leaving her to do the same.

She observed Jake through lowered lids. He looked fearless and strong—like he could cope with whatever came next.

Little did he know. He'd fathered three healthy children and had no idea what could be waiting for them on the other side of the door.

Chapter 7

It seemed the moment they entered the ultrasound room, everything moved at superspeed. The nurse prepped Lilly for the procedure, chatting constantly, mostly with Jake. Lilly's cheeks flamed when the nurse lowered her blanket and arranged her gown. Her embarrassment mystified and annoyed her. Jake had seen her wearing far less and had let her know with softly murmured words and exquisite touches how much he liked and appreciated her naked form.

When the nurse turned her back, Lilly tugged at the hem of her gown. The extra inch or two of modesty eased a bit of her tension but not for long. Her anxiety went through the roof when the door opened and Dr. Paul entered, her street clothes visible beneath a lab coat and those funny little paper slippers covering her shoes. She greeted Lilly and reached for the clipboard the nurse had set on the counter.

"I'm guessing you're the baby's father," Dr. Paul said to Jake while flipping pages.

"Yes, ma'am."

She nodded, her lips pursed in concentration. "How are you doing, Lilly?" She handed the clipboard to the nurse, who dimmed the overhead lights, and then faded into a corner.

Jake stood by Lilly's left shoulder, his position giving him an unobstructed view of the monitor screen.

"I'm doing much better," she told Dr. Paul. "The bleeding and cramps have stopped. There's probably no need for an ultrasound."

Dr. Paul lifted the blanket covering Lilly's lower half. Though the exam was conducted discreetly and efficiently, she suffered another bout of acute embarrassment. She didn't relax until Dr. Paul pulled the blanket back into place.

"I understand your concerns, Lilly, but we really should see what's going on with you. If only to rule out certain things like ectopic pregnancy."

Everything Dr. Paul said made sense, and Lilly was certain it was in her own and the baby's best interest. Her heart, however, still hadn't healed from her previous losses and cried out, "Not yet."

Jake's touch, soft and gentle on her shoulder, lent her courage.

"Nothing invasive," she insisted. "I won't risk a miscarriage."

"We'll use an abdominal probe. I will, however,

ask you to reconsider if the test shows anything out of the ordinary."

Lilly involuntarily gasped when Dr. Paul applied a lubricating gel to her abdomen. The nurse turned on the ultrasound machine, and the screen came to life.

"This might feel a little cold." Dr. Paul delivered the warning a mere second before the probe came to rest on the tiny rise of Lilly's exposed belly.

She tensed, every muscle in her body turning to stone. As much as she dreaded hearing bad news, she couldn't take her eyes off the screen. A swirling black, white and gray image appeared. Dr. Paul moved the probe, and the image gradually came into focus.

"There we go," she said, her tone warm and a little excited. "Mom and Dad, say hello to your baby."

Lilly paid strict attention to every nuance in her doctor's voice, listening for the tiniest hint of something wrong. There was none.

"See here." Dr. Paul indicated a small pulsating shape in the center of the screen. "We have a nice, strong heartbeat."

Lilly repeated the words in her head. They seemed almost too wonderful to be true.

Dr. Paul went on to point out the baby's head, feet, spine, lungs and even a small face. Lilly's breath caught at the sight, and her chest ached with indescribable longing.

"Measurements are good, well within normal range." Dr. Paul continued to move the probe.

"Can you see what sex the baby is?" Jake asked.

"Don't tell us," Lilly said in a rush. It was enough to know the baby was growing normally.

"I can't tell anyway." Dr. Paul squinted at the image. "The umbilical cord's in the way."

"So, everything's fine?"

The hope in Jake's voice echoed Lilly's. She marveled at their shared anticipation and how natural and right it felt. They were two expectant parents, enjoying their first baby pictures.

"Well." Dr. Paul's tone changed to one of caution. "I can't say with complete certainty that everything's fine or that your baby is perfectly healthy. Many problems aren't detectable with a simple ultrasound, especially at this stage."

How well Lilly knew that. Her first child's ultrasound had shown nothing of concern, and her pregnancy had been relatively trouble-free for the first couple of months.

Before her mood could sink lower, Dr. Paul offered reassurances. "But I can tell you this baby is thriving and looks normal for a twelve-to thirteen-week-old fetus."

Tears leaked from the sides of Lilly's eyes. Christmas was almost a month away, but she felt like she'd gotten her first present. Maybe now she could tell her parents about the baby when they came for the holidays.

Jake reached for her hand, and she grabbed it, grateful for his strength.

Dr. Paul's faint smile disappeared. "To be absolutely sure, we could perform additional tests. When you come in for your next appointment—"

"No more tests. Not yet."

"Don't you think we ought to hear what your doctor has to say?" Jake asked softly.

"I need something positive to hold on to if I'm going to make it through the months ahead. You've given me that today," she told the doctor.

"We could have more positive news," Jake said.

"I want to hold off. Please. Just a little while longer. I promise to reconsider if I have more…incidents."

"Okay."

"What?"

"I said okay. If you're willing to take the chance, so am I."

"Really?" She tilted her head to get a better look at him.

He smiled encouragingly. "You and I are going to make a beautiful baby together. I don't see how anything else is possible."

Lilly stared at Jake, searching for any indication of insincerity. The face gazing down at her was open and honest and full of joy, the same kind of joy that burst inside her during those rare moments when she wasn't worrying herself sick.

"We're almost finished," Dr. Paul said, distracting Lilly and returning her to the present. She advised her on what to do when she got home and until her next visit. "Call if you start bleeding and cramping again." After making final notations on the chart, Dr. Paul told Lilly she could go home. "I don't want you driving, though."

"I'll take her," Jake said.

"What about my car? I can't leave it here."

"I'll arrange for someone from the center to drive it home for you." He let go of Lilly's hand only because the nurse needed him to move.

She wondered if he'd hold her hand again when they started down the hall and was a little disappointed that he didn't. He waited outside the treatment area so the nurse could help Lilly dress in private, but he was standing right there as soon as she stepped around the curtain. When his palm came to rest lightly on the small of her back, she said nothing, although she felt quite capable of walking on her own. She could probably walk all the way home, she realized with a surge of happiness.

We have a nice, strong heartbeat.

Dr. Paul's voice resounded in her head. Making it even better, Jake had stood by her, agreeing with her decision to decline further tests. It had been a long time since she'd left a doctor's office or medical facility in such high spirits.

She touched her belly, wishing—imagining—she could feel the heartbeat she'd viewed on the monitor. Maybe this time things would be different, and she'd be blessed with a healthy child.

Jake pressed the elevator button. She observed him as they rode down to the ground floor. If she did get her wish, she'd be faced with deciding just how much to let this man into her life.

"Over here," he said once they were outside. He led her to an older-model pickup parked crookedly and illegally in a tow-away zone.

She stopped and stared. "What happened to your truck?"

"I was in a hurry, and this one was available."

"I can't believe the police didn't give you a ticket," she said, inspecting the windshield when they got closer.

"If they did, it'd be worth every penny."

Lilly paused. That was one of the nicest things Jake had ever said to her. "Thanks for coming today. I'm glad you did."

He opened the passenger-side door for her. "I'm glad you called me."

She considered for a few seconds, then came to a decision that wasn't nearly as hard as she'd thought it would be. "Next week at my regular appointment with Dr. Paul, you can come with me into the exam room."

"You sure?"

"So long as you behave." She smiled and in a teasing tone added, "No getting bossy and taking charge on me."

"I don't do that."

"Yeah, right," she said then let out a "hmm" when it became evident she couldn't climb into the truck without a stepping stool. Not if she was obeying the doctor's orders to avoid strain.

"We might have to take my car. I'm not sure I can get in."

"No problem." He stooped as if to lift her into his arms.

"Wait!" she squeaked and stopped him with a raised hand.

He straightened, effectively trapping her between the truck seat and the hard, unyielding length of his body.

She discovered she'd wrapped her arms around his neck, where, against her better judgment, they lingered. Their eyes locked, and though she knew she should remove her arms and scoot away—if that was even possible—she didn't.

Holding Jake wasn't just for old times' sake. She truly cared for him—more than he cared for her—which was one of the main causes of their breakup.

Not that her feelings for him weren't reciprocated. There was no mistaking the tenderness shining in his hazel eyes or the sexy half-smile that both charmed and irritated her. She caught herself staring at his mouth, which was so close that kissing him would be a simple matter of rising onto her tiptoes.

Lilly resisted. It would be sheer madness. The emotional highs and lows of the last three hours had left her vulnerable and she was confusing Jake's attentiveness with affection. Or something stronger. Thank goodness sanity returned. Before she could completely withdraw her arms, he clasped her by the waist and pulled her toward him. She held the sides of his face, thinking she'd put a halt to his intentions. But the keep-your-distance tactic became a loving caress as her thumbs brushed the faint stubble shadowing his jaw.

His hands slipped inside her jacket and glided up her rib cage, stopping just below her breasts, which were pressed against the confines of her bra. Breasts that were fuller than the last time she and Jake had been intimate.

"Jake." The stern objection she'd planned to deliver came out sounding like an invitation.

One he accepted.

The instant their lips touched, Lilly surrendered to him. The arms she'd almost removed tightened around his neck, and she opened her mouth, encouraging him to deepen their kiss with low, throaty moans. Jake obliged, and the passion she'd never truly lost during the months since their breakup flared to life and burned brightly.

This was unquestionably a mistake and something she'd regret later. But for now Jake's strong fingers kneading her skin though her shirt, his tongue and lips tantalizing, were exactly the emotional balm she needed, and she took every ounce of comfort he was willing to give.

The blazing intensity of their kiss lasted several minutes longer, then slowly began to ebb. Their mouths drew apart but their embrace continued. He seemed to sense that she needed more time before he let go. Sliding her hands to his shoulders, she waited for her breathing to calm.

But at his next words, her breathing stopped completely, and her hands fell limp at her sides.

"Marry me, Lilly."

"I can't marry you, Jake! Not now."

"It doesn't have to be right away. We can wait a few months."

He hadn't expected Lilly to squeal with delight at his spontaneous proposal but neither had he anticipated the absolute horror on her face or the tears filling her eyes. Lots of couples married because of a pregnancy. Surely she'd expected him to propose eventually, or at least bring up the subject of marriage. He'd certainly been considering it since she'd told him about the baby.

She raised her hands to her lips. "Sorry. I didn't mean to overreact. I'm just so surprised."

Okay, he was wrong. She hadn't thought about marrying him. Jake didn't know whether to be hurt or amused.

He took a step back and rested his hand on the passenger door, deciding to be philosophical. His timing was off. Lilly'd had a difficult day and was clearly drained. He shouldn't have sprung any unplanned announcements on her, much less propose. His retreat came to a grinding halt when she abruptly burst into sobs.

"Hey, what's wrong?" He moved closer and put an arm around her. "Don't cry, sweetheart. Everything's going to work out fine."

Jake was prepared for her to push him away. But she didn't, and instead nestled her face in the crook of his neck, her sobs so wrenching she shook from head to toe. He let her cry, glad that she was turning to him, and rubbed her back. Eventually, she quieted but made no effort to move. He liked holding Lilly, so he said nothing for several minutes.

"Let's get in the truck," he suggested softly when she seemed ready.

She released him and wiped her cheeks. He helped her climb into the cab, then went around to the driver's side and got in, too.

"I feel so stupid," she said when he shut his door.

"Don't. This is a hospital parking lot." Rather than start the truck, he set the keys on the dash. "Crying people are pretty common. Marriage proposals, probably not so common," he added wryly.

"I really botched that, didn't I?"

The truck was an older model, so it had a bench seat, and Lilly could sit near the middle with her legs angled toward Jake. He took a chance and put an arm across the seat back. She didn't recoil. But she didn't lean in to him as she had before, either.

"I botched it more. The next time I ask you to marry me, I'll do it right. Ring, flowers, down on one knee."

"Oh, Jake."

He thought for a second she might start crying again. When she didn't, he blundered on, hoping to get past the awkward moment and onto some meaningful conversation.

"I'd like us to be married when the baby's born. Is that so wrong?"

"No, if anything, it's sweet." She sighed. "And under different circumstances, I'd probably want the same thing."

"Different? Meaning…what?" he asked when she didn't elaborate.

"I already had one marriage fall apart under the stress of a child with special needs. I don't want to go through that twice."

"You're not going to lose this baby, and I'm not like your ex-husband." He cut her off before she could disagree. "Okay, I know you have plenty of reason to doubt me."

"You did break up with me."

"This is different."

"How can I be sure?"

"You could be sure if we were married."

"That didn't stop Brad from leaving." She tried to smile but failed miserably. "Everything is so damn complicated."

"The only way to uncomplicate it is to talk to me." The truck cab was beginning to warm up. He would have taken off his jacket but he didn't want to remove his arm from the back of the seat.

"We have to be realistic," she said. "The reasons you ended our relationship haven't changed. Your daughters are still upset about Ellen remarrying, still hate the idea of a stepfather. You can't possibly think they'll be happier about me and our baby."

"They'll come around sooner or later."

"You didn't believe that two months ago. Something tells me you still don't. And what about Le-Anne?"

"What about her?"

"She was scared to death of Jimmy Bob that day

at the center. How do you think she'd react to a new sibling who's born with birth defects?"

"You saw the ultrasound. This baby's going to be fine."

"Which doesn't change the fact that your daughters will be furious with you. It's not a good way to start a marriage, is it?"

Ellen was doing just that, but the thought didn't console Jake. Briana and her mother were hardly speaking. He didn't want the same thing to happen with him.

"I really didn't plan on having another baby," Lilly said haltingly.

"I know that."

"I was on the pill."

He nodded. "I know that, too."

"You had sex with me believing I was protected. And I *was*…or I was *supposed* to be, anyway. Only I wound up pregnant. You're a decent guy, Jake. You probably think it's your duty to marry me."

"I do feel responsible. But I should. You didn't get pregnant alone."

"You're missing the point." She struggled visibly for control. "I won't trap you in a relationship with me. That wasn't the deal. And I'd never forgive myself if I came between you and your girls."

Jake scowled. "Is that why you think I'm here? Because you trapped me?"

"I'm worried that's how you feel."

"Believe me, I don't."

"Maybe not today. Tomorrow could be another story."

"Did your ex-husband accuse you of trapping him?"

Pain flashed in her eyes. "He made it clear when he left that my inability to give him healthy children was a big factor in the divorce."

"He's a jerk." Jake had another word for Lilly's ex but refrained from saying it out loud. "There are other options for couples in your situation."

"Adoption was out. He wanted a biological child."

"He must have had a giant ego."

"Be honest. Most men want their children to be their biological offspring."

"Not all."

"This coming from a man with three daughters."

Jake didn't dispute her. Ellen had gotten pregnant so easily, and their three girls had been born without a single complication. If he was honest, he'd admit he couldn't understand what Lilly's ex-husband had been through or why he felt the way he did. He could only see how much the man had hurt her.

"Doctors can do some pretty incredible things nowadays," he said.

"That's true. And in vitro fertilization using donor eggs might have been an option if we'd had the money. After Evan, our finances were wiped out." She leaned back in the truck seat, her posture defeated. "I think it was easier for Brad to divorce me and find a woman with normal DNA than wait until we could pay off our bills and save more money."

"He remarried?"

"Six months after the papers were finalized. He and his new wife had a baby a year later. I understand from mutual friends that she's expecting again."

"Jeez, Lilly."

"I won't pretend I'm not bothered by it."

"You wouldn't be human if you weren't."

"I'm happy for him. Really." She turned and offered Jake a watery smile. "I just want some of that same happiness for myself."

"You'll have it." He lowered his arm and squeezed her shoulders. "If you find yourself doubting it, remember the ultrasound."

"That was wonderful." Her smile widened.

Jake wanted to kiss her even more in that moment than he had earlier and almost surrendered to temptation. But a white coupe with "Security" painted on the side pulled even with the truck, crushing his impulse. The uniformed man inside beeped his horn.

"It appears my luck's run out," Jake said.

"I'm surprised it lasted this long." Lilly slid over toward the door and fastened her seat belt.

He half wished she'd slid closer to him. The ride to her place would be considerably more enjoyable with her snuggled beside him.

"Look, I jumped the gun with my proposal earlier." He eased the truck onto the road and into Payson's small-town version of rush-hour traffic. Dusk had settled and lights everywhere were coming on. "But I want you to know I was sincere."

"I'm touched. Really."

Lilly laid her head back. Only then did Jake notice

the fatigue marring her lovely features. She must not be sleeping well, which wasn't good for her or the baby. He wished there was more he could do for her. He wished she'd *let* him do more. So far, she'd stuck to her decision and refused his assistance. Until today…

Maybe he was making progress after all.

"I can't saddle you with a sick child," she said, a hitch in her voice. "That's not fair and not what you bargained for when we got involved."

"You wouldn't be saddling me. I want our child to have my name, and I want you to have the assurance that I'll be a responsible and committed parent." The intensity of his words gave him pause. He was certainly a different man from the one who'd run fast and hard a few months ago. Was the baby responsible? More likely the baby's mother and his changing feelings toward her.

They'd reached her house, which was located in one of the newer developments that had been built during a recent economic boom. Jake turned into her driveway and cut the engine. Lilly immediately opened her door. So much for sitting and talking a while longer.

"Will you at least *consider* marrying me?" They stopped on her front step. She didn't invite him inside, and he tried not to read more into that than was there.

"I won't dismiss the idea entirely. That's the best I can offer."

He hated settling; he was a man who went after what he wanted and didn't quit until he got it.

"Have dinner with me Friday night?"

"I…" She shoved her hands in her coat pockets and hunched her shoulders against the cool evening air.

"Hear me out before you say no." Jake knew he had only this one chance to sway Lilly's opinion regarding them. She was on home ground and retreating more and more by the second—physically and emotionally. "I think we should see each other twice a week. Socially. Doctor and hospital visits don't count."

"You want to…date?"

"We're having a baby. Like it or not, we'll be seeing quite a bit of each other for a long time to come." He'd rather it was across his breakfast table every morning, but she'd rejected his proposal. "Don't you agree we'll be better parents if we're on good terms?"

"Of course. But dating?"

"Think of it as two friends hanging out."

She sent him a mistrustful look.

"We can shop for maternity clothes and baby furniture. Go to yoga class. Drink herbal tea while I listen to you complain about your water retention. Whatever friends do."

That earned him a chuckle.

But she quickly sobered and asked, "No pressure? Strictly social? I can't handle it if you're popping the question every time we go out."

He placed a hand over his heart. "Scout's honor."

"I suppose we could try." The crack in the wall she'd erected widened. "See how it goes."

Her enthusiasm left a lot to be desired but Jake took what he could get. "Good. How about I pick you up at seven on Friday?"

"Why do I think you have another agenda?"

Because he did—that of further exploring their renewed and deepening relationship.

He could understand Lilly's rejection of his proposal; she wouldn't act impulsively where her child was concerned. His goal was to take the necessary steps to help his daughters adjust to a blended family and to make sure Lilly's decision to marry him was well thought-out and deliberate. That it was a decision she'd never regret.

And if he had to woo her one dinner date, one yoga class, one shopping spree at a time, he'd do it gladly.

Chapter 8

Lilly emerged from the restroom stall and went directly to the sink. After washing her hands, she automatically checked her blouse and tugged it into place. The strategic folds hid her gently rounded belly but wouldn't for much longer, not at seventeen weeks pregnant. She couldn't believe how fast the weeks had flown by and that it was January already. Any day now she'd have to start telling people—apart from the handful she already had. And *they'd* learned only after she'd gone a full three weeks without any spotting or cramps.

Her parents had expressed mixed emotions. They knew how much Lilly wanted children but were understandably concerned about her ability to endure the loss of a fourth child. And though they'd wisely said little, they were also unhappy about her unmarried state. To her relief, Jake hadn't mentioned his proposal when he'd come over Christmas Eve for dinner and to meet her parents. Lilly had hoped he might bring his daughters, too, so that she could get to know them better. But he hadn't, probably because she was starting to show. Nor had he told them about the baby yet.

Lilly's boss and his wife had been next on her list of people to tell. After explaining her circumstances, they'd agreed not to say anything to the staff until Lilly was ready.

She cradled her middle and whispered a soft prayer for the life growing inside her. The baby who'd first turned her world upside down now completed it. Granted, she spent half her day anxious and agitated, but the other half was spent imagining herself holding a healthy, beautiful baby. Could Dr. Paul be right? Would a different father, a different DNA combination, make the difference?

Jake seemed to think so.

Keeping to their agreement, they'd gone out twice a week for the past five weeks, and it wasn't the hardship Lilly had expected. He took her to dinner a lot, which accounted for some of her recent weight gain. But they also went on day trips, like a hike through the easy trails at the ranch or renting a paddle boat at nearby Commodore Lake—with Jake doing most of the paddling.

They had fun together, but then, they'd had fun before their breakup, too. Their instant and natural camaraderie had been what attracted her to him in the first place. Jake was helping to take the pressure off their new relationship by not bringing up the *M* word again, although she doubted that would last.

Truth be told, she'd entertained the idea of marrying him once or twice. Okay, three or four times...a week. Her reasons to wait still outnumbered her reasons to accept his proposal. If her pregnancy continued to progress well and their relationship strengthened, that might not be the case in another few months.

The door to the restroom banged open, and Miranda walked in. Her face lit up at seeing Lilly, and rather than go into a stall, she joined Lilly at the sink.

"Whatcha doing?"

"Making myself presentable." Lilly smoothed at her hair, hoping Miranda didn't see through her ruse.

"There's a piece sticking up in the back."

Lilly stood immobile while Miranda patted down the flyaway strands.

Miranda held a special place in Lilly's heart because her case was so tragic. When she was two years old, she'd fallen six feet onto concrete. Broken bones weren't the worst of her injuries; she'd suffered a three-inch fracture in her skull that had left her mildly mentally disabled.

"Thank you," Lilly said when Miranda was done.

She grinned. Like a lot of the center's clients, she enjoyed being helpful. "I fix my sister's hair a lot."

"That's nice."

Miranda leaned over the sink until her face was only inches from the mirror and inspected her teeth.

"When your baby's born, can I watch it for you?"

Lilly went stone-still except for her heart, which jumped inside her chest. "What makes you think I'm having a baby?" she asked haltingly.

"You're getting fat. My sister got fat, too." Miranda spun around and patted her own pudgy tummy.

Lilly hid her mortification by returning to the sink and flipping on the cold water faucet. If Miranda had noticed her condition, others must have, too. What a fool she'd been to believe she was successfully camouflaging her pregnancy with loose-fitting clothes and bulky sweaters.

"Did I say something wrong?" Miranda asked, her smile faltering.

"No, not at all." Lilly stalled by washing her hands again. She couldn't leave the restroom, not until she'd composed herself and convinced Miranda to keep her secret. The young woman was a notorious blabbermouth.

"Aren't you happy about the baby?"

Anyone who thought special-needs individuals weren't observant had another thing coming.

"Of course I'm happy. I just wasn't ready to tell people yet."

"Why not?"

"The baby might be sick." *Might not live.*

Miranda gawked at Lilly's stomach. "How can you tell when it's still inside you?"

"I had problems before."

"Sick how? Like strep throat? I had that once."

"No, not like strep throat. More serious." Lilly couldn't bring herself to be upset with Miranda. She was just trying to understand. "Sick isn't the right word. The baby could have physical problems and not…" How to say it without hurting Miranda's feelings? "Not be able to walk or talk."

"Like me." Miranda held out her foot, the one with the specially constructed shoe to compensate for her fibula, which was three inches too short. "My leg's messed up, and I don't talk real good."

"You talk fine." Too much sometimes, Lilly wryly thought. She realized that if she didn't return to her office soon, one of the staff was bound to come looking for her. "And your limp is hardly noticeable."

"Why you all worried then?"

"The baby could have so many things wrong, it would never be able to leave home and might need machines to stay alive."

"That sucks."

Yes, it did.

"I have to go, sweetie." Lilly patted Miranda's shoulder. "Please don't tell anyone about the baby until I say you can. Okay?"

"My mother doesn't tell people about me, either."

"I can't believe that," Lilly said vehemently, although admittedly she didn't know Miranda's mother. Her sister always brought her to the center.

"Sometimes, when she thinks I'm not around, she says she only has one daughter."

"Oh, Miranda." Lilly could have cried.

The young woman screwed up her face into an angry scowl. "I bet if you had a kid like me, you'd be the same way."

Lilly pulled Miranda into a fierce hug. "If I had a daughter like you, I'd be so happy and so proud, I'd tell everybody I met about my beautiful girl and how much I loved her."

"Then why don't you tell people about the baby?"

"I will. Soon."

"Why not right now?"

Yes, why not? Didn't she believe what she'd told Miranda?

"Okay, let's do it. Together." Lilly drew back and took Miranda by the shoulders. "Thank you."

"For what?"

"Reminding me of something important I'd forgotten."

"What's that?"

"Unconditional love."

"I don't get it."

"Don't worry." She pushed open the door. "I'll explain later."

"Wait, I gotta pee."

Lilly laughed as Miranda dashed into the bathroom stall. When she was done, they left the restroom together and went into the main activity room. Miranda bubbled with excitement. The others must have sensed something was up because all eyes were on them.

"I have an announcement," Lilly said when she reached the center of the room.

"Is Big Ben okay?" Jimmy Bob asked.

"Our mule is fine."

"Are we still going to the ranch tomorrow?"

"Shut up, you goon," Miranda scolded. "This isn't about you or that dumb mule."

"This is about me," Lilly said and waited for everyone to quiet down. "I'm very, *very* pleased to tell you that in five months or so, I'm going to have a baby."

Dead silence followed her announcement…for about three seconds. Then the entire room broke into applause and cheers. Those who could get up on their own rushed over to Lilly, hugging her, kissing her and offering her their best wishes. If any of them had suspected she was pregnant, they didn't say.

For the rest of the afternoon, she rejoiced with the center's staff and clients. No doubt her fears and worries would return the next morning. But she didn't let that stop her from treasuring every second of the afternoon and she could hardly wait to tell Jake.

"So, we're officially out of the closet?"

"Yes."

Jake pressed the phone closer to his ear and smiled. Lilly had called to say she'd finally felt comfortable enough with her pregnancy to go public, and elation rang in her voice. It was nice to hear. With each passing week, Lilly and their child became more and more important to him.

"Well, good. I guess now I can do the same."

"You haven't told anyone?"

He absently stirred a pot of steaming vegetables on the stove. The girls were due any minute, and he hadn't seen much of them the last week. They'd stayed with him for ten days straight after Ellen's New Year's

Eve wedding while she and her new husband went on their honeymoon. In exchange, he'd let her have his regular weekend. Reports from the family grapevine were that the reunion hadn't gone well. Apparently Briana and her mother remained at odds, and none of the girls had yet to warm up to their new stepfather.

Jake allowed himself a brief feel-good moment. He was first in his daughters' hearts, and as long as he stayed there, he could tolerate another man living in his home.

"I did tell Carolina a couple months ago," he said to Lilly. "The day you went to the emergency room and had the ultrasound. She denies it, but I'm pretty sure she's told her mother. And if she did, you can bet my mom knows, too."

"What about the girls?" Lilly asked.

"I haven't said a word to them."

"Are you going to?"

"Yeah, soon. I may do it tonight. Ellen's dropping them off." Jake could only postpone the inevitable so long. Before he and Lilly could move forward, his children had to be told. Everything.

"Do you want me to be there?"

"Thanks." Lilly's offer and what it implied wasn't lost on him. "But I think I'd better tackle this alone. Depending on how they handle the news, maybe we all can get together one evening next week."

"I could make dinner. Or how about if I throw everything in a cooler and bring it over there?"

"I'd like that a lot." He imagined Lilly and his

daughters sitting around his kitchen table, the all-American blended family, talking and laughing.

The vision promptly evaporated in a puff of smoke. Unless he and Lilly conquered the hurdles facing them and won his daughters over, those family dinners were going to be stilted and possibly angry.

"Do the girls like baked ravioli?"

"If it's cheese ravioli, yes."

"Great!"

Jake wished he felt as hopeful as Lilly sounded. He really did want that dream of everyone at dinner to become a reality. The girls were aware he and Lilly went out sometimes. Tonight he would tell them that he and Lilly were serious. Let them get used to the idea before he broke the news about the baby. With their home life at their mother's in such turmoil, he felt the need to proceed slowly.

He couldn't wait too much longer, however. Payson was a small town and tongues wagged.

"I hear a car outside," he told Lilly. "I'd better go."

"Call me later if you need to talk."

"What if I don't need to talk and just want to call?"

"That's okay, too," she said softly and hung up after saying goodbye.

He headed to the door, more optimistic than he'd been a few minutes ago. His progress with Lilly had been slow but was now moving in the right direction. It gave him confidence that everything would eventually work out for the best.

"Hi." He stood on his porch, waiting for the stampede.

His daughters tumbled out of Ellen's car, the candy-apple red convertible her husband had brought her as an engagement present. Jake wondered how long the shiny paint would last in the rough, mountainous terrain where they lived and how long until Ellen tired of driving a vehicle so ill-suited to a family with three active children.

LeAnne and Kayla nearly knocked him over. Before they could land in a heap on the porch floor, he swept them into his arms.

"I missed you so much. How are Grandpa and Grandma Pryor?" Over the weekend, Ellen had taken the girls and her new husband to Phoenix for a short visit with her parents.

"Good," Kayla chirped and extracted herself from beneath Jake's arm. Of the three girls, she was the only one who resembled Ellen, inheriting her mother's flashing blue eyes and thick brown hair.

"What's for dinner?" LeAnne demanded, pushing open the door. She reminded Jake of his late sister and was a Tucker through and through.

He caught sight of LeAnne's hand. Her fingernails, normally chewed to the quick, were long, bright pink and covered with tiny decals.

"I'm glad to see you've stopped biting your nails." He couldn't say he liked her choice of polish, though.

"Oh." She held up her hand and wiggled her fingers. "These are fake."

"Fake nails? Aren't you a little young for those?"

"Mom bought them for me," she said, bounding into the kitchen.

Jake grumbled under his breath.

Briana was the last one inside and slow to join them at the table. When they started eating, she was mostly silent, answering only when asked a direct question and then limiting her replies to one or two short sentences.

"Anything wrong, honey?" Jake asked.

"Nothing."

He passed out the chocolate brownies he'd swiped from the dining hall earlier that day when Olivia wasn't looking.

His kitchen manager's last day was almost upon them. Finding her replacement had been a problem and had consumed much of his time recently. Then, yesterday, his other cousin, Corrine, Carolina's sister, called to tell him she'd decided not to re-up after eight years as a warrant officer in the army and was looking for a job. Next to Lilly's continued good health and lack of pregnancy problems, it was the best news he'd had all month.

"Briana's mad because Mom didn't let her drive her new whip over here," Kayla said with a sneer.

"Whip?" Jake asked.

"It means car."

"Huh." When did his bookish, somewhat nerdy daughter start using teen slang?

"Shut up, Kayla," Briana snapped.

"No fighting at the table," Jake warned both of them. "You know the rules."

Briana sulked. Kayla, unaffected, devoured her brownie. Jake said nothing more in an attempt to restore harmony; he wanted everyone in good spirits and receptive when he told them about Lilly.

After helping him clean the kitchen, the two younger girls vanished into the family room to watch TV. Jake didn't ask if they'd finished their homework—the rule was it had to be done before they came over. Because high school tended to be more demanding and Briana was often busy with extracurricular activities, she sometimes got stuck finishing up a reading assignment or report while at Jake's.

When she retreated into his office, he didn't ask any questions. Forty-five minutes later, he knocked on the door and entered, not surprised to find her on the internet.

"Researching?"

"American history." Her tone conveyed just how little she liked the class.

He crossed the room to stand behind her, automatically scanning the Web page she had open. He was glad to see an article about the Industrial Revolution. Not that he didn't trust her, but in her current mood, he wouldn't have been surprised to catch her instant-messaging with a friend.

"I know you're upset about not being able to drive your mom's car, but try and understand. You've just got your learner's permit. The convertible has a standard transmission and a lot more power than you're capable of handling with your limited experience."

"I drive the tractor, and it's a standard."

"Your mom's convertible isn't anything like the

tractor. Plus, it's dark outside, and the roads are still slick from the last snowstorm."

"How am I supposed to get experience if Mom doesn't teach me?"

While he hated seeing Briana's unhappy frown, he was inclined to agree with her mother on this issue. "I've got to pick up your sister's asthma prescription at the drugstore. What if we ran to Payson real quick, and I let you drive the Buick? The drugstore's right next to the ice cream place. I'll treat."

Her expression brightened. "I'd rather go to Java Creations."

"The coffee house?" Jake must have heard wrong. "You don't drink coffee."

"Dad," she said on a sigh. "Everyone from school goes there."

Briana drank coffee. Kayla used slang. LeAnne wore fake nails. His little girls were growing up so fast. Before long, less than two years to be exact, Briana would be leaving for college, finding a job—not necessarily on the ranch—meeting a guy and getting married. Kayla and LeAnne wouldn't be far behind. When that day came, he'd be alone.

No, not alone. He'd be with Lilly and their child.

A baby.

Diapers, late-night feedings, spitting up on his dress shirts. Then later, learning to ride a bike, the first day of school and another trip to Disneyland.

Jake was about to have a second family.

His knees buckled. "I need to sit down," he said and stumbled toward the easy chair.

"I thought we were going to Payson?"

"Oh, yeah. You'll have to drive. My stomach's queasy."

"That's the point, remember me driving?"

"Sorry."

"Jeez, Dad. What's with you?"

"Nothing. I'm fine."

He did feel a little steadier by the time all four of them piled into his old Buick. Then he remembered his plan to tell the kids about Lilly. The closer they got to the coffee shop, the more his agitation increased.

He considered postponing it, then was hit by a terrifying thought. Lilly had told the staff and clients at Horizon about the baby. Briana spent two or three afternoons a week with them at the ranch. It was possible—no, likely—that someone would mention Lilly's pregnancy to her. Briana was smart, she'd do the math and figure out he could be the father.

Difficult as it would be, he'd have to tell his daughters everything tonight.

Java Creations was packed, and the patrons, with the exception of Jake, Kayla and LeAnne, looked like they were regulars, Briana included. The two younger girls ordered hot chocolate. Briana got some decaf latte concoction with an extra shot of skim milk. Jake's request for a plain cup of black coffee was met with borderline disdain from the barista. He almost choked when she told him the total price, but kept his complaint to himself. If four overpriced beverages smoothed the way for his talk with the girls, he'd pay double that.

They grabbed a tiny table near the back, the only one available. It became abundantly clear to Jake the instant they sat down that a noisy, bustling coffee house was no place for a serious discussion, not with Briana hopping up every couple of minutes to greet friends.

"The best-laid plans," he muttered. No one heard him. "Let's go," he said when Briana returned from her third venture. Kayla and LeAnne were finished with their hot chocolate, and his stomach, uneasy to begin with, was rebelling against the coffee.

"Do we have to?" Briana glanced up from her cell phone. "It's only eight o'clock."

More like eight-twenty, and they had to be home by nine on school nights. Jake was running out of time.

"I have something to tell you. All of you," he added.

"What?" LeAnne perked up. Briana and Kayla eyed him suspiciously.

"Nothing bad." Jake's assurance made no difference. Briana and Kayla slunk out of the coffee shop. LeAnne skipped. "Wait just a minute," he said when Briana went to start the car.

She huffed and threw herself against the seat back.

He ignored her theatrics and mentally steeled himself for the task ahead. His daughters had been through so many upheavals in recent years. He couldn't possibly expect them to welcome another one, much less feel enthusiastic about it. Only the fear that Briana might learn about Lilly from someone else kept him going.

"You remember Lilly Russo?" He said the words he'd been practicing in his head during the drive there.

"She works at the center." Briana rolled her eyes. "Comes to the ranch all the time. The two of you dated for a while and still go out sometimes. But you're *just friends*." She mimicked him by drawing out the last two words.

"That's right."

"Are you dating her again?" Kayla asked, slouching in the corner of the back seat and fiddling with the hood ties on her jacket.

Jake reached over and patted her knee. Briana's constant bickering with her mother had taken center stage of late, and the other two were often, if unintentionally, ignored. He vowed to change that, starting right now.

"We are dating again. Sort of. And have been for a few months."

"Define *sort of*," Briana demanded.

"We're seeing a lot of each other."

"Are you getting married, too, Daddy?" LeAnne's innocent question triggered a shock wave that rippled through the car's occupants.

"No, I'm not getting married." *Not yet.*

"Okay. You're dating. Seeing *a lot* of each other," Briana emphasized in a clipped voice. "No big deal."

"Actually, there's more to it." He had their attention. It burned into him like three hot spears. But there was no going back. Not now. "Lilly's having a baby. She's due in July." He didn't add that she might not carry to term or that the baby could be born with birth defects.

One step—one bombshell—at a time.

"You're dating a pregnant woman?" Briana's expression changed, going from disbelief to confusion to outrage in a matter of seconds. Jake's prediction had come true; she'd done the math. "*You're* the father."

"Yes." Jake winced slightly. Falling off the pedestal was much harder than he'd imagined.

"Oh, my God! I don't believe it." Briana clasped the sides of her head with shaking hands. "First Mom cheats on you, then divorces you, then marries the guy she cheated on you with—"

"Briana!" Jake cut her off. He wasn't sure how much her younger sisters knew about their mother's previous relationship with their stepfather.

"You got that woman pregnant." She glared at him, her eyes ablaze with fury and—the thought of it turned his stomach to lead—disappointment.

"First of all, she's not 'that woman.' Lilly is a very nice person. You told me yourself you liked her."

"That was before I found out she was screw—"

"Enough." Jake clenched his teeth and took a moment to calm down. "We didn't plan on her getting pregnant. But regardless, I'm happy about it. Lilly's always wanted to have children and hasn't been able to.… This is her chance to be a mother."

"So, you're just a sperm donor?"

Where did Briana learn this stuff? School? TV? "No. I'm going to be an active, involved parent. Which is why Lilly and I are dating."

He looked into the backseat. LeAnne had crawled over to sit beside Kayla.

"It would be nice if you were active and involved sisters."

"I like babies," LeAnne said in a small voice. "Can I hold it and feed it?"

"You bet." He returned her tentative smile with a grin. Then he recalled how she'd acted with Jimmy Bob, and his grin dimmed.

Kayla remained silent and stone-faced, staring at the floor. Her reaction bothered him more than Briana's anger. His oldest daughter, at least, was venting her feelings, not locking them inside.

"Don't expect me to get within ten feet of the little rug rat," Briana spat.

So much for hoping she'd babysit. "Please don't raise your voice at me." Normally, he'd take a sterner tone with her but he cut her some slack tonight.

"Are you going to move in with Lilly?" LeAnne asked.

"No. I'm staying right where I am."

"Are Lilly and the baby moving in with you?"

"Maybe. Some day."

"Great!" Briana slammed her fist on the steering wheel. "I get to lose my room at your house, too."

"You're not going to lose your room."

"Right." She jammed the key in the ignition, and the Buick roared to life. "Mom said the same thing. But somehow I had to give up my bedroom and move in with *them*—" she jerked her head at her sisters "—so butthead Travis's butthead son could have his own room when he comes to visit us."

"Shut the car off, honey."

"I want to go home."

"Then let me drive. You're too upset."

"I'm not upset," she hollered. "And you promised I could drive."

"Briana, don't." Jake unbuckled his seat belt.

"Daddy!" LeAnne burst into tears and tried to climb into the front seat.

"Stay there." He gently pushed her down.

"Why does everything have to change?" Briana flipped the radio on full blast and shouted, "Why can't we go back to the way we were?"

"Shut the car off, and let's talk." He reached for the key.

Briana beat him to it and threw the car in Reverse. "I don't want a stepdad. I don't want a stepmom. And I sure as hell don't want a new baby brother or sister."

Lilly's worries about his daughters and their reaction to her and the baby were coming true.

Briana suddenly hit the gas. Tires spun, grappling for traction on the dirt parking lot.

Jake raised a hand to shield his eyes from the sudden glare of oncoming headlights. "Briana, watch out!"

He was too late. The car bucked and lurched to a stop as metal collided with metal.

Chapter 9

"Are you all right?" Even though Lilly had spoken to Jake on the phone, been assured he and his daughters were unharmed, she choked up when she saw them in the emergency room waiting area.

He stood, and they went into each other's arms. "Thanks for coming," he said.

"I'm just glad you're out here and not in the operating room." She glanced down at his two youngest daughters huddled together in the chairs beside his. "Where's Briana?"

"She went to the gift shop to get us some bottled water. Kayla and LeAnne were thirsty."

"Was the other driver injured?" She reached up and lightly touched the small shaved spot and butterfly bandage on the side of Jake's head.

"No, fortunately. And the girls are all fine. I wouldn't have been hurt, either, if I hadn't unbuckled my seat belt. That rearview mirror packs a mean wallop." He grunted in disgust. "I didn't want to come here, but the police officer insisted when the damn cut kept bleeding. Then I couldn't get hold of anyone."

Though it was selfish of her, Lilly was glad his parents and cousin, Carolina, hadn't answered his calls. "Is your truck driveable?"

"We were in my old Buick, which is a tank, and it was only going a few miles an hour. The other car fared worse."

"Where'd you leave the Buick?"

"At the coffee house. The manager said we could park it there overnight. I phoned the repair shop, and they're sending a tow truck in the morning to pick it up."

"That's good."

"I know it's late and a huge imposition but can you take us to my place?"

"Of course."

"I've already called Ellen and told her the girls will be staying with me tonight." He looked down the hall and let out an impatient breath. "How long does it take to buy bottled water?"

"I can wait here with Kayla and LeAnne if you want to go search for Briana."

"Do you mind?"

In answer, she sat down in the chair he'd vacated. "Go on."

"I'll be right back," he told his daughters. "Stay here with Ms. Russo."

They nodded, the older one sullenly, the younger one more hesitant.

Lilly leaned in their direction the moment Jake started across the waiting room and gave the pair her most winning smile. "You don't have to call me Ms. Russo. My name's Lilly."

"I'm LeAnne."

"I know. I remember."

"Daddy says you're having a baby."

So, he'd told his daughters tonight. Did breaking the news have anything to do with Briana's fender bender at the coffee house? Lilly thought it might.

"I am."

"He says the baby will be my little brother or sister."

"That's true."

LeAnne's chatter was more curious than friendly but far better than her sister's silent hostility. Lilly swallowed her disappointment. She'd so wanted Jake's daughters to be happy about becoming part of her child's life.

If the baby was born normal.

Lilly wouldn't force them into a relationship with a child like her son, Evan. That would be traumatic, particularly for LeAnne, and too much to ask.

"I like babies," LeAnne said.

"I like babies, too. And kids." Lilly smiled, hoping for even a tiny response. No such luck.

LeAnne looked confused, and Kayla just plain ignored Lilly. She took the slights in stride. She had a lot of experience dealing with uncooperative clients determined to hate their circumstances. Given time, she was confident she could get along with, if not win over, Jake's youngest daughters.

Jake and Briana appeared at the end of the hallway. Lilly took one look at the teenager and knew her worries about Jake's other daughters paled in comparison to her fears about his oldest. Everything, from Briana's surly expression to her rigidly held arms, shouted anger and misery.

Lilly stood. "Guess we're ready to leave." She strived to maintain a pleasant and unconcerned tone. Inside, she was quaking.

She and the two younger girls walked toward Jake and Briana, meeting them near the exit. Lilly tried to make eye contact with Briana but the girl stared at the floor or the wall, anywhere except Lilly.

"Where's my water?" LeAnne asked.

"We didn't get it," Jake answered, his jaw hardly moving.

"But I'm thirsty."

"You'll have to wait."

Obviously, something had gone wrong at the gift shop.

"There's a convenience store up the road," Lilly said.

"Do we have to stop?" Briana whined. "I just want to go home."

Okay, thought Lilly. Not the right time to try impressing his daughters with helpful suggestions.

Outside, Briana resumed her fixation with the ground in front of her feet. Jake took the younger girls' hands, and they crossed the parking lot. "Which way?" he asked Lilly.

"Over here."

They wove between parked cars in an awkward, silent conga line. A familiar tow-away zone triggered memories of the day six weeks ago when Jake had met her here and Dr. Paul had performed the ultrasound.

It suddenly struck Lilly how different tonight was from then and how different her feelings were for Jake. Little by little during the past weeks they'd grown closer and she'd started falling for him.

Or was that falling for him *again?*

"I'm hungry," LeAnne complained as they neared Lilly's car.

She removed her keys from her purse and pressed the button to unlock the doors. "I have some crackers in the glove compartment." She reached for the driver's side door.

Briana, one step ahead of everyone else, already had her door open.

"That's all right," Jake said. "She can wait to eat until we get home."

"I don't mind sharing." Lilly winked at LeAnne as she opened the door.

"He said she can wait!" Briana wheeled on Lilly. "Quit trying so hard to be the nice girlfriend so we'll like you and be okay with you having our dad's kid."

"I'm...sorry I didn't—"

"Briana!" Jake exploded. "That was rude and uncalled for."

A strange and unexpected sensation bloomed in Lilly's middle. She placed one hand on the car roof to steady herself. Her other hand went to cradle her belly. She was vaguely aware of Jake barreling around the car.

"Lilly! Are you all right?"

She tried to nod but didn't quite manage as tears filled her eyes and blurred her vision.

"Is it cramps?" Jake took her arm and held her firmly, supporting her.

She leaned on him, waiting for the sensation to recede and—please, oh, please, God—return.

"No. Not cramps." She couldn't stop crying. "I just felt the baby move for the first time."

"You did?" Jake's grin stretched from ear to ear and his grip on her arm tightened. He kissed her temple and covered her hand with his. "That's great, sweetheart."

"Yeah, great," Briana grumbled. Then she turned around and stormed off.

Briana was conspicuously absent during Lilly's next visit to the ranch. Lilly, Georgina, Austin—a recently hired caregiver—and a van full of clients had arrived nearly an hour ago, and the teenager had yet to make an appearance. Lilly didn't think she would. Not after the other night when she'd stomped off, leaving Jake to chase after her and bring her back.

The drive from the hospital to Jake's place had been

long, tiring and strained. Lilly and the girls hadn't exchanged six words. To compensate, Jake talked enough for everyone until he'd grown weary or ran out of patience or both. The kids couldn't escape her car fast enough when she pulled into Jake's driveway. His goodbye to her had been brief, though warm. Lilly had fallen into bed minutes after getting home, only to be awakened a few hours later by another fluttering in her abdomen.

How could a single night be so wonderful and yet so awful?

Lilly had anticipated a chilly reaction from Jake's daughters, but it still cut to the quick. Not for herself—she could survive being the bane of the girls' existence, right up there with their stepfather—but the baby would be their little brother or sister. She'd expected more from Briana, given her caring attitude toward the people from Horizon.

Excited chattering roused her from her ruminations. A dozen or so guests milled near the gate to the corral, watching a trio of young ranch hands bring out and saddle the horses they'd soon be riding. Dressed in spanking-new cowboy hats and boots, their jeans bearing designer tags, the guests looked every inch the greenhorns they were. One of the ranch hands went around to each person, passing out bright yellow plastic ponchos in case the weather turned bad.

The sight of so many people took a little getting used to for Lilly. Bear Creek Ranch had closed down after New Year's Day and had reopened this week on Valentine's Day for the new season. She and the center's clients had gotten used to having the place pretty much to themselves for the past six weeks. Lilly hadn't minded in the least. The ranch in winter was breathtaking with its snow-capped trees, wreaths decorating every door and smoke billowing out of the lodge's redbrick chimney.

If not for the cold, she'd almost want winter back.

A young child wailed despite his mother's attempts to calm his fear of horses. Lilly knew she should go check on the group from Horizon and see how they were doing, but she had trouble motivating herself to do more than sit and observe the goings-on. Since reaching her fifth month recently, her pregnancy had wreaked havoc with her energy levels. In the mornings, she felt she could tackle ten things at once. But by the afternoon, she was completely exhausted and fighting fatigue.

The golf cart's distinctive chugging sounded from up the road. Lilly automatically checked to see if Jake was in it and jumped off the log bench where she'd been sitting as soon as she recognized him.

So much for fighting fatigue.

She immediately began fussing with her pullover sweater and slacks. She'd started wearing maternity clothes since announcing her pregnancy and, silly as it might be, she wanted him to see her in them. To her great disappointment, Jake hailed Gary Forrester instead, and the two of them disappeared into the stable office. Ranch business, Lilly thought glumly. Well, she'd just have to catch him on his way out.

Jimmy Bob emerged from the barn and meandered

toward her, his demeanor pitiful. This was his first trip to the ranch in almost a month, and now Briana wasn't here. No wonder the poor guy was depressed.

"How's Mr. Deitrich doing?" Lilly asked. The older man's Alzheimer's hadn't gotten better since he had started coming to Bear Creek Ranch, but his family reported that he'd become a little more cooperative at home and they were happy with any improvement.

"Fine," Jimmy Bob answered distractedly. "Cleaning out the stalls."

"Good. What are you up to?"

"Looking for Mr. Forrester."

"He's in the office with Mr. Tucker. What do you need?"

"The keys to the tractor."

"Did Mr. Forrester say you could drive it?"

"That's why I need to find him."

Lilly was relieved to learn that Jimmy Bob was seeking permission. He'd become surprisingly skilled at driving the tractor, but she didn't want him thinking he could take it any old time.

"You should probably wait a few minutes until they're done."

"Okay." With a heavy sigh, he plopped onto the bench.

Lilly bit her tongue, more to suppress a chuckle than to stop herself from reminding him that was where *she'd* been sitting. Besides, it was a good excuse for her to go check on the clients and staff. Anything to take her mind off Jake.

"You stay right here," she instructed Jimmy Bob. "Don't move."

"I promise." He nodded enthusiastically.

"I'll be back in three minutes."

Jimmy Bob had proven himself to be reasonably responsible and, as a result, they'd gotten accustomed to giving him a little more freedom than the other clients.

She went first to the barn, intending to chat with Austin and see how he was doing with Mr. Deitrich. The older man had a tendency to slip away and wander off. One time, they'd found him in a stall brushing down a horse. Luckily, the old mare was quiet and not the high-strung gelding Gary Forrester used for endurance riding.

Loud footsteps echoed through the barn aisle. Lilly stopped and spun around. For a brief second she thought Jake might be hurrying to meet up with her. Instead, the child who'd been crying earlier tore into the barn, his mother and an older child in hot pursuit. They caught up with him at the first stall—where he'd mistakenly tried to hide—and carried him kicking and screaming back to the group of guests waiting to mount up.

Lilly tried not to be judgmental of parents and how they handled their children but in her opinion the heated swimming pool or a game of Ping-Pong might be a better afternoon activity for that family.

Mr. Deitrich was emptying a wheelbarrow of manure into the Dumpster and happily carrying on a conversation with someone only he could see. Lilly would rather he talk with Austin, and went to find out why the rookie caregiver wasn't within visual distance of the older man.

A high-pitched scream brought Lilly to a halt. It was closely followed by a woman's angry shouts. A sense of dread came over Lilly and she changed direction, rushing back the way she'd come. Had something happened to one of the center's clients? Who was the last one riding Big Ben? If only she could remember.

It was immediately apparent when she emerged from the barn that the young child she'd seen earlier was the one screaming and his mother was the one yelling. In the next instant, a ranch hand hauled the boy off the horse he'd been sitting on and placed him in the woman's arms. Sobbing hysterically, the child clung to her, wrapping his legs around her waist. The outraged mother lit into the poor man, raising her voice even louder to be heard over her child's cries. To his credit, the ranch hand merely stood there and took it.

The other guests backed away slowly, as if the scene was too ugly and too embarrassing to be part of. Lilly decided they had the right idea and turned toward the barn.

She glanced back over her shoulder. The few remaining guests were meandering off. In their wake stood a lone young man, his head hung in shame.

"Oh, no!" Lilly's eyes darted to the bench, though she knew it would be empty, and her stomach dropped to her knees. This was her fault. She shouldn't have left to go find Mr. Deitrich.

Breaking into a run, she hollered, "Jimmy Bob!"

He raised a miserable face to her.

Short of breath and near frantic, she took him by the arm. "What happened, honey?"

"Is this your son?" The woman redirected her anger at Lilly.

"No, but he's in my care. I'm the administrator of the local adult day care center. Jimmy Bob is one of our clients."

"Well, you need to keep better track of them," she said with a sneer. "My boy was almost injured because of him. If that horse had reared...well, you can bet my attorney would be in contact with yours."

"Please." Lilly did her best to remain calm. Firing back at the woman wouldn't help the situation. "Tell me what Jimmy Bob did."

"Is there a problem?" Jake stepped from between two people who had stopped to gawk, Gary Forrester on his heels.

"Who are you?" the mother asked. Her son had stopped crying and began kicking his legs to get down. She frowned but held tight.

"One of the owners here. How can I help you?"

She seemed quite pleased to be talking with someone in authority. "This...person—" she indicated Jimmy Bob "—took my boy when my back was turned and put him on that horse. Any...*idiot* could see he's scared to death and didn't want to ride."

Lilly disliked the woman's use of the word *idiot*. This, however, wasn't the right moment to educate her on name-calling or labeling special-needs individuals.

Jimmy Bob began to stammer. "I d-didn't m-mean

nothing, Ms. Russo. I just w-wanted to help. Like I help Samuel and Joey and Miranda ride B-Big Ben."

"It's okay, Jimmy Bob." Lilly patted his shoulder.

"Excuse me, but it's not okay." The mother finally let go of her son, who hit the ground and dashed off to join his brother. "People like him shouldn't be allowed near young children. They certainly shouldn't be allowed to wander around a guest resort *unsupervised*." Her laser-beam glare traveled from Lilly to Jake. "I can't believe that you, as one of the owners, would permit it."

"Please accept my apologies," Jake said cordially, every bit the businessman. "I'd like to invite you and your family to stay an additional night, compliments of the ranch."

"We're leaving tomorrow. I have to be back at work."

"Another time, then. The front desk will issue you a gift certificate good for a year."

"I expect a full refund for the ride, since we're not going."

"Of course. If you'd like to take your sons fishing, I can have someone drive you to our private fishing hole."

"I suppose we could do that." Appeased, the woman called to her sons.

While she and Jake made the arrangements, Lilly escorted a distressed Jimmy Bob over to the bench. When he finally calmed down, she reminded him of the rules and his promise to stay put.

Austin appeared about the time she finished. "What happened?"

"Where have you been?"

"The bathroom. Joey had an accident."

"Where's Georgina?"

"With Mr. Deitrich now. She was with me. Joey threw a fit and wouldn't let me clean him up. Georgina had to help."

Obviously, they were becoming too comfortable at the ranch and too trusting of their clients.

Lilly also owed Jake an apology. The boy's mother might have been rude and insulting, but she'd also been right—the people from Horizon did need constant supervision and she had failed to provide it.

"Hey, Jimmy Bob."

She jumped at Jake's voice. What if he'd come to tell her their deal was no longer working and she had to find a new home for Big Ben?

"Are you okay?" He approached Jimmy Bob and clapped the young man's shoulder.

"I didn't mean to hurt that kid."

"You didn't hurt him. But from now on, let Little José help with any of the children, okay? That's his job, not yours." Jake reached into his pants pocket and pulled out a set of keys. He held them out to Jimmy Bob. "Can you hook the flatbed trailer to the tractor by yourself or do you need help?"

Jimmy Bob exploded into a huge grin. "I can do it."

"Gary will meet you behind the barn in ten minutes. There's a lot of hay to load."

"Thanks." He threw himself at Jake, hugging him fiercely.

Jake returned the hug. "See you later, pal."

Just when Lilly thought she knew the father of her child, he'd surprised her. "You didn't have to do that," she said, her mouth curving into a smile. "Jimmy Bob was left alone, and he shouldn't have been. Trust me, it won't happen again."

"The truth is that woman is nothing but a pain in the rear. The front office has received four complaints from her already."

"Still, Jimmy Bob shouldn't have taken her son and put him on that horse."

"No, he shouldn't have. But he meant well, and he only beat Little José to it. Both boys went riding with their father yesterday and loved it. The kid was pitching a fit for his mother's benefit."

Lilly stared at Jake in disbelief. "Then why did you give her a complimentary night?"

"I didn't like the way she talked about Jimmy Bob."

"Me neither, but that's no reason to reward her."

"It shut her up, didn't it?"

"Jake." Lilly's throat tightened. For what seemed like the hundredth time that day, she cursed her out-of-control hormones.

"Hey." He tugged her into his arms.

She knew better than to let him hold her in front of the ranch employees, and she sure as heck shouldn't let him do it with Georgina, Austin and the clients nearby. It violated every professional standard she held herself to. But Jake had defended Jimmy Bob and treated him like any other person.

More than that, Jake's arms felt good wrapped around her, as if they belonged there.

"What's this?" He set her aside with a lingering once-over. "New shirt?"

"Yes." She laughed and turned to give him a view of her silhouette.

"I like it. Shows off your baby bump."

"I like it, too."

"Are you free on Saturday night?"

"I could be."

"It's my aunt Millie's sixtieth birthday. We're having a private party for her in the dining hall after dinner. Will you come?"

She hesitated before accepting. This wasn't a simple dinner invitation. Jake was, in essence, bringing her home to meet his family. *All* of them. Including his daughters, who, as far as Lilly knew, were still unhappy about her and the baby.

He'd evidently read her mind. "We can't go on avoiding the girls."

"You're right. I just don't want a scene to put a damper on your aunt's party."

"Several of my tenants are going to be there. You're bound to have met some of them. You can use them for cover."

She laughed. "It does sound like fun."

"I'll pick you up at five-thirty."

"Okay."

He gave her a quick, almost platonic kiss on the

lips. The tingle coursing through her, however, was a solid ten on the Richter scale.

"I hate to leave," he said. "I have an appointment back at the office."

"And I have to find Mr. Deitrich."

Jake had hardly disappeared before Lilly began having second thoughts about going to the party with him. Until now, her biggest concern had been his children. She hadn't worried much about the rest of his family, assuming they were like hers, loving and supportive.

But what if the Tuckers weren't? What if they felt just as strongly about her and the baby as the girls did? Could that be the reason Jake had said so little about his parents?

Now she wished she'd asked him before he left instead of letting herself become distracted by his kiss.

Chapter 10

Lilly had met most of the Tucker family before, many of them at the Labor Day cookout just before she'd started dating Jake. But she hadn't been wearing maternity clothes then, and he hadn't introduced her as the mother of his child.

It did make a difference.

There were wall-to-wall Tuckers at Millie Sweetwater's birthday party, and the vast majority of them didn't know how to take Lilly. Reactions ranged from hostility to friendliness, uncertainty to curiosity, with Jake's daughters clearly at the negative end of the spectrum.

Jake's mother fell somewhere in the middle. She sat across from Lilly at one of the large tables, trying hard to include Lilly in the dinner conversation, showing an interest in the baby by asking questions—questions that most expectant mothers would be delighted to answer. Questions that indicated Jake's failure to mention Lilly's medical history.

"Have you picked out a color for the nursery?"

"Not yet." Lilly nibbled on her barbeque chicken.

"That's right. You don't know the baby's sex." Mrs. Tucker's glance took in Jake as well as Lilly. "Have you decided on any names?"

Lilly shook her head. "We're still tossing ideas around."

Mrs. Tucker's expression showed signs of strain. She'd gotten similar answers when she'd asked if Lilly had scheduled a maternity leave and enrolled in a labor class.

How could she explain that she was waiting to learn the baby's health?

"Are your parents coming out when the baby's born?"

"My mother is. She should be done with school by then." Lilly relaxed. Here was a safer subject.

"School? Is she a teacher?"

"No, she's studying to be one. She and my dad came out over Christmas during semester break."

"Yes, Jake mentioned that. You must miss them, living so far away."

"I do."

Jake reached for her hand under the table. "Unlike the Tuckers. We tend to live on top of each other."

"Which is just the way I want it, young man." Mrs. Tucker's scolding was filled with warmth and affection. She turned her attention back to Lilly. "I hope to meet your mother when she comes."

"I'm sure she'd like that, too."

"If you need anything, please call me."

"I will."

It was a promise she very much hoped to keep—because Mrs. Tucker, despite her obvious reservations, was the type of sweet, kindhearted woman Lilly wanted as a grandmother for her child. Especially because her own mother was so far away. Lately, she'd been missing her parents. Their visit at Christmas had been too brief for Lilly and she was thrilled her mother had agreed to return when the baby was born.

Jake remained by her side at dinner and for most of the party that followed. But eventually, duty called. His cousins had planned a *This Is Your Life* activity to celebrate their mother's birthday that required Jake's participation. For the last half hour, Lilly had sat in the audience, convinced that if she listened hard enough, she'd hear her name on everyone's lips.

If she thought this was bad, how would Jake's family react after the baby was born?

How would they act if the child had severe birth defects?

"Hello, Miss Russo." LeAnne bounded up to Lilly, her genuine smile standing out in a sea of polite, yet reserved ones. She laid a hand on Lilly's stomach. "Can I feel the baby move?"

"It's a little early for that."

"You said you felt the baby move." LeAnne frowned in confusion. "Why can't I?"

Her expression was so serious, Lilly had to laugh out loud.

"What's wrong?"

"Nothing." Lilly moved LeAnne's hand higher on the small mound of her belly. "Try this."

LeAnne puckered her lips and concentrated.

Lilly abruptly stopped laughing. Would this child look like her or Jake? Would he or she have Kayla's button nose, LeAnne's dimples or Briana's stubborn streak?

"I felt something!" LeAnne beamed, showing two missing teeth on the bottom.

"You did?" Lilly thought it might have been her stomach gurgling and not the baby, but she played along, delighting in the moment and her budding relationship with Jake's youngest. Whatever could or would or had gone wrong tonight, she'd have this memory.

"I'm going to tell Daddy."

Before Lilly could stop her, LeAnne scampered off, and Lilly was left alone once more. But not for long.

"See, we Tuckers aren't all bad." Jake's cousin Carolina sat down in an empty chair beside Lilly.

"I never said you were," Lilly replied casually, as yet undecided about Carolina's motives.

"You have every reason to think badly of us," she said with mirth rather than rancor in her voice. "Especially if you judge the lot of us by Briana."

"She's a teenage girl."

"She's a lot like her mother. Very intolerant when everything in her world isn't perfectly to her liking.

But have no fear. If you can give her time, she'll mellow, and one day you won't even remember what annoyed you about her."

"I can hardly wait."

Carolina grinned. "I bet you can't. And no matter what she claims, Briana loves babies. More than LeAnne. She could put herself through college on the money she's earned babysitting."

"No kidding!"

"There's one of her regular clients as we speak." Carolina pointed to a young couple with a baby Lilly guessed to be about a year old. "That's Natalie, our manager of guest services, and her husband, Aaron. He's another of the ranch owners."

"I've met Natalie in the office," Lilly said, "and spoken to her on the phone. I didn't realize she was married to one of the owners."

"Aaron is a Tucker purely by association. He was married to Jake's sister, Hailey. She left him her share of the ranch when she died."

"Oh." Lilly's mind raced. She knew Jake and his manager of guest services were friends. She assumed it was because they'd both grown up on the ranch. Not once during their acquaintance had Jake mentioned that Natalie's husband was his former brother-in-law.

"Yeah, *oh,*" Carolina mimicked Lilly. "Things were pretty strange there for a while, very awkward if you catch my drift. We're over it now," she added airily, "and everyone gets along great. One big happy family." She nudged Lilly with her elbow. "It'll be that way for you, too. Don't worry. You just have to hang

in there. Give us Tuckers a chance to work through
our shock and jump off our high horses."

A commotion at the front of the room distracted
Lilly before she could answer.

Carolina rose. "I have to go. They're bringing the
cake out. If I'm not there to sing 'Happy Birthday,'
Mom will disown me, and I do love being a member
of this family." She held out her hand and when Lilly
clasped it, said, "So will you."

Lilly joined in the singing, though her mind remained on her conversation with Jake's cousin. Afterward, while the cake was being served, she did attempt
to see the people at the party through different eyes. It
had been selfish of her to assume that only she, Jake
and his daughters had been affected by their baby. Or
that no one else cared.

She'd also been shortsighted, forgetting that even
bad situations—like losing her first three children—
could bring some good. Her marriage might have
ended but she'd grown closer to her parents, discovered strengths in herself she didn't know she possessed, left an unfulfilling job for one she loved and
met a man who supported her unconditionally where
their unborn child was concerned.

Definitely some good.

She watched Jake eat cake and joke with his family, and her heart stirred with emotion. It wasn't due
to hormones, not this time. Her feelings for him were
real and growing stronger by the day. Soon she'd have
to deal with them and try to figure out what the future
held. But not here and not tonight.

As if he sensed she was thinking about him, he glanced up. His eyes, brimming with amusement a moment ago, turned dark and intense. Desire sparked inside Lilly. She hadn't felt anything this powerful and this consuming between them in a long time. Not since the night they'd made love in his hot tub.

Neither of them broke eye contact. Not even when Jake set his plate of half-eaten cake on the table and strode toward her. Lilly didn't remember standing but all at once she was on her feet.

"I'll get your coat," he said, escorting her from the room.

"Shouldn't you say goodbye to your family?"

"I'll call them tomorrow."

"I don't want to be inconsiderate." Or ruin the progress she'd made with LeAnne and Carolina.

Jake's cousin interrupted her conversation with an older couple to wave at Jake and Lilly on their way out the door. Lilly wasn't quite sure what to make of Carolina's knowing look and decided it was friendly.

Jake had driven his old Buick, so she didn't have to climb into the truck cab. Recently back from the repair shop, it looked as good as new. At the main highway, he turned left, toward Payson and her house. With each mile they drove, her pulse quickened.

What had altered between them so suddenly? And what would happen when they reached her door?

Lilly knew the answer long before they arrived at her house and had not one qualm about her decision. Jake wasn't merely the father of her child. She cared for him—far more than when they'd first dated. And he reciprocated her feelings more than when they'd first dated, as he'd repeatedly demonstrated in recent weeks.

"Would you like to come in?" She inserted the key in her front door.

"Are you absolutely sure?"

She heard his unspoken concerns and tried to put them to rest. "Very sure."

He cupped her cheek, then slid his fingers into her hair. She tipped her head back, giving herself over to the sensual tingling his touch evoked.

"I'm glad."

He lowered his head and skimmed the sensitive skin along her jawline with his lips, heightening her already soaring arousal. She'd completely forgotten about their surroundings. A passing car brought her to her senses.

"We should go inside."

Jake reached around her and opened the door. A rectangle of soft light fell on them from the entry-hall lamp Lilly always left on, illuminating them from the shoulders down. Jake's face remained in shadow, his expression hidden, his thoughts and feelings a mystery for her to discover during the night ahead.

Inside the house, Lilly removed her jacket. Jake took it from her and hung it along with his in the hall closet. She went into the kitchen, mostly because she was unexpectedly shy and uncertain of what to do next.

The sink felt like a safe place, so she went there,

turning on the small overhead light. "Would you like something to drink? I have beer in the fridge."

"No. I'm fine." He came up behind her and rested his hands on her shoulders. He nuzzled the collar of her dress aside and pressed his lips to the hollow at the base of her neck. "It's okay if you've changed your mind."

She all but melted as his warm breath caressed her exposed skin. "I haven't changed my mind." Being with Jake before had been wonderful and exciting. Now that they knew each other on a deeper level, had spent countless hours in each other's company, she could only imagine how much better their love-making would be.

He lowered one hand to clasp her waist. His palm came to rest on her rounded belly, and she involuntarily leaned against him, her back flush with his muscled chest. So much for leaping to conclusions. Jake wanted her with the same ferocity she did him.

"I can't wait to hold our baby," he said in her ear, his voice low and rough as he tenderly stroked the mound beneath which their child lay.

"Jake." If she could just be certain he'd feel the same after their baby was born.

In that moment, with his arms embracing her and his mouth tantalizing her, it was easy for her to believe he would.

"I want you to know I care about you," he said, turning her slowly to face him.

She could see the truth of his admission shining in his eyes, and it thrilled her to the core.

"I always have," he continued, his hands sliding to her hips and pulling her closer, his potent half-smile mesmerizing. "I can't tell you how glad I am you walked into my office that day with your proposition about the mule."

"Really?"

"That suit you were wearing was hot as hell."

She laughed. "I was trying to be professional."

"Business women are sexy." He seduced her with quick, light kisses. "You're sexy."

"I'm fat."

"You're having a baby. My baby. There isn't anything sexier than that."

He claimed her mouth in a fierce and possessive kiss that stole her senses. This was the Jake she remembered, the one who'd made exquisite and incredible love to her before their relationship had come to an abrupt halt.

His hands circled her waist, then moved up her sides. When he stopped just short of covering her breasts, she moaned in frustration. Winding her arms around his neck, she raised her hips to meet his, nestling his erection in the junction of her legs.

He stopped kissing her in order to draw a ragged breath. She thought he might take her into her bedroom. Instead, he stepped back and in one fluid motion, unsnapped his cowboy shirt and pulled it off. His undershirt followed. Both landed on the counter.

Lilly stared. She'd recalled every detail of his chest and torso, or so she'd believed. Their nights together weren't something she'd easily forget. Memory, however, paled when compared to reality. Jake was fit and strong and his muscles beckoned her fingertips, enticing them to trace the smooth contours. His skin, a healthy bronze even in late February, invited her lips to touch and taste.

She was helpless to resist, and she reached out to him.

He captured her hand in midair, and she murmured a protest.

"Not yet." He turned her hand over and kissed the inside of her palm, sending shivers dancing down her spine. "I want to see you first."

"Here? In the kitchen?"

"Kitchen, bedroom, anywhere you'd like. Just don't make me wait."

"The solarium?" Lilly asked.

Jake groaned his approval and swept her into his arms. He carried her down the hall and to the small room off the back of the house. The original owners had chosen to enclose the back porch with insulated glass and fill it with green plants that thrived all year long, even in the cold of winter. Lilly had added to the room by purchasing a double-wide chaise longue. She liked whiling away a lazy weekend afternoon, reading or napping in the bright sun.

At night, the solarium remained warm for hours. And if the stars were out in abundance, like they were tonight, the view was spectacular—the perfect setting to rekindle a romance.

Jake set her on her feet, and she picked up the blanket she kept on the chaise longue, spreading it over the cushion. She felt his eyes on her, heard him unbuckle his belt. His jeans rustled as he pulled them off, and his boots thudded when they hit the tile floor.

She straightened and might have begun undressing herself if not for the touch of his fingers brushing aside her hair and tugging on the zipper of her dress. The fabric slowly parted, and she stepped out of her clothes.

Jake stroked her shoulders, her back, her upper arms. "You're so beautiful."

Any worries she'd had that he might not find her body as attractive as before her pregnancy disappeared when he turned her toward him. The solarium was dark, starlight and a half-hidden moon the only illumination. But Lilly didn't need to see Jake's eyes to sense the raw hunger burning in them. She could feel it—almost touch it—the sensation was so powerful.

She lowered herself onto the chaise, pulling him down beside her. He resisted, one knee propped on a corner.

"I didn't bring any protection."

She laughed. "I think it's a little late for that."

He remained sober. "I haven't been with anyone since our breakup. I haven't told you that before, but it's important to me that you know."

She met his intensely probing gaze. "You're the only man I've been with besides my ex-husband. The only one I've wanted to be with."

Jake came to her then, covering them both with the blanket. Beneath it, his hands roamed her body and together they discovered the changes resulting from her pregnancy.

He kissed her mouth, her neck, her collarbone and her breasts. His lips lingered on her stomach, his fingertips brushing its gentle rise. Lilly sighed when his mouth continued downward, and his hands parted her legs. Jake had the ability to make her feel utterly cherished, and tonight was no exception. He brought her quickly to the edge but she stopped him before she tumbled over.

"What's the matter?" he asked, his breath tickling her.

"Nothing." She tugged on his arms. In response, he positioned himself over her, his weight on his bent elbows. "Everything's just right."

"I don't want to hurt the baby," he said.

"You won't," she assured him and inhaled sharply when he entered her.

Their lovemaking had always been wonderful. But it was more so now, sweeter and infinitely more satisfying because of the months they'd spent getting to know each other and the intimacy brought about by creating a child.

She climaxed, calling his name. His release came moments later, and she held him through it, wrapping herself around him. Afterward, they snuggled under the blanket, talking softly and watching thin, wispy clouds drift past the stars.

"Are you sure we didn't hurt the baby?" He tenderly rubbed her stomach with his hand.

"Dr. Paul told me weeks ago I could resume normal sexual relations as long as I took it easy."

"Funny. I don't remember her saying that."

"It was during a phone call."

"And you didn't tell me?"

"At the time, I wasn't having any normal sexual relations to resume."

"I'm glad we waited."

So was she. Too much, too soon was one of the reasons their relationship had failed.

Jake's cell phone buzzed from beneath the chaise. "Sorry." He kissed her on the lips before rolling over and fumbling in the dark. "That's strange," he said, checking the caller ID as he sat up.

"What?"

"Someone's calling me from my house." He put the phone to his ear. "This is Jake Tucker… Sweetie, what are you doing there?" he asked. "All right, calm down." Another pause. "No, I'm…with Lilly." He groaned under his breath. "Lower your voice, please." This time there was a considerably longer pause, then he said, "I'll be right there. Don't leave, you hear me?" He ended with "Call your mother and let her know where you are," and hung up.

"I'm almost afraid to ask," Lilly said when he was done.

Jake shoved the fingers of one hand into his hair. "Briana's at the house. She had another fight with her mother and drove there from the party. In the old maintenance truck, of all things."

"I didn't think she had her license."

"She doesn't. Only her learner's permit." He blew out a long breath as he stood, then began throwing on his clothes. "She went to the house, expecting me to be there." He sat back down to put on his socks and boots. "I'm not sure which one of us is angrier. Me at her for taking the truck and driving without a license, or her at me for not being at the house when she arrived."

Lilly wrapped herself in the blanket, collected her clothes from the floor and walked with Jake to the kitchen, where he retrieved his shirts. "Is she upset about us being together?"

"Not so much."

Lilly had heard Jake's end of the phone conversation and suspected he was minimizing his daughter's reaction.

"I hate leaving like this," he said at her front door after a last kiss.

"Briana needs you."

He stroked her cheek with the pad of his thumb. "There's a lot I was going to say to you tonight. I feel bad about not getting to it."

Lilly did, too, but didn't add to his guilt by saying so. "You'd better hurry."

"I'll call you tomorrow," he said and left.

She closed the door after him, her emotions at odds. Jake was a family man; it was one of his most attractive qualities. Lilly couldn't be angry at him for going to his daughter when she was in trouble. And she couldn't be mad at Briana, who was having difficulty coping with the many unhappy changes in her young life.

And yet, she *was* angry. Or, at least, frustrated and confused. Everyone at the party had seen her and Jake leave together, including Briana. Had the girl's stunt been a deliberate attempt to sabotage Lilly and Jake's relationship?

She was afraid the answer was yes, and that Briana might never accept her and the baby.

"She wouldn't have run away if you hadn't left with your girlfriend."

"Briana didn't run away. She went to my house."

Jake cursed his good cell phone reception. Usually, three miles outside Payson his phone quit working. But bad luck and an open passage in the mountains made it possible for Ellen to go on and on, blowing the incident with Briana out of all proportion. What else was new?

"She stole a vehicle."

"She took a ranch truck without permission and called me the minute she got to my house to let me know what she'd done and where she was." Not to mention hurl unkind accusations, which he'd chosen not to address in front of Lilly.

"Her behavior's out of control. We have to do something about it."

"You're right, Ellen. Maybe we should consider family counseling. For Briana and all of us. I could use some advice on how to deal with the girls." And how to bring harmony to their relationship with Lilly and their soon-to-be-born sibling, but he refrained from mentioning that to Ellen.

"Sure, blame them for your problems," Ellen said with disgust. "Briana's only giving us grief because you got that woman pregnant."

"Me? What about you? You're the one who—"

Fortunately, at that moment, Jake's phone died. He snapped it shut and tossed it on the passenger seat. What he needed to do—more than argue with his ex-wife—was think about what to say to Briana. Her actions might be sympathetic and understandable to a degree, but that didn't make her unauthorized use of a ranch vehicle, let alone what she'd said about Lilly, acceptable.

He pulled in to his driveway and parked beside the old truck. Angry as he was at his daughter, a small part of him took pride in her. He knew from personal experience that the truck drove like a tank. Briana had managed to make the three miles from the ranch to his house in the dark and on a narrow, winding mountain road. It seemed he'd been wrong, and she was capable of handling her mother's new convertible after all.

Briana sat curled on the couch in the family room, the TV on, but muted, and her iPod earphones in place. She yanked out the earphones and turned off the TV when she saw him.

"Before you start in on me, I admit I screwed up. I shouldn't have taken the truck without permission."

"Taking the truck without permission is the least of your mistakes. You broke the law. Your mother and I have good reason not to let you get your driver's license."

"Dad! You wouldn't." She shot upright. "That's not fair."

"I didn't say we'd do it." He sat on the opposite side of the couch. "Only that we have good reason. But rest assured, there will be a punishment."

"I figured as much." She sat back down, hugging the corner cushion.

"Why'd you do it, Briana?"

"I told you, Mom and I had another fight."

"That's not what she said."

"Whatever."

"Briana."

His needling succeeded in unleashing her anger. "Why'd you have to leave early—with *her?*"

"I brought Lilly to the party. Of course I took her home."

"And stayed there."

Yes, he'd done that, and it had been worth it.

"Lilly and I are involved. We're having a baby together."

"You don't have to remind me."

Okay…it was obvious reasoning with her wasn't going to work. "If you'd told me—"

"I couldn't. You left." Briana's face crumpled, her anger apparently spent.

Jake realized in that moment he'd been missing something important. "Why did you come here, sweetie? What's really bothering you?"

She wiped her nose with her shirtsleeve and said in a tiny voice, "I wanted to talk about moving in with you. Permanently."

"I see."

"You could act happier."

"It's not that. You know how much I'd love to have you live here. But your mother and I have an agreement."

"She has no say. I was talking to some other kids at school, and I'm old enough by law to decide for myself which parent I want to live with."

Who needed an attorney when they had informed friends? He tried a different approach.

"You'd be moving away from your sisters."

"Not really. I'd see them every day at the ranch. And Wednesday nights and every other weekend."

"Is that enough?"

"It is for you."

Ouch! "Let's talk about this some more tomorrow. I'm not opposed to the idea," he said before she could interrupt him, "but there's a lot to consider."

Like Lilly and the baby moving in. Many of Briana's problems with her mother stemmed from her feelings of being displaced, physically and emotionally, by her stepfather and periodically visiting stepbrother. The same thing could happen here with a new stepmother and baby, especially one who might need a lot of attention. "I want you to be sure you'd be moving in for the right reasons, not because you had a fight with your mom and you're mad at her."

"Yeah, I get it." Some of her defiance returned. "Everything's changed now that you knocked up Ms. Russo."

"Briana!" It took every ounce of his willpower not to respond in anger.

"Oh, please. What about all those talks you gave me on being responsible and abstinence and waiting until you're ready. Weren't *you* listening?"

He cringed inwardly. Was talking about sex with your children ever easy? Jake weighed his words before speaking them. He couldn't mess this up.

"Lilly and I didn't have indiscriminate sex. We care a lot about each other. We were also responsible and used protection. Unfortunately, it failed. Or not unfortunately, depending on how you look at it."

"What do you mean?" she said snippily.

He'd been planning to wait until next weekend to tell the girls about Lilly's medical history. Now might be better.

"Lilly's been pregnant before. Three times."

"She has kids?"

"No. Two of the babies were stillborn. The last one had severe birth defects and didn't live long."

"Oh." Not unexpectedly, his news appeared to disturb Briana.

"Lilly has a genetic disorder. I don't understand much except that she's always wanted children and hasn't been able to have them. Her doctor thinks her chances are better with this baby because he or she has a different father. And I care about Lilly and I want her to have a healthy baby."

"What if the baby's not healthy?"

"Then we'll cross that bridge when we come to it."

"You'd be stuck. You'd have to pay for that kid."

"I've never thought of myself as being 'stuck' with any of my children."

"Because it's your duty."

"A duty I've always enjoyed. I love you girls."

Just when he assumed he was getting somewhere with Briana, she showed him how very far he still had to go.

"Well, *your* duty shouldn't have to be *my* duty," she said and sprang up from the couch, snatching her iPod. "You're trying to make yourself sound all noble and everything, giving Lilly the kid she's always wanted. But the truth is you got her pregnant, and now we're all forced to put up with that baby in our lives whether we like it or not. A baby who could be born screwed up or even die. How fair is that?"

She fled the family room and ran down the hall. A few seconds later, Jake heard her bedroom door slam.

Some time passed before he moved from the couch. Briana might have thrown a childish fit but he couldn't dismiss her feelings or the painful points she'd raised. He wanted to be a good father to Lilly's baby. But in so doing, was he being a lousy father to his daughters?

Chapter 11

Lilly studied her computer screen, scrolling through the photographs one by one. Her mother had taken the pictures at the enlistment party of their neighbor's son, Peter, and emailed them to Lilly together with a long, newsy letter. The last photo showed him in uniform with his wife and their young baby, Peter's military cap perched crookedly on the child's little head. They all looked so happy and so...complete.

For several seconds, Lilly envied them. Fortunately, the emotion didn't last. She had much to be grateful for, including a job she loved that gave her tremendous satisfaction. If she never attained that complete family, she'd still have a wonderful life.

But, oh, it would be nice to have at least one child....

She imagined pictures of her holding a baby, Jake

by her side. Would he be her husband or simply the father of her child? He hadn't proposed to her again, but as the weeks passed with more good reports from Dr. Paul, Lilly expected him to pop the question again any day.

She only wished she knew how she'd answer him if—and when—he did ask.

Lilly dashed off a quick e-mail to her mother. She thanked her for the pictures, told her about Jake's aunt's birthday party last week, and assured her of how well her pregnancy—nearly six months and counting—was progressing. She also officially accepted her mother's offer to fly out when the baby was born, saying they'd firm up a date later. Lilly's mother wouldn't be satisfied with that response, but she'd have to live with it. At this point Lilly refused to make any more plans than the bare minimum because of the risk that they'd change or become unnecessary.

She was both elated and scared to be approaching her third trimester. It was around this time that she'd lost her first baby, and she couldn't help recalling that terrible day. Sadly, those memories were sabotaging her happiness—and her relationship with Jake, which also seemed to be going well.

Clicking the send button, she exited her email program and shut down the computer. Jake was due any second. They were going to the Payson Rodeo, an annual event that drew thousands of people to the small town and had filled the ranch's guest cabins to capacity.

What made this outing special was that they were

having lunch with his cousin, Carolina, and her boy-friend, then meeting Jake's family at the rodeo where they'd all sit together. Briana, along with other students from her school, was performing in the opening ceremony.

Jake arrived on time, as usual, and walked Lilly to his Buick.

"I thought we'd be driving in your truck," she said, taking his hand.

"Carolina and Denny decided to come with us rather than meet at the restaurant. Then they'll hitch a ride home with my folks after the rodeo."

It was then that Lilly noticed the couple in the back-seat. "Great." She liked Jake's cousin. Though they weren't quite friends yet, they'd been getting along well since the night of Millie's birthday party. "I finally get to meet the boyfriend."

"One of them." Jake shot her an amused look. "I think she has two on the string these days."

Lilly had gotten an earful about Carolina's dating habits. From Carolina, not Jake. His cousin made no secret of the fact that she had zero intention of settling down, or at least not for years.

The trip to the restaurant went quickly. Lilly took an instant liking to Denny, Carolina's guy *du jour,* and the four of them savored a lovely meal in the outdoor dining area of the restaurant. But Lilly's nerves kicked into high gear the moment the rodeo parking lot came into sight. She had yet to make the kind of progress with the rest of Jake's family as she had with Carolina and LeAnne.

His two youngest daughters sat in the bleachers beside their grandparents. Next to them were the For-resters, Gary, his wife, their daughter, Natalie, and their granddaughter, a squirmy and very pretty toddler.

Natalie's husband, a former national rodeo cham-pion, wasn't with them. He'd retired from the circuit after his first wife, Jake's sister, Hailey, had died, and he now worked for a radio broadcasting company. Jake and Lilly had stopped by the station's booth on the way to their seats to say hello to him.

Jake helped Lilly up the aluminum steps to their seats in the bleachers. The girls scrambled over to him as soon as he sat down, chatting excitedly about their day and what he'd missed so far—namely the petting zoo, cotton candy and a trip to the icky portable toi-lets. Everyone moved and shifted to accommodate the change in seating arrangements.

For the second time that day, Lilly experienced a stab of envy. It was much harder to rationalize the emo-tion away when happy families surrounded her. Jake's daughters hung all over him, their small hands resting on his shoulders and knees. Even harder to deal with was Natalie's toddler, who giggled and squealed and reached her chubby arms out to her grandparents in a bid for attention.

Lilly might have gone on feeling sorry for herself if not for LeAnne.

"Hi," she said, squeezing in beside Lilly, displacing her father in the process.

"Hi, there."

Without asking, she put her hand on Lilly's stomach. "How's the baby today?"

"Good. Sleeping now, I think. He or she hasn't moved much since lunch."

LeAnne lowered her head until her mouth was inches from Lilly's protruding stomach. "Hello, baby." She gently patted Lilly. "Can you hear me? I'm saving all my old toys so I can give them to you when you get older."

Lilly lifted her hand, hesitated, then tentatively touched LeAnne's hair. The little girl had included Lilly in her family circle, and she was enormously moved.

She glanced up to find Jake staring at her, his expression tender and paternal. "What if the baby's a boy?" He addressed LeAnne but grinned at Lilly. "He might not want to play with your Barbie dolls."

"I'm not giving him my Barbie dolls." LeAnne abruptly sat up. "He can have Ken. I don't like Ken all that much anyway, not since the dog chewed his arm."

Lilly's laughter vanquished the last of her envy. However things turned out with Jake and the baby, she had a new friend in LeAnne and another reason to be grateful.

If only forging relationships with the rest of Jake's family were as easy. His parents' greeting to her bordered on reserved, and Kayla kept her distance, always making sure either Jake or LeAnne was between her and Lilly.

A loud electronic screech pierced the air, causing one or two nearby people to raise their voices in protest. The arena speakers crackled to life, and a male voice came on, announcing the start of the rodeo, which would run through Sunday. Sponsors were acknowledged and thanked, concession stand and restroom locations identified and a brief summary of events listed. The emcee finished with a rousing welcome to fans and participants alike and with that, the opening ceremony began.

A gate at the far end of the arena opened. Arizona's reigning rodeo queen galloped out on a stunning palomino horse, a flag of the United States held high. Everyone stood. As she circled the arena, the national anthem played. When it was over, the audience cheered and took their seats. More riders followed, some dressed in period and Native-American costumes, some carrying banners.

"Look!" Jake's mom shouted. "There she is."

Briana burst from the gate with six other riders. Bright turquoise sashes identified them as the high school's equestrian drill team. They trotted in unison to the middle of the arena, where they performed a series of complicated dressage maneuvers.

Lilly was impressed. She'd seen Briana ride at the ranch and practice her barrel racing, but nothing like this.

Jake's mother leaned into his father, and they shared smiles that were both proud and sad. "She looks just like Hailey did at her age."

"Like you did, too." Mr. Tucker patted his wife's leg.

Watching Jake's parents, Lilly felt a small connection with them that she hadn't before. They'd lost a child, and that realization gave her pause. Could his parents' reaction to her be based on the fact that they didn't want their son to experience the same type of tragedy they had?

The drill team executed their last moves and lined up in the center of the arena. On cue, all seven horses went down on one knee in an elegant bow. The audience applauded wildly, showing their support for the hometown girls.

Lilly jumped to her feet, clapping and calling Briana's name. She didn't realize what she was doing until Jake joined her, and so did the rest of his family. Lilly sat back down only when the drill team had exited. Jake put an arm around her and drew her close. They exchanged a lingering glance before he let her go.

The crowd finally quieted, and the first event was announced.

Lilly didn't see the saddle bronc rider explode out of the chute. Kayla stood in her way. She'd crawled over her father to get to Lilly.

"Were you really happy for my sister, or were you faking it in order to impress my dad?"

"Kayla," Jake said sharply.

"That's all right. I'll answer the question." Lilly looked Kayla straight in the eyes. "Your sister Briana and I don't always get along. Neither do you and I. That doesn't mean I don't appreciate her hard work and her talent, whether it's with her school drill team or at the ranch. I cheered for your sister because I was genuinely impressed with her performance. And I would've done exactly the same thing even if I was sitting alone on the other side of the arena, and your dad didn't know I was here."

"Okay," Kayla said after a moment and sat down. On the other side of Lilly. Not next to her father.

Again, everyone shifted in their seats.

No one, Jake especially, seemed to mind.

"Good morning."

"Morning to you, too." Lilly snuggled closer to Jake, her cheek against his chest, her hand draped over his middle. Sunlight seeped through the partially open blinds, casting horizontal lines across the foot of the bed.

"Go back to sleep," he said, tracing the outline of her ear with a fingertip. "Just because I need to get up early doesn't mean you do."

"I wish you didn't have to go to work today."

"Me, too. But we have a lot to do to get ready for the annual breakfast ride. It's only six weeks away."

"Natalie said last year Aaron put the whole thing together in three weeks."

"It's bigger this year. And he wasn't a newlywed then."

Lilly almost hadn't expressed her wish that Jake stay home out loud, afraid he might misunderstand and assume she was ready to take another leap in their relationship. She was glad to see he'd treated her remark for what it was, a longing to extend the nice time they'd had, starting with lunch and the rodeo and ending with making love in his bed.

They hadn't been intimate since the night at her

place, when Jake had left in a hurry because Briana had "borrowed" one of the ranch trucks. Thankfully, there'd been no interruptions last night. When Jake suggested Lilly come home with him after the rodeo, she'd agreed without reservation. Briana had been occupied with her equestrian drill team and wasn't likely to pull a repeat stunt. The younger girls went home with their grandparents. No one was quite sure where Carolina and Denny had disappeared to—nor was anyone concerned.

Jake hadn't told Lilly until later that he needed to wake up early for work. As much as she would've liked to sleep in for another hour or two, tucked securely in the crook of his arm, she understood. The annual breakfast ride raised a considerable amount of money for the Hailey Reyes Foundation, a nonprofit organization founded by Aaron and named in honor of Jake's late sister. The foundation and the projects it funded were near and dear to his heart.

"I'll call you a little before lunch." He kneaded the small of her back. His strong fingers managed to find the very muscles that ached from sitting for hours in the bleachers. "I should be done by then and I'll swing by to pick you up and take you home. Unless—" his voice roughened and his hand moved lower "—you're willing to stay here another night."

"I don't have a toothbrush," she said around a yawn.

"Borrow mine."

"Or clothes."

"I have a pair of old gym shorts you can wear and plenty of sweatshirts."

"What about underwear?"

"Go without," he murmured seductively.

His palm slid up to her hip, and he pulled her against him, his breath coming faster. She anticipated finding him hard and ready and wasn't disappointed....

After his exquisite and thorough attention to her needs the previous night, she couldn't imagine being aroused again for at least a week. The desire winding through her and heightening her awareness was unexpected and thrilling. She embraced the sensations and returned the attention he'd paid her. When Jake finally entered her, after she'd driven him nearly crazy with her hands and mouth, she was already on the verge of climax.

She held out as long as possible. The instant they changed positions so that she straddled his waist, she lost every last shred of control. Seeing Jake caress her swollen breasts, run his thumbs across her nipples, sent her soaring.

Afterward, they lay in each other's arms, totally exhausted, completely satisfied and utterly content. Jake's idea of going back to sleep appealed to Lilly, and she closed her eyes. The lull lasted only a minute.

"Oh!"

"What's wrong?" Jake asked, immediately alert.

"Nothing." The glow within her blossomed and reached her lips. "The baby moved."

In the last month, the flutterings had given way to small jabs and jolts. Both her stillborn babies had hardly moved. She'd been too inexperienced during her first pregnancy to know that wasn't normal. During her second pregnancy, she prayed every day for even the tiniest twinge. There was none.

Evan had been different. He'd kicked and squirmed and wiggled and rolled. But then, his deformities weren't as severe as his brothers'.

Lilly's smile faded as happiness turned into anxiety. If only she could be sure this child would be born normal, then she'd be able to enjoy her pregnancy just like any other expectant mother. No sooner did the idea of asking Dr. Paul about having another ultrasound enter her mind than she dismissed it. She'd been so happy these last few weeks and couldn't bring herself to spoil it by finding out the baby had problems.

"Let me feel." Jake put his hand on her abdomen. "Where was it?"

"Over here." She moved his hand higher and to the side. They waited for several seconds but nothing happened.

"I guess he's taking a nap," Jake said, his face glum.

Lilly didn't know whether to feel sad or relieved. He wanted so much to share her pregnancy and took pleasure in the simplest things. But becoming attached meant that Jake would be devastated if the child didn't survive or was born like Evan.

They hadn't known each other when Hailey died. Lilly had started working at Horizon six months after the accident. She'd heard how long and profoundly he'd grieved the loss of his sister from some of the staff members at the center and more recently, from Carolina.

Lilly didn't want Jake to endure that kind of loss

again but knew of no way to protect him other than by distancing herself. He wouldn't stand for that, and she didn't want to stay away. Not after last night.

Her musings were disrupted by a sharp poke in her side.

"Hey! I felt something." Jake's face lit up. "Was that the baby?"

"Yes."

It was impossible not to take delight in his excitement. How wrong she'd been to think a devoted father and family man like him would ever be able to remain emotionally uninvolved with his unborn child.

And wasn't she the luckiest woman on earth to have him as the father?

He groaned. "There are days I wish the ranch would run itself." Planting a quick kiss on her lips, he hopped out of bed. "Stay right here."

"I really should get up." She threw back the blankets.

"Why?"

"To make coffee." Lilly didn't offer breakfast as Jake usually ate with his family in the dining hall at the ranch.

"That'd be nice."

While he showered, Lilly found those old gym shorts he'd mentioned and put them on, along with a tattered long-sleeved T-shirt he'd left hanging on a hook in the closet. In the kitchen, she found a canister of coffee and brewed a pot. When he came out to join her, dressed, shaved and ready for work, two steaming mugs were waiting on the table.

"Thanks," he said, sitting down.

"I figure I owed you after all the meals you've been feeding me lately. Lunch and dinner just yesterday."

"A hot dog and chips at the rodeo concession stand isn't what I call dinner."

"I had *three* hot dogs, if you remember." She attributed her enormous and embarrassing appetite to all the walking they'd done and the fresh air.

"You ate two. The baby ate one."

She started to make a snappy comeback about her weight but his sudden seriousness gave her pause. "What's wrong, Jake?"

"I like seeing you at my table, wearing my clothes."

"Oh." She sipped at her coffee, buying herself a few precious seconds to think. "Don't look too closely, I'm not at my best in the mornings."

"You're always beautiful."

She raised her mug. "Who needs sugar for coffee when Jake Tucker's around?"

He sat back in his chair, studying her critically. "You know how I feel. I want to get married before the baby's born."

"I do know, and I understand your reasons. But you have to understand my reasons for waiting to make any definite plans until later."

How long would it take her to get over Brad's ruthless abandonment and her fear of history repeating itself? Jake was a great guy. She was probably crazy not to at least consider marrying him. It was obvious he was trying and that her continued resistance hurt him.

"Okay. Forget the wedding. Move in with me."

"That sounds pretty definite."

"Not as definite."

"Your daughters may not agree, and if our relationship is going to succeed, we have to consider them."

"I also have a right to be happy."

"And what if the baby's stillborn or like Evan?" Lilly's throat burned. Their conversation was bringing back too many sad memories. "Do I move out after the funeral?"

"Not if you don't want to."

"There'd be no reason to stay."

"How do you know?" He pushed his plate aside and waited until she met his gaze. "Maybe there would be."

"We'd only be living together for the sake of the baby. If there is no baby…" She didn't finish.

"We have a lot of time yet."

God, she hoped so.

"Things change," he continued. One corner of his mouth turned up. "You could even fall in love with me."

Lilly didn't answer him for fear the unsteadiness in her voice would betray her. Not only could she fall in love with Jake, she was probably halfway there already.

An hour after Jake left for the ranch, Lilly began wishing they'd risen earlier so he could have taken her home. She'd cleaned the kitchen, checked the refrigerator and decided there were plenty of fixings for lunch—he said he'd be back by one at the latest—then tidied the bedroom, showered and dressed. Even after all that, three and a half long hours stretched before her.

Perusing the bookcase in the living room, she found a semi-interesting novel among the many testosterone-infused ones and curled up on the family-room couch, using a pile of throw pillows to support her back.

Her breakfast, for some reason, wasn't sitting well. Odd that oatmeal should bother her when the three concession-stand hot dogs the day before hadn't. Partway into the second chapter, what Lilly assumed was an upset stomach became mild twinges. Fearing cramps, she laid her head back on the cushion and tried to relax.

She must have dozed off because she was abruptly awakened by the sound of the front door opening. Was Jake home? She glanced at the digital clock on the entertainment center. How long had she been asleep? She climbed off the couch, a groan escaping her lips. Her legs and lower back were stiff from her awkward position on the couch, and her right hand tingled from lack of circulation.

"Jake?" She turned, her balance a little off, and massaged her stomach. The twinges hadn't lessened during her nap.

A figure appeared in the doorway.

It was hard to tell which of them was more startled, Lilly or Briana.

"What are you doing here?" Briana's eyebrows came together.

Lilly's first instinct was to defend herself. After all, she had every right to be there. But then, so did Briana. This was her father's house and, unlike Lilly, she didn't need an invitation.

"I'm waiting for your dad. He'll be here about one o'clock."

Lilly didn't elaborate but suspected from the further narrowing of Briana's gaze that she'd guessed Lilly had spent the night. Her father's gym shorts and T-shirt were probably a dead giveaway.

"Terrific," Briana grumbled and shot past Lilly, through the family room and toward the kitchen.

Lilly echoed the teenager's sentiments exactly. She bent to retrieve the book she'd been reading and rearrange the pillows on the couch when she was stabbed by a sharp pain in her lower back. Her first thought was the baby, but her concerns lessened when the pain began to recede. That would teach her to take naps curled in a tight ball. She wondered if Jake had any non-aspirin pain reliever in his bathroom cabinet—and how Briana would react if she saw Lilly going into her father's bedroom.

Briana reappeared from the kitchen, carrying a tall glass of orange juice. Ignoring Lilly, she plopped down on the opposite end of the couch from where Lilly had been sitting, grabbed the remote control and turned on the TV, adjusting the volume to one decibel below ear-splitting.

Lilly got the message and began to leave. Jake's back porch had a gorgeous view of the mountains. She'd read her book and wait there. A thought occurred to her and though it wasn't her place to ask, she did so anyway, her tone casual rather than accusatory.

"By the way, how'd you get here?"

"I didn't drive if that's what you're getting at," Briana snapped. "A friend dropped me off."

Well, that was good news. At least Briana and Jake wouldn't have another argument when he got home.

"I wondered if you'd be at the rodeo again today."

Briana's answer was to hunker down, her attention glued to the TV.

If she didn't want to talk, why didn't she just go to her bedroom? Lilly thought testily. It was almost as if Briana was staking a claim, challenging Lilly for position. Since Lilly was the one leaving, it appeared that Briana was the winner.

Lilly got only two steps away when Briana's head popped up over the back of the couch.

"Just because you're my dad's girlfriend, don't assume we're friends." She stared at Lilly, her eyes huge.

"I'm not assuming anything," Lilly answered calmly and would have continued to the porch if not for a sudden rush of moisture between her legs.

"There's something on your shorts." Briana's voice had a strange quality to it. So did her expression.

Lilly looked down and her legs nearly collapsed out from under her. Head swimming, she reached for the nearest handhold, which happened to be a coatrack. It teetered precariously.

"Are you okay?" Briana had stood and was coming around the couch.

Good thing, because Lilly was going to need help and fast.

Jake's gym shorts were soaked in blood.

Chapter 12

Dear God! It was happening again.

Lilly felt as if her legs were refusing to obey her brain's signals and function correctly.

"Should I call my dad?" Briana's voice, thin and scared, came from far away and did nothing to reassure Lilly.

"No. Nine-one-one."

"Do you need help?"

"Just call."

Lilly stumbled to the couch, her hand clutching her belly. There was so much blood, she could feel it collecting between her legs, dripping down her thighs. If she sat down, she'd ruin the furniture's upholstery. But she really should be lying flat with her feet elevated. She remembered that much from the previous stillbirths.

Where had Briana gone?

Lilly battled a wave of acute dizziness. She had to remain calm. Stress made things worse.

She heard Briana then, speaking on the kitchen phone, giving the operator Jake's address. Lilly was grateful for the teenager's presence. She'd been alone when she lost her first baby and had called the paramedics herself. Her ex-husband had met her at the hospital but by the time he arrived, it was too late. The baby was stillborn. Because of all the tests she'd had, her second stillbirth had been expected—which hadn't made it any less painful. But neither tragedy compared to the sorrow she'd endured when Evan had died.

"They're going to be a while," Briana said. She stood in the doorway between the kitchen and living room, her cheeks a startling shade of white.

"How long's a while?"

"Half an hour. Maybe more. The lady said traffic is backed up all through town because of the rodeo."

Half an hour! It might be too late by then. The ranch was closer. Jake could be here in ten or fifteen minutes.

"I changed my mind. Call your father."

"I'll drive you to the hospital." Briana took a tentative step forward.

"What?"

"I'll drive you."

"How will we get there?"

"Dad keeps a spare set of keys to the Buick in his office." She swallowed nervously. "It'll be faster."

Briana was right. And what did the lack of a driver's license matter at a time like this?

"Get some old towels. Lots of them. Hurry," Lilly added when Briana was slow to react.

She waited on the porch while Briana backed the old Buick out of the garage and pulled it around. Lilly had shoved a towel in the loose gym shorts in an attempt to contain the bleeding. To her surprise, Briana left the car running and jumped out to help her down the steps and into the rear seat, where Lilly lay down atop more towels.

"Thank you," Lilly said, well aware that she was trusting the life of her unborn child and possibly even her own to the hands of a fifteen-and-a-half-year-old girl who didn't much like her.

About five minutes into the twenty-five-minute drive, Briana started ticking off the names of familiar landmarks they passed. "The highway department storage yard's coming up."

It helped Lilly to know where they were and how much longer it would be until they reached Payson Regional Medical Center. From her prone position in the backseat, she couldn't see much more than patches of blue sky and the tops of pine trees flickering past. The view was strangely pretty and very surreal, like a scene in a movie shot from an abstract camera angle.

"We're at Thompson Draw," Briana said.

Lilly focused on the baby, evaluating each sharp stab of pain, each clenching of her abdominal muscles.

Was she having another episode of cramps or premature labor? When was the last time she'd felt the baby move? Had Dr. Paul been mistaken? Had resuming sexual relations harmed the baby?

"Little Green Valley."

The bleeding seemed to be slowing, or at least it felt slower to Lilly. She didn't dare move. Instead, she prayed. For the baby, for herself, for Jake and for Briana. Mostly for Briana, that she had the skill to get them safely to the hospital and not crash the car in the process.

"We're in Star Valley," she said, with less tension in her voice.

They were on the outskirts of Payson.

Thank God. The cramps—definitely not twinges—were strong and occurring more frequently. This was too much like her previous stillbirths, and Lilly began to fear the worst. Covering her face with her hands, she held back a sob.

One child, one precious baby. Was it too much to ask?

Briana slammed on the brakes hard, propelling Lilly forward. She threw out an arm, catching herself before she rolled off the seat.

"Sorry. A car cut in front of me."

There was that scared-little-girl voice again. Traffic was bad because of the rodeo and the thousands of tourists in town. It was just as well Lilly couldn't see more than telephone poles, billboard signs and second-story windows.

"How are you doing, Briana?"

"Okay. What about you?"

"Hanging in there." Barely. Lilly was soaked in sweat, covered in blood and scared as hell. "I'll make it, don't worry."

She conveyed a calm she was far from feeling. Briana was having enough trouble driving as it was. She didn't need to know her passenger was close to falling apart.

"What's happening?" Lilly asked. They'd slowed to a crawl, and she wanted speed. Lots of it.

"We're in downtown Payson. It's packed." Briana hit the brakes again and uttered a swear word her father wouldn't want to hear. "Sorry. People are everywhere."

Maybe Lilly should have waited for the paramedics. Then, a wailing siren would have cleared the way for them.

"If you see a police officer, flag him down. He can escort us to the hospital."

They didn't see a police officer, but a mile and fifteen grueling minutes up the road, traffic grew considerably lighter. Not long after, Briana swung the Buick into the hospital parking lot. She drove straight to the emergency room entrance, flung open the car door and began yelling, "Help, help!" before her feet hit the ground.

Lilly rose up on one elbow and called, "Briana, wait."

But she was already halfway to the double glass doors. An unbearable pain forced Lilly onto her back again. A minute later, Briana returned with two nurses.

"Get a gurney," the first nurse said to the second after taking one look at Lilly. "Can you sit up, honey?"

"If you give me a hand."

The two nurses, one of them a man, were joined by additional medical staff. Lilly was lifted onto the gurney and pushed inside. They flew past the waiting room where she'd met Jake and the girls the night of Briana's fender bender and went straight to a treatment room.

"Wait out here," the male nurse told Briana.

Lilly hadn't realized until then that Briana had come along. "Call your dad for me," she said over her shoulder.

Briana nodded, her eyes wide, her lips set in a grim line.

After that, Lilly forgot about everything except saving her baby.

Jake sat in the chair by Lilly's bed and watched her toss and turn, fighting the effects of the medication she'd been given to help her rest. Even in sleep, her white-knuckled fists clutched the blanket and deep creases appeared on her normally smooth forehead.

The last three hours had been a nightmare for all of them. Her especially, of course. He'd seen the blood-soaked gym shorts before a nurse put them in a bag, and his stomach twisted into a terrible knot. It must have been many times worse for Lilly. And Briana.

He glanced over at her, sitting in a chair by the window, and smiled. His little girl impressed him. She'd gotten Lilly safely off the mountain and to the hospital. Quite a feat for someone who fainted at the sight of blood. There would be no punishment for driving without permission. If anything, he might sign the old Buick over to her on her sixteenth birthday.

"It's getting late. Why don't you call your mom for a ride home?"

She looked up from the magazine she was reading. "I'll wait for you."

All the rooms in the maternity ward were private and comfortable, providing ample room for family and friends.

"We might be here awhile. Possibly all night."

"No problem." She went back to flipping pages in the magazine.

"Okay." Jake didn't argue, he liked having her with him.

A few minutes later, Briana stood and stretched. "I'm going to the cafeteria. You want me to bring you back a sandwich?"

"No, thanks, sweetie. Not right now." His appetite had deserted him the moment she'd called to tell him about Lilly. He couldn't remember ever feeling so afraid and so helpless.

On second thought, he could. The day his sister died.

Not long after Briana left, Lilly stirred and moaned softly. Jake jerked forward in the chair and took her hand, rubbing the back of it with his thumb. Her eyes fluttered open, then went wide.

"The baby—"

"Is fine for now." He smiled reassuringly. "You're both fine."

"I only remember bits and pieces after the IV was inserted." She closed her eyes and sighed heavily. "I was in premature labor, wasn't I?"

"Yes, but the doctors stopped it." Thank goodness. At thirteen weeks early, there was practically no chance of their baby surviving and certainly not without serious problems. "Dr. Paul said she'd be by in a little while to talk to us. You're to sleep as much as possible and not get out of bed for any reason."

"I'm not going anywhere." She curved the hand with the IV needle protectively around her stomach.

"Are you hungry? I can page a nurse and have someone bring a tray."

"Not hungry. I am thirsty, though."

"Here." Jake poured Lilly a glass of ice water from the plastic pitcher on the nightstand beside her bed.

She took the glass and with his help, raised her head enough to drink from the straw. "Thanks." She grimaced.

"Are you okay?"

"Just a stitch in my side. It's gone now."

Something in her demeanor bothered him, and he couldn't quite put his finger on it. She seemed distant and distracted. It could be the medication. Or her exhaustion. More likely, worry. She'd almost lost the baby and probably would have if she'd waited for the paramedics to arrive or traffic had been worse.

"If you're hungry, go ahead and eat," she said, star-

ing out the third-floor window at the late-afternoon
sky. Distant mountains against a vivid blue backdrop
did little to soften the bleak view of the hospital parking lot with its acres of asphalt and concrete pillars.

Maybe it was their mood that was so bleak.

"I'll wait for you. The nurse told me they could
bring two trays."

"I'll be okay myself if you need a break or want to
go home." Lilly didn't—or wouldn't—meet his gaze.

Jake had done much the same when Hailey died.
But Lilly hadn't lost the baby, giving them reason, to
Jake's way of thinking, to comfort each other, not re-
treat into themselves.

"Lilly." He waited for her to look at him. "Please,"
he added when she didn't.

Finally, she turned her head.

"You had a close call. But you're all right now. The
doctors stopped your labor, and the baby's stable." He
nodded at the monitor beside her bed, the one that dis-
played the baby's vital signs. "You have to keep believing that everything's going to work out."

"It was awful." Her voice cracked. "You weren't
there."

"No, I wish I had been." He gripped her fingers
fiercely. "But I'm here now, and I'm not leaving this
hospital without you."

Her eyes brimmed with tears. "I just wish I knew
for sure that the baby's healthy."

Jake handed her a tissue from the box on her nightstand. "He is. Dr. Paul did an ultrasound when you
came in and said everything was fine."

She wiped her damp cheeks. "No, I mean normal."

"We could know for sure if you'd have those tests she recommended."

"And what if the tests come back with abnormalities?"

"Then we'll deal with it."

Admittedly Jake didn't always understand her. She knew he fully supported her decision not to terminate the pregnancy, regardless of any test results. So, why not have them and be better prepared for the outcome, whatever it might be?

It made perfect sense to him. But then he hadn't lost two sons and watched a third slowly die.

"Easy for you to say. You can't imagine what it's like to carry a baby that you know is probably not going to live long enough to be born or will die soon after."

No, he couldn't. Nor could he consider asking Lilly to go through it again.

"I see you're awake." Dr. Paul came into the room and stood at the foot of Lilly's bed to retrieve her chart. "How are you feeling?"

"All right," she said.

"Still cramping?"

"No, just sore."

Dr. Paul returned Lilly's chart to the bed rail. "Your labor's stopped for now," she said, studying the monitor screen. "And the baby's no longer in distress."

"For now?" Trust Lilly to key in on those words.

"First, let me reassure you that premature labor isn't necessarily connected with birth defects. Women with normal babies can go into premature labor. There are a dozen reasons for it. Our greatest concern is what we can do to prevent it from happening again."

She outlined her plan for the remainder of Lilly's stay in the hospital. At some point, they would take her off the intravenous drug used to impede her contractions and put her on an oral medication. Whether or not she went into labor again would determine further treatment.

"I'm venturing to say that when you're sent home, and I feel confident that you will be, you'll be on strict bed rest."

"How strict?" Lilly asked.

"You can get out of bed to use the bathroom, shower and dress."

Lilly gaped at Dr. Paul. "That's it?"

"That's it. Flat on your back as much as possible."

"For how long?"

"Depends on your progress. A week or two. The rest of your pregnancy if necessary."

"What about work?"

"They're going to have to get by without you for a while."

She glanced over at Jake. "I don't want to lose my job."

"You don't want to lose this baby, either," Dr. Paul said firmly. "And you will if you don't take it easy. You had a close call today, Lilly. Your body's giving you a warning, and you have to listen."

"Talk to your boss," Jake said. "He's been understanding so far."

"He has. But I wasn't asking for an indefinite leave of absence. The center can't run for long without an administrator, and he's too busy with the new one in Apache Junction to oversee both places."

"Let's worry about that later, after your premature labor's under control."

"You're right," Lilly said resolutely. "This baby's the most important thing. I'll figure something out. Maybe I'm eligible for temporary disability. I can call Social Security."

Jake didn't add that he'd see she had everything she needed and cover any costs her insurance didn't. They could discuss that another time, when they were alone and Lilly was feeling better.

Dr. Paul moved beside Lilly's bed. "Obviously, the longer you carry the baby, the better his or her chances of survival. Which is why you have to remain on strict bed rest. Gravity isn't your friend. Neither is stress."

"What if I go into labor again?"

"That will depend on how far along you are and if we can stop it with medication."

They discussed a few more details about Lilly's condition, the possibility of depression ensuing from the enforced inactivity and the extreme measures available if bed rest didn't do the trick. Jake hoped they proved unnecessary.

"I'm going to give you the name of a counselor," Dr. Paul went on. "You may find it helpful to talk to someone who's treated patients in your situation."

"What about tests for the baby?" Jake asked. "Are there any we can do?"

Lilly gasped softly. "Nothing invasive."

Dr. Paul considered. "Lilly's right. Amniocentesis and other, more conclusive tests come with risks. In her present unstable condition, those risks are even greater. To be on the safe side, we can do another ultrasound before she leaves the hospital."

After giving Lilly a brief examination, Dr. Paul said, "I have to leave. But I'll come back early tomorrow before office hours. Try and get some sleep. It's the best thing for you."

"Is there any reason Jake needs to stay?"

"Only if he wants to." Dr. Paul paused on her way to the door and addressed Jake. "She's doing fine for the moment if you want to go home. The nurses will call if you're needed."

"I'd rather stay," Jake told Lilly once Dr. Paul had left. It wouldn't be the first time he'd crashed on a hospital waiting-room couch.

"What about Briana?"

"I'll take her home and come back afterward."

"You don't have to keep me company."

"I want to."

Lilly resumed staring out the window.

Jake once again had the feeling he was being ignored or dismissed, and he didn't like it.

"Mind telling me what's really wrong?"

"What are you talking about?"

"You're acting strange, Lilly."

She turned her cheek into the pillow. "It's been a difficult day. I nearly lost my baby. I'm entitled to act a little strange."

"I agree you've had an awful day, but I think there's more to it."

"I'm simply exhausted."

Jake wondered if he'd been reading more into Lilly's behavior than was there.

"Sorry," he said. "I get pushy sometimes. It's a bad habit of mine. I'll leave you alone so you can get some sleep." He'd travel no farther than the waiting-room couch he'd been thinking about earlier, but Lilly didn't need to know that. Later, if Briana changed her mind, he'd take her home and then come right back.

He stood, stretched and leaned over to give Lilly a kiss. She surprised him by opening her eyes. Then she lifted her head and clung to his shirt front.

"Forgive me," she said miserably, pulling him close.

"For what?"

"Acting prickly and out of sorts. I'm just so scared."

"I know, sweetheart. But don't be. Your labor's stopped. The baby's doing well."

"What if we go through all this, stop the labor and save the baby, and he's born with the same birth defects?"

"It won't happen."

"You don't know." Her voice was rough with emotion. "You can't know. No one can."

"I have faith. So should you."

"What if I lose you, too?"

"Impossible." It was on the tip of his tongue to tell her he loved her. Instead, he said, "You're stuck with me."

"That's what Brad said." Lilly let go of Jake's shirt and dropped back onto her pillow. "Only he divorced me."

The door cracked open, and Briana poked her head around the corner. "Can I come in?" she asked in a low voice.

Jake started to answer, then realized he should wait for Lilly.

"Yes, please," she said.

Briana stood by Jake's chair. "How are you doing?"

"Better than a few hours ago."

"Yeah." She chuckled nervously. "That was a pretty intense ride. I freaked when the van pulled in front of me."

"I want to thank you, Briana," Lilly said. "You saved my baby's life, and I can never repay you."

"Really. It's no big deal." Briana tried to appear unconcerned but Jake knew better. He'd seen her horror-stricken face when he'd arrived at the hospital. Comforted her as she shook from head to toe.

"It is a big deal," Lilly continued, "considering you have every reason to resent me and the baby. Somebody else—somebody with a less generous spirit—might have left me to fend for myself."

"I don't resent either of you," Briana said adamantly, then added in a whisper, "not anymore."

Never had Jake loved his oldest daughter more. No wonder Lilly fought so hard to have a child of her own. He wouldn't trade parenthood for anything.

"I'm very glad," she said, also in a whisper. For the

first time since Jake had been at the hospital, a faint smile touched her lips. "I know it's a lot to ask, and if you say no, I'd understand completely." Her fingers plucked nervously at the sheet.

"What?" Briana asked.

"I'm not sure how long I'll be in the hospital. Another day or two, anyway. Maybe longer. Is there any chance you can help supervise the clients when they're at the ranch? If you're busy with school—"

"No problem. I'll help. I like doing it."

"Thanks. It's means a lot to me."

"It means a lot to me, too." Jake took his daughter's hand and kissed the back of it.

"Dad." Briana looked pained. "Don't go all mushy. It's embarrassing."

"It's unavoidable. Just wait until you're a parent." He coughed abruptly. "On second thought, let's hold off on that for another ten years, okay? You're not ready. *I'm* not ready."

His remark earned him a groan.

"I'm going to check out the gift shop," Briana said and held out her hand. "Can I have five dollars for another magazine?"

"I'll walk you to the door."

"Oh, Dad." She rolled her eyes.

Jake touched Lilly's hand. "I'll only be a minute."

"No hurry." Her eyes had drifted shut.

Good, he thought, she needed her rest.

Jake detained Briana just outside Lilly's hospital room. He left the door partially open in case she called out or the monitors beeped, indicating the baby was in distress.

"I really appreciate what you did today and what you're going to do for Lilly." He pulled her to him. "You're a great kid."

"Maybe not so great." She withdrew from his hug.

"Why would you say that?"

"I'm still mad at you, Dad."

"What for?"

"You made me, Kayla and LeAnne start to like Lilly. And Leanne can't wait to be a big sister."

"Sorry, but I don't see anything wrong with that."

"Yeah? Well, what if Lilly loses the baby? Or it's born…sick like her other ones? The two of you aren't the only people who're going to be hurt and sad." Her voice caught, and she struggled for control.

Jake was momentarily stunned. He hadn't thought of that. He'd been too focused on getting the girls to accept Lilly and a new sibling.

"Grandma, too," Briana added. "She's crocheting baby blankets and stuff."

"We have to believe the baby's going to be fine."

"But what if it's not?" She sniffed and wiped her eyes with the back of her hand. "I don't want to lose a little brother or sister, too."

"Shh, don't cry." Jake kissed the top of her head because he really didn't know what to say. Maybe Lilly was right not to plan too far ahead. "I'll see you in a little bit."

Briana left once he'd handed over a five-dollar bill.

When he went back into Lilly's room, he noticed

that her eyes were open. She quickly closed them and turned her head toward the window. Within seconds, her breathing slowed.

Jake sat in the chair, unsure if she'd heard any of his conversation with Briana. And if she had, what she'd made of it.

Chapter 13

"Hey, Mom." Lilly stepped out of her bathroom, fresh from the shower, a towel around her hair. "You don't have to do that."

"I don't mind." Claire Russo was in the middle of changing the sheets on Lilly's bed.

"I'll help." She reached for a clean pillow case.

"You'll do no such thing, young lady. No lifting or exerting yourself. You heard the doctor."

"It's a *pillow*."

Claire pointed to an antique pine chest Lilly had purchased soon after moving to Payson and kept at the foot of her bed. "Sit."

Lilly complied. She'd been on strict bed rest since coming home the previous week after an eight-day stay at the hospital. In addition to showering, dressing and using the bathroom, she was allowed to eat at the kitchen table. That was all except for moving twice daily between the bed and the couch.

The disadvantages of being bedridden were numerous, inactivity being the worst. Her life revolved around the TV, the phone, emails and surfing new-mother internet websites, in-bed exercises, Sudoku puzzles, napping and visitors. The novelty had worn off by day two.

She retrieved a comb from her bathrobe pocket and began working on the knots in her hair.

"Here, let me do that." Claire abandoned making the bed and took the comb from Lilly's hands.

Not for the first time since her mother had traveled from Albuquerque last week to stay with her, she felt like a little girl again. It wasn't all bad. True, her mother often got carried away, and the fussing and hovering irritated Lilly. But other times, like now, when her spirits were low and sinking lower by the minute, she enjoyed the pampering.

The anticontraction medication Dr. Paul had put Lilly on had some unpleasant side effects. So did the one that aided in developing her baby's lungs. The eight glasses of water a day she was required to drink made her wake several times during the night and stumble to the bathroom.

She didn't mind. Every imposition, every sacrifice, would be worth it in the end, or so she prayed.

Dr. Paul dropped by every Tuesday and Friday to examine Lilly. They'd vetoed in-home monitoring equipment. In Dr. Paul's opinion, it was costly and did nothing to prevent preterm labor. She'd expressed satisfaction with Lilly's progress and hinted at the possibility of upgrading her to modified bed rest in a few weeks. She would still have restrictions but nothing as difficult as lying on her back twenty-two hours a day.

Lilly missed going outside. She missed work more. The phone calls from her boss and staff—once frequent enough to be considered bothersome—had dwindled significantly. The thought that they were learning to cope without her contributed to Lilly's low spirits. As did her money concerns and the lack of a steady income. Though she'd gladly give up her job—and her paycheck—for a healthy child, she loved the center and loved feeling needed.

Groaning softly, she shifted her weight to her other hip, which only marginally relieved the chronic stiffness in her neck and back. Pillows and hot showers helped, as did the daily back rubs her mother gave her, but the pain never truly went away and always returned a short while later.

"Your dad called this morning." Claire braided Lilly's hair and tied it.

"Is he miserable without you?"

"He's managing. Your brother's checking in on him every day."

"How's *he* managing?" Lilly's father alternated between being the most annoying and the most terrific guy in the world. The same could be said about her brother.

"Okay. When they're not at each other's throats, they're getting along great."

"If I haven't told you lately, Mom, thanks for coming out."

Claire resumed making the bed. "It's been a while since your dad and I had separate vacations. I'm sort of enjoying it."

"Taking care of me is no vacation."

Lilly was well aware of how much trouble she was, most of it unintentional, some of it admittedly not. She was her father's daughter, after all. And strict bed rest wasn't fun. There were days, like today, when the tedium really got to her. Fortunately, her mother was well-practiced in the art of patience.

She wasn't the only one. Jake, who visited Lilly almost every day, ranked right up there with her mother.

"It's not as bad as you think," Claire said, turning down the comforter and plumping the pillows.

Lilly half sat, half lay in bed, her back against the headboard.

Without asking, Claire took a bottle of lotion from the nightstand and perched on the edge of the mattress. She placed one of Lilly's feet, swollen from water retention and from being unable to walk, in her lap and began rubbing lotion into it. Lilly almost cried, the massage felt so good.

"How long do you think you can stay?"

"Don't worry about that," Claire said, unconcerned.

"What about school? You've worked so hard." Her mother's lifelong dream was to teach, and she'd returned to college the previous year to obtain her teaching degree.

"I can take the classes again next semester."

Lilly hated being such an imposition but dreaded the day her mother would leave. Fussing and hovering aside, she'd come to depend on her and didn't know how she'd survive if her bed rest continued for three more months. Who else would see to her every need, fix her meals, entertain her, act as her personal secretary and rub her aching back and swollen feet?

Jake.

He'd do considerably more for her if she let him. Her mother's continued stay was a built-in excuse to keep him at arm's length and one Lilly frequently used.

She couldn't explain the change that had come over her since nearly losing the baby. From the moment she awoke in the hospital bed, reliving the terror of her previous stillbirths, she'd been reevaluating her and Jake's relationship. Hearing his conversation with Briana outside her door had strengthened her concerns and doubts and her commitment to wait until after the baby's birth before deciding how she and Jake should proceed.

Claire started on Lilly's other foot. "I told your dad when he called this morning that I'm here as long as you need me. He and school will both be there when I get back."

Though it was selfish of her, Lilly wanted that date to be well into the future. Every day she went without going into labor was a blessing. She'd been studying premature birth during her convalescence. Modern medicine had made great strides in recent years, but a child born twelve weeks early could suffer grave complications.

Lilly also visited websites dedicated to parents of preemies and read many stories that gave her hope and encouragement. If she could just hold on...

The phone on her nightstand rang. She reached over and picked it up, checking caller ID first.

"Hello, Jake."

Claire grinned at Lilly and left the bedroom. She could tell her mother approved of Jake and wouldn't mind having him as a son-in-law. She also liked his girls, who'd visited a few days ago. Neither Lilly nor her younger brother had children yet, and it was obvious her mother had been bitten by the grandchild bug.

"How you doing today?" Jake asked.

"Oh, fine." Lilly tried to sound chipper.

He wasn't fooled. "Something wrong?"

"I didn't sleep very well last night." It was the truth, but not why she was down in the dumps.

Dr. Paul had warned Lilly about possible mood swings and depression caused by isolation and inactivity. Lilly, to her displeasure, had become a statistic.

"Maybe I can cheer you up."

"How's that?"

"Lunch. I thought I'd stop by Ernesto's and pick up some Chicken Marsala."

No wonder her mother liked Jake so much; Chicken Marsala was one of her favorite dishes. Did Jake know or had he hit the mark by sheer luck?

Lilly's first instinct was to refuse his offer—that unexplained need to keep him at a distance rearing its head again. She didn't, however. Her mother deserved a nice lunch, one she didn't have to cook or clean up after.

"Thanks. That'd be great."

"Is eleven okay? It's a little early but I have to be back at the ranch by one."

"Sure." The ranch. Another place Lilly missed.

From all reports, the riding program was going well. Briana, true to her promise, helped the center's clients as much as possible. There'd been no more incidents since the one with Jimmy Bob and the little boy, thank goodness, and corrective shoeing continued to minimize Big Ben's lameness.

Of all the new ideas Lilly had introduced at Horizon, this was the best. She only regretted that she wasn't still an active part of it.

Soon, she told herself and tried to imagine her and Jake standing by the corral fence, their baby in a stroller. The image didn't quite come into focus.

"I have an appointment with some people you may know," Jake said, cutting into her thoughts.

"Who?"

"Jimmy Bob's parents." She could hear a smile in Jake's voice.

"Really! What for?"

"To discuss hiring him on part-time."

"Are you serious?"

"Sure. He's doing a good job. The hands like him, and he's a hard worker."

"Be honest. He's doing a mediocre job."

"What he lacks in ability he makes up for in enthusiasm. Besides, I'm not paying him much."

"Jimmy Bob must be thrilled."

Lilly was grateful and deeply touched. Part of the center's goal was to teach skills that special-needs individuals could use in the outside world. One of them actually landing a job, menial and low-paying though it might be, was cause for celebration.

"He doesn't know yet."

She wished she could be there. "What a nice surprise."

"I'll let you get off the phone," Jake said. "See you in a few hours."

"It's not like I have a lot to do." For someone who supposedly believed her feelings had changed, Lilly was reluctant to hang up on Jake. Her world had shrunk so much recently, and he was a link to what lay beyond it.

"You sure you're okay, sweetheart? You sound kind of down."

"Nothing some Chicken Marsala won't fix." She knew he worried about her frame of mind.

"Everything all right with the baby?"

"Yup. Kicking up a storm this morning."

"Glad to hear it."

They said their goodbyes, and Lilly returned the phone to its cradle. Thinking about Jimmy Bob brought a smile to her lips and gave her the motivation she needed to get out of bed and dress. In honor of the lunch Jake was bringing, she opted for stretch slacks and a maternity smock rather than the sweat-pants or lounging pajamas she usually wore.

She padded out to the couch where she'd lie until Jake arrived. Her laptop sat on the coffee table, and next to it, the TV remote. Changing her mind, Lilly went to the solarium instead. TV and email held no appeal for her this morning.

The chaise longue, bathed in warm morning sun-light, released a flood of memories of the night she and Jake had made love there. How different things had been then. She and Jake were exploring their new relationship and optimistic about the baby. Now she fretted endlessly about the baby's health and whether she and Jake cared enough about each other to make a go of it. He was certainly trying.

Thank goodness his daughters' feelings had changed—or maybe not. Briana's conversation with Jake outside Lilly's hospital door had given her more worries and further complicated the situation.

"There you are." Claire stopped just inside the so-larium and rested her hand on the door. "Need any-thing?"

"No. And don't fix lunch," Lilly added. "Jake's bringing it. Chicken Marsala."

"How nice." Claire's face lit up, probably as much at the prospect of seeing Jake as eating one of her fa-vorite meals. "How long's he staying?"

"I'm not sure. Why?"

"I have to run to the post office, then drop off those DVDs we rented."

"I don't need a babysitter, Mom."

"It's not that. I figured you might like some private time with him." When Lilly didn't respond right away, Claire asked, "You two having problems?"

"You mean besides my high-risk pregnancy and the odds of our child being born with severe birth defects?"

"Jake seems like the sort of man who can handle it."

"Only because he doesn't know what he's in for."

"Don't underestimate him." Claire's tone softened. "He isn't like Brad, and you shouldn't lump him in the same category."

"He isn't like Brad. But then, Brad wasn't always such a jerk, either. He changed after Evan was born."

"That's true."

"I wish I could be sure that Jake wouldn't change, too, if the baby's born with a trisomy disorder."

"Thank you for lunch, Jake." Claire gathered their plates from the table and carried them to the kitchen sink. "It was delicious."

"Anytime." He'd grown fond of Lilly's mother in their short acquaintance and had the impression the feeling was mutual. "Let me help you with those."

"Nonsense. You stay put. I'm just going to throw these in the dishwasher and then get out of your hair."

Taking in Lilly's carefully averted gaze, he couldn't help thinking there was a conspiracy at hand. But not one in which she willingly participated. He didn't mind Claire's less-than-subtle matchmaking attempts; he'd been wanting to get Lilly alone for over a week and had been carrying the small ring in his pocket every day, just in case.

Thanks to Claire, his wait was over.

"Couch or bed?" he asked Lilly.

She raised her head. "What about the solarium? I could do with a different setting."

He wished her smile was less forced and more genuine. Chronic bed rest was no fun, and he was becoming concerned about her. Each time he visited, she seemed more despondent, more troubled, more introverted. He had a plan, one he hoped would lift her spirits and give her something to look forward to.

If it didn't backfire. She'd turned him down once before.

"Solarium it is." He pulled her chair out and rested his hand lightly on her back as they left the kitchen.

Claire's parting goodbye smile was everything he wished Lilly's was. What would her mother say if she knew his intentions? His gut instinct told him she'd approve. Believing he had an ally boosted his confidence and convinced him he was doing the right thing.

The lush, earthy scent of green plants surrounded them the moment they stepped through the door. Sunlight streamed in through the skylights and glass windows, warming the rocks and stone walkway beneath their feet.

"I don't think I've ever been here during the day. It's beautiful."

Lilly sent him a look that said she remembered every detail about the night they'd made love here. It was an experience he wouldn't mind repeating during the day. Later. After the baby was born.

She gingerly eased herself onto the chaise. The only other piece of furniture in the solarium was a patio chair at the other end. Jake considered bringing it over but then Lilly scooted sideways and said, "Sit here."

His heart beat faster. Everything was falling into place perfectly.

They didn't cuddle quite as cozily as they had before. Nonetheless, it was nice to sit beside her, and, after several minutes of small talk, Jake sensed her relaxing. The time continued to tick by and when the right opening didn't come, he began to get nervous. He'd have to leave soon in order to meet Jimmy Bob and his parents at the ranch.

Jake decided to make his own opening.

"What's the latest Dr. Paul says about you carrying to term?"

"She hasn't quoted percentages." Lilly made a face. "I think she's being intentionally vague."

"Why?"

"So I'll focus on the positive. Everything I've been reading says the possibility of going into preterm labor again is high. Stress increases the chances."

"I might have a solution," he said, smiling.

"What?" She seemed more wary than excited.

He reached in his pocket and pulled out the ring. The single sapphire, set inside a circle of tiny diamonds, glittered in the sunlight.

Lilly gasped softly. "Jake."

"It was my grandmother's. My grandfather gave it to her on their twentieth anniversary."

"It's beautiful," she said in a voice hardly above a whisper.

Jake took her left hand in his. "I botched my first proposal. I wanted to do this one right."

She curled her fingers into a fist, preventing him from slipping the ring on, and said gently, "I can't accept. The ring or your proposal. You know that."

He'd anticipated the possibility of her refusal and had come prepared to convince her to accept. "Why not? We're getting along really well."

"We are. But compatibility isn't enough of a reason to marry."

"It's a start. And giving my child my name is a hell of a good reason. So is supporting him. Taking care of him. Taking care of *you*."

Her shoulders sagged. "We have too many problems to work out before we can consider marriage."

"Not so many." His smile dissolved into a flat line.

"What about where to live?"

"My house is bigger."

"Mine is closer to the hospital if the baby needs constant attention."

"Fine. Your house. I'll commute to the ranch."

"What about the girls?"

"No problem. They like you."

"I meant, where would they sleep on the weekends? I don't have enough bedrooms."

"Sleeping bags on the living room floor."

"That'll go over big."

"Then we'll stay at my house on those weekends."

"What about the rest of your family?"

"Carolina thinks you're great."

"Your parents don't."

"That isn't true. My mom was really happy when we first started dating."

"Yeah, but back then I wasn't pregnant with a child that could have severe health issues. And you were in a slump because of Ellen's engagement. Your mother was glad to see you moving on. It didn't matter who with."

"She told me the other day how much she respects and admires you."

"Which isn't the same as being ecstatic at the prospect of us marrying."

Lilly tensed and moved away. Only an inch or two but Jake noticed.

"My parents will come around, just like the girls and Carolina have."

She shook her head. "How could we even have a wedding? I'm not allowed to stand up for longer than it takes to walk from the bedroom to the living room."

"We'll get married here. In the solarium."

"On the chaise longue?"

"Why not? We won't invite many people. Have a justice of the peace perform the ceremony."

"I don't want to get married lying down. And what about a dress?"

"Your mom will help."

"I want to pick out my own dress."

"We'll have a big wedding after the baby's born. Invite everyone from the center."

"That's a lovely idea, but no."

"Why wouldn't you invite them?"

She sighed as if he were being intentionally obtuse. "I meant no to a wedding, not to inviting the center's clients. Which, now that you mention it, is another concern of mine."

"The clients?"

"Kayla's uncomfortable around them, and the center is a large part of my life."

"She'll feel more comfortable in time."

"She's a little girl and can't control or evaluate her feelings."

"I'll get Jimmy Bob to help."

"He may have Down's syndrome but he's physically fit, capable of learning and able to function independently to a certain degree. Nothing like Evan. How do you think Kayla will react to a brother with a misshapen head and shrunken limbs?"

"You're being unnecessarily harsh."

"I'm speaking from experience."

"I know she'll get over her fears."

"Brad could hardly bear to look at Evan. It tore me apart to watch them together. I can't go through that again."

"The fact is, none of this may come to pass."

"You can't know for sure until it happens." Lilly pushed up on one elbow. "And neither will I."

"I've supported you and stood behind you during

this entire pregnancy. I've let you set the pace and call the shots, even when I didn't agree with you."

"And I appreciate that."

He suppressed his irritation. "This is my baby, too, Lilly. I have a right to make some of the decisions regarding him—or her. Including giving the baby my name."

She opened her mouth to speak, then promptly closed it.

"You can't do it all alone. You're going to need help," he said before she'd regained her composure. "*Especially* if the baby's born like Evan. I can be that help."

Her expression softened and for a moment, she was the Lilly he knew and understood. "I feel like I'm hurting you, and that's not my intent. But you're not facing reality. You have this fantasy of a perfect family. You and me, your daughters and our baby, all happy and healthy and loving."

"Don't you have the same fantasy?"

"Yes, on occasion. Then I remember what I went through with Evan and Brad."

"What exactly did your ex-husband do to you?"

"Besides disappoint me and abandon me when I needed him the most?"

"The death of a child should bring people closer together. It did for my parents, but I guess they're the exception."

"So was Brad, but not the way you think." Lilly's voice dropped to a hush. "Evan was only two months old—not nine—when Brad packed his bags and left me. He never visited the hospital again after he moved out. Although he called regularly, I didn't see much of him until Evan died. I was stupid enough to think he might want a reconciliation, but a week after the funeral, he served me with divorce papers."

Jake took a much-needed minute to recover. Lilly hadn't told him that part of the story. "I'm sorry, sweetie. It must have been awful for you."

"Awful doesn't come close to describing what I went through."

"I'm not like Brad. I won't leave you."

She turned tear-filled eyes to him. "Do you love me, Jake?"

"I…of course."

"I shouldn't have to ask you that or insist you tell me." Her smile was painfully sad.

"No, you shouldn't." He considered saying the words now but realized they'd sound shallow and forced and that wouldn't advance his cause. If only he'd said them at the hospital when he'd had the chance.

"We can be parents to this child without being in love," she said, folding her arms across her chest and hugging herself, "But we can't have a good marriage without it."

"I wouldn't have come here today with my grandmother's ring if I didn't love you."

"You asked me to marry you before—out of duty, not love."

"That was true once, but not anymore. I've changed

since then." He wished he could convince her he meant what he said.

Her eyes pleaded with him to understand. "It would be different if we knew the baby was healthy."

"We *would* know if you'd consented to the tests when Dr. Paul first suggested them and it was safe."

She scowled and withdrew. "Now you sound like Brad."

Jake stood up, his boots hitting the tile floor with a thud. He could take pretty much anything she threw at him but he was tired of constantly being compared to her ex-husband.

"I don't get you sometimes." He shoved his grand-mother's ring in his jeans pocket.

If Lilly saw him do that, she gave no indication. "How so?"

He swung around to face her. "You're doing exactly what you got mad at *me* for doing six months ago."

"Which is?"

"Slamming on the brakes just when the other person wants to step up the relationship."

"This is entirely different!"

"Why? Because you're the one doing the brake-slamming?"

"I have a good reason."

"You have lots of reasons. I'm beginning to wonder if you stay up at night thinking of them."

"That's not a very nice thing to say."

"I love you, Lilly. I want to marry you." Jake stepped toward the door, or, more accurately, was propelled to move by a surge of resentment. "You're right, I should've told you before, but I thought I was showing you how I felt by proposing."

"Jake, please don't leave like this." She pushed to a more erect position. "Can't we just keep going on the way were until after the baby's born? Then decide to get married?"

"There's something I've been wondering about you and Brad for a while now." He raked his fingers through his hair. "Did Brad really leave you?"

"Yes. Why would you ask me that?"

She looked so vulnerable, sitting on the chaise while he loomed over her. If he hadn't been so furious, if he hadn't risked his ego, only to be kicked to the curb, he might have kept his stupid mouth shut.

But Jake knew he didn't handle rejection well, in business or personally. He wouldn't keep asking Lilly to marry him, wouldn't keep offering to help her, only to be turned down. And he wouldn't leave her house today without saying what was really bothering him.

"I'm just wondering if maybe you misread the situation with Brad."

"I don't think it's possible to misread someone abandoning you." Her eyes flashed with indignation.

"Did he?" Jake started toward the door. "Or did he get tired of you always shutting him out?"

"Is that what you believe I did?"

"It's what you're doing to me, what you've been doing to me all along. And I'm finally getting the message."

She didn't try to stop him, not that he would've gone back. His pride wouldn't have let him.

He walked through the kitchen and was glad to encounter Claire, back from her errands. Angry as he was, he didn't like the idea of leaving Lilly alone.

Claire took one look at him and blurted, "Did something happen? Is Lilly okay?"

"She's fine."

"Are *you* okay?" she asked with concern.

He stopped in midstep. "Call me if you or Lilly need anything."

"That sounds like an I'm-not-coming-back line."

"Bye, Claire."

He nodded and left the woman he'd hoped would be his mother-in-law. His thoughts, however, were on her daughter, the woman he'd hoped would be his wife.

How could something that had seemed so right a few hours ago turn so wrong?

Chapter 14

"Physically, you're doing great." Dr. Paul packed her stethoscope into a black carrying case she'd set on the chest at the foot of Lilly's bed. "I'm thinking we can upgrade you to modified moderate bed rest. At least on a trial basis. See how it goes."

"What does that involve?" Anything sounded better than the strict bed rest Lilly had been on for three solid weeks.

"You can get up for four hours a day. Not one minute more." Dr. Paul wagged a warning finger at Lilly. "Two two-hour intervals. One in the morning, one in the afternoon. The remainder of the time, bed and couch. If you continue to do well, I'll consider increasing the four hours to six. But you have to be good."

"I will." Lilly felt like a newly paroled prisoner. "I promise."

"No exercise, no lifting, no carrying, no driving and no walking long distances. If you have to go someplace, someone takes you. Sit as much as possible."

The restrictions didn't leave Lilly many choices. Still, it was an improvement. Even sitting on a bench in the park up the road would be a refreshing change. Better yet, the one by the corrals at the ranch. She could watch the center's clients ride Big Ben.

On second thought, maybe that wasn't such a good idea. What if Jake showed up? They hadn't spoken much since their argument last week. Though he called regularly to check on her, he talked mostly to her mother. The few times she'd answered the phone, the conversations had been short and stilted.

If only he hadn't proposed. They could have gone on the way they were until the baby was born.

And what way was that? Her holding him at arm's length?

What Jake accused her of was true. Lilly had spent a lot of time this last week thinking. Convalescence was good for that. And she'd concluded that she'd been fooling herself if she'd believed a man like him would be satisfied with the arrangement simply because it was what she wanted.

Not that it *was* the arrangement she'd wanted. She dreamed of the kind of close and loving marriage her parents had. And his parents. The kind of relationship she'd envisioned back when she and Jake had first started dating...

When she hadn't been afraid he'd leave her. Afraid he wouldn't love her as much as she loved him.

Fear ruled Lilly's life and had from the day she'd learned she was pregnant. Fear she'd miscarry. Fear the baby would be born like Evan. Fear Jake would abandon her like Brad. And as much as she wished she could conquer it, she couldn't. It ate away at her like acid, and she was powerless to stop it.

She told herself she'd refused Jake's proposal in order to protect him from hurt and give him an out. In truth, she was the one who wanted protection, who wanted an out. She who was afraid to make the commitment he did so easily.

But knowing the motivation behind her actions didn't change the outcome or bring her insight into how to fix it. But, oh, if only she *could* fix her relationship with Jake.

Because her greatest fear these days was that if the baby was born normal and healthy—as increasingly seemed to be the case—she would have pushed Jake out of her life, out of *their* lives, for nothing.

"Did you call Karen DeSalvo?" Dr. Paul asked.

"Who?" Lilly blinked to clear her head.

"She's the psychologist whose name I gave you at the hospital."

"No, I haven't."

Dr. Paul sent Lilly one of her trademark kind smiles. "I wish you would. She's very good and very compassionate."

"I'm fine."

"Is that why you drifted off for several minutes just

now?" She patted Lilly's hand, the gesture doctorly. "What you're going through would depress anyone. For someone who's lost three children, it must be excruciating. The inactivity, the seclusion, the solitude, can't be helping." Dr. Paul scratched something on a piece of paper. "Talking to someone, learning what you can do to cope, might make the remaining weeks easier."

Lilly fingered the note with the name and phone number Dr. Paul gave her. "Now that I'm able to get up and out for a few hours a day, I'm sure my frame of mind will improve."

"I hope so. And that you'll continue to do well. Returning to strict bed rest can be rough once you've had a taste of freedom."

"I'll take it very easy so that doesn't happen."

"Forgive me for being nosy but, as my patient, your welfare, and that of your baby, is critical to me." Dr. Paul tilted her head inquiringly. "I'm curious to know if there's more to your despondency than the pregnancy."

"There isn't."

"Jake called me the other day."

Lilly pulse tripped. "He did?"

"He asked how you were doing."

"What did you tell him?"

"Nothing, of course. I'm prohibited by law, which I explained to him. His call, however, concerned me, especially when he indicated that you and he weren't talking much."

"We had an argument last week."

"Well, it's understandable and not unexpected. This is a trying period for both of you. Add to that the fact that your hormones are out of whack, you're on a variety of medications, several with significant side effects, and you've been confined to bed. No matter how sympathetic a man is, and Jake *is* sympathetic, he can't fully relate to what you're going through. He certainly can't if you don't discuss it with him."

She sighed. "I realize I need to quit dodging his phone calls."

"Karen DeSalvo can help you both. Please consider making an appointment."

"I will."

"I have to go." Dr. Paul patted Lilly's hand again before rising. "Remember, don't do too much on the outings. And if there's the slightest change or problem, call me immediately."

After a final exchange, Dr. Paul left. Lilly put the piece of paper with the psychologist's name and number on it aside. She would think about calling, but not today. First things first. She had two hours of freedom ahead of her and she knew exactly what she wanted to do with them.

"Mom!" she called, slowly sitting up. Her bare toes touched the carpeted floor.

"Honey, what are you doing?" Claire exclaimed on seeing her.

"I've been paroled. Sort of."

Lilly explained her modified bed-rest routine while she changed into regular clothes, combed and rebraided her hair and dabbed on a small amount of makeup. When she'd finished, her mood was better than it had been in weeks.

"I need you to drive me somewhere," she said.

"Where?" Claire answered.

Lilly's eyes sparkled back at her from the bathroom mirror.

"I want to stop by work."

Lilly lived fifteen minutes from the center. She figured she could spend well over an hour there before having to return home and to the couch. Long enough to visit everyone and solve the one or two problems that surely needed her attention.

The streets and buildings she and her mother passed on the drive to Horizon looked a little strange to Lilly. Familiar, yet different somehow. It made her realize how much being confined to her house for weeks had affected her, and she appreciated her reprieve that much more.

It also made her miss Jake. He'd become a vital and intricate part of her life and, despite their argument, always would be. They'd created a child together, a healthy one, God willing, and would be forever tied to each other because of that, regardless of the outcome.

Had she been able to conquer her fears, overcome her mistrust, stop making excuses, their bond might not be one distanced by many miles and with communications conducted through third parties.

The thought was a sobering one.

And not her first in the week since Jake had left.

She'd blamed Brad for leaving her because it was

easier than admitting her part in the demise of their marriage. Easier to hold her head high after the horrible manner in which he'd handled their divorce. She'd blamed him because, in her mind, he'd deserved it.

Jake wasn't anything like her ex-husband and Lilly couldn't believe she ever thought he was. He'd forced her to examine her former marriage and ask *what came first?* Brad's withdrawal or her pushing him away?

There were days Lilly wasn't sure which—and days she knew and didn't like the answer. Was it too late to change? She hoped not.

"We're here," Claire singsonged.

The sign in the parking lot triggered a sudden pang in Lilly's chest. It seemed as if she'd been away from the center for years instead of weeks. It wouldn't surprise her to find new faces among the familiar ones.

What she hadn't expected to see was a woman sitting behind her desk, head bent over a calculator. Shock rendered Lilly immobile. Her mother had to nudge her along.

"Lilly!" Miranda, guardian of the front entrance and first to notice everyone who came in, tumbled out of her chair. "You're back."

She was joined by nearly everyone in the room.

To Lilly's annoyance, they blocked Lilly's view of the woman seated at her desk. Standing on tiptoe didn't help.

"Careful," she warned Jimmy Bob in a gentle voice when he hugged her a little too exuberantly.

"Sorry. I missed you."

"I missed you, too. All of you." Her smile encompassed the entire room.

"Have you come back to work?" Apparently, Mr. Deitrich was having one of his good days because he recognized her.

"Not yet. I hope to after the baby's born." If she wasn't spending every day at the hospital. "I just came by for a short visit."

"Who the hell is *she?*" Miranda gave Claire a stern once-over.

Lilly might have asked the same question about the woman in her office.

Claire endured Miranda's scrutiny without flinching. "I'm Lilly's mother. I'm staying with her."

"Hi." Jimmy Bob greeted Claire as he did anyone who was a friend or the friend of a friend. He hugged her.

Claire hugged him back.

"Give the poor girl a break." Georgina pushed through the crowd. She'd waited while everyone else had their turn with Lilly. Now, she was demanding equal time. "Can I get you anything? Cold water or some coffee?" offered Georgina.

"A chair." Lilly rested a hand on her protruding stomach. "I'm supposed to sit as much as possible." The commotion generated by her return had tired her more than she'd expected.

"Come on." Georgina guided Lilly toward the back of the room.

"Mom, will you be okay?"

"Miranda's going to give me the grand tour." Claire slung an arm around her new buddy.

Lilly had to dole out three more hugs before she and Georgina escaped to a small seating area behind a partition. Clients sometimes used this corner when they were high-strung and needed a place to calm down.

Within seconds, the center and its occupants returned to normal.

Lilly sank into one of the straight-backed chairs. She would've liked to inquire about the center, how they were faring without her and *who* the woman in her office was. Georgina, however, insisted on finding out about Lilly.

"You doing okay?"

"Pretty good." Lilly summarized the last few weeks, focusing on her pregnancy and omitting anything about Jake. Georgina didn't appear to notice, but then Lilly had always been closemouthed with her co-workers when it came to him.

"I'm so glad. We've been worried sick about you. It must be incredibly difficult, being confined to bed."

"I'd say I'm getting used to it but I'd be lying."

"Please tell me you're coming back after the baby's born."

"I hope so."

Lilly wanted nothing more. There was a limit to the amount of medical leave she could take before she risked losing her job. The FMLA didn't apply in her case because the center employed less than fifty people. She was completely dependent on her boss's generosity. And though the baby came first, she needed an income. As it was, she'd been drawing on her retirement account to make ends meet, and that would only last so long.

Jake's pledge to take care of her and their child echoed in her head.

No. Supporting her wasn't an option. She'd made it on her own for years and wouldn't stop now. Helping with the baby's expenses, yes. That was different. And when he or she was born, Lilly would take Jake up on his promise.

There. She'd made a decision about the baby, and it wasn't as hard as she'd thought it would be.

"I can't believe how much this place has changed in such a short while," she told Georgina.

"It isn't the same without you."

Lilly couldn't hold her tongue any longer. "Who's the gal in my office?" She didn't add *my replacement.* Her heart ached just to think the words, much less speak them.

"Her?" Georgina's grin widened. "That's Alice. She's Jake's assistant from the ranch."

"Oh." Lilly hadn't recognized her. "What's she doing here?"

"I assumed you knew."

"Knew what?"

"She's been coming in every afternoon for the past week. To pick up the slack."

"You're kidding."

"No. She's pretty good, too. Not like you, of course, but who is?"

"Dave hired her?"

"Technically, she's a volunteer."

"That's very nice of her." Lilly was only casually acquainted with Jake's very efficient, very professional and not over-friendly personal assistant. "I wouldn't have pegged her as the type to volunteer."

"She's all right when you get to know her. Which is fortunate since she'll be here until you return. Jake arranged it."

"I'm confused."

"He pays her to work here."

"He does?"

"He comes in most afternoons, too."

"He does?" Realizing she sounded like a parrot, she shut up.

Georgina fidgeted. "Did I mess up by telling you this?"

"No. Not at all." In all their conversations, which weren't many lately, Jake hadn't said anything about either of them helping out at the center.

"Good. Because he's been really great. And the girls, too."

"Girls?" Lilly wasn't sure she'd heard right.

"His daughters. The two youngest ones come in with him after school sometimes. Of course, they aren't much help, but they sure are cute and very entertaining. The clients love them."

"LeAnne *and* Kayla?"

"Yes."

Kayla! Who would have guessed?

"If you stick around a few minutes," Georgina said, "he'll probably show up."

"Really?" Lilly's hand went to her hair. How did it look? Had she chewed off her lipstick?

"That's not all he's done, either. Dave's been going crazy running both centers. He swore if you were out for another two weeks, he was going to replace you. Jake went to Dave and convinced him to keep your job indefinitely. In exchange, we get Alice. Jake's mother helps out, too, once a week. She does the filing and takes the deposit to the bank."

"His...mother?"

"Yeah. And whatever's left, he handles. I guess running Horizon isn't too different from running a guest ranch."

Lilly sat there, dumbstruck.

"He's a great guy, Lilly," Georgina said. "And absolutely nuts about you."

"You think so?"

"How many guys would pay their assistant *and* give up their afternoons to cover for you until you came back to work?"

"Not many."

"Damn straight."

Of everything Jake had ever done for her, this was the sweetest, the kindest, the most generous. He—and his daughters—had proved their willingness to make the center a part of their lives and do whatever it took to help Lilly.

Thank God he hadn't given up on her.

Her heart seemed to tighten, then expand as it filled to bursting with love for him and his family, every one of whom was dear to her. All the barriers she'd erected between her and Jake, all the excuses she'd made to maintain those barriers, fell away, leaving her exposed and vulnerable and finally able to give herself to him heart and soul.

"I'd better find Mom and bail her out." Bracing a hand on the table, Lilly stood. She felt suddenly light and unencumbered. It was true; she still had the same number of burdens to carry. But they weren't as heavy because she shared them with Jake. "Miranda's probably talked her ear off."

Claire was talking, all right. But with Jake, not Miranda. He'd apparently arrived while Lilly and Georgina were in the break room. He wasn't alone. A half dozen of the center's clients completed the circle surrounding him and Claire.

Lilly moved slowly into the room, observing him from a distance. He hadn't noticed her yet. No one had. They stared at him as if he'd hung the moon.

So did she.

In the next instant, he looked up and caught her watching him.

Her breath lodged in her throat.

Something must have flashed in her eyes—or was it the involuntary step she'd taken?—because his smile went from expectant to ecstatic.

All at once, he was across the room, then standing beside her. Taking her in his arms, he held her as if she were everything in the world to him.

"I was wrong," she said, pressing her face into his neck.

"Me, too."

It was enough for now. Later, they'd sort out all the misunderstandings and take back the angry words they'd said.

"I love you, Lilly." He withdrew only enough to place his hand on her stomach. "You and the baby. And I always will, no matter what."

She didn't doubt him and never would again. "I love you, too."

"I'm hoping what they say is true." He reached into the front pocket of his jeans.

"What's that?"

"About the third time being the charm." He withdrew his grandmother's ring. "I've been carrying this everywhere with me. I didn't have the heart to put it away."

"Oh, Jake!"

"Will you marry me, Lilly? Be my wife and the mother of my child?"

Claire started crying. She wasn't the only one.

Tears sprang to Lilly's eyes, and her throat closed, which made accepting Jake's proposal difficult. She finally managed a hoarse "Yes."

He slipped the ring on her finger. It fit as though it was made for her. The way she fit in Jake's life and he in hers. They sealed their commitment with a lingering kiss. She hardly heard the whoops and cheers from the center's clients and staff over the pounding of her heart, which was and would forever be joined with Jake's.

Epilogue

"Ladies and gentlemen, may I present Mr. and Mrs. Jake Tucker."

At the minister's announcement, the group of people on the porch of Founder's Cabin applauded. Lilly's lips still tingled from Jake's kiss, the one that had united them as husband and wife. On her finger, a simple gold band nestled beside his grandmother's sapphire ring.

They'd opted for a very small wedding, immediate family and a few friends, and had pulled it together in a matter of weeks. Still bedridden for most of the day, Lilly couldn't have managed without her mother, who'd stayed on, and Jake's mother, who was quite possibly the best mother-in-law in the world.

There was no reception line. Instead, everyone converged on the bride and groom, showering them with hugs, kisses and good wishes. Lilly knew she should lie down soon but was too excited.

"Come see Big Ben." Jimmy Bob, dressed in his groomsman's suit, beckoned Lilly and Jake to accompany him. "Me and Briana fixed him up."

He led the newlyweds to the porch railing. The old mule was tied to the hitching post in front of the cabin, a wreath of spring flowers on his neck. He was more interested in trying to eat them than showing them off.

"Thank you, Jimmy Bob." Lilly kissed his cheek. "And you, too." She embraced Briana and might have pulled back if the teenager hadn't continued to cling to her.

Of all the wedding presents Lilly had received, that was the best.

"Are you hungry?" Jake asked, stealing her away to a corner of the porch for a moment of privacy.

"Not really."

"Tired?"

"No, but I should be—"

An odd sensation, unlike any she'd previously felt during her pregnancy, rippled through her middle. Grimacing, Lilly held her stomach.

"Sweetheart, are you okay?"

"I don't think so." Suddenly, her water broke, soaking her dress and the porch floor. "Jake!"

Carolina rushed forward. "You two go. I'll take care of everything here."

He wasted no time helping her to his truck. Lilly knew as he buckled her in the front seat that there was no stopping this premature labor. She prayed that at thirty-three weeks, she was far enough along, and the baby would be safe.

Please, please.

The wedding guests gathered in front of the cabin and waved goodbye. Jake held Lilly's hand the entire way to the hospital and all through her labor, which lasted a mere forty minutes. If he hadn't driven like a madman, they might have become parents somewhere along the road to Payson.

"It's a girl," Dr. Paul said and lifted up a wriggling, squalling baby.

"A girl!" Lilly fought to sit up straight. "Is she all right?"

Jake was beaming. "She sure can cry."

Dr. Paul brought the baby over and laid her in Lilly's arms. "She's small but looks perfectly healthy. Do you hear me, Lilly? *Perfect.* Ten fingers and ten toes. You have your baby."

Lilly cradled her beautiful new daughter in one arm. The other, she wrapped around Jake.

"You're not sorry you have another girl?"

"Are you kidding?" He kissed the top of her head, then their daughter's damp brown hair. "Boys are overrated."

"What should we name her?" Lilly asked, laughing and crying at the same time. Finally, after all these years, she'd beaten the odds.

"I was thinking…."

"Yes?"

"Hailey, after my sister."

"And Claire, after my mother?"

"Hailey Claire Tucker," Jake said with pride, slipping his index finger into the baby's small fist. She instantly stopped flailing and looked at her parents with unfocused eyes. "I like the sound of that," he said.

"I like it, too."

Lilly gazed down at her daughter, then over at Jake. Joy bubbled up inside her. In one day, she'd become a wife *and* a mother.

"We did it," she said. "We have a baby."

"You did it."

All those pictures of ideal families she'd tried to imagine and couldn't suddenly came into sharp focus. Soon they'd be a reality. They'd cover the walls of the home she shared with the man she loved and the child she'd always wanted.

Lilly sighed contentedly. The wait had been worth it.

* * * * *

We hope you enjoyed reading

WILD ABOUT HARRY
by *New York Times* bestselling author
LINDA LAEL MILLER and

WAITING FOR BABY
by *New York Times* bestselling author
CATHY McDAVID!

Both were originally
Harlequin® series stories!

Discover more heartwarming contemporary tales
of everyday women finding love and becoming
part of a family or community from the
Harlequin® American Romance® series.
Featuring small-town settings and irresistible
cowboys, Harlequin® American Romance®
stories are must-reads.

 HARLEQUIN®

American Romance®

Romance the all-American way!

Look for four new romances every month
from Harlequin American Romance!

Available wherever books are sold.

Picking up the bouquet, Cliff said, "These are for you."

"Thanks." Scarlett accepted the flowers and, with both
hands full, set them back down on the table. "You didn't have
to."

"They're a bribe. I was hoping you'd go with me to the
square dance Friday night."

The community center had finally reopened nearly a year
after the fire. The barbecue and dance were in celebration.

"I…um…don't think I can. I appreciate the invitation,
though."

"Are you going with someone else?" He didn't like the
idea of that.

"No, no. I'm just…busy." She clutched her mug tightly
between both hands.

"I'd really like to take you." Fifteen minutes ago he probably
wouldn't have put up a fight and would have accepted her loss
of interest. Except he was suddenly more interested in her
than before. "Think on it overnight."

"O-kay." She took another sip of her coffee. As she did, the
cuff of her shirtsleeve pulled back.

He saw it then, a small tattoo on the inside of her left wrist resembling a shooting star. A jolt coursed through him. He hadn't seen the tattoo before.

Because seven days ago, when he and Scarlett ate dinner at the I Do Café, it hadn't been there.

"Is that new?" He pointed to the tattoo.

Panic filled her eyes. "Um…yeah. It is."

Cliff didn't buy her story. There were no tattoo parlors in Sweetheart and, to his knowledge, she hadn't left town. And why the sudden panic?

Scarlett averted her face. She was hiding something.

Leaning down, he smelled her hair, which reminded him of the flowers he'd brought for her. It wasn't at all how Scarlett normally smelled.

Something was seriously wrong.

He scrutinized her face. Eyes, chocolate-brown and fathomless. Same as before. Hair, thick and glossy as mink's fur. Her lips, however, were different. More ripe, more lush and incredibly kissable.

He didn't stop to think and simply reacted. The next instant, his mouth covered hers.

She squirmed and squealed and wrestled him. Hot coffee splashed onto his chest and down his slacks. He let her go, but not because of any pain.

"Are you crazy?" she demanded, her breath coming fast.

Holding on to the wrist with the new tattoo, he narrowed his gaze. "Who the hell are you? And don't bother lying, because I know you aren't Scarlett McPhee."

Look for MOST ELIGIBLE SHERIFF *by Cathy McDavid next month from Harlequin® American Romance®!*

HARLEQUIN®

American Romance®

ROMANCE THE ALL-AMERICAN WAY!

Save $1.00 on the purchase of

MOST ELIGIBLE SHERIFF

by Cathy McDavid,

available March 4, 2014, or on any other
Harlequin American Romance® book.

Available wherever books are sold, including most bookstores,
supermarkets, drugstores and discount stores.

Save $1.00

on the purchase of
MOST ELIGIBLE SHERIFF by Cathy McDavid
available March 4, 2014,
or on any other Harlequin American Romance® book.

Coupon valid until May 4, 2014. Redeemable at participating retail outlets
in the U.S. and Canada only. Limit one coupon per customer.

52611315

5 65373 00076 2 (8100)0 11901

NYTCOUP0214

REQUEST YOUR FREE BOOKS!

2 FREE NOVELS
FROM THE ROMANCE COLLECTION
PLUS 2 FREE GIFTS!

YES! Please send me 2 FREE novels from the Romance Collection and my 2 FREE gifts (gifts are worth about $10). After receiving them, if I don't wish to receive any more books, I can return the shipping statement marked "cancel." If I don't cancel, I will receive 4 brand-new novels every month and be billed just $6.24 per book in the U.S. or $6.74 per book in Canada. That's a savings of at least 22% off the cover price. It's quite a bargain! Shipping and handling is just 50¢ per book in the U.S. and 75¢ per book in Canada.* I understand that accepting the 2 free books and gifts places me under no obligation to buy anything. I can always return a shipment and cancel at any time. Even if I never buy another book, the two free books and gifts are mine to keep forever.

194/394 MDN F4XY

Name   (PLEASE PRINT)

Address   Apt. #

City   State/Prov.   Zip/Postal Code

Signature (if under 18, a parent or guardian must sign)

Mail to the Harlequin® Reader Service:
IN U.S.A.: P.O. Box 1867, Buffalo, NY 14240-1867
IN CANADA: P.O. Box 609, Fort Erie, Ontario L2A 5X3

Want to try two free books from another line?
Call 1-800-873-8635 or visit www.ReaderService.com.

* Terms and prices subject to change without notice. Prices do not include applicable taxes. Sales tax applicable in N.Y. Canadian residents will be charged applicable taxes. Offer not valid in Quebec. This offer is limited to one order per household. Not valid for current subscribers to the Romance Collection or the Romance/Suspense Collection. All orders subject to credit approval. Credit or debit balances in a customer's account(s) may be offset by any other outstanding balance owed by or to the customer. Please allow 4 to 6 weeks for delivery. Offer available while quantities last.

Your Privacy—The Harlequin® Reader Service is committed to protecting your privacy. Our Privacy Policy is available online at www.ReaderService.com or upon request from the Harlequin Reader Service.

We make a portion of our mailing list available to reputable third parties that offer products we believe may interest you. If you prefer that we not exchange your name with third parties, or if you wish to clarify or modify your communication preferences, please visit us at www.ReaderService.com/consumerchoice or write to us at Harlequin Reader Service Preference Service, P.O. Box 9062, Buffalo, NY 14269. Include your complete name and address.

ROM13R